SPELLS AND JINGLEBELLS

A Collection of Paranormal Cozy Shorts

CONTENTS

CHRISTMAS BONUSES!

TWO MAGICAL BONUSES FROM US TO YOU!

We hope our stories bring extra enchantment to your holiday season! We had such a great time writing these for you that we decided to add two fun bonuses.

A Magical Scavenger Hunt

We've chosen a single holiday object and woven it into each of our stories so that it appears in every story at least once. Figure it out for a chance to win an Amazon gift card and free books!

14 Days of Christmas

From December 10 through Christmas Eve, five random entrants per day will win a full-length book from one of our authors.

Go to this page to enter both contests or visit our Facebook page to enter and spend the holiday season with us!

THE GHOST HUNTER WHO SAVED CHRISTMAS

Beechwood Harbor Magic Mysteries

DANIELLE GARRETT

SUMMARY

It's Christmastime in Beechwood Harbor, a sleepy coastal town that's teeming with paranormal beings. The local children are waiting eagerly for the sound of sleigh bells and reindeer hooves, but in the days before Christmas Eve, their dreams turn to nightmares and a rash of hysteria threatens to overshadow the big day!

Local ghost whisperer Scarlet Sanderson already has her hands full with her thriving floral business and an impending visit from her uppity parents. But when she hears that there's a revenge-hungry super-elf on the loose, she can't sit on the sidelines. Together with Holly Boldt, a powerful witch, they have to stop the elf from stealing away every child's dreams of Christmas before it's too late.

CHAPTER ONE

W hen battling through the holiday season, I'd found it helped to make friends with the local baristas. As many of them as possible. Especially the kind, thoughtful ones who knew just when to slip you an extra shot—or three—of espresso. In the quaint, seaside town of Beechwood Harbor, there was only one coffee house. Luckily for me, Siren's Song was staffed by some lovely baristas, all of whom noted the bags under my eyes and took pity on my poor, sleep-deprived soul.

It was my first year as a businesswoman, having opened my own floral design shop earlier in the year. I was a skilled florist, but between the holiday-party centerpieces, Christmas garlands and wreaths, and the several dozen potted poinsettias I'd been slinging all over town for the past two weeks as preparations reached a final fever-pitch, I was exhausted.

I started each day feeling like a hopped-up hummingbird yet somehow ended up moving like a turtle trudging through a vat of peanut butter by the end of it. My assistant, Lizzie, was trained up and helping as best she could, but the printer continued to spit orders in such a steady flow that I wasn't sure we'd ever make it to the bottom of the stack. As soon as one batch of deliveries was loaded into the back of the company van, I'd turn around and find ten new orders, still warm from the always-buzzing machine.

And then there were the ghosts.

In addition to general holiday chaos, I had the extra task of sorting out the qualms of those who weren't quite resting in peace. Since my eighth birthday, I've been able to see and speak with ghosts. Call it a blessing or a curse. I go back and forth most days. Recently, a whole host of needy specters had wormed from the woodwork and spent the day vying for my attention.

My loyal ghost-friends Gwen, Hayward, and Flapjack did their best to keep the hangers-on at bay, but there was only so much they could do. And, to be honest, even the usual trio was starting to grate on my nerves a little bit.

So, when I made my plans to spend the Friday before Christmas in Seattle, doing my last-minute—okay, fine, *all* of my—Christmas shopping, I made sure the ghosts in my life knew it was a spirit-free zone. On my way back to Beechwood Harbor, I took it slow and made a pit-stop at Siren's Song to stretch the solo outing a little bit further.

"Hey, Scarlet!" Holly Boldt called from the front counter. She had a broom in her hands and if not for the presence of the shop manager, Cassandra Frank, I would have cracked a joke about her using it to fly home. She was a witch after all. It was a rare moment when I needed Flapjack, the ghost of my childhood cat, there to tell the joke on my behalf. He was a royal pain in the rear, but at least he kept me laughing.

"Hello, Holly. Cassie." I stepped deeper into the cozy shop, letting the warm, espresso-scented air envelope me and melt away the layer of snowflakes dusting my coat. "Am I too late to get a latte?" I asked, shifting my gaze to the espresso machine to Holly's right. The blue lights on the front were flashing and I hoped that meant it was still ready for one more round.

Holly grinned as she sidestepped to lean the broom against the nearest wall. "Not a problem. How many shots do you want?" She glanced up at the copper-faced clock on the wall. It was creeping up on eight o'clock. The coffee shop had been running extended hours to keep up with the surrounding retail shops in the small town.

I sagged against the counter, dropping down to rest my weight on my forearms and peered up at her. "Load me up."

Holly went to work and within seconds, the rich, comforting scent of dark-roast espresso wafted to my nose, reviving me ever so slightly. I perked when the shots finished pouring. She raised the two shot glasses and I grinned. "Hit me."

Holly laughed. "Living dangerously."

"More accurately, I have about three dozen presents to wrap and when that's done, assuming I don't end up hog-typing myself in Scotch tape, I get to move on to deep-cleaning my entire apartment so I can minimize snide comments from my ever-doting mother when she arrives with my father in the morning."

Cassie and Holly both winced and I adored them for it. It was always good to have friends who *got it.*

Holly bumped a switch and the steam wand kicked on, turning the silver pitcher of almond milk into a fluffy, warm dream I could wrap myself in before hunkering down to work. I started to pull out my debit card but Cassie shooed my hand away when I tried to pass it over the counter. "It's on the house. An early Christmas gift."

I lifted an eyebrow. "Fine, but you can't stop me from doing this," I insisted, digging out a couple of bills from my wallet and dropping them into their tip jar.

"Thanks, Scarlet."

Holly snapped the lid on my latte and handed it over with a knowing smile. "We've got pretty much everything wrapped up around here. Want to sit with us while we wait for the clock to wind down?"

"Sure."

Cassie grabbed a ceramic mug covered in painted red mittens and took it to one of the two percolators. She pulled the lever and an amber liquid filled her cup. The savory scent of apple and cinnamon mingled with the lingering espresso and Cassie raised the mug to her nose and breathed deeply. "Is there anything more festive than hot apple cider?" she asked, a dreamy look in her eyes.

Holly grinned and retrieved a travel mug from beside the espresso machine. "I don't know, you'll have to take that up with the pumpkin-spice people."

Looking at me, Cassie asked, "Looks like you'll have to be the tie breaker, Scarlet."

I held up my latte. "What can I say, I'm a hazelnut gal any time of year."

"Boo!" Cassie jeered, a grin on her face.

Before I could defend my position, the door opened, sending a chilly blast rippling through the shop. I tucked my chin into my coat, protecting the back of my neck from the frosty blast of air.

"Good evening," Holly said, setting her mug back down. She brushed her hands off on the front of her apron as she returned to her place at the cash register. "How may I help you, ladies?"

Three women trooped into the shop, vacant stares on their wind-burnt faces. Having spent the entire day weaving in and out of an outdoor shopping mall, I knew the look of my fellow last-minute shoppers well. They were haggard and suffering through a bout of festivity fatigue.

The tallest of the three stood in the center and was the first to approach the counter. She tried a smile, but it was tight and dull. "I think we'll take three pumpkin spice lattes. Extra shots in all three, please."

Holly rang it up and then gave Cassie a meaningful smile. Although, clearly none of the women were in the mood to argue the merits of their preferred holiday beverage. Once the women paid, they shuffled to the other end of the counter even though there was no one waiting behind them. Or in the entire shop, for that matter. They'd hit the bottom of their fuel tanks and switched over to coasting. Since all of them looked to be in their early to mid-thirties, I imagined they all had children at home and a laundry list that could beat mine up and take its lunch money.

I lingered at the bakery case. Despite my surplus of things to do, it was nice being away from the shop. My apartment was right above the retail and studio space of my flower shop, so even when I was home, it wasn't much different than being at work. Besides the local take-out restaurants, I hadn't gone much of anywhere over the past few weeks. If Holly and Cassie had time to sit and chat for a few minutes, I was willing to hang around. My mother would just have to accept that there were dust bunnies under my couch. And yes, she was the type who would likely check when she figured I wasn't looking. That was another perk to having ghosts swirling at all times. Flapjack would no doubt give me a full report.

"I just hope they will help the kids sleep tonight," the taller woman was saying when Holly killed the steam wand.

"Ugh. No kidding. Am I a terrible mother for wanting to slip some brandy in Garfield's bottle?" the brunette asked with a sheepish smile.

"No. But you *are* a horrible mother for naming your child *Garfield*," a mocking voice interjected.

I cringed and then shot a stern look across the counter to where a silvery-purple Himalayan sat casually cleaning its whiskers. "Flapjack," I hissed in a whisper, turning my head away from the trio of worried moms.

"What?" He paused, his fluffy paw lifted to his mouth. "You know I'm right."

That was really beside the point.

I looked at Holly and saw her lips curled in, trying to smother a laugh. Despite my multiple requests-slash-orders that he stay away from the coffee house, Holly informed me that my once-childhood-pet turned talking ghost cat, was a regular visitor who liked to sit on the counter and crack jokes about the patrons most afternoons.

"Well, if that makes you horrible, then I'm a full-fledged monster. I've been thinking about putting noise-cancelling headphones on, popping open a bottle of wine, and pretending the kids don't exist long enough to take a bubble bath."

The other two moms gave sympathetic laughs.

Holly smiled at the women and passed over the first latte. "Are your kiddos prepping for all-night Santa patrol on Christmas Eve?"

The shortest woman shook her head and accepted the latte. "They're terrified of Santa!"

The smile dropped from Holly's lips. "Oh? How come?"

Flapjack stretched. "I'll bet they got one look at that hobo they hired to play Santa down by the carousel and decided they'd rather go without presents than have him climb down the chimney."

I rolled my eyes at him. A city council member's out-of-work nephew was playing the local Santa this year. Marvin was a little rough around the edges, but Flapjack's characterization was hardly fair.

I made a mental note to lecture the snarky feline on the merits of charity and goodwill, especially this time of year, a little later, though it wouldn't get me very far.

"It started a couple of nights ago," the tall woman started, heaving a sigh before continuing. "My son, Bradley, told me that he saw someone outside his window. We checked all over, but couldn't find any sign of footprints in the snow in the yard or around the house. We figured it was just a bad dream and tried to move on."

"But then, the next day, my daughter Izzy was having the same issue. The kids were talking about it the next morning at the skating rink."

The last woman nodded. "My son, Dwayne said he saw someone and he has it in his head that it was Santa. But, not the happy, jolly version from the movies. He's had the same nightmare three nights in a row. We've tried everything, but around midnight, he wakes up screaming."

The other two women nodded, clearly it sounded familiar.

"Poor little guys," Holly said, her lips twisted into a pensive expression.

"Only a couple more nights until Christmas. Hopefully a pile of shiny presents will take their minds off this boogeyman," the taller woman said.

"I imagine that will do the trick." Holly smiled and handed over the final latte.

The women thanked her and then turned to leave. Cassie rounded the counter and followed a few steps behind the trio as they made their way out of the coffee shop. It was five minutes past closing, so when they were a little way down the sidewalk, she locked the front door and flipped over the wooden sign to the *closed* side.

"Holly, I'm going to get a jump on the payroll. Scarlet, if I don't see you before Christmas, I hope you have a good one."

"Thanks, Cassie." I smiled. "You too."

She twinkled her fingers and then disappeared into the back.

Holly watched her go and then slowly shifted her gaze to me. "Are you thinking what I'm thinking?"

"Erm, well, I doubt it. I was wondering how much of a fit my mother would pitch if I copped out and used gift bags this year."

Holly giggled but it faded quickly. "Actually, I was thinking about what those mothers were saying. About their kid's night terrors. What are the odds that three separate kids would have the same nightmare in one night?"

I took a long sip and shrugged one shoulder. "I don't know. If they all talked about it, maybe it was a power-of-suggestion kind of thing."

I narrowed my eyes when she didn't look convinced. "You don't think it's a..." I trailed off, glancing at the arched entry to the back room to make sure Cassie wasn't coming back out. She and Holly were best friends, but she had no idea about Holly's powers or my own. "A ghost?" I finished, daring a whisper.

"I don't know. It seems suspicious." Holly shifted her gaze to the front window, staring at the snow furling in the pools of light cast by the street lamps.

Flapjack yawned. "You ask me, some mall Santa went on a bender and wandered through the wrong neighborhood on his way back home."

"They said they checked for footprints in the snow outside and didn't find any," I hurried to point out. "Pretty sure a drunk wouldn't have been so careful."

"I think I know what's going on," Holly said, meeting my gaze. "Have you ever heard of the Red Snowman?"

CHAPTER TWO

"The *Red Snowman?*"

Holly glanced over her shoulder, ensuring we were still alone. "He's a little bit of a legend, but his calling card is a rash of nightmares. And he only ever comes out at Christmas time."

I held up a hand. "Okay, hold on. What are you talking about? Is he an actual snowman?"

Holly laughed. "No, no. He's an elf."

"Obviously, Scar," Flapjack quipped, flicking his tail.

I scowled at him. "Like you've heard of him."

I'd been able to see ghosts since I was a child, which had proved to be a gateway into the supernatural world. While I'd never been to one of the concealed supernatural cities, called havens, I knew of them and the host of creatures and stories that came from them. Granted, after spending time with Holly and her household of supernatural friends at the Beechwood Manor, I'd realized that my knowledge was more like seeing the tip of the iceberg.

"All right, so this Red Snowman, is he dangerous?" I asked Holly, ignoring Flapjack.

"The story is that he tried to duel with Santa Claus to be King of the North Pole. When he lost, he went on a mission to ruin Christmas for as many children as possible. He invades their dreams, feeding them nightmares and making them afraid of Santa."

"That's horrible!"

Even Flapjack looked appalled, which was a rarity.

"With the Christmas season growing longer and longer each year, it gives the Red Snowman more time to spread his poison," Holly continued. "If he's here in Beechwood Harbor, we have a chance to stop him!"

"If he's so terrible, why hasn't someone stopped him already?"

"I'm sure they've tried. Santa himself likely has elves on the case."

My head spun. Even with my supernatural knowledge, I guess I'd still somehow slipped Santa into the make-believe category. Apparently, that had been a mistake.

"Great. Just what I need." I sighed heavily and leaned into the counter. "Is it so much to ask that all ancient elves on a power trip leave us alone until *after* my parents are back in Arizona?"

Holly started. "Oh, right! Your parents are coming in. Bat wings."

"Scar usually uses stronger words for it." Flapjack snorted.

I scowled at him, but couldn't argue. He was right. Since they'd announced their plans to visit me, I'd been on edge. I should have seen it coming, especially as their only child, but when they hadn't made the trip for Thanksgiving, I'd figured I'd make it through the holiday season unscathed.

Holly tapped a finger against her lips. "Tell you what, I'll see what Posy's up to tonight, but maybe you could recruit some of your ghost friends. They can keep an eye on things around town and alert us if they see Red."

"Sure. Organizing a supernatural neighborhood watch should be a snap with my overbearing mother helicoptering over my every move."

"Right. They don't know about the whole ghost thing."

I laughed, the sound hollow. "Yeah, I stopped trying to convince them that Flapjack here was a real ghost back when I was nine. I'd probably be living in a nice, padded cell right now if I'd kept at it."

Holly cringed. "What time do they get in? Are you driving to Sea-Tac tonight?"

"No. I just got back from Seattle actually." I looked up at the clock on the wall. My cleaning hours were rapidly shrinking away. "They're flying in on a private jet to the airfield up in Copalis."

Holly let out a low whistle. "Fancy."

"They'll be here at seven-thirty tomorrow morning."

"Got it." Her green eyes shifted back and forth as she considered our options, reminding me of one of those kitschy *Felix the Cat* clocks.

I pushed away from the counter, resigning myself to leaving the warm coffee house. "Tell you what, I'll get Gwen to call an emergency meeting. Can you come to my apartment after you're done here?"

"Sure," Holly agreed. "I'll be done here in a little while and then I'm off work until after Christmas anyway. Granted, I have a list of potions to make for my Last-Minute Lucy customers."

I smiled. "Speaking of..."

She cocked her hip. "You too?"

"I just need something for sleeping," I said, pressing my palms together.

"Easy enough." She backtracked a few steps and grabbed an eggplant-purple purse from the set of hooks in the hallway. She rummaged through for a few moments, her eyes focused on the bright green satin lining of the bag, and then came up with two small vials pinched between her fingers. "My last two! But they're all yours."

"You're a lifesaver!" I exclaimed as she dropped them into my cupped hands. "How much do I owe you?"

Holly flapped a hand. "On the house. I'm always happy to help my friends."

I grinned, a streak of mischief tugging at the edges. "Technically, the potions aren't for me..."

She arched an eyebrow. "Oh?"

Flapjack flicked his tail, his once-blue eyes gleaming as he looked up at me. "You're going to dose your mother. Aren't you?"

Heat crept over my cheeks, but I didn't deny it. "Only if she really gets on my nerves. A few drops in her after-dinner green tea and I'll be able to get some time to myself."

Flapjack snorted as he lifted his gaze to Holly. "You might want to make a fresh batch. I have a feeling two vials aren't going to be enough to get her through the next week."

I rolled my eyes at him. "Any chance you know someone who is dying to get a mouthy ghost-cat for Christmas this year? I happen to be willing to part with one."

Holly giggled at the scowl on Flapjack's face. Disgruntled, he launched off the counter and stalked toward the door, his tail twitching at the tip.

When he was gone, Holly smiled at me. "He's something else, isn't he?"

I sighed. "I just wish I knew *what*."

My shop, Lily Pond Floral Designs was only a quick drive from the coffee house, so within minutes of leaving Holly, I was hauling bags up the back stairs to my apartment, taking slow, careful steps to avoid slipping on the ice-encrusted wood. There was a second staircase inside, but I didn't want to track through my retail space in my wet boots. I'd had the floors refinished before Thanksgiving and was still babying them. The plastic handles of my multiple shopping bags dug into my wrists and I let out a sigh of relief when I finally dumped everything onto the couch.

Flapjack was already inside, pestering Hayward—formally known as Sir Hayward Kensington III. "Where's your ghoul-friend? Scar needs to talk to her."

"Flapjack," I warned.

Hayward looked at me. "Good evening, Lady Scarlet! It looks as though your expedition was quite prosperous!" He surveyed the pile of bag and the packages overflowing from them and lifted his thick brows. "*Quite* prosperous indeed."

I reached for the paper bags that were from the grocery store and hauled them across the small apartment to the kitchen. I shoved aside a peppermint-stripe candy dish and plopped the bags onto the counter. I didn't have quite the flair for design that my mother has, but I indulged in a few decorations this time of year.

"Hello, Hayward." I put away a carton of eggs and crossed back to get a bag of frozen green beans. I cringed as I chucked it into the freezer, making a mental note to take the trash out before I started cooking. My mother would be horrified if she knew the produce was frozen, not fresh. And she definitely couldn't find out that the apple pie wasn't homemade...

"I think I've got most everything. The challenge is going to be wrapping it all when I really need to start cleaning this place." I paused my unpacking and drew in a haggard sigh. "Oh, and on top of that, there's some kind of Christmas gremlin running around the neighborhood, scaring children."

"Oh my!" Hayward jolted so hard he nearly lost his formal top hat. He'd died at the Vienna Opera House during the encore—he'd been so moved by the performance, he'd lost his footing and toppled right out of his prominent balcony, three floors up. He'd been cutting a dashing figure through the afterlife ever since.

"That's why she needs to see your paranormal paramour," Flapjack teased.

I shot him a glare. "Are you done yet?"

"Oh, not even close."

Scoffing, I rolled my eyes. "Well, while you think up more clever nicknames, how about you make yourself useful and go find Gwen and help round up the others. See if Sturgeon's available. He's always good in a pinch."

Flapjack twitched his tail, pausing just long enough that I thought he was about to argue, but then he hopped off the couch and sailed right through the carpeted floor when he landed.

"Sorry about him," I told Hayward, folding up a paper bag and depositing it in the cupboard below the sink for reuse later. "He's especially annoying this time of year. Somehow all the extra merriment and joy floating around only makes him snarlier. It's a phenomenon for sure."

Hayward joined me in the kitchen, wearing a serene smile. "Oh, it's quite all right, Lady Scarlet. Actually, I've recently heard a little riddle I can use to get him back. Would you like to hear it?"

"Erm, sure?"

He leaned in conspiratorially, grinning like a mad hatter. "What do you call a cat on the beach at Christmastime?"

"I—uh ... I don't know."

"Sandy Claws!" he bellowed before breaking into rumbling laughter.

"Oh, Hayward."

"What? Isn't it clever?"

I shook my head.

"Drafts," Hayward said.

"Besides, if you start trying to fire back, you'll only encourage him," I added, putting away two loaves of bread. "Trust me, it's best to ignore him."

"Hmm. Perhaps you're right, milady." Hayward floated from the kitchen, slightly crestfallen. He swirled around, his formal coattails fanning behind him. "Now, tell me about this gremlin."

"Ugh. I don't know very much about him. Or if that's even what we're dealing with." I paused, frowning at how easily I'd inserted myself into the problem. It was my curse in life; the inability to stay away from the strange and curious. I figured that's how I ended up with Flapjack following me around for the better part of the last two and a half decades. If that isn't some kind of curse, then I don't know what is.

I put away the last couple of bags of groceries and left the kitchen. "Anyway, there are some children in the neighborhood who are suffering from nightmares about Santa Claus. Holly says it sounds like this elf that goes by the name Red Snowman."

"That's not very intimidating, is it?" Hayward replied, his mustache bristling.

I shrugged. "I don't know. All I know is that Holly wants to try to stop him while he's here in town, so I need all the ghosts Gwen can enlist to search for him. Have you seen her today?"

"No, milady." Hayward looked down at his gloved hands.

"What's wrong?"

"In truth, I've been avoiding her."

I cocked my head. "Why?"

He met my eyes. "I got her something for Christmas, but don't know how to—well, how to present it to her."

My brows knit together. "You got her an *actual* gift?"

Hayward reached into his formal jacket and fished in the breast pocket. It was a strange sight, considering all of him was borderline transparent: his attire, skin, and hair were all the same fuzzy silver-purple hue. He produced a sparkling necklace, the color of starlight with a solitary heart-shaped pendent.

I pressed my hands against my mouth and stifled a gasp.

Hayward flinched and retracted the necklace. "Do you think it's too—"

"It's *perfect!*" I whispered. Lowering my hands, I leaned in closer to inspect the delicate pendent. "I've never seen anything like this, Hayward. Where on earth did you find it?"

"Sturgeon introduced me to a ghost jeweler. I'm not entirely sure how it works, but he assured me that Gwen would indeed be able to wear it, as she would have in life."

I reached out, intending to touch it, but my fingers passed right through and the familiar cold rush surged through me, as though I'd made contact with a ghost. "Wow!"

"Will you help me find a way to show her?"

"Of course!" I glanced up at the wooden clock on the kitchen counter beside my Portuguese Word-of-the-Day calendar. "I'm sure Flapjack will be back soon. He usually knows where to find her. Listen, I need to get this place cleaned up, but I promise that I'll help you find a good time to present Gwen with her gift."

"Thank you, Lady Scarlet." He slipped the necklace back into his pocket and headed for the door. "I'll go out and make sure Flapjack is staying on task."

I smiled. "You're going to tell him the Sandy Claws joke, aren't you?"

Hayward quirked his eyebrows. "I simply cannot help myself, milady."

With that, he disappeared through the front door.

I laughed softly to myself and then sprang into action. My mother would no doubt find out about the bakery-bought pie and the frozen green beans, but there was no way I was going to let her find a speck of dust on any surface of my apartment.

CHAPTER THREE

F lapjack and Hayward returned with Gwen and half a dozen other ghosts in tow an hour later. It never ceased to amaze me how well-connected Gwen was around town. As the harbor's resident gossip-hound, she knew everyone—both the living and the not-so-much—and managed to keep me updated on everything going on in the small community. Whether I wanted to be or not.

Still, for all her oversharing, she was downright useful, especially in a crisis, and volunteered to be my head ringleader (AKA ghost wrangler). I'd learned long ago that when dealing with needy spirits, it was best to keep regular office hours.

"This is so exciting!" Gwen exclaimed, swirling around the Christmas tree I'd barely managed to get up and decorated two nights before. "I just love Christmastime, don't you, Scarlet?"

Despite the sheer exhaustion of working non-stop long days, the stress over my parents' impending visit, and the seasonal money crunch, I couldn't help but pause and take a moment to appreciate the glittering tree and the fragile ornaments dancing in the lights. It had to be some kind of deeply-rooted magic, intertwined with the season itself, that had the power to draw everyone to the wonder and joy, even amidst the chaos it often brought with it.

"I do," I answered Gwen, returning her warm smile. "What do you normally do on the actual day?"

As much as I enjoyed her company, I'd asked that she spread the word that I was not to be disturbed on Christmas Day. Even Hayward and Flapjack were on strict orders to make other plans. It was awkward enough ignoring them when I was at work and had customers or Lizzie buzzing around. Ignoring them at home, with my parents there, would be nearly impossible. My mother's internal radar was finely tuned to my every move and I knew there was no chance I'd avoid her notice entirely if my eyes kept zooming to one ghost or another.

"Holly has invited us to a special dinner at the Beechwood Manor!" she answered, smiling dreamily at the twinkling star at the top of the tree. "Most of the ghosts around town will be there."

Everyone in residence at the Beechwood Manor was a supernatural being; a witch, vampire, shifter, and of course, Posy the landlady was a ghost herself. It was the perfect place for ghosts to have a party.

"That sounds like fun. I wish I could go, too." I frowned, then remembered the vial of sleeping potion in the pocket of my jeans and smiled again. "You know, I think I'll try to stop by."

Gwen clapped her hands together, though it produced no sound. "That would be so fun, Scarlet!"

My eyes darted across the room to Hayward, who was smiling at Gwen while she wasn't looking. I made a mental note to ask if he wouldn't mind waiting to present Gwen with her gift until I got to the party. I'd waited a long time for him to finally make his intentions known, and I didn't want to miss a moment.

"So, Scarlet, tell me why you've called us all here." Gwen floated away from the tree and landed at my other side. She caught Hayward's eye and smiled.

A knock at the door interrupted my efforts to organize my thoughts. "That'll be Holly," I told Gwen, starting for the door.

Holly and her boyfriend, Adam St. James, a dog-shifter, waited on the welcome mat.

"Hello, Adam. Nice to see you again," I said, ushering them inside. "Come on in. It's not that much warmer in here, but it's a little bit better than out there."

"You two are always so cute," Gwen sighed, a dreamy look in her eyes as she noted their matching scarves and stocking hats.

Adam smiled and picked up the edge of the scarf. "Two-for-one special."

Holly laughed. "He's so romantic when he bargain shops."

Adam playfully elbowed her and then wrapped his arm around her waist and pulled her against him before planting a kiss on her rosy, windblown cheek.

"I was just telling everyone about the Red Snowman," I started, turning back to face the assembled ghosts.

"The Red Snowman?" one of the ghosts repeated, sending a ripple of whispers through the group. From the looks on their faces, none of them recognized the name.

"Holly, why don't you explain."

She took over, giving a condensed version of the joy-thieving elf. By the end, all those gathered were muttering angrily to one another. For the most part, they'd all lived in Beechwood Harbor or the neighboring towns their whole lives and now choose to continue into their afterlife. The idea of someone walking in and disturbing the local children felt like a personal assault on the town they all loved so much.

"A walking nightmare wandering through Beechwood," Adam said when Holly finished explaining. "What else is new?"

Holly raised her hands. "What we're proposing is a neighborhood watch until Christmas is over. If you can all organize amongst yourselves, I think we can have eyeballs on most neighborhoods without too much trouble. If you see anything strange, report directly to me. Scarlet is not to be disturbed unless absolutely necessary." She smiled at me. "Anything else?"

"Not that I can think of. Other than a thank you to all of you for volunteering. If this Red Snowman is wandering around town, I have no doubt that we'll be able to find him and send him packing!"

A chorus of whoops answered me.

Gwen raised her hand, delivering a rallying cry. "Let's go! We have a Christmas to save!"

The ghosts poured from the room, all evaporating in the blink of an eye, leaving Holly, Adam, and me behind. They said their goodbyes and went out to catch up with the ghosts. When the door closed behind them, I sighed, and wished I were with them instead of fighting my way through housework.

Seven o'clock came all too soon and when I peeled myself from my bed, I worried I might have caused permanent damage to the old-school alarm clock on my nightstand after the final slam I'd delivered to the snooze button. I pulled my phone from the drawer and was jolted fully awake by the series of text messages letting me know my parents had already landed and were on their way into town. I'd volunteered to drive up and collect my parents from the airfield as it was only an hour up the coastline, but they'd insisted they would find their way to me. It turned out to be a good thing, as I barely managed to shower, dress, and put on a pot of coffee before they were knocking at my door.

I smoothed my hands over my still-wet ponytail and then pulled the door open. "Hello, Mom and Dad. You made good time. How was the flight?"

Jack and Lynne Sanderson were every inch the king and queen of suburbia. My father was an investment broker who had enough money squirreled away to retire ten times over. My mother, a psychologist by profession, had retired from work once I was born and when I was in my school-aged years, busied herself with volunteer work for a myriad of organizations in between brunching with the other upwardly mobile women of Scottsdale.

My mother frowned and stripped her gloves off. "I think the pilot must have been partaking in some buttered rum, pre-flight. Whose recommendation was he, again?" she asked my father. "Surely not Raphael's?"

My dad ignored her question and stepped inside, opening his arms to me. I embraced him, breathing in his familiar scent. "Merry Christmas, pumpkin," he said against my ear.

"Merry Christmas, Dad." I took a step back and waved my hand at the small hallway. They'd been to my apartment once before, not too long after I'd moved. It was a one-bedroom, one-bathroom space that was only slightly larger than their walk-in closet back home in Arizona. "Come on, let me get you set up in my room."

We slipped into an easy small talk as they got settled into the room. My mother continued her griping about the supposedly drunk pilot and my father asked me about business. I took them on a tour of my flower shop and then we went to McNally's, a local restaurant that boasted a mean brunch menu.

When we returned later in the afternoon, my mother strode into the kitchen. My heart sank as she started peeking through my cupboards. One by one, she found the frozen beans, unbaked apple pie still in its bakery box, and half a dozen other ingredients she would deem unworthy of a Christmas feast. Sure enough, her lips quirked into a twisted pucker. "Oh, Scarlet, dear. It looks like we'll need to make a trip to the grocery store. I thought you'd already picked up everything we would need?"

"Mom, we can use everything I bought. It's just not the way you're—"

"Busted now, huh, Scar?" Flapjack said, appearing at my mother's shoulder.

"Scarlet, dear, is something wrong?" my mother asked, her raised eyebrow and stilted tone clearly indicating that it would not be acceptable if something *was* wrong.

"Um. No. Not at all."

It was Christmas time after all. Everything had to be as perfect as it was in the encapsulated scenes depicted in her collection of snow globes she meticulously set out each year. I'd lost count of them a few years ago, but she kept at least twenty just along the six-foot mantle above the fireplace in the formal living room. They popped up all over the house; guest bathroom, dining room centerpieces, entryway table, and last year she'd even thought to put some on the banister of the front porch.

"Excuse me for a moment," I said, nodding at Flapjack.

My mom nodded. "I'll get started on a list."

I rolled my eyes and went to the bathroom. Flapjack was sitting on the counter by the sink when I flicked on the lights and closed the door. "What's going on? Did they find the Red Snowman last night?"

"No. I don't think there even is such a thing." Flapjack swished his tail and looked at the door. "How's it going with Middle-Aged Ken and Barbie out there?"

"So far, I've learned that my curtains are too *loud*, I need a new mattress, and that I can't be trusted to go grocery shopping without supervision."

He snorted. "So, really, a seven out of ten."

"Yeah." I sighed. "Just waiting for her to start prodding me about my love life and when I'm going to get around to giving her a pack of grandchildren."

"She's probably saving that for Christmas dinner."

"Gee, I can't wait."

By the time I went to bed that night, sprawled across my second-hand couch, I tossed and turned, coming up with imaginary arguments to all of my mom's *instructions* at the grocery store, as though I was nothing more than a helpless child, playing make-believe. It was always so convenient how she managed to forget that I'd spent nearly a decade on my own traveling the world, and while I'd occasionally needed their financial help, I'd done it on my own two feet. I might not know how to pick out the perfect pineapple or make biscuits from scratch, but I knew three languages, had more stamps in my passport by thirty than most people managed to get in a lifetime, and I'd single-handedly opened and ran a flower shop in a town I'd never even visited prior to signing my lease.

Eventually, somewhere around midnight, I managed to shift my brain to less blood-boiling thoughts and started wondering if Flapjack was right and the Red Snowman was some kind of urban legend. Flapjack's visit hadn't lasted for long, but before he left, he'd told me that the search would be continuing that night, and that as it was Christmas Eve, it was likely the last chance to catch the ancient, mischief-making elf. If he even existed. It was hard to imagine anyone running through the neighborhood infecting children's Christmas dreams with nasty horrors, but there were a lot of things I'd heard of that seemed far-fetched right up until I saw them come to life right before my eyes. There was a good chance the menace was real. When a voice and cold blast of air woke me, I jolted upright, my eyes scanning the moonlit room for signs of him.

Instead, I found Flapjack, sitting at the foot of my bed.

"What's going on? You aren't doing that creepy thing where you watch me sleep again, are you?" I asked with a scowl.

"Turns out that I was wrong." Flapjack twitched his fluffy, feather-duster tail. "The Red Snowman is real."

CHAPTER FOUR

"Gwen went with Hayward to get Holly and Adam. You're coming with me."

I swung my legs over the side of the bed and stuffed my feet into the mid-calf faux-shearling boots I'd kicked off before climbing into my makeshift bed. They had rubber soles, and while I wasn't sure they were quite the optimal footwear choice for chasing a Christmas-hating elf, I couldn't say for certain they *weren't* perfect. After all, this was my first angry-elf-hunting mission.

And hopefully my last.

My fleece-lined sweatpants would fight off the sub-zero temperatures but I shoved my arms into my thick winter coat and grabbed my satchel from the hook by the door before grabbing my keys and hurrying out the door. I moved as quietly as I could, because when it came right down to it, the idea of dosing my mom with Holly's potion made me squeamish and I hadn't been able to follow through.

"Where is he?" I asked Flapjack, only once the apartment door was closed behind me.

"In the Lilac neighborhood. It's just like Holly said. He's standing outside a window and there's a chain of light coming from the room on the other side. It's downright spooky, Scar."

I cringed. "Did anyone say anything? Or try to stop him?"

"No."

"Good." I fumbled through my keyring, my fingers already growing stiff from the cold. I found the one I needed and hurried across the small parking lot behind the row of shops and unlocked my custom-painted delivery van. Flapjack appeared in the passenger seat and we set off into the night.

I parked a few houses down from the one Flapjack indicated and looked around, waiting for signs of Adam or Holly. Surely they would have been faster than me?

"There he is!" Flapjack shouted, arching his back.

I followed his wide eyes and saw what looked like a small child bolting across the street. There was no mistaking him. He wore an all-red outfit, made from some shiny material that glittered under the frosty pool of light from the street lamps positioned on either side of the street. Midway across, he jumped high into the air, clicked his heels together, and vanished, leaving behind nothing but the echoing sounds of the jingle bells on the toes of his slippers.

"Great. Now what?" Flapjack huffed.

"There's Holly. And ... Adam?"

A large black dog was at Holly's side. I'd known Adam was a dog-shifter, but the beast beside Holly came up past her hip and was twice as wide as any domestic dog I'd ever seen. Gwen and Hayward and two other ghosts followed in their wake.

I jumped from the driver's seat, shut the door softly behind me, and hurried to catch up to them. "He vanished!" I said. "He was there, right at that window." I pointed, indicating the spot. "Then he ran across the street and disappeared."

"Slippery little thing," Holly said.

I nodded and then gestured to the ghosts. "Everyone, fan out. Maybe he's still close by."

Holly and I found him two streets over, standing on his tiptoes to peek into yet another window. We crouched behind a row of hedges, watching him for a moment. A beam of light filtered from the window. The elf glowed as it surrounded him like a ribbon around a wrapped package. His eyes were closed, as though in some kind of blissful Zen.

I started forward, but Holly stopped me. "Wait," she whispered. "If we rush at him, I have a feeling he'll vanish again. We need a way to trap him."

I looked to Adam, the massive dog sitting on her other side, his dark eyes trained at the elf.

"Oh! I have an idea," I whispered, looking back at Holly. "Wanna use some of that voodoo you do?"

She smiled. "What did you have in mind?"

I dug into my satchel and pulled out a silver sphere.

"Your ghost trap?" she asked, one brow arched.

"Technically, it's a soul keeper. I've never tried it on anything other than ghosts, but in theory, at least, it should work on anything. Can you charm it to look like a snow globe?"

"I think so." She rubbed her hands together, conjuring up a ball of light. Her lips set in a firm line as she concentrated on the small silver ball. Magic poured from her fingers, feeding into the sphere and after a moment, the edges changed and became transparent and a little snow village formed inside the orb.

"Now, the only catch is that he has to *willingly* enter the trap."

Adam turned, cocking his head in a quizzical way.

"That seems like a tall order," Holly whispered.

"I think we can do it. Just hold onto the globe, okay?"

She nodded.

I peered over the edge of bushes, the elf's light was starting to fizzle out, flickering like a candle burnt to the wick. In the moment before his eyes opened, I jumped up from my hiding spot. "Stop right there!"

The elf started and turned to run, but was a half a heartbeat too slow.

Holly let a stunning spell fly and hit her target dead center. It pushed him back against the wall of the house. That's when Adam made his debut. The shaggy dog silently entered the yard and the elf's eyes doubled in size. "N—in—nice doggy!"

Holly frowned and folded her arms. "We know who you are, Red Snowman."

"And what you're doing. You're poisoning these children's dreams and turning them into nightmares. You want them to be afraid of Santa Claus because you're jealous of the attention he gets this time of year. Shame on you!"

Adam growled.

The elf shook his head, his range of motion limited by the hold of Holly's spell. "No, no. You've got it all wrong!"

Before I could argue, a muffled scream sounded from the room he'd been drawing power from moments before.

Cringing, I turned to him. "You were saying?"

"Okay! Sometimes that happens, but it's not my *intention*."

A light turned on in the room and Holly ducked. I drew back away from the window, while Adam's beast-form and the elf's head were well below the window eave. "The parents are taking the kid to bed," Flapjack reported, his tail dangling below the window as he hovered mid-air.

The light went off and Holly straightened to her full height.

The elf quivered, the spell wearing thin. His face screwed up, his eyes nearly squeezed closed. "Everyone thinks I'm a cheat!" he wailed. "A fraud! I can't get a job at the workshop and no one else will take a chance on me. This time of the year always reminds me of those stupid rumors and I have to find some happiness somewhere! I discovered that I can ... borrow ... it from the children. They usually have more than enough to spare! They're not supposed to even notice it's missing!"

I gave the darkened window a pointed look. "Safe to say, they've noticed."

The elf worked his hands together. "Sometimes I take too much. When that happens, well, it opens the door for a nightmare."

"That's despicable!" Holly added, scowling at the elf.

Adam padded closer, baring his teeth.

The elf howled, his pleas unintelligible.

I held up a hand. "I have a solution. A place you can go where it's Christmas all the time."

The elf's eyes went wide. "You—you do?"

I looked at Holly and she held up the trap, disguised as a snow globe. "You can have the whole place to yourself, but you have to agree to go and never come back."

He looked at Adam again and frantically nodded. "Okay! I'll go!"

With his permission, I muttered the password to the enchanted trap, and the elf soared up into the air and shrank down, smaller and smaller, until he was barely half an inch tall. "It worked!"

We peered into the snow globe and sure enough, Red Snowman was there, already gleefully conducting the Christmas train as it careened around the track in a figure eight. He would have his run of the place; including the miniature version of Santa's own workshop. He was trapped inside the globe but in a way, was getting what he'd always wanted.

"Doesn't look too broken up about it, does he?" Flapjack asked, hovering over my left shoulder.

I flapped a hand at him. With my mother in town, I'd had more than my fair share of someone watching over my every move.

"I guess the real question is what do we do with it?"

"Not a problem." I held out my hand and grinned at her. "I know someone who would just *love* to add this to her collection."

Flapjack snorted. "You're bad, Scar. So very, very *bad*."

I laughed. "She'll hardly even notice it, not with the six dozen other ones she has hanging around the house."

Holly cocked her head. "Won't she notice the little elf running around inside?"

I shrugged one shoulder. "I'll tell her it's some kind of new technology. A holograph or something."

Holly walked with me back to my delivery van. I opened the back doors to get a box to put the globe inside but stopped short, cringing at the pile of unwrapped gifts waiting for me. "You wouldn't happen to have a gift-wrapping spell, would you? I ran out of time yesterday and ended up stashing everything down here."

She laughed and waved a hand, sending the boxes to one orderly stack on the other side of the van. I waited, eagerly anticipating her next spell, when she stopped and rolled up her sleeves. "Sadly, no. But I'm a fast wrapper. Hand me some tape and paper and let's do this!"

Laughing, I found a box for the globe, tucked it inside with a sheet of spare tissue paper, and handed it to her. I pulled a roll of tape and bright green wrapping paper from one of the shopping bags and passed them over to her side of the van.

We worked side-by-side, wrapping the pile of gifts. I occasionally caught Holly out of the corner of my eye, using a twirl of her fingers to form a bow. She might not have a particular spell, but she couldn't help adding a little magical flair. Within half an hour, the gifts were wrapped and packed into the large box I'd used to bring them down to the van in the first place. Holly flicked her hand, levitated the box, and sent it flying up the back stairs to land softly at the front door. "Save your back," she said with a wink.

"You're a lifesaver, Holly."

"My pleasure."

"Wait right here," I told her, holding up a finger. I dashed inside the back door of my flower shop and grabbed one of the few remaining potted poinsettias from the front counter. I quickly—though without magic—tied a bow to the front and rushed it out to present to Holly. "Just make sure Boots doesn't start munching on it. Pretty sure poinsettias are bad for cats, magical or not."

Holly laughed and promised me she would keep it from the tubby tabby cat that served as her familiar, and then gave me a quick embrace. "Have a Merry Christmas, Scarlet."

I smiled. "Merry Christmas, Holly."

Hayward and Gwen were alone in the shop when I went downstairs after stashing the presents. I hung the delivery van keys up on their rightful peg and walked in on them sharing a sweet kiss under the mistletoe I'd hung in the front window display. Silently, I tiptoed back into the shadows, smiling to myself as I caught sight of the sparkling necklace resting against Gwen's chest.

"Merry Christmas, Hayward," I whispered and then slipped up the back stairs to return to my bed.

If you'd like to know more about Scarlet and her only-*slightly* haunted flower shop, you'll want to pick up The Ghost Hunter Next Door, the first full-length novel in the Beechwood Harbor Ghost Mysteries series.

As for Holly, you can find her in my original series, the Beechwood Harbor Magic Mysteries, starting with Murder's a Witch.

ABOUT THE AUTHOR

From a young age, Danielle Garrett was obsessed with fantastic places and the stories set in them. As a lifelong bookworm, she's gone on hundreds of adventures through the eyes of wizards, princesses, elves, and some rather wonderful everyday people as well.

Danielle now lives in Oregon and while she travels as often as possible, she wouldn't call anywhere else home. She shares her life with her husband and their house full of animals, and when not writing, spends her time being a house servant for three extremely spoiled cats and guardian of one outnumbered puppy.

Follow Danielle Garrett online:
  Website
  Facebook

WITCHING FOR A MIRACLE

TEGAN MAHER

SUMMARY

What do you get when you combine magic and teenage attitude? A witch stuck in a snow globe, that's what. Shelby Flynn's tired of being treated like a kid and when she finds herself in trouble for yet another simple mistake, she wishes for a perfect life.

Unfortunately, she has a lot to learn about perfection and finds out the hard way that growing up has nothing to do with age and being independent doesn't mean that you don't occasionally need a little help.

Now it's going to take a miracle to get her home to the ones she loves so she can prove she's the witch they know she can be. Lucky for her, that's what Christmas is all about.

CHAPTER ONE

I laughed as my best friend Emma shoved me forward along the snowy path that led from the school to the center of town.

"We're so totally up the creek without a paddle if Principal Larson finds out we're the ones who did that."

"Well, since we're the only witnesses, I guess we're in the clear, then."

We turned around to take one final look at the school fountain. The lighting reflected festively off the newly colored Christmas-green plume of water erupting from the center.

Our home-ec class had decorated around it earlier with red bows and garland, but it just hadn't looked complete to me. That's when I'd hatched the plan, then shared it with Emma, who'd embraced it with open arms. Cody, my straight-laced boyfriend, had been a little harder to convince.

As my Aunt Addy would say, he'd been as nervous as a long-tailed cat in a room full of rocking chairs while we were adding the green food coloring to the water, but had finally relaxed once we were within a couple of blocks of the diner and a half-mile away from the school.

I nudged him with my elbow. "So how does it feel to be one of the bad kids?"

He tried to maintain his frown of disapproval, but couldn't. He burst into a grin. "A little weird, but that fountain really does look cool." He leaned down and gave me a quick kiss. A little thrill ran through me that had nothing to do with the remnants of adrenaline from the prank. I was still dumbfounded that such an amazing guy had picked me.

The pinks and blues from the neon lights shining from the windows of the diner lit Emma's face as she rolled her eyes. "Jeez. Get a room you two."

She stomped the snow off her boots and pulled the door open. The warmth of the diner felt great after we'd just walked for a mile in thirty-degree weather. My stomach rumbled as the smells of bacon and hot coffee permeated my half-frozen nose.

The Starlight Diner had been a gathering place for teenagers and adults alike since the mid-50s. Becky, one of the owner's daughters and the fourth member of our little group, rushed over to us. "Oh my god, Shelby! Y'all did it, didn't you!" she whispered, her green eyes sparkling with excitement.

"Why, whatever are you talking about Rebecca? We've just been out for a stroll, admiring the Christmas decorations around town," I replied as I peeled off my coat and slid into a booth.

"Oh bull, Shelby. Don't feed me that." She had the best alibi ever if we got busted, but have no doubt that she was just as guilty as we were —she'd provided the commercial-sized bottles of green food coloring purloined from her mama's baking supplies. She slid onto the red fake-leather booth across from Cody and leaned in. "What does it look like? Did you take pics?"

Emma rolled her eyes. "Oh sure. We just snapped away, then went ahead and uploaded them to Instagram. Oh, and we did a Snapchat with my mom, too. She was real proud of us." She shoulder-bumped Becky. "Of course we didn't take pics, dingbat."

Becky raised a brow. "Keep it up. I'm the one bringing your food."

"Baloney. You know you wouldn't." Em narrowed her eyes at her. "Would you?"

Becky gave her a smug smile. "Hmm. Makes you wonder, doesn't it? Maybe you oughta be nice to your waitress." She propped her elbows on the table, a move her mama would smack her for if she saw it. "Fine. Are you guys eating?"

My stomach was past the point of patience and growled again, this time loud enough for everybody to hear it. Cody laughed. "I think that's a yes."

I nodded. "No joke. Walking all the way to the school and back made me hungry. Will you ask your mom to make me my cheeseburger? I'm starving." By mine, I meant a bacon cheeseburger with avocado, jalapenos, tomato, and extra mayonnaise.

Cody wrinkled his nose. "I swear you only eat that because you know nobody else will ask for a bite."

I gave him a half grin. "Nah, that's just a bonus."

Becky went and told her mom we were there and returned carrying a tray full of ketchup bottles. She plopped down in the booth and married them while we talked about the fountain and the upcoming class Christmas trip to the Georgia Aquarium in Atlanta to check out their annual Festival of the Season.

We'd raised money all year to go, and it was going to be the highlight of the school year. Becky's mom brought our food out to us, and just as I squirted ketchup on my plate, my phone dinged with an incoming text. My sister Noelle wanted me to grab bread on my way home. I looked at the time at the top of my phone and gasped when I saw that it was nine-forty.

"Em, we only have twenty minutes to get home." My mouth was watering as I gazed longing at my burger, but there was no way I was going to be able to get everybody home in time if we finished our food. Taking it with us wasn't an option because as far as the parental units knew, we'd been at the diner for the last hour—plenty of time to have eaten. I couldn't think of a valid excuse to fill the missing time.

The thought of abandoning the juicy, oozing burger with the tips of crispy bacon peeking out from the edges of the bun made me want to cry. Both Emma and I had missed curfew last night, though. Being late two nights in a row wasn't an option.

Cody and Em groaned but started to get up.

"You know," I told Emma thoughtfully, "Cody's car is already at my place and his curfew isn't until ten-thirty, and Will's out of town." Will was Cody's uncle and guardian. "We could scarf down our food then haul butt to the farm. I'll pull around to the barn where Noelle won't see us, then just port you home." By port, I meant teleport. I'm a witch and so is Em, but she doesn't really have to ability to move from one place to another, at least not as well as I do, so I'd have to take her.

"I don't know," she said, doubtful. "If something goes wrong, you could get in big trouble. Or something could happen to us. That's a pretty new trick for you and you've never taken anybody else with you."

I'd been working hard—unless you asked my sister—to master my powers because, unlike most witches who had a chance to grow into theirs, mine had been bound when I was young, which is a long story for another time. Anyway, they had sort of attacked me all at once when I took a serious hit to my head last summer. I was getting pretty good at porting though, and had confidence.

I scoffed. "Every time I've done it the last month, I've been dead-on. C'mon. Aren't you hungry?"

She stared at her chicken tenders wistfully. "Yeah, but—"

"But nothing. Eat."

Cody spoke up, his eyebrows drawn together in concern. "Shel, I don't think that's a good idea. Em's right. You're already on thin ice with the council and that's a pretty complicated spell. What if you don't get it exactly right?"

He was referring to the Witch's Council. I was currently being tutored—translate babysat—by Camille, Em's mother, who was a member of the Magical Oversight Committee.

I dug into my cheeseburger, getting a little irritated. "I can do the spell just fine and we're not gonna get caught," I said around a mouthful. "Just eat."

They didn't look convinced, but dug into their food. We scarfed down our dinner in just over five minutes and jumped in my car. By the time we pulled into my yard, we had three minutes left to get Em home. I pulled around the side of the barn and Em jumped out and met me in front of the car.

"Text me later," I told Cody and gave his a quick peck.

"You text me as soon as you're back here and both of you are safe," he told me back, worrying his bottom lip.

"Stop worrying." I grasped Em's hand, then centered myself and pictured the sidewalk outside of her house. I pulled the spell together and felt the magic swirling around us. Just as I uttered the last words, Noelle screeched my name from the porch. It grabbed my attention at the exact second I should have been directing all of my focus on our destination, but it was too late to stop the spell. I shut my eyes and hoped for the best.

"Emma Rose Payne! What in *tarnation* do you think you're doin'?" I heard Camille yelling at the same time I landed with a thunk, startled both by her voice and by something wiry poking me in the butt. I opened my eyes and my heart dropped to the floor. Instead of appearing on the sidewalk out front, we'd landed square in the middle of Em's living room, right on top of the opened box of Camille's brand-new, unassembled fake Christmas tree.

And to make matters worse, Aurora Darkmore, the president of the local chapter of the Witch's Council, was sitting on the couch, her glass of eggnog halfway to her mouth.

I was so dead.

CHAPTER TWO

I heard Em squeal and assumed she was suffering the same pincushion experience I was. I struggled to get out of the box, finally rolling onto the floor and shaking off a couple of the top-tier limb pieces that had wrapped around my wrist in the struggle. Of course, when I pushed myself up, more of the limbs tumbled out onto the floor and made an even bigger mess.

I didn't realize until I managed to make it to my feet that the room had gone silent. Camille was staring at us—well, at Em— cringing and wide-eyed, with her hand over her mouth. Aurora looked thunderous. She slammed her eggnog down onto the table so hard that the sticky contents splashed over the side, then pulled Em's granny's Christmas afghan off the back of the couch and marched toward us, holding it out and looking to the side. What the heck?

Turning, I looked at Em and groaned. She was standing there in her bra, doing her best to cover her girls with her arms and a piece of plastic Colorado Blue Spruce.

She snatched the afghan from Aurora and fled to her room without looking back. Camille was glaring at me with her arms crossed and Aurora was terrifyingly emotionless as Em's door slammed behind her.

"It's totally not Em's fault." I said with my hands out. "This is all on me. It was my idea—"

"Of course it was your idea," Camille bellowed. "It's *always* your idea! I'm not saying that Emma doesn't pull her fair share of knot-headed shenanigans, but this! This has you written all over it. Danger-ous, reckless, arrogant. Transporting two people is difficult for an expe-rienced witch, let alone one who's barely learned to light a candle with her magic."

She pointed toward the door, so disgusted she wasn't even making eye contact. "Just go, Shelby. I can't even look at you right now. What if you'd left behind something other than her shirt? You know, like her arm?"

Tears welled in my eyes as I looked up the stairs at Emma's closed door. Aurora's gaze was stony and Camille's was so angry that I just wanted to shrink into a ball. I had to make her understand I didn't mean it. "I'm sorry," I said, tears running freely down my cheeks, blur-ring my vision. "It was an accident."

She just shook her head. "No, Shelby. It wasn't an accident. An accident, by definition, is unavoidable. This was just you being over-confident and screwing up." She heaved a sigh and shook her head. "I'm calling Noelle. You can wait on the porch. Don't you dare try to magic your way home or I swear I'll bind your here and now. And don't call Em. I think it's a good idea if you two spend some time apart."

Resentment bubbled in my chest as I walked out the door and settled on the top step. The Christmas lights wrapped around the porch posts blinked merrily and I just wanted to rip them down as I thought about the events of the last twenty minutes. It's not like I landed us in Peru, for cripe's sake.

Okay, so maybe I should have listened to Em and Cody and just eaten the grounding for being out past curfew, but what was the point of having magic if I couldn't use it? I sat there and stewed for the fifteen minutes it took Noelle to get there. I had no doubt she was gonna take a strip of hide off me, too. Yay.

When she finally pulled up, I shoved to my feet and trudged to the truck. She pushed the door open from the driver's side but didn't say anything when I got in. She just waited for me to buckle up and then pulled away from the curb. We made it almost all the way home before I couldn't stand the tension in the car anymore.

"Just get it over with."

She glanced at me out the corner of her eye. "Get what over with?"

"The butt chewing. I know it's coming. I can see it on your face."

She lifted a shoulder. "Why'd you do it? Why not just cowgirl up and take the grounding for being late? Do you understand what could have happened, to either, or both, of you?"

I crossed my arms and glared out the side window, clenching my jaw. "Of course I know what could have happened," I snapped. "But it didn't, did it? Magic always carries a risk but I've been practicing. I would have landed us just fine if you hadn't hollered at me when you did."

"So this is my fault?" she asked. I could tell by her tone this wasn't the time to keep pushing.

"No. It was nobody's fault. I mean, yeah, it was my idea, but I didn't do anything awful. I missed my mark by a few yards and missed pulling her shirt along with us. It's not that big a deal." I really did understand exactly what could have happened and just the thought of it made me shiver, but being talked to like I was ten was getting old.

"Do you have any idea what went through my mind when I walked down to the barn and saw poor Cody standing there holding Em's shirt? I felt your magic all the way up at the house. I don't know why you think you can hide something that big from me. But when I saw him holding that shirt, I about lost my everlovin' mind worrying that one of the hundred awful scenarios flashing through my brain was what had really happened."

She turned her head and studied my face as we pulled up in front of the house. The colored lights that Noelle and I had strung along the eves and porch railings twinkled. A light snow coated them, giving them a soft, cozy glow, but the holiday good cheer of just a few hours ago was completely gone. Now they just seemed to be mocking me.

"Nobody's out to get you Shelby," she said softly, reaching out to brush my hair back off my forehead. I turned my head away and shifted my body so she couldn't reach me but didn't look her in the eye.

"Well it sure doesn't feel that way. Every time I try to do something even a little bit grown up, all I get is grief. Why can't you respect that I'm almost an adult?" I fought to keep the petulance out of my voice because I wanted a real answer.

"Oh, sugar. There's a huge difference between being *almost* an adult and being one."

"Yeah? Well I'll trade you places, then." I pushed open the truck door and jumped out, nearly plowing over Max, our talking donkey on the way.

"Hey! Watch where you're going, you impudent child." He took a potshot at me with a back hoof, and with the way the night was going, I was surprised he missed.

Noelle called out to me before I made it to the door. "Chill out in your room for a while, then we're going to talk."

I pushed the door open so hard the pinecone wreath crashed to the floor. I snatched it up and shoved it back on the hanger, then bolted past the brightly decorated Christmas tree straight to my room.

CHAPTER THREE

I flung myself on my bed but was too anxious to sit still. My room was huge and at first I paced, but then, as I cooled down, I started to think. My eyes fell on the antique snow globe that Noelle's friend Sarah had given me the year before. It was right after our Aunt Adelaide had passed, and I was so lost.

Sarah said it had comforted her when she needed it most, and hoped it would do the same for me. Surprisingly, it had.

When Addy showed up a couple of weeks later as a ghost, it was the happiest day of my life. She was pretty much the only mom I'd ever known; my real mom—her sister—died when I was four. Noelle remembered her, but all I had were flashes. When Sarah gave it to me, Noelle said that anytime I ever needed a quiet place to go, just shake the snow globe and pretend I was skating my worries away on that pond. Since then, I'd used it as a kind of thinking piece.

I flipped it upside down and watched as the snowflakes drifted silently onto the village, coating the shoulders of two couples skating on a pond in the center of town. "Sure does look perfect in there, doesn't it?" I jumped when Addy appeared beside me. Since becoming living-impaired, as Noelle liked to say, she'd pretty much lost her respect for boundaries.

"Yeah, it does," I said, not taking my eyes from the village.

"It's not, you know. There's no such thing as perfect, baby. At least not in the way you think of it. Every dog has a few fleas."

No matter what she said, it looked a whole lot better than here. There was a man sitting on a bench beside the pond, watching the skaters. I always thought he looked a little out of place because he wasn't smiling and carefree like all the other people in the snow globe were. He looked more ... thoughtful, I guess. A little dog lay on the bench beside him, resting his head on the man's leg.

"Well I know for a fact nobody thinks *I'm* perfect," I said. "They all pretty much think of me as a screw-up. Even Em. She stayed in her room when Camille threw me out. She made me wait for Noelle on the porch and it was freezing." Tears welled in my eyes and I brushed them away, irritated that I was letting it get to me. "She said I had to stay away from Em for a while."

Addy heaved a sigh that was a habit left over from when she was living. "Sugar, don't nobody think you're a screw-up. We're just worried about you because you sure don't seem none too concerned about yourself. You could have killed Em tonight, or yourself. You know that, right?"

I lowered my eyebrows and focused on the snow globe, fighting tears. I was used to Noelle getting her tail all twisted, but Addy was usually on my side, or at least not against me.

"And I know *why* you were rushing, too."

I glanced up at her, startled.

"Me and Belle"—Belle was the former owner and current resident ghost of the Clip N Curl beauty parlor—"were out lookin' at Christmas lights and saw you three sneakin' up the hill to the school and decided to follow."

I gave the snow globe another good shake. "Awesome," I said, voice flat. "You gonna rat me out?"

She moved closer so that I had to look her in the eyes. "No. But I am going to punish you myself for lying to Noelle. Schoolyard hijinks are the least of your problems right now, and I don't wanna give the council any more ammunition, but it does fit a pattern, Shel. It's almost like you're *trying* to get into trouble, or just don't care. What's going on?"

"Nothing," I mumbled. "I'm almost an adult and I'm sick and tired of being treated like a little kid."

"Well then," she said as she started to fade out, "maybe you should stop acting like one." For a long time after she was gone, her words echoed in my head.

I glanced back down at the ice-skating couples and the happy little town that surrounded them. Families were building snowmen together and the warmth of the lights glowing from the windows of the Victorian building made me want to go inside. It seemed so welcoming, and they all looked so happy.

Thoughts of Cody drifted through my mind. I wondered if he was mad at me, too. I leaned my head against the windowsill and imagined it was the two of us ice skating on that pond. No curfews, no nagging, no Witch's Council, no punishment for stupid stuff. Just us and all the time in the world to explore that adorable, perfect little town.

I felt the swirl of magic around me and started to panic. I hadn't called upon it. I put the globe down and tried to rein it in, to stop it, but I felt the pull of the vortex that accompanied a port and everything went dark, as it always did.

CHAPTER FOUR

The first things I noticed when the fog began to clear were that I was teetering on what felt like two tight ropes, and everything was blindingly white. I flung my arms out to balance myself, but was too late; I landed on my backside with a solid thunk so hard my teeth rattled. The ground beneath me was hard and cold but I took a minute to look around before trying to stand. A familiar voice sounded behind me.

"Shelby, what did you do? Where are we?" It was Cody, and like me, he was sitting on the ground. Unlike me, he looked pissed. The cold was seeping through my gloves and snow was gathering on my eyelashes. I realized we were sitting on ice. I held up my finger to silence him as I took a minute to examine our surroundings. Snow blanketed everything—the pine trees, the buildings, the pond we were sitting on.

The pond.

Aw crud. My shoulders sagged; we were in my snow globe.

I turned to him and cringed when he glared at me. "I think maybe I ported us into my snow globe somehow." Scrunching my eyes shut, I waited for his reaction.

"You what? It sounded like you said you ported us into your snow globe." He was looking around, clenching his jaw as he realized what he was seeing. I mean, he'd never paid much attention to mine in particular, but the structure of snow globes are pretty distinguishable. A whoosh of air passed me and the other couple—the couple that was *supposed* to be there—skated by, nearly taking off my fingers.

I scowled and jerked my hand back. "Hey! Watch it!" I yelled, but they didn't so much as turn around.

"We need to move," Cody said as he pushed to his feet. I tried to follow suit, but it felt like I had on lead shoes. I groaned when I saw why—I was wearing skates that were so white they matched the snow, with little red pompoms on the toes. In fact, we were both wearing the same red snowsuits as one of the two pairs of skaters had been, and there was only one other couple besides us on the ice.

No way this was happening.

"Do you know how to ice skate?" I asked.

He was already standing, and reached down for me. "Yes. I do. Though I have to say I never thought I'd be using the skill to keep somebody from chopping my fingers off on a pond inside a snow globe."

I took his hand and let him haul me up. I couldn't risk looking at his face to see if he was kidding because it was all I could do to stay upright. Plus, I couldn't take the disappointment that was probably written on his face.

"C'mon, Shel," he said as I almost fell for the third time. "It's not much different than roller blading and I know you can do that."

Oh sure. It was *just* like that. Not. But I could hear a trace of irritation in his voice, so I tried a little harder.

Using him as a brace, I managed to scramble to the side of the pond and up the bank to a cast-iron bench painted Christmas red. While I was catching my breath, I checked out our surroundings. It looked way different from this perspective.

The couple skating on the pond never looked away from each other as they jumped and dipped. The families building snowmen together smiled and worked as a team and the townspeople decorating the giant tree in the town square hung each bulb and string of lights just so. Even the carolers were perfectly in tune.

Everything was exactly as it was supposed to be. Except, something was missing. I looked around again, paying attention to each detail. It was the man—we were sitting on the bench the man usually sat on. The one with the little dog.

I looked around. He was nowhere in sight, but everything else was exactly as it should be. Why would he be different?

Then, before I could give it more thought, reality struck. We were in a snow globe; nothing was how it should to be. It was a model of a town, not a real town. Nobody should be moving. Christmas lights shouldn't be twinkling. Carolers shouldn't be singing. Skaters shouldn't be skating. Cody was staring around, but I couldn't tell if he was amazed or terrified. Or both.

"Okay, now that we're not in danger of losing fingers to the dipping duo out there, would you please tell me what's going on?"

I pushed down the panic and looked at my folded hands, then up into his eyes, begging for understanding. "I don't know. One minute I was sitting in my window thinking how perfect it looked in here, and how I wished it were me and you out there on the ice, and the next ... well, the next, here we were."

He scrunched his eyebrows together in a gesture that I'd come to recognize as his thinking expression. "Gimme some context. Why did you wish that? Start with what happened after you ported with Em. All I know is Noelle came running outside mad as a wet hen, then when she saw the shirt, I thought she was gonna pass out."

I took him through the whole story, starting with how Noelle had distracted me and I'd accidentally landed us in Camille's living room, right up until we landed on the ice.

"It was an accident," I finished, and it sounded old and lame even to me.

He searched my face for a few seconds then sighed. "Well, at least you can get us out of here, right?"

I chewed on my lip. I wasn't sure whether I could or not, but I didn't want to tell him that. It wasn't like I'd just ported us from one place to another. I'd called him from a distance, shrunk us both, and animated the entire snow globe. I was proud of my progress, but I had no idea where to even start because I had no idea how I'd *done* it.

"Right?" he prodded, his brows up.

I pasted a cheery smile on my face, if for no other reason than to keep my fear at bay. "Of course I can. But since we're here anyway, let's chill out for a little bit," I said, hoping to buy myself some time. After all, it was my mess and I was perfectly capable of fixing it. I just needed some time to think about it first.

He looked around, a worried frown creasing his brow. "I don't know. I think we should probably go home."

My face dropped. "Come on. Can't we spend just a little bit of time in here before I have to go back and deal with Noelle and Camille? I'm probably not gonna see daylight for months by the time they're done with me. Will's out of town, so it's not like you'll be reported missing."

I saw the moment he gave in and smiled.

"You suck. You know that, right?" He smiled and 'shook his head. "Stuck in a snow globe. Definitely not an experience I would have considered a possibility six months ago."

We'd met when I was magically skipping stones across Keyhole Lake and he busted me. That wasn't too long after he lost his parents, and he'd been there for the same reason I was—solitude and a place to think without people asking questions or expecting anything of him.

"Yeah," I sighed and laid my head on his shoulder. "Me neither."

I shrugged off the woe-is-me feelings as it finally sunk in that we could do whatever we wanted to do. In there, we were adults. I took his hand and headed to a corner of the pond where the sliding slashers didn't seem to go. "Now, teach me to ice skate!" After all, that's what I'd come there to do.

CHAPTER FIVE

I t didn't take me long to get the hang of it and soon we were skating around hand in hand, avoiding the other couple and having a blast. We'd been on the ice for probably a half-hour when I skidded to a stop after racing him across the ice. I almost face-planted into the bank, but he caught me.

"I'm parched," I said, out of breath as I steadied myself. "Let's go find something to drink."

"We will, but first I want to show you something." He took my hand and pulled me closer to the other couple but near the edge, where we wouldn't be in the way. We were standing beside a small pine tree that was decorated with red and silver ribbons. Little clusters of snow tipped the end of each branch. Just like everything else in here, it was picture-perfect. I said as much.

He tilted his head and looked at me for a second, then pulled me in front of him and rested his chin on my shoulder. "Look at their path," he said, motioning to the couple. "Look at their faces when they come past."

They skated by and performed a complex jump and twirl, then skated to the other end and back around, then back and into the same routine. Their expressions never changed and they never averted their eyes from each other. They just skated and smiled at each other.

I gasped when I realized what he was trying to show me. He gently let go of me, making sure I was stable first, then went to the tree and pushed it over.

"Honey, there's no such thing as your concept of perfect. I know that's why you pulled us in here, and you've mentioned it several times, but what you imagine just doesn't exist. No matter how great something looks on the surface, there's always something at least a little off. But perfection is in the eye of the beholder. I think you're perfect. Everything about you makes you the girl I love, warts and all."

I wrinkled my nose. "Eww. I get the concept, but can we say freckles or something instead?"

He laughed and kissed my nose. "I make a grand declaration and reveal one or the great truths of the universe, and you pick out the word wort. See, that's one of these wort—freckles I was talking about. The ability to completely pick out what you want to hear and nothing else. C'mon, Hagatha," he said, dodging me when I swatted at him. "Let's get you something to drink."

We headed back toward the bench and collapsed onto it, and the missing man flitted through my mind again. Once we sat down, though, the problem of how to un-work my spell to get us out of the globe popped back to the forefront of my mind. I bent over to unlace my skate, trying to recapture exactly what I'd been thinking and feeling when I felt the magic. Somehow, that was the key.

Cody cleared his throat and looked at the socked foot that I'd just pulled free of the skate. "Whatcha gonna put on once you take those off?"

Ah crap on a cracker. He was right; I'd magicked us in here wearing skates. I was just glad that I'd thought of warm clothing, even if it was in the form of 70s-style jumpsuits.

"Maybe one of the shops has shoes," I said.

He leaned back on the bench and crossed his legs, his skate resting on his knee. He grinned and I wondered again how I'd gotten so lucky. "Oh yeah," he said. Did you happen to bring your Winter Wonderland

Visa with you? Or should I just put it on my Magic Village Mastercard?"

I slapped his skate but smiled back. "There's no need to be a snow globe smarty-pants. I think I have an idea." I placed my hands over my skates, summoning the magic I'd need to turn them into regular shoes.

He took my hand and touched my face. "Sweetie, I think it's time to go home."

Dread clawed at me and I kept working and reworking the pieces of our predicament in my head. Not only was I unsure about how to get us out, I wasn't exactly thrilled about going back to face my fate, either. I'm sure they had a grand punishment cooked up for me. The happy feelings I'd had since we landed in the globe faded away into resentment. Still, it's not like I could hold us in there forever. Surely by now they'd had a chance to realize how badly they'd overreacted.

I squeezed his hands and confessed my fears about the magic involved. "The spell has to be different, more complicated that just porting, and," I looked down at our hands, "I don't know if I can get it right."

"What do you mean it's different?"

"I mean, somehow I did more than just port us in here. We're three inches tall, or I guess we are, I pulled you all the way from your house, and we literally took the place of the skating couple I'd wanted to trade places with, clothes and all, when the magic happened." I slapped my forehead. "Oh, man! I wonder what I did with them." My voice was rising in pitch and I was talking a mile a minute.

"With who?" He asked.

"The skaters!" Did I pull them out? Or did I just make them disappear? My mind rabbit-trailed, chasing all the possibilities.

He snapped his fingers in front of my face to get my attention.

"Rude!" I said.

He rolled his eyes. "Yeah, okay, whatever. But you need to focus. What were you feeling when you worked the spell?"

I thought about it. "I was mad because everybody thinks I'm a screw-up and because I'm tired of never getting any respect." I lowered my voice and he had to lean forward to hear me. "I was also worrying you'd finally reached the end of your rope with me. I wished that we were in here, with no outside pressure or hassle."

He ran a hand over his hair. "I think we need to figure out another way. No offense, but I don't want to risk leaving behind any critical parts."

I looked around at the fake town full of fake people. They didn't look so perfect anymore. "I'm not seeing any other options. Besides, I got us in here, so I have no doubt I can get us out. Just give me a few minutes to think about how to organize the spell."

He looked doubtful and opened his mouth to say something, but before he could, the ground shuddered and a cloud passed over us, taking it from full daylight to dusk inside our little bubble. I jumped to my feet and pulled fistfuls of defensive magic into my palms.

CHAPTER SIX

The cloud obscuring the light slowly came into focus, and suddenly I wished it hadn't. I took a couple of deep breaths like Camille had taught me, and released the magic, then looked up into one of the four faces on the planet I did *not* want to see right then: Noelle's. And if the color of her face was anything to go by, she was about to give me both barrels. I groaned and closed my eyes, preparing myself mentally for the battle I knew was coming.

"What in the name of all that's holy have you gone and done now?" She put her nose down so close to the globe that little twin plumes of fog covered a quarter of our sky.

I tried to answer, but apparently the glass was one-way. Nice to see my lucky streak was still holding—I couldn't even defend myself. She stood back and two more faces took her place. Nice. Now we had three of the four. Camille glared down at me, but Addy put her hand on her arm. Noelle stepped back into sight.

"We all just need to calm down. I don't think this was anything she did on purpose," Addy said.

Camille humphed. "That about sums up her life recently. A whole string of *accidents*. Look where the coddling got her." She flung her hand at us. "Locked in a snow globe, and she dragged Cody along with her. Now what are we supposed to do? You know she's not going to be able to clean this up on her own—I don't even know if Aurora will be able to do anything about it."

That went through me like a hot knife through butter. I was sick of being talked down to. I may have made this mess, but I was going to clean it up, too. I grabbed Cody's hand and let my rage fuel my magic. They were going to see once and for all that I wasn't the child they all took me for. The Christmas lights inside the globe dimmed and the lamp in my room flickered.

Noelle frowned and realized what was going on. She narrowed her eyes and pointed that stupid mom-finger at me. "Shelby Kay, don't you even think—"

I tuned her out and pictured the two of us in my room, clothed, whole, and full-size, and felt the magic melding to my will. It felt right! The vortex built and I felt my reserves drain; I only had one shot at this and it was going to take everything I had to get us both back, but I poured everything I had into it.

Just as the magic pulled us through, something grabbed my ankle and my focus shifted. A brilliant white light flashed, and for just a split second, I felt a weird sense of comfort mixed with ... elation?

As quickly as the vacuum of space sucked us through, we were on the other side, except something wasn't right. And not in a *look we landed on a bed of hundred-dollar bills* way.

Surprise, surprise.

CHAPTER SEVEN

T he fog cleared and Cody and I were back, full-sized, but still wearing the tacky red snowsuits. Two out of three. I'd take it. Addy, Noelle, Camille, and Rae were staring back and forth between Cody and a little brown dog with a big heart-shaped patch of white hair over his left eye, eyes wide.

I frowned. Where did the dog come from? Some scruffy old guy—like forty-five or something—who I didn't recognize came up from behind me, scaring the bejezus out of me. He knelt and called to the mutt, who came running and tried to jump on him, but went right through him instead.

"I'm so sorry," he said to me when the dog sat down and cocked his head at us. "I think I might have thrown a wrench in the works."

My family moved in to hug Cody, but Addy was the first one to ask about me, probably because she couldn't actually hug him.

"It's all well and good you're back but where in the Sam Hill is Shelby? And where did the mutt come from?" She looked at him suspiciously.

"Oh dear sweet baby Jesus," Raeann, our cousin and Noelle's best friend, gasped. "She done went and turned herself into a dog!"

Noelle and Addy did a double take at the pup and Addy swooped in to get a closer look. To his credit the little dog held his ground, even though he could obviously see her.

Aurora, a large woman who enjoyed wearing turtlenecks year-round —don't ask me why because they did *nothing* for her figure—pushed forward, nearly knocking Noe and Rae down. "Don't be ridiculous. Give me the beast."

The little dog hunkered down and growled at her.

"Don't try me, mutt, or I'll turn you into a cat." The dog seemed to understand, because he stopped growling. He didn't exactly look pleased, though.

Green light pooled at Aurora's fingertips and she wiggled them over the dog. "Reveal!" she commanded. Everybody stayed still and watched for a few seconds, until the pup poked his nose out and licked her hand.

Noelle shook her head. "Nope, definitely not Shelby. "She'd have bit her."

I stepped forward, irritated. "All right. HAHA. I get it. I was stupid. Again. But don't ignore me. Noelle, you know that makes me crazy." I was really starting to get ticked because that's what she used to do when we were kids and I was being annoying. Or she was being mean. Whichever.

The look of concern on her face was real, though.

"Noelle, can you sense her?" Addy demanded.

I started to get scared when my sister froze and schooled her face into the expression that I'd come to know all too well over the last few months. She was reaching out to me with her mind. She wouldn't be doing that for real just to mess with me. They really couldn't see me!

Usually, as soon as she started psychically knocking, I felt her familiar presence. Not this time.

I looked back at the man who, apparently, was only visible to me, and growled. "I'll ask you one time: What did you do? Why can't they see me? Why can't she talk to me? And why is your dog visible but we aren't? Are you some kind of crazy, evil spirit or something?" Hysterical laughter bubbled into my throat and I threw up my hands. "Like you'd admit to being an insane, evil spirit. God, Shelby," I said to myself. "Get a grip."

"I can explain—," he started.

I held my hand up, silencing him, and turned my attention back to Noelle. That little worry crease between her eyes was on full display. Lately it was there almost constantly because she sweated *everything*. Seriously. Like, she couldn't let anything go. It was irritating, because before Addy'd died, she'd been a different person.

She'd been carefree. She'd driven too fast. She laughed all the time. She ditched class sometimes—I know because I caught her a couple of times and blackmailed her for rides to the movies.

Now she was just ... a fun sponge. She had no concept of spontaneity or risk-taking. She'd gotten better at it since she started dating Hunter, the local sheriff, but she was still pretty buttoned up.

All eyes were back on Cody, but he was looking wildly around, calling my name. He held his hands out toward my family helplessly. "She was *just* here! She was holding my hand."

Rae's face lit up and she stepped back over to my window seat. "She's probably still in the snow globe. You know her magic is spotty at best sometimes. And that was a doozy of a spell she just tried to pull off."

Camille and Noe joined her while Addy hovered over the top for a bird's eye view. They picked the globe up and turned it gently so that only a little bit of the snow poofed up.

When they realized I wasn't in there, Noe, Rae, and Addy started talking at once, throwing around ideas and what-ifs. Something felt off as I watched them, but it took me a couple of second to put my finger on what. I couldn't sense any of their emotions.

Camille looked shaken, but she yelled over them. "Ladies! Panicking won't help. We need to calm down, and look at this rationally. We need to start with how they ended up in the snow globe to begin with. Cody?"

Cody stepped forward and gave the Reader's Digest version. Yes, I know what that means. I'm young, not illiterate or culturally delayed.

When he was finished, Camille pinched the bridge of her nose. "Okay, so when you left the globe what did you feel? Were you holding her hand the whole time? When did you stop feeling her hand?"

He concentrated. "I think I felt her hand right up to when we landed here. I was still holding it when I opened my eyes and saw you guys. Then, nothing. Oh, I do remember hearing the dog bark right as we got pulled away out of the globe and there was this huge flash of white light.

Throughout the whole story, the four women listened without interrupting.

"So after I said hello to you guys, I turned to congratulate her on a spell well done, but she was just gone."

Camille's eyes were troubled. "This is really not good."

Noelle, who always seemed to have a handle on pretty much every-thing, asked, "Why? What are you thinking? Do you know what happened? Do you know where she's at?"

"I'm not sure, but I think so, yes."

When she paused, Rae made the rolling, get-on-with-it gesture. "Spit it out. We ain't got all day to find her."

Camille cringed. "Actually, I don't know if you *can* find her. I think she's stuck between the two worlds."

Addy blew out a relieved sight. "Oh, the in-between. Well then, there's the answer. I'll just go looking for her. That's my world."

"No, it's not," Aurora said. "You're on an entirely separate plane from the one she's talking about. It's an earthly plane, or at least sort of. Imagine a page of a book. You open the book and there's page one. That's where we"—she motioned to all the living people in the room —"exist. You turn the page and there's page two. That's where you exist. But there's that tiny little sliver of paper between them. *That* is where I think Shelby is."

"Okay," Noelle asked. "So how do we get her back?"

Addy spoke up this time. "I've heard of this before but thought it was just a fairy tale to keep young kids entertained and to teach a small life lesson. I had no idea it was a real thing."

"Oh, it's real, all right. Rare, but real. It was a topic in one of my Magical Errors classes at the academy. The problem is that, according to all the documentation, you're not supposed to be able to come back from it. It's a void."

"Well," Noelle said. "That's kind of good news, then. If there's one thing Shelby's good at, it's doing things she's not supposed to. I just have to keep faith in that until she figures out a way to communicate with us."

I moved up to her to hug her and my arms just went right through her like Addy's do ours. I turned to the guy and sighed. Like it or not, we were in it together, so I needed all the information I could get in order to come up with a plan.

Cody and the girls shuffled out of my room with the little dog lagging behind, looking at us. "C'mon boy. I don't know who you are, but you're staying with us for a while," Rae said, then flipped the light off behind her when he followed, still glancing over his shoulder. Noelle flipped the light back on and looked around my room as if she was searching for something—me.

"Leave it on please, just in case." With a final glance around, she pulled the door shut behind her.

CHAPTER EIGHT

A s soon as the door closed, I spun on the man.
"Fan-flippin-tastic! What did you do? Whatever it was, you messed everything up. You heard her. Nobody's ever gotten out of this before. Tell me everything. How did you get in the snow globe to begin with? How did you know that Cody and I were going to port when we did? Why didn't you approach us when we first got there?"

He looked down at his toes as I fired off the questions, and the shadows of his face stirred my memory. I pointed my finger at him. "Wait just a doggone minute. You're the dude from the bench beside the pond."

He took a deep breath and released it, then motioned toward my window seat. He took a chair next to it. "Sit down if you want the entire story. It's gonna take a minute."

"Well, it appears as if time is the one thing we have more than enough of." I was probably a little more sarcastic than I should have been considering I was stuck in some in-between plane with a guy who might be a serial killer. But really, could I even die, anyway?

"Let's start with the basics. What town are we in?"

"You're kidding, right?" He just looked at me, waiting for the answer. "We're in Keyhole Lake, Georgia."

70

He puffed out a little sigh of relief. "Good. I thought so, but I needed to make sure. It's not like it's something you ever talk about. My name's Gary, by the way."

I held up a hand. "Hold up, there *Gary*, the way you said that kinda implies you know me."

He looked at me like I was a little slow. "I've lived in your snow globe for right at a year, if I've managed to keep track of the days right, though sometimes time skips around in there some. It's not exactly like I was eavesdropping, but if you were standing close to the ball, I could hear you. And man, no offense, but you're kind of a whiner."

I looked at him suspiciously, ignoring the jibe. "You could just hear me?"

He nodded. "Yes. Just hear. I mean, I could see you when you were looking into the globe, and it was a pain in the backside when you shook it, but the rest of the time, you were just a voice."

"Anyway," he continued, "I bought the snow globe originally for my wife Melody on our wedding day almost a decade ago. She collected them, but that was her favorite. I found it at a junk shop." His lips quirked up into a sad smile. "I think it was just sentimental value. She was diagnosed with leukemia a couple of years ago and passed away right before Thanksgiving last year."

He paused and looked at the globe, lost in memory. "All I could do was look at that stupid snow globe and wish that I had her back again and that we were one of those couples on the ice, together and happy. Looking back, I was so lost in my own grief that I didn't even stop to think about how horrible it was for our daughter."

Movement outside my window caught my eye; Cody was walking around in the yard, and he looked totally lost. I noticed it was daylight out instead of dark and Gary's comment about time skipping around in there penetrated my brain.

I needed to hurry this along because we'd already lost at least one night. I rolled my finger at him. "Okay, skip the gooey parts and cut to the place where you got sucked into the globe so I can fix this, hopefully before Cody leaves."

"You know, that's one of your biggest problems. You're selfish. It's always about you. I'm sitting here telling you that I've been locked in your snow globe for a year and that my wife died just before that, and all you care about is that your boyfriend is leaving."

I sighed. "I'm sorry. I just don't see the relevance. How is that going to help me get us out of here?"

He just shook his head. "You really do have a lot of growing up to do."

Before I could protest, he started speaking again. "One day I was looking in the globe, pining and holding Levi—that's my dog—and the next, I was sitting on the bench in the snow globe. I've been there ever since. How did you end up in there? I heard part of your conversation with your aunt Addy, but what were you actually thinking when you were zapped in? And how did Cody end up in there with you?"

It was weird to me that he knew so much about my life that he called the people close to me by name. He must have known what I was thinking because he raised his brows. "Hey, it was no picnic for me either. Seriously, I knew teenage girls were flighty and egocentric, but you gotta be the queen. You have no idea how glad I've been a few times when you finally quit woe-is-meing and turned off the lights.

My brain tends to focus on random details when it's working on something in the background, like it was doing now. "So how did you eat and shower and ... you know ... all of that while you were in there?"

He raised a brow. "Of all of the things that have to be rattlin' around in your head, *that* was the question you chose to ask first?" He scratched his nose. "The answer is that I didn't. It was like time was suspended, sort of. I didn't get hungry. I didn't sweat. I didn't even grow a beard."

I started to think how weird that was, but then remembered we were talking about being locked in a snow globe. Weird was subjective.

Let's go see what's going on with my family. Maybe they've thought of something."

I headed to the door and reached for the knob, but my hand passed right through it.

"Holy crap," he said. "For a kid who's so book-smart, you ain't got much common sense sometimes. We don't have a form on this plane." He pushed past me and walked right through the door.

I scowled. "I'd have figured it out."

"Sure you would have." He stopped to let me pass, then followed me to the kitchen. Noelle and Rae were sitting at the table with their heads in their hands and Addy was floating above them.

"Well," he said. "It doesn't look like any mountains are getting moved in the next half hour. I'm going to go see my daughter."

"And how exactly do you reckon you're gonna do that? We can't exactly drive, you know."

"Yeah, I do know. I also know we're not on the physical plane, so those laws probably don't apply to us." He was still smirking as he faded out of site.

CHAPTER NINE

A short while later, Addy's friend Belle showed up and the four of them spent two hours tossing suggestions back and forth. The problem was obvious. I wasn't alive or dead. I was just ... I don't know what I was, but I wasn't on a plane where either side could reach me.

Suddenly, Noelle dropped her head in her hands and began to sob. I rushed over to her, but wasn't able to do anything other than stand there helplessly.

"This is all my fault! I should have taken more time and found a way to make her understand how dangerous magic can be. She just kept pushing the boundaries and—"

Rae frowned and put her hand on Noelle's shoulder and I was glad. She'd make her feel better. Tell her it wasn't her fault she had to work and that I was almost a grown woman who could fend for myself.

"You did everything you could, sugar. Don't you dare beat yourself up. You've worked two jobs to manage this place and take care of her. We all tried to get her to understand magic is no joke, but she's so hell-bent on proving how big and bad she is that it didn't matter what any of us said to her. In her mind, she knew more than any of us did."

Hey! That wasn't true all! I looked to Addy.

She hovered over Noelle, frowning. "Raeann's right, honey." Wait, what? "Shelby's a good girl. She's just headstrong and hasn't matured enough yet to appreciate what others do for her, or understand that we have her best interests at heart. I blame myself for spoiling her."

Camille snorted as she pulled open the fridge to refill her tea glass. "You two need some perspective. Shelby makes her own choices. She's no dummy. She knows exactly how dangerous magic is," she said as she filled her glass. "She just thinks the rules don't apply to her. I don't know how she got them sucked into the globe to begin with, but she had the four most powerful witches in Keyhole here to find a way to safely get them both out, but as usual, she was damned and determined to prove she knew more than we did."

Rae nodded. "I love her, but Camille's right. We were right there, but before we had a chance to find the best way to do it, she had to show off. It doesn't make her a bad kid, just an immature one that, so far, has been lucky enough that her pranks haven't hurt anybody."

I felt like somebody'd hit me in the forehead with an axe handle, but at the same time, I hung my head. If I was honest with myself, I knew they were right. That stung.

I started to feel sorry for myself, but Gary's words about my woe-is-meing drifted unbidden through my head. I'd been such a bratty jerk. And now it might be too late to make a change.

Gary popped back in right then. "Hey princess. You look like somebody just took your favorite teddy bear."

I relayed what they'd just said about me.

He hmphed. "It's the absolute truth. You're way too big for your britches. They molly-coddled you and didn't let you learn your own lessons. That's how people learn humility, consideration for others, and consequences. Oh, and how to respect your elders." He waited a few seconds then added, "And my trip to see my daughter was a flop, thanks for asking. Apparently they've moved."

"I'm sorry to hear that," I said automatically, not really paying attention to what he was saying. Tears welled up in my eyes. Was he right? Were they all right? I thought back over the last year or so since my magical problems had started. I didn't get full use of them until I was sixteen, and everybody was so far ahead of me. Em already knew how to use hers, though she was still finding new talents.

When my powers were unbound, I was already taking classes with Camille because sometimes they would break through the binding, and things would go sideways. Glasses would break, I'd swing my hand and the dishes would fly from the table, or some other disaster would happen. Then when I got full control, they still made me take lessons even though things came easy for me. But was I really that bad? I thought to the incident last night with Em.

If I set aside my ego for a minute and looked at it realistically, that could have gone really bad and I hadn't really considered that before I did it because I was so sure I had it handled. And what was worse was that she hadn't wanted to do it. I'd bulldozed her into it. I thought I was just being confident, but she'd had magic longer than me; she knew.

The women had been talking in the background, but Emma's name caught my attention. Noelle has asked Camille how she was.

"She's gonna be okay. Thankfully it was just a patch of hair that got left behind with her shirt. It'll grow back." What had happened to Em? I stepped closer and waited for more explanation and was startled when Noelle apologized.

"I'm so sorry Camille. I felt her magic stir and I yelled for her, but she was already gone."

"Don't you dare apologize for Shelby's behavior. She's seventeen years old."

The alarm on Noelle's phone chimed and she shut it off and pushed to her feet. "I have to get to work. Bobbie Sue tried to make me take the evening off, but really, what can I do different here than there? Plus, they're gonna need the extra hands."

Gary's little dog had been sleeping at Noelle's feet, but when she stood up, he raised his head. When he caught site of Gary, he hopped up and trotted toward us, whining and wagging his tail.

Rae raised a brow. "What's he doing?"

I guess to her it looked like he was getting excited at thin air. Her gaze traveled to the wall behind us.

"There's nothing on the wall." She peeked out the front curtain. "And there's nobody outside."

Addy's gaze sharpened. "What if she's here?"

Noelle spun around and started right at me, or I guess through me. "Shelby? Are you here? If so, please find a way to let me know. Move something if you can."

I reached out and tried to move Camille's tea glass, but my hand just passed right through. I growled in frustration and tried again. "It's not gonna work," Gary said. "I've tried half a dozen times." I turned away, dejected.

CHAPTER TEN

For lack of anything better to do, we decided to follow Noelle to work. It seemed we were the only two beings on this plane—small blessings, I guess—but it only gave you one person to hang out with, too. In the scheme of things, though, it would have sucked to be dodging serial killers or evil spirits while I was dealing with some serious come-to-Jesus moments.

When we got there, I followed Noelle over to the waitress station. While she was tying on her apron, Bobbie Sue hustled out from the kitchen and gave her a hug. "Any news yet?"

Noe stuffed her server book into her apron pocket. "Nope. Not so far. Not even a glimpse." She paused. "I think she's around, though. The little dog that came back with Cody has acted weird a couple of times, barking or whining at thin air. You know they say dogs are sensitive. I wish we knew where he played into all of this."

"What kind of dog?"

"Just a little brown mutt. Except he's got the cutest little heart over his eye." She pulled the pic up on her cell.

Bobbie Sue frowned and rubbed her chin. "I know that dog from somewhere."

Noelle shrugged. "I've never seen him before. He's a cute little thing. If only he could talk."

"Well if there's anything I can do, you just let me know, sugar," she muttered, lost in thought as she headed back to the kitchen.

"Sure thing."

Noelle went off to take an order, which was boring, so I followed Bobbie to the back. I'd been coming and going from that kitchen all my life, but I still liked to watch her and her husband Earl cook. That man was a genius with meat.

"Any news?" He turned the meat slicer off and waited for her to answer.

"No, 'ceptin I think I recognize the dog that came back with Cody."

"What dog?"

"When he reappeared, he had a little brown dog with a heart-shaped patch over his eye."

He stepped to the swinging door that led to the dining room and poked his head out. Noelle must have been standing close to the door because he barely grunted, in true Earl style, for her to come back there.

She had a roll of silver garland in her hand when she stepped in. "Whatcha need?"

"Show me the pic of that dog."

Gary had joined us in the kitchen when Earl had called for Noelle. He was all excited. "I forgot—Earl's gonna recognize him. We used to take him fishing with us all the time."

She pulled it up on her phone again and handed it to him. He looked at it and took a huge breath. He pinched his lips together and looked at Bobbi Sue. "You should recognize him," he told her. "That there's Gary Rossi's dog. The one'ut up and disappeared with him last year."

The color drained from Bobbie's face, but Noelle just looked confused.

"Who's Gary Rossi? The name's familiar but I can't place it."

"That's Sarah's uncle. He disappeared straight outta his room last year a coupla months afore Christmas, and his little dog, too. That's Bonnie's daddy."

Sarah was the other girl who worked with us at Bobbie Sue's. She had her own little boy, Sean, and was raising her five-year-old cousin, Bonnie. Now that they explained, I knew exactly who they were talking about.

"Okay, but now the question is how Gary and his mutt are related to Shelby, or at least to the snow globe, right?"

Earl nodded. "Yup. That about sums it up. Gives you a place to start, anyway. Might try askin' Sarah at the party tonight."

Gary glanced over at me. "What party?"

I slapped my forehead. "Tonight's their annual Christmas party. They get together—"

"Yeah, I remember. Earl dresses up as Santa, and everybody brings a covered dish. Somebody always brings the most incredible apple pie shine."

I smiled. "Yeah, that'd be Rae, the dark-haired girl that was at my house." She makes it every year for Halloween, Thanksgiving, and Christmas. I got into a batch of it once." I felt kinda like hurling just remembering it. "It was delicious going down. Not so much coming back up."

He chuckled. "Yup, that's how shine always works. It's a dog that bites back."

For the first time since we'd found ourselves in this predicament, I laughed. "Ferreal!"

CHAPTER ELEVEN

When the subject of us and Gary's disappearance appeared to be closed and a half a dozen attempts to speak to them failed, we decided to walk around town for a while until people started showing up to the party. I brought him up to speed on what had happened in Keyhole Lake over the last year.

We're a small town located—surprise—on a keyhole-shaped lake. The town wraps around the round part of it, which makes us a prime location for tourists looking to go boating, swimming, or camping.

"I assume Hank's still sheriff." He curled his lip like he'd just eaten something bad.

"Nope," I said, popping the p at the end. "He finally got his *just desserts* over the Fourth of July weekend this summer." I snickered. Sometimes I crack me up. Gary wasn't as amused as I was, since he had no idea what I was talking about, so I explained. "He was poisoned by a mixed berry pie. Fell dead as a doornail right in his plate of barbecue."

"Well ain't that just some of the best news ever." He scratched his whiskers and grinned. "I always hoped he'd come to a *sticky end.*"

Okay, that was pretty good, even for an old guy.

"Did they find who did it?"

I shuddered, not because I was queasy thinking about Hank being killed, but because, due to a weird series of events, Noelle and I were almost killed, too. "They did." I said, and left it at that.

We walked in silence for a while just admiring the decorations. I was playing our problem over in my head, trying to figure out a way to get us out of the mess we were in. It started snowing while we were in the town square, those big, fluffy flakes, and I admired how pretty they looked as they settled on the colored lights wrapped around the fence that surrounded the park.

The town Christmas tree, located in the center of the park, twinkled with thousands of multi-colored lights, and the nativity scene looked peaceful situated between the tree and the fence.

After a while, he said, "You know, this may not be any of my business"—I hate it when people say that, because they're usually right —"but you don't have it as bad as you think you do. Being locked in that snow globe gave me time to ponder. To put things in perspective. Just like you tend to do, I was focusing on what I didn't have instead of what I did."

He seemed lost in thought as we made the circle around the park, passing businesses with windows decorated for the annual Christmas contest. I admired the huge tree in the center from all angles and tried to pick out the ornaments that we'd made for it.

"Sure, I lost Melody and it was horrible, but I still had my daughter and a niece and nephew. More importantly, I lost sight of the fact that my daughter lost her mama. I wasn't there for her because I was too lost in myself. And I disappeared right before Christmas, when I should have been trying to make things good for her. Instead, I made them a ton worse." He glanced over at me.

"You're the same. You complain all the time about how bad you have it, but you really don't. You still have your aunt, in some form, anyway. Noelle works like a dog to put food on the table and make sure you have nice things. When was the last time she bought *herself* a two-hundred-dollar pair of boots?"

I thought back to the Shyannes that she'd given me for my birthday a couple months ago. I blushed. Rather than being grateful for the boots, I'd been a little disappointed because I didn't get the eighty-dollar blingy belt to go with them.

"Not for a long time, I guess." I replied, feeling like a real troll as I thought of the forty-dollar knock-offs she'd just bought herself because she'd already Shoe Goo'd her old ones twice.

He nodded. "Yeah. But do you think she regrets giving you those? No. Because that's what being mature is about—willingly taking care of the people who depend on you, even if it means sacrificing sometimes in order to see them smile." As if he'd read my mind, he continued, "She was putting your laundry away the other day and told your aunt she wished she could have afforded the belt, too, because she knows you really wanted it. Just so you know."

Wow. Could I be any more horrible?

He elbowed me. "Don't kick yourself. Just do better. You're at a tough age, but it's time to start thinking about somebody other than just Shelby."

Now that he'd put that into my mind, I couldn't stop thinking. Noelle's boots, The T-shirt I'd bought for Rae for Christmas then decided to keep because I liked it. I gasped. My best friend popping into her living room topless in front of her mom and the head of the Witch's Council, apparently missing part of her hair, too. Everything snapped painfully into focus. Addy was right. I acted like a spoiled little kid.

I needed to get back because I had some making up to do, but it seemed like we were going to need a miracle to make *that* happen.

CHAPTER TWELVE

By the time we strolled back to Bobbie's, the place was full. There were several kids, including Bobbie and Earl's adopted son, Justin, racing around in front of the store and lobbing snowballs at each other, laughing and talking good-natured smack.

Inside, most of the adults were all decked out with blinking Christmas bulb necklaces, Santa hats, or reindeer ears, and ready for the ugliest sweater contest later. And boy, was there some serious competition.

Earl was already in his Santa costume, making his way toward his throne with a bag of presents over his shoulder. As always, a place had been built where the salad bar used to be until Bobbie Sue had watched a documentary on sneeze-guards.

Noelle, Sarah, and Bobbie had done a great job making Santa's throne and building a wonderland behind him using white sparkling fabric with lights, presents, and even a cardboard gingerbread house.

A wave of sadness washed over me as I realized I was supposed to help. We'd planned to make Christmas cookies before we came, then drink punch and sing Christmas carols while we decorated, just like we'd done last year. Noelle was arranging snacks on the table and I noticed the worry lines around her eyes. She wondered over to the checkout counter where we'd each hung our stocking, and she ran her fingers over the one with my name on it. A single tear ran down her cheek.

I walked up to her and tried to lay my hand on her shoulder, but of course it passed right through her. Rae came up beside her and hugged her for me.

"Any word yet from Aurora or Camille about what we can do to get her back?"

Noe shook her head. "What are we gonna do, Rae? She's so young. What if there are terrible things in there with her? What if we don't get her back?"

My heart ached because I'd done this. If I'd just listened and let them do what was best, we probably wouldn't be in this mess. Sure, Gary had thrown a wrench in the works, but if I'd waited, no doubt Aurora, Camille, Noelle, and Rae would have put together a spell with enough forethought and craft that it would have gotten us all out.

I didn't hear Rae's reply because Gary grabbed my arm and pointed to where Santa Earl was sitting. There was a little blonde girl with giant blue eyes sitting on his lap. "That's her! That's my Bonnie."

We rushed over just as Earl asked her what she wanted for Christmas. "I know you can't give me what I really want," she said in a small voice, her little head bowed so that we could barely hear. "So I guess just anything will do. I've been a good girl, but I thought I was a good girl last year, too, but Mommy went to be an angel, then Daddy went away, too."

Earl heaved a big sigh and looked at Bobbie Sue, helpless. He wasn't much for emotions on a good day, and this situation put him clear out of his depth. Bobbie shrugged helplessly, her eyes shining with tears.

Just then, Cheri Lynn floated in, all dressed up like Santa's helper in a little red costume with white fur trim and white go-go boots. The skirt was a little short, but she tended to drift a little toward the risqué side of the dress code. Considering she'd been a dancer in life—pole, not barre—she was dressed fairly conservatively, all things considered.

She glided up to us and looked at Bonnie. "Why's that little angel so sad, Shelby? She's breakin' my heart."

I started to answer, then realized that she'd talked to me. I spun around to face her. "Cheri, you can see me?"

CHAPTER THIRTEEN

She looked at me, confused. "Well of course I can see you. You can see me, right?" She patted down her outfit and checked her hair. "Why wouldn't I be able to see you?"

"Cheri, this is important. Can you see the man with me?"

Cheri looked over at him and her eyes grew round. "Holy sh-Moses! Gary Rossi! Where on earth have you been for the last year?" She narrowed her eyes. "Shame on you. Up and disappearin' on that youngin without so much as a by-your-leave. She's been adrift as a kite in a hailstorm. And poor Sarah. She's been workin' her fingers to the bone to put food in their bellies."

Gary hung his head and I could see the resemblance between him and his daughter. "I didn't mean to. Somehow I managed to curse myself into a snow globe and had no idea how to get back out." He motioned toward me with his head. "Shelby here did the same thing to her and Cody, but she managed to magic them out. I grabbed hold, but she only planned on taking the two of them out, so she and I got stuck in the in-between."

She looked at me, curious, then looked closer. "What's he mean, the in-between?"

I shrugged and gave her the book example that Camille used.

"But then why can I see you if Addy can't?"

I bit my lip right as Noelle slipped by carrying more finger foods. "I don't know, but will you catch her right now and have her meet us in the kitchen? Rae, too?"

"Of course, sweetie pie. Gimme two shakes."

I looked at Gary, excited. "This may be our miracle!"

"But how does Cheri Lynn being able to see us get us any closer to being free?"

I scowled at him. "If nothing else, we have somebody who can communicate for us. That's more that we had five minutes ago."

"True that," he said as Noe and Rae pushed the doors open to follow us into the back.

As soon as we were back there, Noelle started firing off questions and looking around, frantic to see me for herself. "Shelby! Are you okay? Are you there alone?" She looked at Cheri Lynn. "Is she okay? Is there anybody with her?"

Cheri sighed. "This ain't workin', sugar. You need to talk to one of us or the other. Talk to her, I'll tell you the answers. Shelby, you can see and hear her fine as frog's hair, right?"

I nodded.

"All right then. To answer you, Noelle, she looks fine, and she's got Gary Rossi with her."

"Gary Rossi?" Rae asked. "Who's Gary Rossi?" Rae hadn't been there earlier for the conversation, so Noelle started to bring her up to speed. Cheri Lynn beat her to it.

"He's Sarah's uncle, the one who up and dumped poor little Bonnie on her."

Cheri'd become a member of our little pack since she'd been murdered several months before, and loved us all. She was giving him the stink eye something fierce.

"He didn't mean to, Cheri Lynn, and trust me, he regrets it. He's been stuck inside a snow globe for a year. He was sad, missing his wife, and wished that they were one of the couples skating on the ice. Then bam! He was in there and couldn't get out. It's not like he's been in the Bahamas."

Cheri Lynn relayed the information.

"Wait a minute," Noelle said. "He was stuck in *your* snow globe?" She narrowed her eyes. "Just exactly what could he see while he was sitting on a shelf in your bedroom?"

Gary sighed, exasperated. "Why does everybody automatically go there? It's not like I'm some pervy, creepy elf on a shelf. I couldn't see anything unless she looked directly into it. And even then, the magic in the globe kept her from seeing me, so don't worry—she didn't see anything weird either."

I arched a brow at him. "What weird things were you doing in my snow globe?"

He pinched his nose. "For the love of god, Shelby. You two are messed up as a mud fence in a rainstorm. Knock it off."

Cheri Lynn had been watching the exchange, smiling.

Noelle interrupted. "I don't know what you're smiling about, but please, feel free to share with the class."

"Okay, she said, waving Noelle off. "Shelby, that's how Cody said you guys ended up in there, too. You made the same wish, right?"

"Yeah, but with slightly different intentions. I wanted to be in a world where it was just the two of us. No rules, no council, nobody to boss us."

Noelle waited for Cheri Lynn to explain, then closed her eyes for a minute. "Okay, so this seems to be a spell of intent. It's not a passive spell. It was placed there specifically as a means to trap people. Or by somebody who was really desperate, then the magic clung."

She turned to Cheri Lynn. "We need to talk to Camille and Aurora. And Shelby, don't try anything. It's you going off half-cocked that got you into this mess. Just wait."

Before Cheri could say a word, I said, "I'm perfectly happy to let them do it. I'm over the whole, *I'm a big girl, now* thing. I just want whoever can fix this to do it."

"Your mouth to God's ears," Cheri said, then relayed it to Noe and Rae. "We'll be right back. I'm just going to call Aurora and Camille."

We left the kitchen and rushed through the restaurant, then skidded to a stop as Levi, who'd been lying under the table eating bits of pork from Bobbie Sue's fingers, came running toward us.

Bonnie saw him and her eyes lit up. "Levi!" Her gaze started darting around the room, frantic to see the one face that wasn't in the crowd. "Daddy? Daddy are you here?"

CHAPTER FOURTEEN

G ary rushed toward her, but as he tried to gather her up, his arms slipped right through her. His gaze was agonized as her turned toward me. "We've gotta do something." He looked from me to Cheri Lynn to Rae. "You guys have to figure out how to get us out of here!"

Sarah had seen the dog and heard Bonnie's cry. She was by her side in an instant and looked up at us. Her eyes settled on Gary and if looks could kill, he'd have been dead where he stood.

"You! After abandoning her for a year, you just waltz right back in here and expect to pick her up and sit her on Santa's knee? Over my dead body." She raced over and picked up a bewildered Bonnie.

"Who are you talking to Sarah? Did you see that little dog? He looks just like Levi!"

Since we were only about ten feet from them, Sarah was looking back and forth between me and Gary. "Shelby! I'm so happy to see you! Noelle told me what happened, but she didn't tell me you made it back safe."

By now, Noelle and Rae were as bumfuzzled as Gary and I were. And Bonnie was struggling to get down so that she could chase the dog.

Cheri Lynn seemed to be the only one with enough clarity to take control of the situation. "Sarah, honey, take Bonnie to Bobbie Sue for a few minutes. We need to talk."

Still glancing back and forth between the five of us, Sarah nodded and did as she asked. It only took her a minute to hand her over to Bobbie Sue, who led her over to the chocolate fountain. Sarah made it back to us in double time. "Now would somebody mind tell me what in the name of little green apples is going on here?"

Cheri Lynn took the lead again and gave her the run-down. Her face paled as the story progressed.

"So let me get this straight. You and I are the only ones who can see and hear them?" Cheri nodded, and Sarah turned to Noe and Rae. "And you two can't?"

"Nope. Not so much as a shadow or a peep," Raeann said.

"So," Sarah said, never taking her eyes off of Gary, "you never left us? At least not on purpose?"

"Never, sweetheart. I was a horrible father after Melody died, but I would have never up and left Bonnie, or you and Sean."

Sarah's chin quivered, but she squared her shoulders. "What do we need to do to get them out? Noelle? You've been talking to Camille, right? What does she say?"

"She says nobody's ever come back from the in-between."

"What in blue blazes is the in-between?"

Noelle explained it again, but I was really getting tired of being stuck between pages one and two. "I can't believe we're this close and there's no solution. Tell Noelle I said so. Tell her and Rae that they're two of the most powerful witches I know and that I know they can do it."

Cheri Lynn did, but then I felt bad when Noe's face fell. I'd meant to be inspiring, but I think I just put more pressure on her. What if we never came out? She'd blame herself.

"Tell her I know this is my fault. I was a snotty, irresponsible, cocky brat and if there's not a way to fix this, then it's not her fault."

Sarah repeated what I said, but it didn't appear to make Noelle feel any better.

Cheri Lynn was looking at Sarah as if she were working a puzzle. "Why do you reckon we can see them when nobody else can?"

Noelle chimed in. "There's only one thing you two have in common. Cheri, your Bebee had the sight, right?"

The ghostly go-go elf nodded, then added, "She had the gift. Said she could walk between the realms, whatever that means."

Noelle turned to Sarah. "And you have a touch of psychic power too, right?"

"A touch," she said, "I've never really done anything with it."

Noelle's face was twisted in concentration, then she turned and strode toward the front door.

"Follow me. I think I have an idea. Or at least an idea for an idea."

Sure. That cleared things right up.

CHAPTER FIFTEEN

Outside, it had gotten completely dark except for all the Christmas lights strung around town. The snow hadn't stopped falling, and a soft blanket of it coated the rooftops and tipped the trees.

The moon hung full and beautiful, crystal blue in that way it can only look when it's really cold outside. The stars glowed and twinkled along with the Christmas lights and I thought how much better it looked than the snow globe.

Noelle called for Addy, and it only took my aunt a second to pop in. "What? Belle and I were getting ready to come in a sing a couple of carols with y'all. Why are you outside?"

"This is more important that caroling," Noelle said, waving her hand. "Can you see Shelby and a guy standing right there?" Rae motioned toward us.

Addy looked straight at us and frowned. "If that's supposed to be funny young lady, you missed the mark by a long shot."

"No, I'm not trying to be funny. Cheri Lynn and Sarah can see them." She brought Addy up to speed right as Camille popped in.

"Let me get this straight," Camille said. "We have two women who both have at least a touch of the gift, though walking between the worlds usually only applies to the world of the living and the world of the dead. There's a chasm in between, which is where Shelby and this Gary guy are. But I still don't understand why anybody, living or dead can see them, because they're neither."

Noelle shook her head. "That can't be. They have to be one or the other."

Addy nodded and crossed her arms. "I agree. Not to get all hippy dippy, but you're either kickin' or you're not." She pointed to Camille then at herself. "You are, I'm not. Ain't no in-between there."

"I agree," said Cheri Lynn. "I've been both. Ms. Addy's right. Ain't no maybe about it. So, what do we do to pull these two"—she motioned toward us with her thumb—"outta the butt crack of existence?"

Sarah'd been quiet up until then, but she stepped forward. "Cheri Lynn, have you tried touching either one of them?"

"No," she answered. "Actually, I haven't. But they look solid to me, just like other ghosts look. Living people look different."

"They look normal to me, too. Solid as everybody else looks to me."

Cheri Lynn floated over and touched my shoulder, pulling her hand back like she'd been burned when she actually touched me. When the shock wore off after a second, she squealed, then moved back in and scooped me into a hug. I could actually smell her candy-and-jasmine perfume as I hugged her back.

"But, does this mean I'm dead, then?" I asked, a little scared.

Cheri pointed to Sarah, who was hugging Gary. "I don't think so."

"Okay then," Camille said. "I've never in my almost-three-hundred years seen anythin' at all like this. Since I can't see them—"

Cheri Lynn's whole demeanor suddenly changed. She shushed Camille as she turned to look at something behind her. "Don't matter if you can see them or not," Addy said as stared over her shoulder in the same direction Cheri was, eyes wide, then dropped to one knee. "Because unless I'm sorely mistaken, we're about to get the miracle we've been prayin' for."

Even I could feel the change. It was like a huge storm was coming; the hairs on my arms stood up and my ears popped.

Cheri Lynn and Sarah had their eyes closed, and their faces looked all peaceful. A pinpoint of light started behind Cheri Lynn, and grew as it came closer. As the voices inside the restaurant lifted high and clear, singing about angels playing near the earth, the most beautiful woman I'd ever seen stepped out of the light, wearing what looked like a white toga with a golden, filigreed belt and circlet. Her blonde hair flowed to her waist, and the light behind her made it look like spun gold.

Gary gasped as she stopped within a few feet of us, and a tear rolled down his cheek. "Melody?"

She rolled her shoulders and a magnificent pair of white-feathered golden wings spread out behind her.

"Yes, sugar." She nodded and smiled at him in a way that made me think she didn't know how to frown. "You've been lost for so long. Now it's time to go take care of our little girl." She turned to me. "And you, Shelby. You have a place in this world—an important one, which is one of the reasons I'm here—but first you need to accept that you have only started your journey and you have much to learn."

I started to drop to my knees as Addy had done because, well, holy geez, there was an honest-to-god angel standing in front of me. She smiled at me and touched my shoulder. "The Flynn witches are power-ful; you're not meant to kneel to any being, but you do need to learn what your place is in this moment in time. Bow your head in humility and embrace your destiny. Your power is a gift, meant for good. Remember that."

She turned back to Gary, who was drinking her in with his eyes, tears streaming down his face. Her gaze turned wistful and she laid her hand on his face. "I'll be waiting on you, but a lifetime will pass before we see each other again. Find happiness, and fill Bonnie's world with joy. For both of us."

She looked at Cheri Lynn and Sarah. "Ready ladies?"

Cheri looked at Sarah. "You know what to do?"

"Weirdly enough, I do now."

"Shelby, Gary, take our hands," Cheri Lynn said as she and Sarah moved to stand face to face, leaving enough room between them for us to stand.

We did as they asked, then they closed their eyes. I had the strangest feeling of being lifted off my feet. Gary and I were literally floating, but it felt like we were being balanced and guided. Each time we'd float a little too close to either of the girls, it was like we'd hit a wall. The only directions open to us were up and down.

The beginning strains of "It Came Upon a Midnight Clear" drifted out to us, the voices of our friends and neighbors blending, each note hanging on the cold night air in near-perfect harmony. Goose bumps raced down my arms as everything around me snapped into sharper focus.

When that happened, Cheri and Sarah smiled and nodded at Melody, and she placed a hand on each of their shoulders. As the final strains of the carol played out, the light grew so bright that I had to shut my eyes, and even though I still felt the floating feeling, it was as if Cheri Lynn was pushing us and Sarah was pulling us.

The chill air brushed my cheek. The light winked out and the feeling of floating went away, and time was suspended for a minute as I looked around. Were we back?

After a split second, Noelle and Rae pounced on me, squealing—even though they're *never* squealers—and hugging me. Sarah ran to Gary and pulled him in for one, too. I thanked Cheri Lynn and Sarah for what they'd done.

"Sugar," Cheri Lynn said, "that wasn't any of our doin'. We just somehow knew what she wanted us to do, and did it. Make no mistake, that's a rare blessing you just got."

I shivered, feeling the cold for the first time since we'd been outside. The crowd inside Bobbie Sue's burst into "Deck the Halls" and suddenly I couldn't wait to be among them.

We made our way inside the restaurant. The decorations seemed cheerier and the lights twinkled a little brighter as I caught my first glimpses of the smiling faces of the people I loved.

CHAPTER SIXTEEN

It was warm inside, and little Bonnie was sitting on Santa Earl's lap singing Jingle Bells with a cookie in each hand and melted chocolate on her face. Everybody looked toward the door as we blasted them with cold air and her little hands went slack, dropping both cookies, as she saw who was walking beside us.

She scrambled off Earl's lap and ran across the room as fast as her short legs could carry her, then stopped a little bit in front of us, staring. Gary bent down and opened his arms, and she jumped the few feet to him. He swung her up and buried his face in her hair, squeezing her, smiling and crying at the same time.

I guess, thinkin' about it, he'd had a pretty big day. He'd been sucked out of a snow globe, dropped between pages one and two, found out his wife was an angel, then got to hold his little girl for the first time in a year. The guy had a right to be a little emotional, all things considered.

After all the hugs and fussin' were done and over with, I called Cody. He'd worked late at the clinic with Will, but came over as soon as he heard my voice. As soon as he got there—after hugging me so hard I thought I was gonna break, he made me promise never to wish we were anywhere else again, and I gladly obliged.

I was happy right where I was, and was ready to admit that I didn't know nearly as much as I thought I did. I was just grateful that, for some reason, the universe had seen fit to send me a Christmas miracle when I surely hadn't earned one.

I went into the bathroom to change out of the horrid red ski suit and Noelle followed me. As I pulled off my ratty sleep shirt—that's what I'd been wearing when I wished us into the snow globe—Noelle grabbed me by the arm so hard she sunk her nails into me. I scowled and tried to pull away from her. "Sorry," she said. "But look." I tried to twist around to see what she was pointing at, but couldn't.

She pulled her compact out of her purse and I backed up close to the mirror. There, right where Melody had touched me on my right shoulder, was an inch-high, reddish-brown mark shaped like a perfect pair of angel wings.

EPILOGUE

An attractive couple sat at one of the cafe tables at Brew4U, sipping lattes and watching the holiday activities going on in the town square.

"It seems to be a quaint little town," he said to her.

She nodded once. "It does. I'd love to give that barbecue place over there a go." Her stomach rumbled as she peered at the sign.

He followed her gaze, then took another sip of his coffee. "Do you think we'll have any trouble adapting?"

"So far, we've fared well," she said, shrugging. "These people seem to be especially forgiving when we make errors. Though I do wonder what a Yankee is. They seem to use the term mostly when we've committed a social blunder."

"Maybe it just means foreigner," he said. "They seem inordinately determined to point out that we're *not from these parts*. Perhaps we should focus on learning the local dialect and rules of conduct."

She hummed, agreeing. "We'll need to find employment and a place to live. I saw a sign when we entered announcing this shop is looking for a barista. I assume that means somebody who makes coffee. It's not a term that was in use in our day, but it can't be too difficult. What would you like to do? You're skilled with animals, but the horse and carriage seems to have been replaced with those automated vehicles."

"I don't know," he said, eying a passing pickup with a wreath attached to the grill with interest. "I'm not particular. Perhaps I can secure a position in the building sector. That can't have changed much. After all, a hammer is a hammer. Or I could learn to repair those vehicles. If it's mechanical, it breaks."

Smiling, she placed her hand over his. "It doesn't matter what we do as long as we're together."

He lifted one corner of his mouth in a loving half-smile. "I'm content wherever you are, love. As long as you never ask me to ice skate again."

Thank you for joining me for Christmas in Keyhole Lake, a small southern Georgia town where the residents are quirky, the ghosts are sassy, and the tea is sweet. I hope you enjoyed reading Witching for a Miracle as much as I enjoyed writing it. Though the main series is written from her older sister's Noelle's perspective, I wanted to give seventeen-year-old Shelby a chance to shine in this one.

If this is the first time you've visited, I invite you to start at the beginning, with Sweet Murder, the first book in the Witches of Keyhole Lake Series, available on Amazon.

ABOUT THE AUTHOR

I was born and raised in the South and even hung my motorcycle helmet in Colorado for a few months. I've always had a touch of wanderlust and have never feared just packing up and going on new adventures, whether in real life or via the pages of a great book.

When I was a little girl, I didn't want to grow up to be a writer—I wanted to raise unicorns and be a superhero. When those gigs fell through, I chose the next best thing: creating my own magical lands filled with adventure, magic, humor, and romance.

Follow Tegan Maher online:
Website
Facebook
Amazon

Or join her readers club here to be the first to hear about new releases, giveaways, contests and special deals. No spam, no more than one email weekly, and your info is safe!

MY, WHAT BIG FANGS YOU HAVE

A Vegan Vamp Christmas Story

CATE LAWLEY

SUMMARY

Christmas dinner with the family has never been so strange. Evelyn is convinced her daughter's sudden weight loss and new liquid diet are a sign of a serious illness or worse. She's going to get to the bottom of the mystery before the dessert course no matter how far it stretches her parenting skills or dents her reputation as the perfect hostess.

Join Evelyn, her daughter Mallory, and their close friends for this heartwarming Christmas story set in the Vegan Vamp world.

CHAPTER ONE

Sometimes a woman has to pressure her child. Sometimes apply guilt. Sometimes it simply takes more than that. What was that saying? Walk softly but carry a big golf club?

My husband had always been the golfer in our family, though he certainly hadn't walked softly. But he was gone, and though I could hardly celebrate the fact that he'd died—that would be heartless—I could celebrate the fact that the cheating oaf had died before either our divorce was finalized or he'd changed his will.

But his absence meant that I was the golfing parent now. It wasn't a role I felt suited me. I'd always been more of a tennis player. But suited or not, it was time to pull that club out. I dialed my daughter's number.

Praise be, the child answered. At least she wasn't so far gone as to duck my calls. "Mother, how are you? I don't have long to talk."

"Mallory, darling, one should always have time for one's mother." I let a slight edge sharpen my voice. "And it has been—oh, let me see—how long has it been since I've set eyes on you, darling?"

A tense silence followed my question. Naturally. Tense silences occurred when one's child hid from her mother—for months.

"Mallory? Are you still there?" I tapped the phone. "The line's gone all quiet."

A beleaguered sigh followed. She must think I was going deaf in my dotage. Well, I was neither in my dotage nor going deaf. "Yes, Mother, I'm still here. And I know it's been a little while since we've gotten together. Work has been..."

"What was that? Work's been demanding? What is it that you do, now that you've changed careers? I'm not sure you've ever been clear on that point, sweetheart."

Mallory had been rabidly avoiding dispensing any information about her mysterious new job, and the opening had simply been too good to pass up. Not to imply that a mother-daughter relationship was a battle. Certainly not. It was more a protracted war in which two parties fought, sometimes together, sometimes apart, against the rest of the world.

"Ah, my job, I...um, I was doing some client work, and then—"

"Client work? What type of client work?" Pressure applied, and now for the walk back. "You know what, darling, that's all right. I'm in a bit of a rush myself. Maybe we can discuss your job later." And then that big golf swing. "At Christmas dinner. I know you wouldn't miss Christmas dinner with your widowed mother."

Reference to my widowed status might seem extreme, but adding a touch of guilt was always wise when dealing with naughty children. I examined my manicure. I really must start bringing my own polish. The new line of products the salon used wasn't holding up. And it wasn't like I participated in any particularly strenuous or arduous tasks. Tennis and yoga certainly didn't count. Although, I suppose life had gotten a little more physical of late with my gentleman friend. What that man could do with his—

"All right. Yes, Mother, I'll see you at Christmas dinner."

"Lovely!" I paused for effect. "And we can be thankful that you won't be coming down with that flu bug that's been going around, since you already had your nasty little run-in with it over Thanksgiving...isn't that right?"

I could almost hear her teeth grinding.

It's never pleasant to be caught in a lie. It served the little reprobate right. Shame on her for skipping out on Thanksgiving dinner with her closest living relative. That had been when I still believed the never-ending excuses. I'd brought around soup, for goodness' sake! The ungrateful child had told me to leave it on the porch. What a way to behave. I'd raised her better than that.

Finally, she said, "I'm sure I won't be sick. You're right, I've already had the flu that's going around. About that... You know, I lost a bit of weight when I was sick. So, I, ah, I'm a little thinner than the last time you saw me."

Since I was as certain my child hadn't contracted the flu as I was of the inauthenticity of Buffy Segal's new four-carat ring, my suspicions were immediately aroused.

Not that my daughter couldn't stand to lose a few pounds. Mallory wasn't exactly round. She was what we used to call pleasantly plump, which had been code for "could probably lose ten or fifteen pounds and look better." But nowadays it wasn't considered acceptable to criticize weight, and I would never want my lovely girl to think she was failing in any way...even if she could stand to shed that little extra she carried around.

If not that fake flu of hers, then what *had* caused her weight loss? Hm. I supposed I'd have to skip it for now. Wouldn't want to get a hasty retraction for Christmas. "Well, then all the more reason to enjoy a lovely five-course Christmas dinner with your mother."

"Ah, and about that, so I've taken up a new diet..."

I waited. This should be good. Mallory did not diet. Not to fit into that special dress. Not to catch that elusive man. Not to increase her energy. Not to shame her slightly pudgier peers. My child liked to eat.

"Anyway, I might not be able to eat much, so don't go to too much trouble, okay?"

Hm. And then a thought dropped right into my head, a terrible, nasty thought. Drugs. My daughter had become a drug addict. She was doing meth and didn't want me to see that she'd ruined her lovely teeth and was wasting away. How long did one take meth before losing one's teeth?

"Darling, are you sure you're all right?"

A long-suffering sigh practically tickled my ear.

She really must think I was deaf.

"I'm fine, Mother, really."

The threat of drugs still loomed, so I wasn't so sure about that. But if she skipped out on Christmas dinner, my new gentleman friend and I were going to have a long chat. As my daughter's roommate, he'd been quite insistent from the beginning that we keep those particular boundaries intact.

He didn't discuss Mallory with me, and I only occasionally used my womanly wiles to get information out of him.

"Oh, sweetheart? I've invited Jefferson to join us for Christmas dinner. The poor dear doesn't have any family to celebrate with."

My daughter muttered, "Of course he doesn't." Then, in a brighter tone, added, "Do you mind if I invite a friend to even the numbers?"

And my heart soared. Every good hostess knows that even numbers implies an even mix of gentlemen and ladies. My daughter had a gentleman friend! I could barely contain my excitement, and it would explain so much. After taking a breath, I said, "Of course, Mallory. You're welcome to invite whomever you choose. I wouldn't wish anyone to spend Christmas alone."

I hung up—and then I pulled out the champagne. With a quick glance at the clock, I added a dash of orange juice. There, perfect for a midmorning libation.

"My daughter has a beau!" *Finally!*—but I would never say such a thing aloud. Not even in the privacy of my own home. I would, however, toast her future happiness.

When I was done celebrating—no mother wants a life of loneliness for her child—I looked at the phone in my hand. I might not be a golfer, but I'd gotten a few good swings in.

Now if only *all* the signs were pointing to this new gentleman friend—and not, God forbid, meth—then everything would be just fine. I'd have to get to the bottom of that particular mystery.

I was up to the challenge. This was my daughter, my only child. For her, I would climb mountains, so solving a little mystery was certainly manageable.

I'd even cook a Christmas dinner that met whatever strange new diet she was claiming to be following. We'd all have a fabulous dinner, while I rooted out the cause of all the recent changes in Mallory's life. And I promised myself that if it wasn't this man, if it was drugs, I could handle it.

I could. I would. I loved my daughter, and whatever was going on in her life, we'd get through it.

CHAPTER TWO

Five days later

Christmas dinner was going to be a disaster.

Months of on-and-off dating and not once had Jefferson's special dietary requirements arisen. I couldn't believe that we'd never shared a meal. We'd attended many events—soirees, award banquets, charity dinners, social luncheons. So many events with food, and yet he never ate a bite. How had I not seen that?

Then I smiled. I knew how. He'd claim to be watching his figure and then give me one of those looks that was just suggestive enough to tell me that he'd happily exit for a private interlude in the library, and all without being so crass as to leer.

The man had a talent. Many talents, I amended, when I considered the occasional side room we'd shared at events. A dark corner for a little hanky-panky, an isolated room for a little more. A sigh escaped my chest. It might not be love, but it certainly was a rather advanced case of full-blown lust.

Jefferson was delectable. The things that man could do made my insides quiver like so much lightly set custard.

And he could dance like a dream. He didn't complain about being kept waiting (a woman must always look her best), was always suitably attired—except for that beard that he refused to shave, but at least kept nicely trimmed—always handled the ordering and the check, and always drove and maintained his car as a gentleman should. He might be ten years younger than me, but that sort of thing wasn't nearly so gauche today as it had been a few years ago.

And then there was his body. His gorgeous body. Unlike so many men in my circle of acquaintance, he hadn't spread more around the middle the longer we'd dated. In fact, Jefferson had initially been, ah, "less than fit" would be the more delicate phrase. But the longer I'd known him, the fitter he'd become. And now... I clasped my hand to my chest. Now, my Jefferson had the body of a Norse god.

He sounded almost too good to be true. But he was real, and he was mine, every delicious, lickable inch of him. And there were many inches to lick. I fanned my face.

What had I been dithering over? I glanced at the pen and paper in front of me. The dinner menu. Yes, dinner. I fanned myself again. So the man had a few dietary foibles. The whole package was worth the trouble.

If only my daughter would reveal the constraints of her own diet, I might be able to plan a proper meal.

A warm glow suffused me. Mallory, dieting! I never thought a man could bring about such a change. But then a darker thought intruded again—perhaps it wasn't a man, but drugs. Surely it wasn't drugs.

I'd been reading up on addictive behaviors and the signs of drug abuse. It was chilling reading.

But there was nothing to be done until I saw my daughter with my own eyes. Then I could decide how best to tackle the problem. A little bit of that warm excitement burbled in my chest again: maybe, just maybe, she was in love. And not a drugged-up junkie.

CHAPTER THREE

Two days later, Christmas Eve, late afternoon

"**D**arling! You're so thin." I immediately regretted the comment. I'd always been thinner than Mallory, and she'd perceived that as an unspoken criticism. And for that to be the first thing I said on opening the door—shame on me. "The dress you're wearing is very flattering. It's a beautiful choice, sweetheart." I kissed her cheek, but her shoulder was tense under my hand.

"You look lovely, Mother." Mallory met my gaze and held it for a heartbeat before brushing past me.

Something was different. She always said I looked lovely. She was a good girl, and I'd raised her with a modicum of manners. But this time —I felt my eyes burn a bit—this time she *meant* it.

Much as I peeked around the front of the house at the drive, I couldn't spot her date.

She glanced over her shoulder and caught me checking. "It's just me. My friend Alex drove separately. He's running late."

She looked rather put out by the fact. Especially considering that she was calling him a friend. Not her boyfriend. Not even her date.

I shut the door then tipped my head. "Work? On Christmas?"

"Oh, I'm not sure." She seemed to consider the question then nodded. "It might be. Alex does some work as an emergency responder."

That conjured all variety of possibilities. Firefighter? Paramedic? Not Mallory's usual type, but whoever could hold my daughter's interest must be fascinating, whatever he did. And there were all those calendars with all those bulging muscles, so maybe he was interesting in *that* way.

"When are you expecting Wembley?"

"I really don't understand why you call him that, dear. His name is Jefferson." I patted the back of my French twist. "I'm sure he'll be here shortly. Jefferson is always on time."

"Okay. I just wondered, because he left our place at least a half an hour before me."

I could feel my cheeks tingle. Most certainly I could expect a lovely arrangement for the table or a festive bouquet for the credenza in the hallway. Jefferson always did the right thing. I was sure that was what had detained him. I'd expected them to arrive yesterday, and I hadn't any idea where he might be retrieving them, because no florist was open the afternoon of Christmas Eve.

As Mallory hung her jacket in the coat closet, her lips twitched. "I thought you didn't approve of women dating younger men. When Francesca had her fling with that twenty-nine year-old, you thought she'd lost her mind."

"Not her mind, dear, her sense." I touched my neck and hair again, only recognizing the fidget after I'd already ascertained that it was as neat as it should be. "Besides," I added in an airy tone, "I haven't a clue about Jefferson's age. It hasn't come up."

Mallory started to cough. She covered her mouth and gasped for breath. Maybe she was coming down with something. Maybe she truly had been sick before. Maybe her immunity had been shattered by all the drugs she was doing. Oh, God.

I rubbed her back, trying to sneak a closer look at her mouth when she lowered her hand. Some of the pictures I'd found online, oh my, appalling.

When she caught her breath, she said, "Wow, Mom, no need to

look so worried. I'm fine. I'm not getting sick, I just, ah, I swallowed wrong...or something." Her voice trailed away to nothing, and she averted her eyes.

That girl was hiding something, and before she left tonight, I was going to find out what.

The ring of the doorbell had me switching to hostess mode, so it would have to wait—for now.

When I opened the door, I discovered a slightly disheveled, very tall man on the doorstep. No, on second glance, not disheveled. He had more than a shadow of scruff, perhaps a week's worth of beard, but he was attired as one ought to be for a family Christmas dinner. Slacks, a button-down shirt, a beautiful tie, but no jacket. He simply had a rakish air about him that his refusal to shave reinforced.

My warmest hostess smile in place, I extended my hand. "Hello. I'm Evelyn Andrews, Mallory's mother. Welcome to my home."

He accepted my hand and shook it with exactly the right amount of pressure, neither so briefly as to slight nor so long as to be forward. "Alex Valois. It's a pleasure to meet you."

That voice. If my daughter wasn't interested in this man, she should be.

"Please come inside." I opened the door wider and gestured for him to enter.

"Thank you for having me. I appreciate being included in your family dinner." He handed me a bottle of wine as he crossed the threshold.

Hm. Perhaps they'd just begun to date? Those didn't sound like the words of a man in a committed long-term relationship. "You're more than welcome, Mr. Valois—"

"Alex."

I nodded. "Alex. We're both very happy to have you. And thank you for the wine." I glanced at the label then looked again. Alex Valois had expensive taste in wine.

Before I could impress—with some subtlety, of course—how welcome a man was in my daughter's life, at least so far as her mother was concerned, the doorbell rang again.

With a touch on his shoulder, I pointed to the bar. "Please, help yourself."

He removed his coat and handed it to Mallory, and I had to peel away my attention from shoulders that had been revealed as surprisingly broad and the lovely shape of his derriere. It was always delightful when a man could fill out a pair of pants nicely.

After depositing the bottle of red wine on the credenza, I opened the door. The doorway was filled with a gorgeous bouquet of white, green, and a pinch of red. Now that would have to go in the hallway. It would make the entryway smell lovely for days. I accepted both the bouquet and a kiss to the cheek before ushering Jefferson inside.

"Mallory, darling, take Jefferson's coat while I put these in a vase. Aren't they gorgeous?" I leaned closer as I passed by. "And your friend Alex brought a divine bottle of red."

"Does that mean I'm forgiven?" Jefferson asked.

I paused en route to the kitchen and gave him a very pointed look. If he couldn't interpret the clear signs of "not now" and "speaking will result in your castration," then he was blind.

"What have you done now, Wembley?" my daughter asked.

"Ah. You two should consider speaking about—" My daughter's glare derailed him, and after a substantial and quite noticeable pause, Jefferson said, "Things."

Mallory flushed, and I noticed, not for the first time this evening, how impeccably she'd applied her makeup. She looked ten years younger. "I don't want to talk about *things*, Wembley."

Jefferson's gaze darted between the two of us, and I caught a calculating look in his eye that wasn't at all familiar.

"All right," he said, nodding and looking much too agreeable. "Just so you're aware of your mother's concerns and the possible stress that she's under—" Surely he wouldn't dare, but I tried to catch his eye, just in case he would. He ignored me and continued, "I've refused to answer her questions about a burgeoning drug problem she's concerned you might have."

My hand flew up to pat my perfectly coiffed hair, and I knew the small gasp I heard was my own.

Talented tongue and magical hands notwithstanding, I might just have to kill that man.

CHAPTER FOUR

The kitchen and a vase for the flowers called. Mostly because I couldn't face my daughter. What if I were wrong and this terrible pall had been created for nothing?

Worse—what if I were right?

And for this shadow to be cast so blatantly over a holiday meal—I was going to kill Jefferson. I had never known him to be so insensitive, so inappropriate. I shoved the drawer that had contained the florist scissors with too much force, and it closed with a sharp thud.

That man. Months we'd spent together. He knew how important my daughter was to me. He knew she and I hadn't been close lately. I could throttle him.

I started to split the stems, but my hand was shaking, so I dropped the scissors.

And where was the handsome devil? He should be here apologizing, begging my forgiveness for his terrible lapse in judgment.

Rummaging through the shelves, I found the perfect vase, and then made myself spend the next several minutes tweaking the flowers until they were just so—plenty of time for him to come and check on me. Plenty of time for him to formulate a heartfelt apology.

But when I'd placed one particular white rose in its fourth and least attractive position, I realized the terrible man wasn't going to apologize. And I was going to have to face my daughter at some point.

So I tidied up the mess, found the perfect place for that innocent white rose, and picked up the arrangement.

Time to face the music.

When I returned to the formal living room, I found the three of them gathered tightly together, looking for all the world as if they were plotting something nefarious.

A truly terrible thought occurred. It *was* drugs, and they were all in it together. Jefferson's income was a mystery—a lady did not inquire when the information was not offered—and he was my daughter's roommate. He claimed he enjoyed the company, but the house was really very small for someone with his income.

And this Alex Valois, he and Jefferson knew each other long before Mallory had come into the picture.

Mallory's reluctance to discuss her new work, her roommate who could afford his own home but continued to share hers, a gentleman friend who also had mysterious employment…

That was it. Alex, Jefferson, and Mallory were manufacturing and selling drugs. And Mallory must have gotten hooked, hence all the weight loss.

My daughter and drugs. My eyes burned.

"Mom?" Mallory saw that I'd returned and left her little band of drug-manufacturing thugs. "Don't get upset. It's not at all what you're thinking."

I willed the tears away. This was Christmas. Christmas Eve dinner was not a place for tears and confrontations. For which Jefferson should be thankful. I targeted him with the look of impending doom.

"We're not discussing this now. Right now, we're having Christmas dinner."

The table was set, the food already prepared except for a few final touches—if one could call it food. Maybe drug dealers and druggies had strange food cravings? Or bizarre dietary needs?

I decided to forgo the preprandial niceties. Aperitifs might be *de rigueur*, but that involved making small talk…with a bunch of drug dealers. Much better to have a table of food between me and them.

"Please, have a seat in the dining room. Mallory will show you the way. I'll just be a moment in the kitchen." I didn't consider myself a particularly cowardly woman, but one was allowed a graceful retreat when entertaining possible criminals. Or so I assumed. I'd only ever hosted the one, and Alan Smith-Sanderson had been suspected of a white-collar crime—fraud, perhaps?—at the time. Not at all the same thing.

Once in the kitchen, I took a few deep breaths, patted my hair into place, and served up the soup course. The *first* soup course. Who ever heard of multiple courses of soup? It really wasn't done. But a good hostess does not question the needs of her guests, she simply accommodates them.

Before loading them on the serving tray, I peeked in on the individual servings of vegan fondue that were baking in the oven, and turned the temperature down.

Vegan fondue—who would have thought? But Jefferson had given me the name of the cheese to use, a neighbor had provided the recipe, and the test batch had been surprisingly edible.

It was time to return to my guests and serve the soup. I was going to put a good face on this if it killed me. I stopped to catch my breath as panic hit. For all I knew, this could be the last Christmas I had with Mallory on the outside. My little girl could be incarcerated this time next year.

That thought could not enter my head or I'd ruin Christmas dinner by crying.

As I returned with the serving tray of soup, I heard Alex say, "You should tell her. You only have a certain amount of time left before—" He stopped abruptly when he saw me enter.

Alex immediately stood, took the tray from me, and placed it on the side table. What drug dealer was ever so polite? Though I didn't have much of a pool for comparison. I gestured for him to have a seat and served the soup. And as I sat down, I said, "Apple and squash soup. I hope you enjoy it."

There were murmurs of appreciation all around the table, which I accepted with a smile. But Alex's comment wouldn't fade away. It kept tapping away in my mind. Mallory only had so much time...limited time...weight loss...a special diet.

And then I realized, and the world fell out from under my feet. "Oh my God. It's not drugs. You're dying."

I couldn't breathe. I was fifty-nine and losing everything. My little girl was dying.

CHAPTER FIVE

"Mother! I'm not dying." Mallory turned to Alex and said, "I told you this was a bad idea. I shouldn't have come."

Now that caught my attention. My eyes narrowed. "Not come to Christmas dinner? When you might not"—my breath caught on a sob —"when you might not be here next Christmas?"

She was breaking my heart all over again. And just when I'd seen a spark of connection—oh, I wanted to cry. This was the worst Christmas ever, worse even than the year we hosted Edward's corporate Christmas party and the neighbors had erected a giant glowing snow globe in the yard. My mother must be turning over in her grave in shame.

"Mom." Mallory knelt next to my chair. She took my hand—the one that wasn't clutching my linen napkin and dabbing at the tears slowly leaking from my eyes. "Mom, listen to me. I'm not dying. I'm not sick." She sighed. "Not exactly. Well, sort of."

I hiccuped. I knew it. She was sick. Why else all the liquids? And vegan cheese? My nose wrinkled involuntarily. No one ate vegan cheese because they *wanted* to. Did they? Although the trial run of the fondue had been quite tasty...

"I might have kept things from you in the past, but I don't lie, not about the important things. I never have." She squeezed my fingers. "You remember what I said when you talked to me about Dad? You were worried that your marital problems were having some kind of horrible effect on my life, so you sat me down to talk about what was about to happen." A look of amusement crossed her face. "Even though I was well into my thirties."

A watery chuckle escaped my lips, taking me by surprise. Even with the threat of a serious illness in my daughter's future, I still found that conversation surprising and funny. That had been the first hint at my daughter's deeply buried and little-used sense of humor.

I dabbed at the corners of my eyes again. "You gave me a top-ten list of reasons to leave your father." I peeked up at her. "You know, I still have that list." I smirked as I recalled numbers three and seven, relating specifically to physical attributes of Lawrence and his latest floozy—Candy.

"See. I was brutally honest then, and I'm being honest with you now. I'm not dying. Not today, and"—she shared a glance with Jefferson—"probably not for a *very* long time. Are we good? Can I go eat the rest of that fabulous soup you made, preferably before it's cold?"

I sniffed. "It's quite tasty chilled, actually, though with the weather what it is, warm is so much better." I sat up straighter. "Of course. Please, go eat your soup, honey."

But I wasn't comforted. Well, perhaps I was a bit, but only a little bit. If death wasn't immediately in the offing, then maybe it was drugs and incarceration that I had to worry about. Or some terrible, lingering illness. Maybe she wasn't going to die immediately, but would waste away over a course of years?

She finished her soup and asked if she might help herself to seconds.

My eyes narrowed as I agreed she might. Perhaps not wasting away, but something was wrong with my daughter.

As I tried to get my breath—my daughter was not dying—I peered at the mysterious Alex. So Alex had told Mallory to fess up to her mother. Handsome, excellent taste in wine, met minimally acceptable standards for appearance and attire, not flat broke (the wine had been quite expensive), and encouraged open lines of communication with her mother. Oh, Mallory needed to keep this one...so long as he wasn't the head of some drug cartel.

When she returned with a second bowl for both herself and Alex, I found I'd only finished half of my own. Nothing to do with the soup, which was quite tasty. There might be something to this vegan diet, if one did the appropriate research and knew the right people to ask. Suzanne from two doors down had given me this and another recipe that had vied for a place on the menu. I hadn't even known Suzanne was a vegan, but apparently she'd joined the ranks not long after one of her teenage children had started refusing to eat anything that came from an animal.

I set down my spoon. I just couldn't finish the soup—tasty or not. Not when I didn't know what in the world was happening with my daughter. I excused myself to check on the vegan fondue, and returned a few minutes later with the tiny pots of faux cheese. I hoped it was filling enough to warrant its place on the menu as the entrée. We only had a light consommé and dessert drinks to follow.

After serving the individual pots, Alex and I used the tiny toasts and various vegetables arranged at intervals across the table to dip into the fondue. Jefferson and Mallory ate it much like a soup. Could my poor little girl not eat any solids at all? I'd thought that a mild exaggeration when she told me.

What little appetite I had left fled as I tried to parse the puzzle of my daughter's illness. What could possible cause such odd symptoms?

I glanced up to find Jefferson sending Mallory critical looks interspersed with intense interest in his fondue.

Finally, Mallory caught his eye and, with her lips pinched, shook her head.

Jefferson set aside his fondue and pushed his chair back a few inches. Looking between me and Mallory, his face took on a grim cast, and my heart did an erratic little hop-skip in my chest.

Jefferson closed his eyes, muttered something to do with Odin, then said, "Oh, please put everyone here out of their misery, Mallory, and just tell the poor woman."

And my daughter growled. Right there at the dinner table, like a heathen with no manners.

I frowned at her. "Mallory—"

"Mom, I'm a vampire."

I blinked at her and shook my head. "Pardon me?"

My daughter, who until this moment had only shown signs of anxiety and mild obsessive-compulsive order, said once more, "I'm a vampire."

My sweet little girl wasn't dying.

She was bonkers.

CHAPTER SIX

"Bourbon milk punch for dessert, anyone?" To heck with the consommé. I needed liquor. I looked around the table, waiting for replies.

Jefferson and Alex both nodded, so I turned to Mallory with my hostess mask firmly in place. "It's made with almond milk, darling. Would you like some?"

She was pinching her lips together, something I recognized from her childhood. She used to do that when she had a secret. This could not be good. Not if there was still more to tell.

How did one have one's child committed? Maybe Alex would know. He worked in that field, didn't he? Although—I peeked at Alex and Wembley from under my lashes as I pretended to fold my napkin. They both looked much too sanguine, given Mallory's revelation. Were they involved somehow with her delusion?

"Wembley's a vampire, too!" Mallory blurted, then blushed a fiery red and mouthed, "I'm sorry," to Wembley.

Group delusion? Prank? They were all on drugs *right now*?

I set my napkin to the side of my barely touched fondue. "I'll just go fetch those drinks, why don't I?"

For the life of me, I couldn't meet a single eye in the room. I slipped out of my seat and made a hasty retreat to the kitchen.

I loved my kitchen. It was a place where I was in control. It was modern and tidy. The fixtures gleamed. Everything had its proper place.

Where was the proper place for a daughter who thought she was a vampire?

And didn't vampires drink blood? Maybe those were last-century vampires. Maybe the vampires of today were juicers, hence Mallory's liquid diet preferences.

I retrieved a tea towel and my lavender water. After liberally spritzing the towel, I sat down at the kitchen table, leaned back, and covered my entire face with the scented towel. I just needed a moment of lavender-imbued silence to contemplate the situation.

I wasn't hiding. A good hostess would never hide from her guests.

Several slow and measured breaths later, I removed the towel. I *was* hiding, and it was lovely. But I couldn't hide forever, I had guests.

I needed to approach this problem in a calm and logical fashion.

Set up an evaluation for Mallory with...who was that man that Suzanne's other daughter, not the vegan one, started to see when she had her breakdown? Dr. Dinmeyer? Or was it Dinmann? Whoever, Suzanne swore by the man. I'd get his information from her after Christmas. But what to do *today*? *Now*?

And with relief, I realized I knew exactly what to do. I'd told my guests I was fetching drinks, and that was exactly what I would do.

For the moment, I needed to prepare those drinks. I could work on the problem as I prepped. I snuck a sip, then another. Maybe things would look better after I just finished off this one drink.

When a strategy didn't present itself after I'd finished my second milk punch, I decided that additional information was required. I needed to find out if my daughter was dangerous. How far from reality had she stepped, and what were these delusions pushing her to do?

Maybe it was all quite harmless, like a personality quirk. Great-Auntie Lula had always been a bit eccentric, and while there had been whispers, she certainly had never been committed...so far as I knew.

Or maybe it was a lifestyle choice. This was the twenty-first century, and embracing different lifestyles was what one did.

Vampirism didn't seem to quite fit that category, but I hardly kept up with all the latest trends.

Drinks prepared and my third milk punch long gone, I headed back to the dining room with my investigative hat on and the drinks tray in my hands. As I passed the lavender-scented tea towel on my way out, I gave it a final wistful glance.

I'd wanted to know what was happening with my daughter. And now that I knew, I was glad. Not that she'd lost her grip with reality, of course, but glad that the problem was out in the open. We could start to deal with it.

Or not.

Because the dining room was empty when I returned. Empty. As in, no guests present. They weren't all just crackers, they were heathens.

Should I look for the wayward bunch of vampires? Except Alex hadn't been slapped with the label. Mallory had only indicated Jefferson in her group delusion. Alex had gone along with it, but...

Oh, I was tired. I was too old to keep up with the trends kids followed these days. That was my last hope, that this was some kind of trend. Otherwise, I didn't see any other way. Mallory would have to be committed.

And then they trooped back in the room, the whole lot of them—and an extra one.

"Hello?" I rose to my feet in dismay. This small family event had just completely spiraled out of control. Strangers were appearing uninvited at the dinner table.

The tiny blond woman was wearing an appalling Christmas sweater and a very put-upon expression. "I'm sorry to intrude, but these idiots seem to have created an unpleasant situation"—she turned to glare at the threesome—"and thought I might be able to help."

My eyebrows climbed. "Are you a vampire as well?"

She hesitated then said firmly, "No."

A whoosh of relief swept through me. Small favors. Now if she'd just explain what she was doing in my home—

A hopeful look crossed her face when she saw the drinks. "Is that milk punch?"

"Yes, with bourbon," I replied with my best hostess smile. Even uninvited strangers should be made to feel welcome—at least, that seemed best until I sorted out who she was and what exactly she was doing in my home. "It's the vegan variety. Would you like a glass?" When she seemed unsure, I prompted her to have a seat. "Please. Mallory will fetch you a glass."

Mallory didn't hesitate. It was like she grew wings, she was gone so quickly.

Before seating herself, the woman said, "My name is Star, ah, Stephanie Kawolski, and it's kind of you to have me. Especially so unexpectedly." She shot Wembley and Alex a nasty look.

Once I sat down, Alex and Wembley both took their seats again. "So, why are you here, Stephanie? I'm sure you have Christmas plans of your own." I glanced at the sweater.

She glanced down and grinned. "A gift from my children. I've actually already eaten dinner with my family. With small children, we schedule early, so I was just wrapping up when these buffoons called me."

"So why are you here?" I asked.

Stephanie looked at Alex. "Yes, Alex. Explain to the very kind woman why I've gate-crashed her quiet family evening."

Except it was Wembley who spoke. "She's here just in case things go amiss. We wanted to be sure that someone who was especially gifted at...ah, counseling was on hand if you didn't take things well."

This woman was no counselor.

"What in the world are you up to, Jefferson? What have you gotten my daughter involved in?"

He raised his hands. "I met her afterward. She was already—"

"I was already a vampire when Wembley met me, Mom." Mallory entered the dining room and placed Stephanie's drink in front of her. "They're quite good. Mom found a great milk substitute."

With a quick, sweeping glance, I found that Stephanie seemed unsurprised by the announcement, Alex was watching me like a hawk —what did the man think I might do?—and Jefferson...Jefferson was so immersed in this fiasco that I wasn't sure I cared what he was doing.

A vampire—what would that man come up with next? I blinked at him. Looked again. Blinked. "Jefferson, are those fangs?"

CHAPTER SEVEN

G iven the circumstances, I was proud of myself.

I didn't faint. I didn't cry. I didn't even scream. I was the perfect hostess...in my mind, at least.

In reality, I wasn't entirely certain what I did.

"Mom?" Mallory held my hand and was tapping it.

It wasn't as if I'd passed out—had I? "Darling, I'm fine." I clasped her hand between my own.

"Are you?" Mallory asked. Then she sniffed. "Mom...how much milk punch have you had?"

"Oh, really?" I shooed her back to her seat, and Alex, as well, when I found him hovering on the other side of my chair. "You ask me how much I've had to drink after you tell me that you're not dying but you're sick, and, oh, by the way, you're a *vampire*?" I shot her a narrow-eyed look. "You may not criticize my drinking habits."

Stephanie chuckled. "Mrs. Andrews—"

"Evelyn, please."

"Evelyn, I might adore you."

At which point my other three guests turned to stare at her. It seemed apparent by their response that Stephanie did not often declare her adoration.

"That's so kind of you say, Stephanie. Would you like some consommé? Or perhaps some fondue? Vegan, of course, but it won't take a moment to reheat."

Stephanie grinned broadly. "No, I'm still full from my family dinner, but thank you so much for asking." She turned to Alex and Jefferson. "Well, boys, what do you have to say to Evelyn?"

I glanced at Alex, but my gaze rested on Jefferson. Much as I peered, I couldn't detect those fangs I was certain I'd seen before.

"Our sincerest apologies for surprising you with an unexpected guest," Alex said.

Jefferson nodded. "Of course, yes. Although Sta-Stephanie is handy in a crisis, and we weren't entirely certain how you'd react to—"

"Your fangs?" I asked. When he didn't deny it, I knew that what I'd seen was real. With a stiff smile directed at my daughter, I said, "And Mallory, do you also have fangs?"

There. I'd said "fangs" twice now without flinching or hysterical laughter. Mother would be proud.

"I do, but they're much smaller than Wembley's," she said, looking oddly chagrined.

My lips twitched, but since my thoughts were hardly appropriate, I wouldn't share them. I couldn't help a quick glance in Wembley's direction, and caught one of his patented, heated come-hither looks.

My cheeks tingled, as did some other parts of my body. The man was so deliciously naughty. And perhaps...a vampire. That was certainly something to explore in more detail. After the dinner guests had gone, naturally.

I clasped my hands together in my lap. "All right, Mallory." I steeled myself. Seeing my lover with fangs was one thing, but my child... "Let me have a look."

An appalled expression crossed her face. "I don't think so."

"I'm your mother, darling. I've seen you in the buff, ill, and completely out of sorts. I can handle fangs." I pursed my lips primly, then added, "Tiny fangs, you said. I'm sure they're barely noticeable."

And when they appeared, I had to remind myself that my daughter had expressed some sensitivity concerning her newly acquired fangs. I pressed my lips together. I would not smile. I would not. But then I did, because there were just so adorable. Especially compared to Jefferson's much, um, *larger* set.

She covered her mouth with her hand, and when she removed it, her fangs had disappeared. Just like Jefferson's. "Happy?"

"No need for sarcasm. Now." I clasped my hands firmly together. "You need to tell me everything. Every single bit of it. And if you leave any important parts out, I will know. I am your mother, and I *always* know."

Stephanie and I shared a look of mutual understanding. She was a mother. She knew exactly what I was talking about.

It turned out that my daughter had met a man, just not the romantic catch I would have hoped for her. She'd crossed paths with a predator who had infected her. As she told me how that had happened and what had followed, I did my very best to be strong. But my poor little girl—

"Mom, don't cry. I'm fine. Really. Aren't I, guys?"

Everyone around the table agreed that, indeed, my daughter was doing quite well. But I still gave her a hug.

With my arms around her, she patted my back and said softly, "And he's dead. He's gone."

The surge of satisfaction I felt was enough to banish my tears.

After I'd taken my seat again, I asked, "What about the blood?" That seemed an important question.

"No blood. I'm a bit of an anomaly there. No blood—it actually makes me really sick, even the smell."

I nodded. That made sense. "You always were squeamish about blood."

Mallory shrugged. "And I guess I still am. Also, no solids, and so far nothing but plant-derived foods."

"But you're saying that's not typical." A mother did try to avoid using the word "normal," and in the case of vampires, that seemed particularly wise.

After a resounding agreement from all present that, no, that was certainly *not* typical, I directed my attention to a certain vampire who had a lot of explaining to do. I pasted a pleasantly inquisitive look on my face. "And you, Jefferson? Do you consume blood?"

Jefferson squirmed in his chair, just like a schoolboy. "I might." One stern look from me, and he said, "Yes, but it's all very civilized these days. No murdering or rampaging."

He might have added "anymore," but I was a lady, so I pretended not to hear.

"Hm." Morbid curiosity had me wondering about the logistics, but how did one ask such a question delicately? Where were the lines of etiquette drawn when discussing how and from what sources one partook of blood?

"Go on, Mom. I know you have questions."

Again, how did one ask such a question delicately? One didn't. One simply asked. "Do you use the bagged or the fresh variety?" I frowned. Would I need to start stocking blood? Perhaps a second refrigerator in the utility room...

"Bagged contains preservatives, and that doesn't really..." Jefferson's gaze locked on my face. He cleared his throat. "Ah, fresh is best."

Alex intervened before poor Jefferson could entirely insert his foot into his mouth. "What Wembley means to say is that there's a bottled version. Collected by donors and then stored in stasis bottles."

"Stasis bottles? That sounds very high-tech." I considered space and hygiene concerns.

Mallory fidgeted. "More *witch*-tech than high-tech"

"Witches. There are witches?"

Mallory nodded.

"Now that's exciting." I'd always had a secret fascination for witches. And there was the neighbor down the way who practiced Wicca. Was there a connection between Wicca and Mallory's witches? But back to the blood, because one must be prepared at all times for guests. "So about these stasis bottles, should they be stored in any special way? Perhaps a dedicated refrigeration unit?" I tapped my finger on the table. "I'm thinking a small unit in the utility room. Oh, perhaps warmed? Do I need special equipment to heat it?"

The scent of garlic made my nose twitch, and I looked up to see my daughter crying. And the more her tears ran, the stronger the scent became.

"Sweetheart, is it possible, I hate to ask, but..." I leaned close and whispered, "Darling, do your tears smell like garlic?"

She sniffled and wiped her face. But instead of answering me, she said, "Mother, I love you."

"I know, honey. I love you too." Silly girl, as if there was anything she could do—or be—that would make me love her less.

I did let loose a discreet sigh of relief. No need for that appointment with Dr. Dinmann, thankfully. I would have to do some reorganizing to find the perfect spot for these stasis bottles of blood, but that seemed simple enough. And a better juicer. The one I had simply wouldn't do. There'd be a lot of juicing happening at the house now.

A few questions still buzzed around in my head. For example, if not vampires, what exactly were Alex Valois and Stephanie Kawolski?

With a smile, I turned my attention to the pair of them. "So, tell me more about yourselves."

I'd get to the bottom of it. After all, they were my daughter's friends. Best to know exactly who she was spending her time with.

I caught a glimpse of her out of the corner of my eye, and realized her tears had left red marks down her face. I leaned close again and whispered, "Darling, I think you need to powder your nose." I nudged her. "Literally."

She laughed. "Yes, Mom, I imagine I do." And she quietly left to do just that.

EPILOGUE

My daughter, a vampire. Heavens, who would have thought? I grinned as I rinsed the last of the dishes. Certainly not Suzanne, down the road. Oh, Lord—or her father. No telling what Edward would have said. That man could be so rigid. I'd never go so far as to say I was *thankful* he'd passed on, but perhaps to be thankful he'd missed this particular stage of our daughter's life wasn't so terrible.

I removed my gloves. I'd forgotten how relaxing washing dishes could be. With the cleaner on holiday for the next few days and so much of the dinnerware not dishwasher safe, it had been unavoidable. But dishes for five people, that was only a moment's work in any event.

The milk punch was looking inviting. Perhaps—no, that wasn't quite what I was craving. I started to towel-dry the last bit of dampness from the dishes.

My daughter a vampire—and Stephanie a witch. She'd been only too happy to exchange numbers with me. I was certain the charming woman felt surrounded by people wholly unlike herself. My daughter, newly turned. And Jefferson had hardly been at his best this evening.

Ah, Jefferson.

I'd decided to send him home. It wouldn't do for him to think he could betray a confidence without some repercussion. Though he had been attempting to bring my daughter and I closer together... No, sending him home had been the right choice. It did feel as though I'd punished myself, but that simply couldn't be helped. Jefferson and I could explore his, ah, vampireness some other time.

Stacking the last of the dishes, I decided on the red that Alex had brought. I was feeling the need to indulge, and for whatever reason, red wine sounded divine. And the man had excellent taste in wine.

Alex was a mystery. He seemed to exude a kind of self-contained confidence, short of arrogance, but intense. And not a word as to *what* he was. Not a vampire or a witch, if there were such a thing as male witches—or would that be a warlock? But his silence on the topic had been noteworthy.

I wondered if Mallory knew that her date—and yes, Alex had most certainly been her date—had a shared history with the now happily married Stephanie Kawolski? It was impossible to miss, if one knew what signs to watch for. And I most certainly knew those signs.

That might make the furtherance of my acquaintanceship with Stephanie slightly awkward, but I liked her. We might not be so very alike, but I sensed a possible friend and perhaps an ally in this world that my daughter had entered.

I'd give her a call next week. Perhaps she could sneak away for brunch or a manicure.

I sat down at the kitchen table with my glass of red (it was truly divine) and my laptop. I'd just have a quick look at that juicer that Suzanne bought recently when her vegan daughter went on a juicing kick. Or was that the other daughter? The one that saw the psychiatrist?

Oh, and what was the brand of that adorable little fridge that the Nelsons had in their bar? That would fit perfectly in the utility room. Also a microwave...

I hope you enjoyed this peek into Mallory's world through her mom's eyes. If you'd like to read more about Mallory's adventures as a vegan vampire, the series begins with Adventures of a Vegan Vamp.

ABOUT THE AUTHOR

When Cate's not tapping away at her keyboard or in deep contempla-
tion of her next fanciful writing project, she's sweeping up hairy dust
bunnies and watching British mysteries. Cate writes and lives in
Austin, Texas (where many of her stories take place) with her pack of
pointers and hounds. She's worked as an attorney, a dog trainer, and in
various other positions, but writer is the hands-down winner.

Cate writes paranormal cozies (Vegan Vamp Mysteries & Death
Retired) and romance (The Goode Witch Matchmaker & Lucky
Magic) as Cate Lawley and paranormal (Lost Library) & urban fantasy
(Spirelli) as Kate Baray.

Follow Cate Lawley online:
Her Newsletter
Her blog
Amazon
Facebook
BookBub

THE MYSTERY OF THE CHRISTMAS DOLL

ANI GONZALEZ

SUMMARY

Christmas in Banshee Creek usually means cold weather, hot chocolate, and lots of toys. But when a haunted doll with a bloody past arrives in the Magical Curiosity Shoppe, Dora Pendragon suspects that the innocent-looking toy is determined to find a new owner. Will Dora solve the mystery behind the doll before it finds a new victim?

CHAPTER ONE

D ecember in Virginia. Ugh. It wasn't as cold as the outer rings of Hades, exactly, but it was close. It had been cloudy all day and the afternoon chill was hard to cope with. I could feel my hands turning blue inside my jacket pockets.

Double ugh.

I ignored the cold and paused in front of my store in jeans and a puffy winter jacket, scanning my surroundings in the dim light.

Back alley? Check.

Broken streetlamp? Check.

Shabby wooden sign with "Magical Curiosity Shoppe" written in creepy Goth script? Check.

Yep, my shop was still here in Banshee Creek, Virginia, USA.

Ensconced in its small brick building, the store looked old and well established, as if it had been sitting there for centuries. The stone steps were well-worn and the front window had a crack. The place looked like the rest of this Colonial-era town, aged and respectable.

A neat trick, considering my shop had appeared in Banshee Creek only a few weeks ago.

And I mean "appeared" quite literally. The Magical Curiosity Shoppe was one of those interdimensional establishments that hopped from one reality to another, causing people to exclaim "Wait, that wasn't there yesterday."

They all looked the same, shabby little shops full of antiques and odds and ends. You never found what you were looking for in those shops, but sometimes you found what you needed. Or, if you were terribly unlucky, what needed *you*.

This wasn't my first time in Banshee Creek. The town sat on a powerful ley line and my wandering shop was obviously attracted to that energy. But my last visit had been several years ago. Actually, almost a century ago. Time flies when you're having fun.

The town hadn't changed much, at least this part of Main Street. It had electricity now and lots of cars, but that was about it. The Colonial-era buildings were still standing and Victorian homes still dotted the streets. Strong magic had that effect. It preserved things.

Things like ghosts.

The town was famous for its many spectral inhabitants. The first thing I was told when I showed up a few weeks ago was that it had been voted America's Most Haunted town.

No wonder my shop kept returning. But why was it still hanging around? That was the question.

I opened the heavy wood door and stepped into the Magical Curiosity Shoppe. Right now I needed heat. Luckily, the shop came prepared and delicious warm air hit my face the moment I stepped inside.

"You look like an ambulatory iceberg, Dora," a gravelly voice said from behind the counter.

I turned, taking off my jacket, as a black and white cat leapt onto the wood counter.

"I feel it too," I replied, removing my wool beanie and letting my long, dark hair loose.

Despite the shop's warmth, I was still shivering. Born, raised and cursed in the balmy Greek isles, it took me a while to understand the northern midwinter traditions about slaying the dreaded winter gods. I understood them now, though.

"Why did you even go outside?" Bubo, my daemon cat, replied, sitting with his tail neatly wrapped around his legs. "You know what the weather is like here. It hailed for three days the last time we were here."

Bubo had many magical gifts, and pointing out the obvious was definitely one of them.

"I just wanted to check the facade," I replied.

Bubo snorted. "It's the same one every time. The only thing that changes is the language the sign is written on."

He was right again. I hadn't actually gone outside just to check the shop's exterior. I was feeling restless.

This was unfortunate given that I, like Bubo, was tied to the shop and thus moved along with it from dimension to dimension. I'd been doing it now for thousands of years, and, frankly, I was starting to feel claustrophobic.

I'd spent millennia trapped inside these four walls. Oh, I had visitors and new items arrived with regularity. The unicorn skeleton was barely fifty years old—an elderly French woman had brought it in when the shop popped up in Paris during the Vichy regime. Yaavik, the balding teddy bear who constantly cursed in Yiddish, had arrived a decade ago, left behind by a rotund young man of Romanian heritage during our last Las Vegas sojourn. The snow globe with the Cthulhu Santa Claus and the ominous "He's Keeping a List" warning—or was it a threat?—had arrived two weeks ago. It had been furtively exchanged for a copper dagger with evil-looking symbols even I couldn't identify.

But it was still the same cramped space with buckling wood shelves, erratic lighting, and a lingering smell of mothballs that filled me with cabin fever.

I was ready for a change. I was magically tethered to the store and couldn't leave it for long periods of time, but I could take a short break. And I really needed one.

Okay, fine. I'd needed a lot of breaks lately. Nothing wrong with that, right?

"I could drop by the bakery again," I mused. "Patricia baked us some cookies yesterday." I scanned the room, looking for the bakery owner's treats. "By the way, what happened to those?"

Bubo gave a discreet burp. "They were very good."

"You could have left one for me," I exclaimed. "Cats aren't even supposed to eat cookies. You're messing up your disguise."

"Did you share any of that coffee drink she brought with the cookies?" he asked. "No, you did not. We are even now."

He had a point, but, still, *cookies*. "What kind were they?"

"The card said 'Chocolate Peppermint Cookies-Cute But Haunted Name To Be Determined.'" He licked his whiskers. "They were tasty too."

"Ha, ha," I said, heading for the door. "That settles it. I'm heading for the bakery to get a drink. Maybe I'll try hot chocolate this time."

"Bring back more cookies," Bubo shouted. "And try not to freeze."

Easier said than done, at least the "not freezing" part. The cold hit me like a wall of ice as soon as I stepped outside. You'd think I'd be able to deal with freezing temperatures after thousands of years in this gig, but no.

I crossed the alley quickly and turned onto sleepy Main Street. December was a slow, lazy time in Banshee Creek, as Halloween, the town's busy season, was long past. A few eccentric tourists arrived to celebrate Christmas with a spooky twist, but the autumn crowds were a memory. Still, a bedraggled group of ghost hunters, bundled up in thick scarves and furry boots with little skull designs, were asking directions from a friendly woman in pink pigtails. She was wearing a purple vest with the word PRoVE spelled in bright yellow letters.

The weird spelling wasn't a mistake. The letters stood for Paranormal Research of Virginia Enterprises, the local paranormal investigations group. PRoVE hosted ghost tours, kept track of the town's paranormal history, and even produced shows about their investigations. They seemed devoted to their craft.

Which is why I gave them wide berth. The shop's magic kept people from becoming too suspicious, but you never knew with the Banshee Creek paranormal groups. They were sometimes more than they seemed.

The street was lined with small shops, all with some kind of paranormal Christmas theme. The candle shop advertised candy-striped peppermint-scented and Yule-log shaped candles. The botánica offered evergreen wreaths decorated with berries and plastic images of ancient mother goddesses. The pizzeria, aptly named "Poltergeist Pizza," had an all-you-can-eat Bloody Krampus Cannelloni special with the tagline "Defeat the Dark God, If You Can."

That did not sound particularly appetizing to me, but the pizzeria was one of the few businesses that were full of people. Bloody cannelloni seemed to be a winner in this town.

The Banshee Creek Bakery was also quite full. It was located in a tidy brick building with a striped pink-and-orange awning and a cute ghost logo, and it had a line of customers coming out the door. That "Yule Love It Smoothie" that Patricia said she was working on must have been a hit.

The front door was covered with town announcements: PRoVE was hosting a competitive Christmastide hike near the lake that sounded absolutely horrifying in this nasty weather. There was also a celebratory "Traditional Quenching of the Booze Cocktail Hour" at the pizzeria, which seemed more appealing. But wasn't that pushing the Christmas theme a bit? Yes, the old pagan festivals involved lots of toasting and drinking, but no one did that any more. Any excuse for a drink, I guess.

I wasn't looking forward to standing in line in the freezing cold, but Patricia's overly-sweet coffee drink was too tempting. Eager for a taste, I stepped behind a young mom who was trying to calm down her hyped-up offspring.

"I want a candy corn cupcake," the little girl said, shaking her ponytail for effect. "The real stuff, not that nasty red, white and green peppermint stuff."

"It's not Halloween," her mom cautioned. "They may not have candy corn."

The little girl shook her head. "It's always Halloween here. After cupcakes, we can go to the toy store." She patted the bag that hung across her body. "I brought my piggy bank."

"I don't think they have a toy store," the mom said, sounding weary. "But we can go to the botánica, if you're looking for a doll. They have that Little Goddesses collection you liked last time."

The ponytail's gyrations grew in intensity. "I want a toy store."

Luckily, the line moved forward and they entered the bakery. I snuck in behind them and soaked in the precious heat. From ugh to bliss.

Patricia O'Dare, the owner of the bakery, smiled from behind the display case.

"Hi, our special today is—"

"I want a candy corn cupcake," the little girl interrupted. "And a hot chocolate."

The mom smiled apologetically. "Make that two hot chocolates."

Patricia grinned at the little girl and reached into the case. "You know what you want, don't you? Here you go. One candy corn cupcake." She took out the white frosted confection triumphantly. "You got our last one. Lucky girl."

The little girl reached up for her treat.

"Laurie will ring you up," Patricia said, gesturing toward the dark-haired woman behind the cash register.

That was my cue. I stepped forward, trying out my friendliest smile. "Hi."

I was still a little rusty at the whole interacting-with-mortals thing, but Patricia didn't seem to mind. She smiled back without reservation.

"Dora," she said, "taking a break? Let me get you the Yule Smoothie." She turned to the back counter, where a tall blender held pride of place. "It turned out delicious—no surprise, since it's basically frozen hot chocolate with toasted marshmallows—and you're going to love it."

"That's exactly what I was hoping," I answered, untruthfully.

I'd been hoping for something hot, but I couldn't turn down Patricia's beloved smoothie. "Do you have any of those peppermint chocolate cookies left?"

She shook her head. "Sorry all gone. I still have some Christmas candy corn cookies left, though. I made extra, but nobody seems to like them." She made face. "I guess this town attracts the purists. Would you like those? They *are* really good, even if not exactly Christmas or Halloween."

"They sound great," I said.

Patricia laughed. "Good. Are you going to the happy hour tonight?

Zach has a special winter sangría recipe made with apple cider. It's downright addictive."

"Sounds wonderful," I replied.

Music and alcohol. That didn't sound bad. I couldn't go, of course. I seldom left the store.

But it was tempting.

I left the bakery in an excellent mood with a frozen hot chocolate smoothie and a box full of cookies. The harried mom was not so lucky, as her tenacious offspring gobbled up the cupcake in record time and dragged her into the December cold in search of a toy store.

"It's around here somewhere," she squealed as she ran down Main Street.

"Sugar," the mom muttered, shaking her head, "always a bad idea."

I walked down Main Street, feeling upbeat. The sun was starting to pierce through the clouds, which, hopefully, heralded an imminent rise in temperature. And speaking of positive future events...

Nah, I couldn't possibly go to the happy hour. That wasn't my kind of thing at all.

Was it?

I turned the corner and saw my store and my mood soured immediately.

Thomas Lane, tall and handsome in black pants and a black military-style parka with lots of unnecessary pockets, stood in front of the door. He was holding a...cage?

At least that's what it looked like. It was a metal box with a handle and air holes. The sides were covered with stickers proclaiming that the contents were "fragile" and "dangerous" and should be "handled with care."

But the biggest sticker was purple and yellow and it said, "Property of PRoVE."

My hearts sank. Like I suspected, the local ghost hunters were more than they seemed.

CHAPTER TWO

"Coffee break?" Thomas asked as I approached, his green eyes twinkling.

He wasn't as young as he looked. He was also handsome in an odd, otherworldly way, with an ageless quality to that emerald glance that made me wary. As far as I could tell, he was human...but there was *something*.

"Just for a couple of minutes," I replied, opening the door. "I'm sorry you had to wait."

"Don't apologize," he replied, following me into the dark warmth of the store. "It beats hiking the hills at negative one hundred bazillion degrees in honor of the Wild Hunt."

Bubo, sleeping on the shelf next to the stuffed raven, gave him a suspicious glance. I ignored the cat, stepped behind the counter, and put my goodies away.

Thomas looked around. "You don't go for Christmas decorations, I see."

True, my shop was woefully plain compared to the other stores in town. But what was I supposed to do? Everything in the store was either haunted, cursed, or just plain dangerous. Should I have put up an evergreen covered in life-sucking vampire beads? Or a wreath covered with murderous cornhusk dolls?

Not exactly the Christmas spirit.

"I didn't have time to decorate," I answered. "And I hear there will be alcoholic celebrations tonight."

Not the smoothest of transitions, but hopefully it would change the subject.

"That, I may show up for." He put the cage on the counter. "But I'm on a different errand right now" He patted the cage. "This is for you."

A preternatural warmth emanated from the enclosure, a telltale magical sign. Like I said, PRoVE was more than it pretended to be. At least they had enough magical prowess to put a force field around whatever was in the cage.

And enough knowledge to deliver it to me.

Oh, joy.

I peered into the cage. There was something inside, but it didn't seem to be moving.

"Is it alive?" I asked.

"Not exactly," Thomas said, sounding amused.

His tone should have annoyed me, but it didn't. There was something oddly compelling about this man.

I reached for the cage's door. "May I open it?"

He stepped back, arms crossed. "It's all yours now. The paperwork is on top."

Interesting. Deliberately or not, he'd completed all the steps necessary to transfer the item to the store. Whatever was in that cage belonged to me now—or rather to the shop.

I opened the cage and peeked inside. The contents still did not move.

I looked up, Thomas seemed unconcerned. He was examining an old Celtic sword hanging on the wall.

"ΠΡΟΣΤΑΣΙΑ," I whispered, drawing a protective shield around myself.

Then I reached into the cage. I felt around until my fingers touched something soft and yielding, covered in fabric.

I slowly extracted the object. It was a doll, fairly old, but also well-maintained, with blond yarn hair and a glittery space suit with a rainbow printed on the shirt. The sleeves and boots were also tricked out in a rainbow print.

It looked inoffensive, almost cheery.

"Pretty, isn't it?" Thomas asked.

"Yes, yes it is," I answered, turning the doll over.

The space suit was carefully mended in the back. Someone had spent a lot of time carefully repairing a tear in the shiny fabric. I flipped it over and examined the face. Friendly blue eyes stared back at me. I noticed that a patch of hair looked slightly lighter than the rest of the doll's mane. That had been repaired too.

These weren't magical repairs. It was mundane patching. Someone had loved this doll and taken care of it.

"What's wrong with it?" I asked.

Thomas shrugged. "We don't know, but it was in a fire two years ago. One person died. The house was boarded up and condemned. We went in last week to tape a show and found it between the rubble. It looked untouched, no smudging, no burn marks, nothing."

I glanced at the cage. "And that merited all of these precautions?"

He smiled and backed toward the door. "Read the paperwork." Then he gave a courtly bow and exited the store.

Gotta hand it to the guy. He knew how to make an exit.

As soon as Thomas left, Bubo leaped onto the counter and sniffed the doll. I sighed, grabbed my drink, and took a long sip.

I really needed it right now. Not only were the local ghost hunters onto me, they were making deliveries.

Not good.

"Doesn't smell like smoke," Bubo said, then sauntered off to examine my cookies. "No magic smell either."

"It's cute," I said, propping the doll on the counter and reaching for the papers taped to the top of the cage.

"Obnoxiously cheerful too," Bubo agreed. "Doesn't look like it belongs here, does it?"

I nodded. The store's merchandise tended to be rather on the decrepit side, lots of sepia tones and various shades of dust and decay.

This colorful doll with its dimpled smile stuck out like a rainbow-colored sore thumb.

I opened the envelope, which contained a printed memorandum from someone named Cassandra Jones, PhD. It looked pretty fancy and had a lot of big words like *Röntgenoluminescence screening, residual ghost possession,* and *pyrokinesis.*

"What does it say?" Bubo asked, leaning over my shoulder to read. "Is it snakes? You know I hate snakes."

"The good news is, it isn't snakes," I replied, scanning the document. "The bad news is...well, there's a lot of bad news."

The gist of it was simple. Found in a fire in California fifteen years ago. One person dead. Tracked to another fire a year later. That one was in Arkansas, two people died, and the doll was found in the house. Five years later the doll appeared in a children's shelter in Idaho. A few days before, a nearby house fire had resulted in three deaths.

The memo went on and on. Dr. Cassandra Jones had tracked the doll through shelters, donation bins, and online listings. It had been bought, sold, and transferred dozens of times, and every single time there had been a fire nearby, sometimes it was a house, other times a business or a storage unit.

But always someone died.

And the doll moved on. This thing had compiled a long rap sheet, and it wasn't even that old.

I was reluctantly impressed. The soul-stealing sword on the wall Thomas had been admiring was five centuries old and it had killed maybe half as many people. This pyrokinetic doll would set a new mortality record for the shop.

Bubo glanced at the ceiling. "Please tell me this place has magical emergency sprinklers."

"Not that I know of," I replied, folding the pages and placing them in a drawer. "We've never needed them before."

The doll stared at me with innocent blue eyes.

I shook my head at it. "You are going to be trouble. I can tell." I scanned the store. "Now, where should we put you?"

"As far away from me as possible," Bubo said, jumping onto his pillow on the top shelf.

He wasn't the only one leery of our new arrival. Yaavik the teddy bear stretched to cover as much space as possible, ensuring that I wouldn't be able to squeeze the doll between him and the Chinese Torture Box. The candle fragments that made up the Hand of Death scuttled around, occupying most of the surface area of their shelf. The Victorian porcelain dolls, always snooty, crossed their lace-covered arms and stared at the rainbow doll with undisguised hostility.

"Look, guys," I said. "Someone is going to have to make room, or—"

I was interrupted by a knock on the front door.

"Hello?" someone asked tentatively, opening the door a crack. "Are you open?"

"Yes, we are." I replied.

The store was always open, at least as long as I was inside. That was part of my magical *geas*.

I recognized the customer immediately. It was the mom who stood in front of me on the bakery line. Sure enough, the little girl with the ponytail followed her into the store.

"See," the girl said, looking around. "I told you they had toys."

The mom frowned, staring at the desiccated raven on the top shelf. "I don't think this is a toy store, honey."

Toy store? I didn't have to glance at Bubo to know that he was rolling his eyes hard enough to dislodge the orbs.

"Yes, it is," the girl said, her inquiring gaze landing on the rainbow doll next to me.

That was my cue. "Welcome," I chirped. "Unfortunately, we don't carry toys, just collectibles and curiosities—"

"You have dolls," the little girl interrupted, eyes still focused on out new acquisition. "I want a doll."

The mom pulled on her daughter's hand. "Their stuff is old, honey. We can stop at Toys 'r' Us on the way back home."

The girl shook off her mom's grip. "They have dollies."

Her eyes were riveted on the rainbow doll.

"And I like this one."

CHAPTER THREE

H er mom glanced at the doll and grimaced. "Rainbow Brite? I haven't seen one of those in ages. This one has to be from the mid-eighties. Did it come in that box?"

"Oh," I said, faking a giggle. "That's just someone's idea of a joke."

"I like it," the little girl repeated in a sing-song voice. "It's meant to be mine."

That phrase made alarm bells ring in my head. I'd heard it many times before.

Luckily, the mom was not affected. She regarded the doll with ill-concealed distaste. "It's older than you are, Ginny. C'mon, we can order something online when we get home."

"But this one is mine," the little girl wailed.

"It's old and probably quite expensive," Mom said.

"I have my birthday money," the little girl whined.

I hid a smile. The items in my shop were expensive, but not in the economic sense. Money had no meaning here.

And Mom was right to keep her daughter away from this doll.

"You asked Santa for an American Girl," the mom replied. "I'm sure he'll bring it."

The little girl looked torn.

"That sounds like a better idea," I said, stuffing the doll back in the cage.

"C'mon," the mom said, opening the door and letting in a blast of cold air. "If we don't get to the ghost tour, they'll leave without us."

With a last mournful glance at the cage, the little girl reluctantly followed her mother out of the shop.

I grabbed the cage and placed it behind the counter. The doll could stay there until I found a permanent place for it.

Bubo leaped onto the vacated spot and started licking his fur.

"Is that its new home?" he asked. "It doesn't seem fireproof enough."

"Why do you care?" I asked, reaching for my drink. "You're an immortal plague daemon."

But I shared his sense of unease. We'd received weird items before, but somehow this felt different.

"One that's stuck in a cat body," he noted. "You try licking ashes out of your fur. I still have flashbacks about trying to clean myself after the Great London Fire of sixteen sixty-six."

Ah, yes, the conflagration that had finally stopped London's worst plague outbreak. The Magical Curiosity Shoppe had been a tiny storefront in Southmark on that night. I remember watching London Bridge burn throughout the night, the acrid smell of smoke and loss clinging to the air.

Then a piebald cat arrived at the shop, tail singed and whiskers burnt off. Once the plague daemon entered the shop, the store disappeared and the Great London Fire was left behind.

The plague had not reappeared, and it wouldn't, not as long as Bubo was locked up in the shop.

With me.

I reached out and stroked the daemon's fur. "Well, I'm not plague-stricken and I've been living in the shop with you for centuries. So I don't think little miss Rainbow Brite is going to burn us down."

"Famous last words," Bubo muttered, his lithe body shivering under my hand.

Why, the poor thing, er, daemon, was really scared. How strange.

And how unnecessary. If there was a way to destroy this store and its contents, I would have done it a long time ago.

"Oh, c'mon," I said, finishing the drink. "Would it make you feel better if I put a fire protection spell around it?"

I could do a quick amulet. It wouldn't do any harm and it may make Bubo feel better.

"Why would I want to protect the doll?" Bubo asked with a snarl. "If you're going to make an amulet, make it for me."

Ah, the cat's majestic self-centeredness had been a haven of stability for me for centuries. Today was no exception.

"I'll do it for the whole store," I said. "How about that?"

Bubo made a face. "As if I care about the rest of you."

That made me laugh. "I'll try not to take that personally."

I would need materials. Lead would be good for a fire protection charm. I scanned the store, looking for something useful. Yaavik the teddy bear had a lead inscription...

But Yaavik had disappeared. The Victorian dolls had followed his lead and retreated into the shadows. Even the unicorn skeleton was surreptitiously sneaking behind the damask curtain.

"You're bone, you idiot," I muttered. "Combustible materials can't protect from fire."

No lead, then. Fine, I could improvise.

I opened a drawer. If I remembered correctly, we should have some iron nails from Roman times in here somewhere...

They were gone. Gee, who knew metal could be so sneaky?

"Don't look at me," Bubo said. "I don't play with murderous metal items. I like feathers and catnip."

"I could go to the botánica," I mused, throwing my empty cup into the trashcan, "and get some supplies."

Two outings in one day? That would be an unprecedented luxury.

But I'd be gathering materials for a protection spell for the shop. Surely that merited a little leeway.

Bubo's eyes narrowed. "You're dying to get out, aren't you?"

"Hey, I'm doing this for you," I replied, already heading for the antique cash register. "You're the one who wants protection."

I pushed a couple of metal buttons at random, then pulled the lever. The drawer opened with a clang and I grabbed a bunch of dollar bills.

I didn't bother to count them. It would be the right amount.

It always was.

"I'll eat all your cookies while you're gone," Bubo warned, as I walked to the door, stuffing the dollar bills in my pocket.

"Do it, and I'll make an ash-attractant amulet instead." I turned the closed sign over. "You'll be licking cinders off your fur for decades."

He glared at me as I exited the shop, locking the door behind me.

But I didn't care. He was right. I was desperate to escape. Even the freezing weather couldn't stop me.

I headed back to Main Street, burying my nose in my cozy scarf to stave off the wind. The botánica was two blocks away and I had to pass the perennially tempting bakery to get there. I walked by quickly, not looking at the specials. Surely Bubo wouldn't eat *all* the cookies.

I finally reached the botánica, a sprawling store with a large sign proclaiming that the place sold books, potions, and spell casting materials, but "exorcisms were extra." The large glass window was covered with posters advertising services and town events, including the PRoVE ghost tours and the upcoming Lughnasadh happy hour. The town businesses all seemed to advertise on the botánica's window because they knew the manager, Kat Ramos, would not mind. Poltergeist Pizza had its menu up and the Banshee Creek Bakery had a flyer advertising its new holiday smoothie. PRoVE had tons of ads for its events, and there was even an advertisement for the Magical Curiosity Shoppe—

Wait, *what?*

I stared at the window in shock. I couldn't quite believe what I was seeing, but there it was, in black and sparkly purple ink: *Magical Curiosity Shoppe Now Open! Visit Us And Find That Precious Item You Didn't Know You Needed.*

Why was there an ad for my shop here? My shop didn't advertise. In fact, it possessed a reality-warping field that kept the curious and uninvited away. The shop's magic wouldn't allow me—or anyone else— to advertise.

So this colorful little flyer shouldn't exist.

I entered the botánica, muttering the Greek word for silence under my breath. That spell ensured that the warning bell Kat used to announce customers would not reveal my presence.

Kat was standing by the bookshelves, chatting with a customer. While she was distracted, I surreptitiously snuck up to the window and grabbed the advertisement, crumbling it up and stuffing it in my pocket.

"Dora," Kat exclaimed behind me. "What are you doing here?"

"Just dropping by," I turned to face her, "and picking up some things."

I froze as I caught sight of her companion.

"Good to see you again," Thomas Lane said with a knowing smile. "Unexpected shopping trip?"

"Something like that," I muttered.

"I'll leave you to take care of our new neighbor, Kat," he said. "Please let me know when my package comes in."

"Don't hold your breath," Kat cautioned. "South American orders take forever."

"I understand," he replied, walking toward the door. "I'm used to it."

I stepped back to get out of his way. He noticed the gesture and his lips curved into an expression that was almost, but now quite, a smirk.

"The fire charms are in the back," he whispered as he passed next to me.

"Gee, thanks," I replied.

But he was gone.

He'd just delivered a pyrokinetic doll to my store. The fire charms comment wasn't just a guess. Thomas knew exactly what was going on.

"Nice, eh?" Kat asked with a wink.

"What?" I replied.

She laughed. "I mean Thomas. He's good looking in that 'hate to see him go, but love to watch him leave' way."

"Oh, sure," I replied, not knowing what exactly she was talking about.

Kat threw her hands up. "His butt. He has a nice butt."

"Oh, *that*."

"But enough about the local attractions," she continued. "What can I help you with?" She glanced down. "Was there something wrong with your ad?"

I followed her gaze to a crumbled piece of paper, lying on the floor between us.

How did the flyer fall out of my pocket?

"I didn't intend to start spreading the word," I replied, bending down to pick up the paper. "I'm not ready for an onslaught of customers just yet." I stared at the paper, which was suspiciously unwrinkled once I smoothed it out. "How did this get here, by the way?"

Kat frowned. "I thought you put it up." She tapped her chin thoughtfully. "It just kind of appeared one day."

"I bet," I muttered, glaring at the paper. "Well, let me know if another appears."

There would be another one, for sure.

"Appears?" Kate asked, looking confused.

"If my, uh, secret benefactor," I said, "decides to put up another one."

Her face cleared. "Sure, I'll keep you posted."

I nodded, knowing perfectly well there was no such benefactor. The shop, it seemed, was being naughty. It wanted to attract customers and was experimenting with new marketing techniques. Lucky me.

I had to figure out a way to deal with that, but first I had to handle the doll.

"In the meantime," I continued. "I'll just get some supplies for a fire protection amulet I'm working on."

"Sounds great," Kat said. "Those are in the—"

"In the back," I replied quickly. "I know."

I passed the bookshelves full of tomes about Voudoun, pre-Christian mythological treatises, and lighter items like the cartoon pamphlet titled *1001 Halloween Jokes for Kids*. The store wasn't big, so I quickly reached the back, where Kat kept her magical materials.

An apothecary chest had little drawers full of stones and crystals, bags of dried herbs hung from an old metal rack, and bundles of twigs hung from the ceiling. I walked around an umbrella stand full of tree branches ready to be turned into wands and staffs, and peered at the burnished wooden chest. I pulled open a drawer labeled "garnet" and took out a smooth, pear-shaped stone with a pre-drilled hole. I found lead fishing weights in another drawer and a leather cord in a third one.

A little pinch of cinnamon and I was done.

I handed Kat the money and she put my purchase in a reusable yellow bag with the botánica's logo and the motto "Exorcisms Are Extra" in gothic font.

"There you go," she said. "Good luck." She glanced down at my bag. "And be careful."

"Careful?" I asked. "Why?"

Her lips turned up into a mischievous smile. "Fire can be a metaphor."

"A metaphor for what?"

She stared at me like I was missing the obvious. "You know, for other things?"

I still didn't understand.

She shook her head in exasperation. "Never mind. Happy spell crafting. I hope to see you at the happy hour tonight."

"Thanks," I replied, heading out the door. "It sounds like fun."

That was a pretty noncommittal response. Stepping out of the store for a coffee break or spell material was one thing, going to a happy hour was quite another. My curse was allergic to fun.

But Kat's comment about the fire still bothered me. Maybe she meant a metaphor for cooking? Or...

I couldn't think of anything.

I returned to my shop, unlocked the door, and turned the sign on the door to "Open."

Bubo was sitting on the counter, next to an untouched bag of cookies, an annoyed look on his face.

"You didn't eat them?" I asked, placing my botánica bag next to him. "Maybe there's hope for you yet."

"It's white chocolate," he replied, curling his lip. "Plus I've been busy."

I frowned. "Busy with what?"

He glanced behind the counter. I walked around the store warily and peered down.

The doll's cage was still there, just where I left it.

But the door was open.

And the doll was gone.

CHAPTER FOUR

"**D**on't look at me," Bubo said quickly. "There wasn't much I could do."

"Did you even try?" I asked, slamming the cage door closed.

The clanging sound reverberated through the shop ominously.

"When the inventory wants to leave," he replied, "it just leaves. Anyway, she *petted* me. You know how I get when someone pets me."

"Let me get this straight," I said, staring into his glowing yellow eyes. "You let a little girl come into the store and leave with a homicidal artifact, just because she stroked your fur?"

Bubo bristled. "You don't have to sound so judgmental. She was very good at it and clearly had lots of cat petting experience."

"The store was locked. How did she get in?"

Bubo yawned, exposing razor-sharp fangs. "It unlocks itself. You know that."

Yes, I did. When an item wanted to leave, it would find a way.

And the consequences were often horrifying.

"But where was her mom?" I asked helplessly.

"Nowhere to be found," Bubo replied. "She brought her kid up right, though. Look, the girl left her piggy bank as payment."

That explained the porcelain pig with the legend "Compliments

From Virginia Union Bank. A Penny Saved Is A Penny Earned" that was on the counter. The sight of it tore at my heart.

"Don't worry about it, toots," Bubo said. "There's nothing you can do."

He was probably right, but I grabbed the doll's paperwork anyway and started to read. Maybe there was something there that could help.

The memo wasn't reassuring, even on a second reading. The first owner of the doll had been a nine-year-old girl from California named Jenny Luna. Her mom had bought her the doll as a present. There was nothing suspicious about the purchase. The doll came from a large toy store chain and was bought with cash, which was normal for the time. There was nothing noteworthy about it other than it was a highly coveted early release of the toy.

And that a few days after, the little girl perished in a fire.

Unlike the other deaths, however, it wasn't a house fire. The girl had died in California in a freak tunnel accident where an oil tanker hit a crashed vehicle, causing an explosion during rush hour. The cars piled up behind the inferno and the passengers were unable to escape in time.

That did not sound like something the doll had caused. Although the fact that the doll had survived the explosion seemed suspicious.

I leafed through the memo until I found the appendixes at the back. One contained photographs, including a school picture of a smiling gap-toothed Jenny Luna wearing a Rainbow Brite shirt.

That girl had really loved Rainbow Brite, loved it so much that she made her mom stand in line for hours to get an early release of the doll.

Loved it so much she'd carried it everywhere.

Loved it so much, she'd died with it.

"It's haunted," I said. "The doll is possessed by a little girl."

Bubo sighed. "Who cares? It's gone and you can't get it back."

"Maybe." I put the papers back. "Maybe not. They said they were going to the ghost tour, right?"

"Yes, they did," he answered, licking his back. "Ironic, considering that the little girl is carrying the specter with her. PRoVE will be pioneering the bring-you-own-ghost tour." He paused in mid-lick as I grabbed the piggy bank. "Wait, you're not going after them, are you?"

I glanced at the piggy bank. It was probably useless...Then I caught sight of the botánica's bag.

"Yes," I replied, emptying the bag. "I'm going after them."

It took a few seconds to thread the leather through the stones and complete the charm. I would have to activate it magically, but that would have to wait until I figured out how I wanted to use it.

"There's nothing you can do," Bubo said, as I tied the knots and put the charm in my pocket.

I paused. He was right.

But, somehow, I couldn't just stay in the store as I'd done before. Someone would drop by the shop and pick up a horribly dangerous item and I would just wave them off and wait for the shop to teleport to its next destination. No muss, no fuss.

But it was different now. I couldn't quite put my finger on why, but I couldn't just stand and watch any more, curse or no curse.

"I can try," I said, grabbing the piggy bank and heading for the door.

"And you can fail," Bubo replied.

"Thanks, I really appreciate the support," I said, turning the knob.

Or, rather, *trying* to turn it. The contraption refused to move.

"I'm not being a party-pooper," Bubo said, flopping onto his back so he could lick his belly. "It's just a statement of fact."

"We'll see."

I stood back and stared at the knob.

"Open," I said in Greek.

The knob slowly gyrated and the door opened.

"That's more like it," I said, exiting the shop with the piggy bank in my hand.

The sun was setting and the alley was crowded with shadows. Main Street still had some light, so I was able to make out different groups of people milling about. A gaggle of teens was lined up for a last cupcake before the bakery closed for the night, and a scattering of couples were waiting for a table at the pizzeria. Happy hour was about to start.

I scanned the street, looking for a ghost tour.

Uh, what did a ghost tour look like? I knew they wore costumes in October, but in December the streets of Banshee Creek were full of anonymous winter coat wearers. PRoVE had tours all over the town, but I wasn't sure where they were.

I walked to the botánica and peered into the window. If I remembered correctly, one of the flyers was around here and it had tour information...

There it was. PRoVE ghost tours...limited openings for the off-season...evening tour of the town.

Thank Zeus there was a map. It wasn't very clear, but it seemed the tour would go down Main Street, turn at the creek, head up towards the library, and then to the park to attend...

The fire festival.

Of course.

"Hi, Dora."

The cheerful voice made me jump. Kat had left her store and come up behind me.

"Why are you holding a pig?" she asked with the air of someone trying to be polite about a strange happening.

I looked down at the ceramic animal in my hands. "Oh, a little girl left it at my store. I'm trying to return it."

"Oh, I hate it when that happens. There's a lost and found in the town hall, but the tourists seldom come back to pick up their stuff."

"I think they're still doing a ghost tour, so I can catch up to them. Can I take the map?"

"I'll get it."

She went back into the store and brought out the flyer. "They will finish near the park because of the—"

"Fire festival." I grabbed the flyer with one hand and held the piggy bank with the other. "I know."

"We have a lot of those," she replied. "You'll get used to them. Caine will light a bonfire and pass out s'mores at the drop of a hat."

"It's not the s'mores I'm worried about," I muttered. "But thanks for the map."

"No problem," Kat said, as I walked away. "I hope you find her."

I hoped so too. I walked quickly down Main Street, dodging stray groups of people. The ghost tour started at PRoVE headquarters, a Second Empire building with a mansard roof, a sweeping front porch, and purple siding with nauseating green trim. It wasn't hard to find.

But no one was there, at least not anyone waiting for a ghost tour. I stood in front of the building and examined the map in my hands, trying to figure out the next stop.

"Are you looking for something?"

Thomas Lane was suddenly next to me, an inquiring look on his face.

"Or someone?" he added, his lip curving into a half-smile.

That's when I noticed he was wearing a "Ghost Tour Guide" t-shirt with PRoVE's all-seeing eye symbol.

Looks like I hit the jackpot.

"Did the last tour leave?" I asked him. "Was there a mom with a little girl?

"We had two tours leave," he said. "I don't remember a little girl."

Two tours? I guess the slow season wasn't slow enough. How did they get enough people for two tours?

"They'll go to the Rosemoor first?" I asked.

"Yes," he answered. "That usually takes a while because that ghost has a complicated history and people like to take selfies with the medicine cabinet."

With the—? Never mind, I wasn't going to ask.

I looked around. "And which way is it?"

He looked at me strangely, then pointed down the street. "It's that way, but they will be turning around soon. They go north and then south and end in the park." He glanced at the piggy bank in my hands. "What happened? Did someone purchase something from your store?" He frowned. "It was the doll, wasn't it?"

Oh, yes. Thomas knew exactly what was going on.

"Yes, someone tried to buy it," I muttered. "I'm trying to undo the transaction."

His face grew hard. "I'll take you."

He started walking toward the street and I ran up to stop him. The last thing I needed was a mortal getting involved in this.

"Oh, I don't need—"

A shout pierced the evening stillness, interrupting me.

"Help me, please."

I turned to see the woman who had entered my shop earlier running towards the PRoVE building, eyes wild.

"My daughter," she sobbed. "Have you seen her?"

CHAPTER FIVE

"She was right next to me," the mom said, gasping for breath. "Then she was gone. Her name's Ginny. Ginny Armstrong. I'm Sheila."

Thomas grabbed his walkie-talkie, suddenly all business. "I'll alert the sheriff. What does she look like?"

"She's five," Sheila said. "Short with brown hair and brown eyes, wearing a Scooby-Doo t-shirt."

Thomas spoke into the radio, alerting both the police and the fire department.

"She came to my store," I said, "and took the doll." I showed her the piggy bank. "She left this behind."

She grabbed the piggy bank, looking relieved. "That's good."

Not the response I expected.

"That means no one took her," she explained. "They would take the money too."

"Would she try to rejoin the tour?" Thomas asked. "Or return to where you started?"

"If we were separated, she was supposed to come back here," Sheila said, pointing to the building. "To the starting point. She was going to wait for me on the porch."

"The sheriff has sent out patrols," Thomas said. "And the fire department is already in the park. They're looking for her."

"I think that's our group coming back," she said. "If she's with them—"

A loud screech interrupted her. I looked up, but was suddenly pushed out of the way.

"Get out," Thomas screamed. The mom tripped over me and we both went down on the sidewalk. The impact knocked the breath out of me and I cried out in pain as my hip and leg hit the sidewalk.

But the sound was drowned out by a huge crash behind us. I turned to see a red van trample the fence and crash into the PRoVE head-quarters' porch.

Sheila held my arm. "We were just there. How—"

"There's someone inside," Thomas interrupted.

He raised his walkie-talkie. "Vehicle crash at HQ. Van's on fire. People trapped."

"It's on fire?" I said, as he ran towards the van.

But he was right. The back door to the van had swung open and I could see small flames inside.

Sheila pulled at me. "Move back. That's a food truck. It could explode."

The van's side said "Calavera Catrina's Mexican Churros" in gothic script. The legend "try our deadly ghost pepper chocolate topping" was written in flowing letters below.

"They have propane tanks for cooking," Sheila shouted, leading me away.

"But Thomas is there," I exclaimed.

He was struggling to help the driver out of the vehicle. Time seemed to stand still until he finally got the driver loose and they ran over to meet us on the other side of the street.

A fire truck appeared, lights flashing, and the firefighters spread out to contain the flames.

"That was fast," I said, as paramedics reached us and led the van driver to a stretcher.

"They were," Thomas gasped for breath, "already on their way."

A paramedic approached him, but he waved her off.

"I'm fine," he said. "But what about—"

"MOMMY."

Sheila turned with a joyful expression on her face. Ginny was running down the side street toward us, the colorful doll held tightly in her arms.

Sheila squealed with glee, then glanced back at the collapsed porch and paled.

"She would've been waiting for me," she whispered in an anguished voice. "Right there."

"Mommy," Ginny shouted again as she ran towards us, the rainbow doll clutched tightly in her hands.

"Sweetie." Sheila enveloped her tightly in her arms. "Where were you?"

"I got lost," Ginny explained. "I know I was supposed to come to the big, green porch and wait for you, but *she* called me."

"Who?" Sheila asked. "Do you mean the police lady?"

"No." Ginny waved the doll in the air. "I mean *her*. Rainbow Brite."

Thomas and I exchanged looks.

"She said I had to come get her," Ginny explained. "So I went to the store and it was open and everything. I couldn't see the doll, but I followed the kitty to pet him and found the box."

Ah, Bubo, you little traitor. You wanted to get rid of the doll and you figured out the perfect way to do it.

Ginny grinned. "She said she'd help me find you *and she did*."

She glanced at the wrecked van, as if only just noticing it. "That looks bad."

"It *was* bad," Sheila answered. "Next time stick by Mommy, okay?" She glanced back at me. "And I think you have to give the dolly back."

As if. That's not the way this worked. The new owners were not able to return the items. The item itself decided when it was time to part, and it's keeper had no—

"Here you go." Ginny pushed the doll towards me. "She wants to go home now."

The thing practically leaped into my hands. I was frozen to the spot, staring at doll's oddly satisfied smile.

"I can't keep her," Ginny explained. "She has to help other kids."

"She does?" I asked.

The doll's smile seemed to grow wider.

Ginny nodded. "She *remembers*." She took her piggy bank back then turned to her mom. "Can I have an Abominable Snowman Milkshake before we leave?"

"Sure, honey," Sheila said, taking her hand.

"Good luck," Thomas said, looking relieved.

Sheila grinned. "Oh, we've had plenty of that, thank heavens."

And she walked off, still holding her daughter's hand.

They left me and Thomas, alone with only a wrecked porch and a smoldering truck for company. Thomas peered at the doll in my hands. He reached out and rubbed out a smudge on the doll's cheek.

"Ashes," he said.

I didn't ask how the doll had acquired a sooty covering on the other side of town. I really didn't want to know.

"There was always one survivor, you know," Thomas said. "A kid."

I didn't ask how he knew that. He'd read the memo just like I had.

"Yes," I said. "I just realized that."

He reached out to stroke the toy's fluffy golden hair. "She always got one kid out."

I nodded. Jenny Luna wasn't able to save everyone, but she always saved *someone*.

"I better take her back to the store now," I said.

Thomas looked up to see a police cruiser parking at the curb. "And I should go talk to the police." He sighed, glancing at the porch. "I don't know how I'm going to explain this to Caine."

I looked down at the doll. "And I don't know how I'm going to explain this to Bubo."

"Who?"

"My cat," I replied. "He...oh, never mind."

It wasn't something I could explain. I would have to deal with my pyrophobic feline on my own.

"Here's a thought," Thomas said, "I could drop by later and we could head to the happy hour."

My heart skipped a beat. "Oh, I don't..."

Wait, was the doll *winking* at me?

"It's going to be a blast," he continued. "But if you—"

"I'll go," I said quickly. "It sounds fun."

"Oh, it will be. Zak has a new—"

The buzzing walkie-talkie interrupted him. He grimaced and picked it up.

"Hey, Caine," he said into the radio. "Everything is under control." He paused to listen. "Yes, Fire and Rescue is here and so is the sheriff."

More listening. Thomas glanced at the damaged building and ran his hand through his hair in exasperation.

"Well, there's good news and bad news." The radio squawked loudly. "You know how the real meaning of Yule is survival over the forces of nature and all that jazz?"

I could hear Caine cursing over the line. That was my cue to go. I had a store to manage, a doll to put away, and an ornery daemon cat who was about to get a big shock to handle. I smiled, stepped back, and waved goodbye.

Thomas waved back apologetically.

"Well," I heard him say as I walked away. "The good news is you're getting a new porch for Christmas this year."

Author's Note: I hope you enjoyed this story. A full list of books is available on my website, www.AniGonzalez.biz. If you join my mailing list you'll get updates on when the next Banshee Creek stories are published and the first three PRoVE novelettes, *One Night with the Golden Goddess, One Night in the Mummy's Lair,* and *One Night in the Chupacabras Ranch,* FREE.

ABOUT THE AUTHOR

Ani Gonzalez writes paranormal romantic comedy and cozy mystery (whew, that's a mouthful!) set in Banshee Creek, Virginia, The Most Haunted Town in the USA. Her books feature feisty, irrepressible heroines dealing with a host of paranormal critters (ghosts, cryptids, pagan gods...the sky's the limit) and mysteries. They find love and laughter (and sometimes corpses) along the way, and readers get to follow them every step of the way.

Follow Ani Gonzalez online:
   Facebook
   Amazon
   Goodreads
   Twitter

A DARK ROOT SOLSTICE: AUNT DORA'S DILEMMA

APRIL AASHEIM

SUMMARY

The fabled Oak Crown has been stolen. Aunt Dora has until dusk to find it, or the world will be trapped in winter for another year.

CHAPTER ONE

A bitter wind swept down the frozen forest path leading from downtown Dark Root to Harvest Home. Dora Maddock, a woman of high-middle age, bowed her head and squared her shoulders as her boots stomped down on the ice. Her hair - more salt now than pepper - rearranged itself around her face with each gust, doing its best to obscure her vision. But Dora knew this path like the back of her veined hand and wouldn't be deterred.

"Not much longer, now," she said to herself, as well as any nature spirit who might be listening. In her youth, Dora had spent a lot of time in the forest, and though it was difficult to get around these days, she still felt awe and reverence for the woods and the trees. It was one of the reasons she loved Dark Root. The tiny town, nestled in a dense forest, was the perfect compromise between modern living and her more primitive roots.

She stopped and leaned against a bare tree, setting her shopping bags down so she could massage the crest of her hip with her strong knuckles. Her bursitis was acting up, as it did every winter. The ache was deep from the walk and she knew that even her strongest willow bark tea would do little to numb it.

"It'll all be worth it," she said, picking up her bags.

A smile appeared on her weathered face as she pictured her four nieces all gathered around the dining room table for the Midwinter's Feast this evening. Dora had secured a goose - and a ham! - but the weight was more than she had anticipated. She should have taken one of the many offers for a ride home, but she was too proud. She'd seen too many women - even those who had a little magick in them as she did - become dependent on others. She wasn't about to be one of them! Even if she did have to fake it, at times. Besides, tonight when she placed the Oak Crown on the altar, the Holly King would relinquish his hold on winter. And then the Oak King would bring warmth to the world again. Today might be the darkest, shortest day of the year, but the wheel kept turning and tomorrow would start the world anew.

She hurried on and soon realized she was limping. Indeed, she noticed that her left footprints were different from her right. Once again, she chided herself for being foolish and not getting a ride.

"I'll just use my broom!" She had said with a wink when the owner of the local cafe had asked how she was getting home.

Bill had smiled and waved her a Merry Solstice before disappearing to attend to more pressing business. Dark Root was bustling with last-minute shoppers and those who'd come for the small town's holiday charm. And the crowds always led to chaos. There had been tales of shops running out of inventory, of the petting zoo losing all its reindeer, and of Mr. Claus kissing a woman who clearly wasn't Mrs. Claus.

At last, her proud Victorian home appeared in an expansive clearing. She said a quick thank you to the nature spirits for getting her back safely, then did her best to keep her footing as she made her way across the open field to the back door of the house. The lingering scents of fruitcake and scones and mincemeat pies wafted out through the kitchen window. Streamers of gray-white smoke billowed up from the chimney, evidence the Yule log continued to burn. Red and green lights draped lovingly around the eaves winked at her with promises of warmth.

Dora stamped her boots free of snow as she searched her pockets for her house key. After the third dive into her left pocket, she found it. Her bushy brows narrowed into a deep point. "Tis the season of

Krampus," she said, looking cautiously back over her shoulder as she slid the key into the lock. "Always stealing things an' tryin' ta mess with people." She felt a prickling sensation on the back of her neck, and whether it was the wind or her imagination or something else, she couldn't ascertain.

She could almost hear her nieces laughing at her as she pushed the door open with her good hip. She'd been telling them stories of Krampus all week, because it was important they know the truth. If they were expected to believe in the light side of Yule, they needed to see the darker side, too. The mischievous imp Krampus was responsible for much of the mayhem during the holidays. He went around dousing Yule logs, stealing oranges, and poking the feet of naughty children while they slept. He didn't leave toys. He took them! Only to throw them over a cliff so no child could ever play with them! Santa didn't bring coal - Krampus did! He was a master of mischief, who took great delight in annoying others, even if that annoyance was simply a key that turned up in a pocket only after it had been thoroughly searched for twice already.

Her nieces might not believe he was real, nor even her magickly gifted sister, Sasha, but Dora knew. Dora kept the old ways, and Dora knew.

It was warm inside the charming kitchen, with pies cooling on the wood-fired stove and a kettle of tea still warming on a burner. A bowl of potpourri crafted of pinecones, orange peels, and cinnamon sticks sat on the counter, inviting health, longevity and abundance into the home. The combined aromas made her stomach growl and she scolded it. "Just a few hours more and we'll be feasting!" she promised. But there was still much to do.

Dora checked the pies and gathered the silver, going over her mental to-do list. It was only then that she noticed how quiet the house was. When she'd left for town that morning, Harvest Home had bustled with the sounds of her nieces, but now all was silent. She hurried into the living room and looked around. An evergreen had been cut and decorated in her absence, and the house was a little less clean than when she'd left it, but nothing else seemed out of place.

Nothing she could see anyway.

Dora sniffed the air. Something was wrong. She stood very still and listened. Was that a bell she heard on the wind? Her eyes widened, yet she held her position, sensing the energy around her. Her nieces were fine; she was sure of it. But the unease didn't go away.

She kept sniffing as she walked around the house. There was a strange, bitter odor in the air. She passed the hearth with its burning Yule log, and an end table, decorated with gold and red candles. Everything still seemed to be in its proper place.

Then, Dora knew. She felt it in her bones as strongly as she felt the bursitis in her hip.

She hurriedly limped into the dining room, where the table was mostly set for the evening meal. Gleaming crystal glasses and silver serving utensils sparkled among a dozen unlit candles. The table was set with the finest bone china, dishes Dora used only once a year.

But the centerpiece – the crown, crafted from golden leaves and meant as a gift to the Oak King – was gone!

And Dora knew for certain that if she couldn't find it, winter would never end.

The woman fell into her overstuffed chair, fanning her face with her hands. "Calm down ol' girl," she said, breathing through her nose. Just because the Oak Crown was missing didn't mean there was foul play involved. Perhaps one of the girls had taken it for safekeeping. After all, she had drilled the importance of the Oak Crown into them that very morning.

CHAPTER TWO

"I 'll be gone most o' the day, girls," Dora said before setting off for town. "Ya'll have yer tasks to keep ya busy, and t'night we'll celebrate the endin' of the darker half o' the year, when the Oak King regains his power o'er the Holly King. If we can keep Krampus at bay, that is."

"Uh – who's Krampus?" her oldest niece, Ruth Anne, asked.

"An imp who wants ta ruin Christmas! Jus' like the Holly King, he doesn't want winter ta end. But the Holly King wants it out o' love fer the winter. Krampus jus' likes ta keep things cold so folks stay miserable. He's always watchin' and will always find a way in, whether through attic windows or down the chimney!"

"Like Santa Claus?" Eve, her youngest niece, asked.

"Nay, nay! Not like Santa. Santa brings cheer! Krampus brings coal! He wants ta ruin the holidays because he hates cheer."

"Sounds like the Grinch," fair-haired Merry said, putting her finger to her chin thoughtfully.

"The Grinch is a fairy godmother next ta Krampus!" Dora said.

By now, Dora had worked up quite a sweat and was pacing about the kitchen. Though she had never seen Krampus herself, she knew he was out there. Her mother had said so. And her mother before that.

"Dora..." Her sister Sasha said, stopping her by pulling her wrist on her next pass. "Perhaps we should talk of this some other time."

Dora pointed to the window, with its early indigo sky. "It's the Solstice. They need ta know!"

Sasha rolled her eyes but let go of her sister and stepped towards the counter, pouring herself a cup of Yule tea while Dora continued.

"The beast is covered in matted brown fur. He can walk on two legs, or four, or e'en on his terrible claws!" Dora raised her hands and crooked her fingers, and monster hooks appeared as shadows on the wall. "*Click. Click. Click.* His claws scrape against the wooden floors as he creeps about, looking fer mischief."

"This guy is Krampus-ing my style," Ruth Anne said, nervously coughing into her fist as her aunt continued.

"His horns are sharp, ready to gore. His eyes are red slits. Ya'll know he's comin' by the jingle of the bell draped around his neck, a bell he must wear ta warn children."

Maggie, who usually kept to herself, pulled on the ends of her coarse red ponytail. She looked around nervously, as if fearing he was close by. "How do we keep him out?"

"Even if ya could keep him out o' the house, which ya can't, he'd still find ya in the woods. But once the Oak King takes the crown, winter will start ta thaw and Krampus will be gone, too."

At that, Dora walked through the vast living room and into the dining room, motioning for her nieces and Sasha to follow. She pointed to a polished silver platter and Ruth Anne removed the lid. Inside was a magnificent crown, crafted of oak leaves and twigs. A collective gasp sounded around the room, followed by a heavy sigh from Sasha, who just folded her arms and let her sister continue.

Dora pointed to two paintings that the girls hadn't seen before, now adorning the dining room wall near the head of the formal table. "The Holly King and the Oak King," she announced. The Holly King looked rather like Santa Claus, the girls thought, with his rosy cheeks, fur coat, bushy beard and a wreath of holly around his head. The Oak King, on the other hand, looked like a Tree Man. Between the two paintings was a wheel, with arrows inside that moved like the hands on a clock.

Sasha lifted a finger and stepped forward. "Normally, I approve of your history lessons, Dora, but not today. Spring will come whether the Oak King takes his crown or not. It is the wheel of life, children, and those hands move on their own. We must not get stuck in the old ways."

"The old ways have gotten us this far," Dora said, tossing pretend salt over her shoulder. "But yer mother's right. Enough o' that! Today is the party! Do ya all have your tasks? I'll need everyone's help ta make this a Solstice feast ta remember!"

"I'll see to it everything is done," Sasha said, then turned to her daughters. "If you have no further questions, you may be excused."

The girls ran off, nearly tripping over each other in a fit of giggles as Ruth Anne pretended to be Krampus, charging at them with her hands up like horns.

"Don't go filling their heads with too much nonsense," Sasha said, once the room had cleared. "Samhain is the time for mischief. Yule is the time for renewal." Sasha looked around the room and noticed that the Yule Fairy, the one that graced Dora's tree every year, was on a high shelf. She pointed a finger at it, and the fairy gracefully floated down, complete with softly flapping wings. "This is the one Merry is to mend, correct?" Sasha said, noting the tear in the blue dress.

"Aye. But I thought ya didn't like squandering' yer magick," Dora said, regarding her sister with one eye closed.

"It is the Solstice," Sasha said. "But don't let it get around." With that, Sasha took her fur coat from the coatrack and waved a hasty goodbye. "I'll be working on the cider back at my house. The girls and I will see you at the feast tonight."

That was the last time Dora had seen the Oak Crown.

Dora looked at the clock. Evening would come in no time! She hefted herself out of the chair and returned to the dining room, hoping that she had simply overlooked it. The platter was still there, with the lid sitting next to it, but the crown was gone. Bits of leaves had been left behind on the table, and Dora noticed that some of them had also fallen to the floor. Though her back wasn't what it used to be, she hunched forward and followed them, all the way to the front door, where all traces disappeared in the snow. Dora took a step outside and was met with a blast of freezing wind that set her teeth to chattering. She looked up and around as she folded her arms across her chest, but there was no sign of the missing crown.

"Girls!" She cupped her mouth with her hands and called into the wind, but there was no response. She went back inside, wringing her hands all the way into the kitchen as she wondered what to do. She had less than a handful of hours to find the crown and place it on the forest altar, or else the world would be trapped in winter for another year!

She should call her sister, Sasha.

But what would Sasha say? Even if she didn't outright berate her, she'd quietly point out her superstitious nonsense. But Sasha hadn't been charged with keeping the tradition - Dora had.

With trembling hands, Dora lifted the mustard-yellow rotary phone hanging in the kitchen. She dialed her sister's number. "Hello?" she said into the receiver as her free hand kneaded her apron belt. "Sasha?"

"Dora? Is that you?" Her sister asked. "Is something wrong? You never call."

It was true. Dora was the type who would listen to your troubles over the phone for hours, yet rarely initiated a call. If she needed to speak to you directly, she'd walk the distance, no matter how far. But time was short.

"Are - are the girls with you?" Dora asked, as casually as she could.

"Not yet. They're not there with you?"

"Uh, no." Dora sucked in her breath, waiting for her chastisement. It didn't come.

"I'm sure they're just finishing up shopping or gift wrapping," Sasha said calmly. "I wouldn't worry about them too much in Dark Root. They run this town. Unless Krampus comes, that is. I'll see you at dinner."

Sasha chuckled and hung up as Dora tried to swallow the lump in her throat.

Dora looked up at the clock - a black cat whose eyes moved with each tick - and noted the time. "I'm not a young woman anymore,"

Dora said, blowing into her palms and rubbing them together. "But I am still a witch, an' I got a few tricks up my sleeves yet!"

CHAPTER THREE

Tea wasn't a requirement for scrying, but it certainly helped.
Dora made a kettle of mugwort and honey tea in order to induce deep meditation, adding in a sprig of cinnamon for luck. She smelled the heady aromas wafting from the kettle, and then finished it off with a pinch of frankincense, for protection. It wouldn't taste very good, but scrying teas rarely did.

Next, she retrieved her wand from the laundry room. She tapped it twice against the wastebasket to remove the cobwebs and dust that had settled on it since its last use. "Have I neglected ya fer so long?" She asked the wand, as she felt the old but familiar tingle in her hand. She could almost feel it twitch with excitement as she rinsed it beneath cool running water to cleanse any stagnant energy.

"Ya'll get more use this spring," she promised the wand. "If we get ta spring!"

Dora looked around the kitchen once more, then nodded to herself - she was ready! She cleared her throat and spun the wand in the air three times - a magical number. Next, she aimed the wand at a high cabinet over the sink where she kept her 'important things'. After considerable focus, and a bit of strain, the cabinet door opened.

She was a short woman, no taller than five feet on her best day, and couldn't see the contents inside very well, but she nonetheless knew exactly where everything was located in her home. Her mind found the heavy crystal globe nestled within a wooden pedestal, and tugged it towards the edge of the shelf. Her telekinetic abilities weren't as strong as Sasha's, and even the wand did little to alleviate the globe's bumps on the ride down from the cabinet, but it landed smoothly on the table, just next to her cup of tea. The cabinet shut itself, having done it so many times in the past that it didn't need her direct instruction.

"I feel young again!" Dora said with a laugh that was a borderline cackle. Magick was limited, even in Dark Root, but this was not a waste! Besides, when spring came again, the magick would replenish itself, as it always did.

Dora drank down her cup of tea in one long draw, then wiped her mouth with the back of her hand. Before even setting the cup back on the table, she felt its hypnotic effects. She was light on her toes, and the world seemed a bit fuzzy and warm. She put on her reading glasses and took her spot at the kitchen table where she conducted all of her business, and peered at the placard on the base of pedestal. It read: *Dark Root Memories.*

She tapped the top of the glass ball and snowflakes began to swirl around the perimeter. When they cleared, a floating calendar appeared in the center of the crystal ball, its pages flipped open to the month of December. Dora found the day she was looking for - today - and tapped it again. A new image appeared, fuzzy at first, but taking shape the longer she stared at it. She placed her fingers on either side of the globe. It felt charged. *Alive.*

Dora exhaled as the image firmed up. "It's not nice ta spy on family," she said to the fairies and house goblins that watched over Harvest Home. "An' I promise, I wouldn't if this wasn't so important."

She gave a confirmatory nod, then relaxed her eyes and let the soothing effects of the tea settle over her. Then, she recited the incantation that came into her head.

"The Oak Crown is missin' and the culprit is near. Show me just how it disappeared."

She tapped the globe with her silver teaspoon three times and the snow inside rose up again. For a moment, there was only a blur and the swirl of the flakes.

Dora tightened her shawl and leaned forward. A scene began to take shape. A pretty young girl with flaxen hair carried an armload full of art supplies to the dining room table. The girl was her niece, Merry. Halfway to the table the girl stopped and looked around uneasily, and shivered. There was something in the house with her. Dora sensed it too, even through the barrier of time.

What was it? Dora's nose was nearly pressed to the glass, as she willed the image to further come alive.

And it did.

It was only for a moment that Merry thought she sensed another presence in the house. Soon, the moment passed and Merry chided herself for being silly. She was the most responsible of all the girls, and if she gave in to superstitions and fears, what example would that set for younger Maggie and Eve?

"There's no one in the house with me," Merry said resolutely, continuing her trek towards the dining table. "I'm absolutely sure of that."

Merry carefully set all the art supplies on the table. She had markers and scissors, glitter and glue, all ready to bedeck and bedazzle Aunt Dora's ancient Yule Fairy into something beautiful.

She lifted the fairy. It was a beautiful doll in a pale blue dress, with hair the same white-blond as Merry's, and wings that spanned two feet. Tonight, it would sit atop the Yule tree for the first time in years, and it was Merry's job to get her ready.

"Be creative," the note her Aunt Dora left her had said. "And take your time. This fairy represents the light of the world. Make her shine."

Merry carefully scanned her supplies as she decided on her best course of action. She thought the fairy's dress should be red or green, to match the colors of the season, but color-changing magick that was beyond her capabilities at the moment. Besides, if Aunt Dora had wanted the fairy to have a red dress, she would have said so.

Her eyes darted around the dining room, searching for a muse. The Yule log popped pleasantly in the fireplace. Dozens of large candles were set in holly rings about the room, waiting for the evening meal when they would be lit. It was a warm and festive feeling, and Merry decided to use that as her inspiration. She lined the doll's wings with gold glitter. Then she pasted on soft blue snowflakes she had cut from felt. She combed the fairy's long hair until it gleamed. Finally, she kissed the doll's head and the fairy immediately regained pink in her porcelain cheeks. Even the subtle crack in her chin had sealed up. The doll looked almost new. Merry's magick was subtle, but it effective.

But the fairy still had a small tear in its dress. Merry looked around the room, wondering how she would repair it. She hadn't brought her sewing kit and she knew her aunt's was upstairs. Her eyes raised to the floor above her. She could go upstairs and retrieve it, but... she still couldn't shake that uneasy feeling.

Merry had never been one to fear her Aunt Dora's home. She had practically been raised here. But after all that talk of... what was the creature's name? Krimpus? Krampus! After all that talk of him, Merry felt unsettled. She knew her aunt was superstitious, but sometimes her beliefs could be downright frightening.

Like the war between the Holly King and the Oak King for instance. She raised her eyes to the pair of portraits hanging on the wall - one of a jolly fat man in furs with rosy cheeks and knowing eyes, and the other of a tall tree-like man who stared somberly ahead. Aunt Dora claimed the two were always fighting for dominion over the seasons. That distressed Merry, but she couldn't say why. Perhaps because if her aunt was right, the whole world counted on her to deliver the crown to the Oak King. The crown that sat on the silver platter in the middle of the very table she worked at.

She decided to finish quickly, and either find her sisters or return home to Sister House. She wouldn't need the sewing kit, if she tried hard enough. She concentrated on the small tear in the gown. Her fingers massaged the fairy's hands, as if in consolation. After several agonizing seconds, the gown began to mend itself. In another moment, it was as if there had never been a tear at all.

Merry smiled brightly, wishing someone were around to see her work. She wouldn't brag or even talk about it, but she did secretly long to be acknowledged. Oh well, it was a good deed and would make her aunt happy. That was all that mattered.

As she dusted the glitter from the fairy's wings, a sudden tingle crept up her spine. There was someone else in the house with her! This time, she was sure. She held as still as she could, and listened. A muffled crash sounded from upstairs, followed by the slow stink of something she couldn't place. Hadn't her aunt said something about Krampus' smell? She couldn't remember.

Merry glanced out the window. Outside, there was a snowy clearing surrounded by a vast and endless forest. The sun worked to make its mark, but the world was too gray, too caught up in the depths of winter.

Upstairs, there was another crash. This time, it was so loud that Merry dropped the fairy on the table and dashed to front door. As she turned the knob, she stopped herself. If there was someone in the house with her - or something - and it was bent on destroying the holiday as Aunt Dora said, she had to stop it. She raced back for the Oak Crown.

She lunged for it, but there was another crash upstairs and the crown dropped to the floor, rolling under the table. By now, the stench was so strong that she thought she might get sick. She could almost hear the Click Click Click of claws on the roof!

"Sorry, Auntie" Merry said, running full speed to the door, not bothering to close it behind her.

CHAPTER FOUR

T he globe fizzled and the snow melted on the ground. Dora had lost the vision. She flicked the globe in frustration, trying to will it back alive, but it was no use.

In the last image, Merry had lost the crown beneath the harvest table. Dora had crossed that path a handful of times already, but for good measure she returned to the dining room, pulling out chairs and looking more carefully. But the crown of oak leaves was still missing.

"It can't be far," Dora said to herself. *Unless...*

What had caused those crashing sounds, and the strange smell? The scent was mostly gone now, though there was a hint that lingered. Dora wouldn't have noticed it had she not experienced it in the globe first. Now, it was just an annoyance, a restrained suggestion that something wasn't quite right in Harvest Home.

Dora returned to the kitchen and poured herself another cup of tea. After a few thoughtful sips, she refocused on the globe, her hands quivering with both fear and excitement. She was rusty from Sasha's 'Magick Moratorium' over the last few years, but it was all coming back to her now.

"Winter frost and jingle bells. Show me where the Oak Crown dwells."

Dora wriggled her fingers over the globe, then blew on the glass. As before, the snow swirled inside the glass sphere. When it settled, Dora was greeted by the image of her youngest niece, Eve. She was sitting at a work station covered in glass bottles, vials, silver bowls and candles. There was even a small black cauldron.

It took Dora a moment to recognize Eve's location. The attic. The life-sized, porcelain dolls that smiled in the background had been denizens of the upper floor longer than Dora had occupied this house. But why was Eve there?

Dora relaxed her eyes, letting the tea and the magickal globe do their work once again.

Eve sat at the small work table she had cobbled together in her aunt's attic. It wasn't much more than a slab of wood, a few bottles, and some spoons, but it was hers, a place where she could practice her spells and charms away from the critical eyes of her mother. Sasha didn't set much stock in incantations that evoked beauty or even love, not when 'there were more pressing issues in the world.' But Eve wondered, what could be more important than beauty or love? Even if she was too young to have a boyfriend, someday she might, and she'd need these essential skills to make sure they didn't run off like her mother's men all had.

But love was for another day. Today, she was helping her beloved Aunt Dora prepare for the Solstice feast and the turning of winter.

Eve lit several large candles and laid out the handwritten note her aunt had pressed into her hand. Aunt Dora had charged her with 'dressing the candles.' It was an easy task, in theory. She would anoint the red, gold, and silver candles with frankincense and myrrh oils, then roll them in cinnamon, ginger, pepper-mint, and a handful of other ingredients. This was to ensure health, wealth and posterity for the coming months.

Eve inspected all the items filched from their mother's business - Miss Sasha's Magick Shoppe. It all glittered and glowed beneath the flickering candles, as enticing as Christmas candy. She blew into her hands and lifted a red candle from its waxed paper, then doused it in myrrh oil. The scent was bitter, and much more powerful than she had anticipated, and she quickly covered her nose. Was it supposed to be that strong?

She attended to the other candles, coating them in frankincense and cedar oils, rolling them in dragon's blood resin or crushed holly leaves. They smelled better, but their look wasn't quite right.

Eve worked on a dozen candles and none of them seemed fit to present to her aunt. Tossing them in a wastebasket beneath her table, she frowned as she noticed that her materials were growing thin. She looked over her shoulder at the solitary attic window, and realized the day was getting on. Soon it would be dark, and the last thing Eve wanted was to be alone in the attic with all the creepy dolls after dusk.

With a dramatic sigh, Eve poured the remaining contents of her oils into a large silver bowl and stirred. The bitter aroma was enough to make her gag and take a step back. She knocked her chair over in her effort to get away. Still covering her nose, she threw the holly leaves, some mistletoe, and a handful of sage leaves into the bowl.

"Frankincense. Myrrh and holly, too. Let's put you all in, and see what you do. I'll add some mistletoe for love. And sage to clear the air above."

The bowl hissed, then smoked! This couldn't be good!

"Uh-oh!" Eve said, as large, belching bubbles rose up to the surface. By now, the stench was so bad her eyes watered. She went to the small window and opened it, but there was no reprieve. The attic smelled like burning rubber, wet towels, and a cat that had been outdoors too long. She had to get out of here. In a hurry.

She ran for the door, knocking over dolls on the way. She could only hope she was alone in the house, and her deed wouldn't be discovered before she could get back and clean it up. If she were lucky, the smell would be gone before her aunt came home.

As she scampered down the stairs, she wondered what she to do about the candles she still hadn't properly dressed. She knew that Aunt Dora had some in a drawer in the dining room. If she grabbed a few of those, and begged for Merry's help, she might be okay.

Eve reached the landing and noticed that Merry's scarf was on the floor. She dashed through the house, calling for her sister, hoping to enlist her help before Aunt Dora or their mother arrived. The front door was wide open but the house was empty. In the dining room, she noticed that the glue on the Yule Fairy's wings were still wet.

Eve spotted the Oak Crown beneath the long table. She picked it up and went to the window, to let air in before the smell coming down from the attic permeated the entire house.

Outside, the air was frigid and the snow was falling hard. Eve would have closed the window again, smell or no smell, were it not for the strange form she saw back near the edge of the woods.

She gripped the crown and peered through the snow. Sure enough, something was approaching from the woods! It was a furred creature with a bowed back, dragging a hurt leg through the snow. And were those horns on its head?

It lumbered towards the house, its brown fur ruffling out around it its diminutive shape.

Aunt Dora was right!

Eve slammed the window shut, nearly catching her finger in the process. She ran for the front door, but as soon as her foot hit the porch, a strong gust of wind yanked the crown from her hand and sent it sailing.

Towards the woods.

Towards the creature!

Eve stopped a moment, turning her head towards the forest, and then towards the path leading home.

"Sorry, Auntie," Eve said, following Merry's fading footprints away from the house.

CHAPTER FIVE

W as Eve okay? Dora licked her index finger and held it to the air, moving it in the direction Eve had run. Yes, her niece was fine. She breathed a sigh of relief as she poured her third cup of tea.

What of the crown? Dora wondered.

And that creature in the yard...

She wished she had gotten a closer look, but the whole scene had passed too quickly. She couldn't blame Eve for running. If she'd seen that thing in the woods, she'd probably have run, too.

Once again, Dora wiggled her fingers above the globe.

"We reap the seeds that we have sown. Show me where the crown was blown."

The crystal ball was slowly coaxed by Dora's words, and the snow rose up once more, momentarily obscuring the image within. When the snowflakes settled, this time Dora was shown the image of the porch and open front door.

She tapped on the thick rounded glass and pulled her fingers apart, stretching the image. Soon, the entire front side of Harvest Home came into view. The porch railing was decorated with a festive garland and the porch had a soft dusting of white powder. Dora spotted the crown, half buried in the snow not far from the doorway. She clapped her hands in gratitude. The crown hadn't been lost after all! It was merely buried beneath the thickly falling snow. She was about to go dig it out, when she noticed something in the globe near the edge of the woods - a furry creature, hunched over and nursing a hurt leg, limping towards Harvest Home.

Dora's eyes widened with every step. *Click. Click. Click.* She could almost hear its fearsome claws. She tried to hurry the image, but the globe took its time. Dora held her breath as the creature approached. When she could finally make it out, she laughed so hard tears formed in the corners of her eyes. The furry creature with the hurt leg was no monster - it was her niece, Maggie! She was wearing one of her mother's hooded fur coats, dragging a sled laden with kindling for the fireplace.

"Yer a fool, Dora," she said, wiping the corners of her eyes before returning to the scene. The image became clearer, and Dora watched as Maggie's full body came into view. She pulled the sled along, stopping now and again to move a rock or kick a log. It was a long trek back from the woods, laden as she was, and Maggie's face gleamed with the effort.

Halfway across the field, Maggie spotted color in the stark white snow. Leaves peeked up at her from the ground, and for a moment Maggie wondered how something was still growing in such frigid ground. Then, she saw that it wasn't a random plant at all, but her aunt's Oak Crown!

"What the..." Maggie's eyebrows bunched as she picked it up. According to her aunt, this was an important artifact, necessary for restarting the wheel. So why was it out here? She ran the sled the rest of the way home, calling "Merry! Eve? Aunt Dora?" The front door was wide open, which was quite odd, but everything else seemed to be in place.

She shed the fur just inside the doorway and dropped it to the ground, even though the coat rack was within arm's reach. Then she took the kindling and the crown to the fireplace, tracking snow the entire way. She sat still a moment, and then let out a long breath. Though she wasn't a fan of the old holidays in the way that her sisters were, she felt honored at having been asked to tend the Yule log.

It had burned for twelve days straight now, and this was its final night. A piece would be saved to light next year's fire, just as a little piece had been saved from last year to light this one.

Maggie relaxed, her eyes drifting over the small flame as she tossed twigs and pine needles and evergreen boughs into the hearth, as well as some dried fruit. She loved the feel of the heat on her cheeks and inched closer. Looking around to confirm that she was alone, she concentrated on the flame, imagining it growing in her mind. She broadened it and lengthened it, until it was roaring. She wasn't surprised that the flame responded, but she was surprised that it molded to her exact image. Maggie was a wilder, and her mother often accused her of having 'untamed magick.' A smug smile appeared on the girl's face as she imagined her mother's pleasant surprise. But Maggie wouldn't tell her. She liked to keep things to herself.

When the fire was roaring suitably, Maggie stood and dusted off her jeans. She still had several hours to play in the woods before she was called to the Midwinter's Feast. She was keen to get back out in nature, away from the eyes and confinement of her family. But the snow was falling harder now, and Maggie wondered if the boredom of staying at her aunt's house, with only a rickety old TV to keep her company, might just be worth staying warm. She looked out the window again and determined that the snow couldn't fall forever. She would wait it out, she decided.

It was strange being at Harvest Home alone. Her aunt was a staple in the house, as much a part of the decor as the sofa or the old television. Mother said Dora had been quite the socialite in her younger days, but those days were long gone. Dora was mostly homebound now, and when she was away there was a tangible difference in the air. It was as if the whole house waited for her to come home before it breathed again.

Was it any wonder that her aunt had freaked herself out? Being here alone in the winter, surrounded by nothing but the woods, had to take its emotional toll. Maggie was young, but she wasn't a fool. Wind chimes could mimic the sounds of Krampus' bells, and birds roosting in the rafters might make the curious clicking sound of his claws.

Click. Click. Clicccccckkk!

Maggie froze, her eyes rolling upwards. The roof!

Click. Click!

There it went again. But it wasn't on the roof, it was at the window!

Maggie squeezed her eyes shut, telling herself it was just her imagination. Aunt Dora had legions of old monsters she named throughout the year. This was just another one. Still, a shiver tickled her spine and she noticed how dim the room was, even though it was high afternoon and the fire was going strong.

She swallowed hard and made her way to the window, still holding the Oak Crown. She parted the curtain and peered carefully outside. As she let the drape fall closed, she caught movement to her right. She twisted her neck and looked as far as she could and saw...

The points of two polished yellow-gray horns, disappearing at the side of the house!

Maggie leapt towards the door, racing around the house in the direction she'd witnessed the disappearing horns. Krampus might be frightening to her aunt, but Maggie could handle him, just as long as she could see him. It was the unknown monsters that scared her most.

Snow pelted Maggie's face. For a moment, she thought she saw the creature's tracks, and she followed them until they disappeared near the edge of the woods.

"Krampus!" she called, feeling emboldened yet silly. "You want the crown, come and get it."

Whether it was the inherent magick of Dark Root, the fierce winter winds, or Krampus himself, Maggie would never know. But as soon as she had spoken the words, the wreath was blasted from her fingertips. She watched helplessly as it sailed into the shadowy forest.

And though Maggie felt at home in these woods she had grown up in, she hesitated. If the creature had scared her aunt, perhaps she didn't need to tangle with it herself? She stared into the trees, wondering what to do. She would tell Merry. Or her mother. Or someone.

Or, she could pretend that she had never seen the crown at all.

She looked back. Her own footprints had already been covered by new snow.

Winter wouldn't really go on forever if they didn't give the Oak King his crown, would it?

She didn't have time to think. She heard a terrible noise in the forest and was certain she saw another flash of the creature's sharp horns.

"Sorry, Auntie," Maggie said, running back towards the house and then down the lone trail that led her home.

CHAPTER SIX

O nce again, the image began to break apart and Dora was left staring into clear glass.

"Not so fast!" she said, blowing on the crystal, as if fanning a flame. The globe responded, pulling up an image as quickly as the last had faded away. There was snow, so much snow, and she was unable to tell if it was from the globe or the wintry landscape. She narrowed her eyes and looked closer, and found the Oak Crown, sailing through the air, winding through the dense trees.

She followed its path with her eyes, and saw it land softly on an extended evergreen bough.

But the crown's peaceful rest was disturbed by a rumbling like thunder. With each boom, the crown slightly dislodged itself from the bough, until it hung from the tip of the branch, like an old Kleenex ready to be discarded. Boom! The noise sounded again, yet the crown valiantly hung on. What was causing those terrible sounds? It was as if the whole earth had opened up and was pulling everything down with it.

"Focus," she said to herself, trying to pan out her view.

The image expanded, and she noticed that it wasn't the whole world falling apart, just that one tree.

"Whew!" Dora said, crossing her chest. When she returned her gaze to the globe, she noticed a small figure at the base of the tree and a glint of silver cutting through the gloom.

It was her eldest niece, Ruth Anne, who had taken an axe to the small evergreen tree.

Whack! The sharpened steel split into the tree. Ruth Anne paused a moment to wipe her brow, then resumed her task. She wasn't a true witch, like her magickal sisters, but she still had a soft spot for nature. Especially trees. Had her own mother asked her to cut one down for the Solstice, she might have argued. But she would never say no to her beloved aunt. Even if it meant a tree had to be taken from the forest.

Ruth Anne reached into its branches and retrieved two pinecones, stuffing them into her coat pocket. With some attention, along with Merry's nature magick, two new trees would grow to replace this one.

After a few more whacks the evergreen fell, scattering the nearby robins and wrens. It wasn't a very big tree, hardly six feet tall and half as wide, but it had a heavy trunk. Ruth Anne wished she had thought to bring a sled, as Maggie had to collect wood.

It was nearly dark but the Sister House wasn't far off, down a small trail and across a field. She'd drag it in, set it up, and if she was feeling particularly charitable, she might even throw on a few decorations. Ruth Anne was sentimental at heart, and though she might joke about her aunt's rustic holiday decor, she enjoyed the tradition of lifting each ornament out of its box and reliving memories of holidays past.

Ruth Anne pulled the tree behind her, periodically letting go with one hand to blow warm air into her mittens. The crunching of snow beneath her boots and the rustling of the boughs as they brushed against other trees were the only sounds she heard in the quiet forest. Ruth Anne realized how alone she felt as the moon and the sun began trading places. She could see why her aunt was spooked about winter - the world was so quiet and slumbering.

Click. Click. Click.

Huh? What made that noise?

Ruth Anne dropped the end of the fir and looked nervously about. Wood-

peckers this late in the year? She held still, cocking her ear, and realized it wasn't a clicking sound but rather a scraping noise. Like sharpened nails being scraped across wood.

"Ruth Anne!" She jumped, looking around for the source of the voice. "Ruth Anne!" The voice called again. But the wind pulled the sound apart until she was uncertain of who had called her or where it had come from. She lifted the base of the tree and ran as fast as she could towards the edge of the woods as the shadows closed in around her.

A flash of brown fur in the distance stopped her in her tracks, and she turned back the other way. Up ahead, she heard the clicking again, accompanied by the softest tinkling of bells. She looked up and down, trying to find the source, but the ringing seemed to come from all around her.

Ruth Anne dropped the tree and forged a new path through the tight woods. Something dropped from a high bough behind her, and she had only a moment to look back and see that it was the Oak Crown before a gleaming horn poked out from behind a nearby tree.

The Krampus was real, and he was with her!

"Sorry, Auntie," she said as she raced for the clearing. She would come back later, she promised herself, as the sound of bells followed her all the way out of the forest. She only hoped she could find the crown again.

CHAPTER SEVEN

W hen Ruth Anne's scene faded, the globe went completely dark. No amount of tapping or blowing on it would stir it again.

Was the crown still out there in the woods? The tree was set up, so Ruth Anne must have gone back for it. Yet there was no sign of the crown, so she had probably forgotten about it. Dora knew the forest well and could probably find it, if Krampus hadn't taken it back to his lair already.

The snow had now stopped falling, though it was still terribly cold and growing darker by the moment. But time was limited. In less than an hour the sun would set, and if she didn't give the king his crown, winter might settle over the world for another full spin of the wheel.

Dora bundled up and headed outside, armed with only her wand and trusty lantern. She sneezed periodically, hoping she wasn't scaring Krampus further into the forest. But if she knew him, he'd stick around. Having the crown, he would want to stay close to see what kind of misery his mischief had caused.

"Krampus!" she called out, cupping her hands as she shouted into the woods. She noticed that her hip hurt less with every resolute step, and even the cold didn't seem to bother her. The only thing that mattered was that crown. "Krampus!" she called again. "I know yer out there and ya have the crown. Hand it o'er and I won't have ta use my magick on ya. I'm rusty. Who knows what this old wand will do if I point it at ya!"

The wind twisted around the trees, shaking loose pinecones and overlaying every other sound. Dora's resolve began to break, as she searched in vain for the crown and found only snow. She eventually sat down on a stump and willed the tears away from her eyes as she issued her apology.

"I'm sorry, Oak King. The Holly King won this time. I was a fool ta not watch the crown myself." She reached into her never ending pockets and drew out an offering of mistletoe and dried fruit, laying them on the forest floor. Then she dried her eyes and went home. It was going to be a sad meal this night, and Dora wondered how she would explain the turn of events to her family.

Click. Click. Click.

Ring!

Scratch!

Dora heard the sounds behind her. They seemed to be coming from everywhere. Were there more monsters roaming the world tonight than she knew?

Every instinct told her to run, but she drew her wand like a sword and turned to face the creatures. Sparks from her wand struck a nearby tree, severing a small branch. She was sorry for the tree, but the fate of spring was in her hands.

"Krampus! I got ya now!" She said as her eyes searched the shadows, following the hoof prints that wove in and out of the trees. She lifted her wand, ready to strike again.

The sound of crunching snow forced her attention to the right, and her lantern light caught a furry creature with large eyes and short pointed horns. She spun the lantern around and saw another horned creature in her peripheral vision.

It took less than a moment for Dora to realize what had happened.

She hadn't found Krampus. She had found a small herd of young reindeer, with bells dangling about their necks. The escapees from the petting zoo!

Dora laughed so hard in relief that she stumbled backwards against a tree. She felt spent, yet relieved.

Dora reached into her deep pockets and produced two small apples, offering each to a deer, while the rest of the herd feasted on the mistletoe and dried fruit she had set out. She petted one, whose collar read: Stan.

There was no sign of the crown, but there was no sign of Krampus either. Perhaps her sister was right. Maybe she clung too much to the old ways.

She said goodbye to the deer and buttoned her coat. She wasn't sure if winter would end. She would have to wait and see. But as she turned to make her way home, another figure emerged from the woods. This was a tall figure with broad shoulders, garbed in a red cloak and fur collar.

Dora gulped as the form stepped from the shadows. Krampus might not be near, but someone was. "Holly King?" she asked as the form stepped forward. She had been so preoccupied with Krampus that she had forgotten that the Holly King had the greatest stake of in all of this - giving up his own crown.

The figure pulled back its hood and Dora's lantern illuminated the face beneath the hood. There was no laughing this time, only a wide smile as she registered recognition.

"Sasha! What are ya doing' here?" Dora asked.

Sasha clicked her tongue. "You were so worked up this morning about the crown, I decided to keep an eye on it myself." Sasha reached into her cloak pocket and removed a hand mirror, and showed it to Dora.

"My crown!" she said of the image that appeared. "An' it's on its altar! But how? No one knows where the altar is located but me!"

Sasha returned the mirror to her pocket and looped her arm through Dora's. "I may not share your beliefs, Dora, but I respect them. I've known the location of the altar for years. In fact, I have a confession to make."

"Yes?" Dora asked as they tramped through the snow-covered field back to Harvest Home.

"I've been the one taking the crown from the altar every year. It wasn't the Oak King. It was me. I'm sorry."

Dora slumped against the front door for a moment. "I shoulda known! How could I have thought the fate o' the wheel depended on me?"

"We all have our parts to play, Dora. Your beliefs add to the magick of the season."

Dora opened the door and tramped inside, Sasha right behind her. The smells of ham and goose and candies and pies greeted them, and she shut the door to keep in the coziness. "Do ya think Krampus is a myth? An' the Holly King, too?"

Sasha removed her fur coat and hung it on the rack as she considered her sister's question. "I've lived in Dark Root long enough to know that no magick should be discounted. I think that anything we truly believe in can be real."

"Alright then," Dora said as she headed into the kitchen. She opened the oven and removed a pan of stuffing, setting it aside. The sound of her laughing nieces greeted her at the back door. They each smiled shyly as they went by, but not one of them volunteered information on their day.

"Its time I let go o' the old ways," Dora said aloud. "The girls deserve more than silly superstition. I frightened them all."

"That sounds reasonable," said Sasha. She patted Dora's shoulder and left the kitchen.

As Dora peeled potatoes, she thought she heard a distant laugh, and her eyes wandered out the kitchen window. She saw something in the woods, for just a moment.

Was it another deer? Krampus? Or even the Holly King?

Dora didn't know.

She could go out to the altar tomorrow and see if the crown had been taken, now that her sister had confessed, or she could just have faith that the wheel would turn on its own.

"Auntie, look!" Merry said, coming in and grabbing her by the fingers. "The fairy is on the tree!"

They stood around the tree, admiring it as a family, and Dora realized it didn't matter if winter lasted the entire year. She was safe, and she was home and loved.

Dora made her way back into the kitchen. "No more superstitious ways," she promised herself. From now on, she was a modern witch with modern ideas.

She stirred the mashed potatoes, then tossed a pinch of salt over each of her shoulders, just to seal the deal.

The End

To read more from April Aasheim, visit her at www.aprilaasheimwriter.com.

ABOUT THE AUTHOR

April Aasheim lives in Portland, Oregon with her family and her familiar: Boots the Cat. When she isn't writing she enjoys hiking, dance fitness, and ghost hunting.

April is the author of the best-selling Daughters of Dark Root series. Her stories have been featured in many anthologies, including two that hit the USA Today Best Seller lists.

Follow April Aasheim online:
Facebook
Website
Twitter

MISTLETOE, MAGIC, & MURDER

Suburban Witches Series

RUBY BLAYLOCK

SUMMARY

Mischa, Ellie, and Poe are more than just best friends and neighbors—they also form a coven of witches living right in the middle of a sleepy suburban town in North Carolina. They make the perfect neighborhood watch and always have an eye on what's going on in their town. So, when a blonde bombshell with a mysterious past moves in, they're understandably curious. Especially when, hours later, another neighbor drops dead.

Did their new neighbor murder their old one? Or did someone else want grumpy Edith Whitlow dead?

It's up to the witches to solve Edith's murder, but with PTA meetings, full-time jobs, and two talking cats underfoot, can they catch the culprit in time for their annual Christmas party?

Meet the witches of Country Acres Coven, Kensleigh Landing East, where the suburbs and the supernatural just happen to overlap.

CHAPTER ONE

"I think blondie bumped off the old hag," Poe Landry muttered between bites of the muffin that her neighbor, Mischa, had brought over to her. It was apple, still warm, and completely delicious in that just-out-of-the-oven way.

"We can't jump to any conclusions," Mischa scolded. She squeezed her peppermint mocha latte between her gloved hands, willing the warmth into them. "I'm sure she's nice."

Poe thought that Mischa was far too generous with her trust. The new neighbor had moved in exactly thirty-six hours ago, and approximately twelve hours later, another woman on Country Lane Close had been found dead.

No one on the quiet cul-de-sac street had liked the old woman. Even Mischa had a hard time finding anything redeemable in the old hag. Of course, Edith Whitlow, the woman in question, hadn't been a witch like Poe, Mischa, or their other friend, Ellie, but the three witches rarely held that against anyone.

Ellie, Mischa, and Poe were a coven of sorts. Somehow all of them had found their way to the Country Acres subdivision and had bought homes on the same street. As far as they knew, they were the only witches in the neighborhood, though they knew that they were far from the only magical beings in Kensleigh Landing East, the small North Carolina town that they lived in.

Mischa was the only married witch in the group. The fact that she was married to a 'normie,' or non-magical being, didn't escape them, but Mischa's husband wasn't phased by the fact that his wife was a witch or that his neighbor had talking cats. Mischa herself had almost forgotten that her husband couldn't cast spells. The fact that they were a mixed-race couple usually caused more raised eyebrows than the fact that Joe couldn't do magic.

"She's got a dog," Ellie said neutrally. She shifted on her feet, trying to keep warm on the icy driveway of Poe's house. The three women met most mornings for coffee and gossip. Mischa had her two kids to take to school and Ellie had to be at work early, but they tried to meet regularly, at least when there was something newsworthy to discuss. And the mysterious leggy blonde who'd just moved into number 618 was definitely newsworthy.

"He's weird," intoned Raven, describing the dog. "He can't even speak."

"That's rich, coming from a talking cat," replied Cleo, licking one icy paw thoughtfully and running it through her own whiskers.

"Well, we can't just stand out here all day," huffed Ellie as she brushed her auburn hair away from her face. "As much as I hate to say it, I have to go to work." She downed the last of her own coffee and patted Mischa on the arm. "Thanks for the muffin, Misch. Poe, stay sober."

The black-haired young woman in Doc Martens shrugged her shoulders. "Hey, it's for medicinal purposes," she called out as Ellie disappeared into her own house.

"She just worries about you. We all do," Mischa chirped. "Save the Schnapps for the Christmas party, okay?" She hugged her friend and nodded at the two talking cats, then sprinted down the sidewalk back to her own house.

Poe cocked her head to one side and considered the house next to hers. She thought she could see the new girl moving around inside near the window. Poe took another swig of her spiked coffee and leaned forward slightly, trying to get a better view of the inside of the house through its cheap lace curtains.

"A picture would last longer," boomed a voice, frightening Poe enough to almost spill her drink.

"Crap!" she muttered, trying to compose herself. Somehow the new neighbor had managed to appear behind Poe in the frozen driveway. And she did not look happy.

"Look," the blonde began, pushing her still-damp hair behind her ears. She was dressed in a business skirt suit and wore dangerously high heels for the icy conditions, but she stood tall and self-assured. "I'm not trying to be rude, but I can't help but notice that you and your friends have been staring at my house for the last half hour."

Poe had regained her own composure. "So you were watching us for the last thirty minutes? Huh. And here I thought we were the only stalkers in the neighborhood." She swigged her drink. "So how do you like the neighborhood?"

Blondie crossed her arms. "Well, considering the fact that I've only been here a hot five minutes, I'd say I haven't really had a chance to decide how I like it." She considered Poe for a long moment, then offered her hand. "My name is Seneca Wolfram. I guess I'm your new neighbor."

Poe accepted the handshake cautiously. "Poe Landry. Nice to meet you." Her words didn't match her tone, which was unenthusiastic at best. Poe didn't get excited too often, and she certainly wasn't going to jump up and down just because the new, very suspicious neighbor happened to introduce herself.

"Have you lived here long?" Seneca asked, rubbing her hands together to fight the winter chill. It was a balmy twenty-four degrees on the street, but the alcohol in her coffee had kept Poe toasty and warm, at least on the inside. Obviously, Seneca hadn't partaken of such a useful beverage.

"Three years," Poe replied. "You from around here?" She batted the ball back to Seneca, keeping the conversation going longer than she'd planned.

Poe rarely had conversations with people other than Mischa, Ellie, and their families. Heck, Poe didn't even have conversations with her own family, at least not if she could help it.

Seneca fidgeted with the sleeve of her shirt, which looked to Poe to be too thin to provide much warmth. "No, I moved here for work," she replied. "And I'm afraid I'll be late if I don't leave soon. I just wanted to come over here and introduce myself so you and your friends could stop gawking at me through the window." She glared at Poe, but Poe simply shrugged.

"Sorry. For what it's worth, we meet out here most mornings. You just happened to be the topic of the day because you're new." Poe drained the rest of her coffee and glanced around for her cats, but they were nowhere to be seen. "I guess I should let you get on with your day." She turned without waiting for Seneca to reply and only looked back when she reached her front door. The blonde woman was nowhere to be seen.

The two cats were waiting impatiently by the front door when Poe reached it. They huddled together, staring at their owner reproachfully.

"She's weird, too," Raven moaned, pushing past Poe and rushing into the warmth of the house.

Poe agreed with him. "She's kind of snooty, isn't she?"

Cleo strolled past Poe with her head held high. "I'll keep an eye on her," she purred. "You just focus on ordering me some of those yummy treats from the online pet store," she added. "I've been a very good girl and I think I really do deserve at least that much for it." The cat collapsed into a heap of silky Siamese fur in front of the fireplace and began washing her paws.

Poe sighed and sat down at her computer, but instead of going to the pet store's website, she pulled up her favorite search engine and typed in her new neighbor's name. Seneca may not have told her much about herself, but that didn't mean that Poe wouldn't know all about her by the end of the day.

CHAPTER TWO

Mischa Henley pulled her minivan into a parking space at the Kensleigh Landing East Bank & Trust parking lot. It was only nine AM, but she was already on her third cup of coffee thanks to the stress of the school run and her other errands. With one child at the middle school and one at the elementary school, Mischa felt like she spent way too much time in her car every day anyway, but she couldn't say no when her husband, Joe, had asked her to drop off a deposit at the bank.

Joe worked in a lumber mill by day but dabbled in carpentry on the side. Specifically, he created artwork from unused bits of lumber and pieces of trees. He'd carved a garden gnome from a block of wood and sold it to an older gentleman who lived in the neighborhood. Mr. Gibbons had paid him with a handful of wrinkled ten dollar bills and a stack of rolled quarters. Mischa hefted the tote bag carrying the money and made her way into the bank, anxious to get rid of the cumbersome cash.

Mischa smiled at the teller as she approached the counter, ready to make small talk while the young woman counted out all the coins in the deposit. She felt bad bringing in so much change, so Mischa had also brought the remainder of her apple muffins as a way to make up for the inconvenience.

"I'll just go and sit over there while you do the deposit," Mischa suggested, leaving the teller with her muffins and money. As she turned to find a seat in the bank's lobby, a tall blonde woman caught her attention.

"Excuse me," Mischa called out, interrupting the woman's walk across the lobby. When she turned around to see who was calling out to her, the woman frowned.

"Were you calling me?" the blonde woman asked.

Mischa smiled widely, hoping that she looked friendly and not like a crazy person. "I think we're neighbors," Mischa said, offering her hand. "I'm Mischa Henley. I live two houses down from you, I think."

Seneca smiled back at Mischa, but it was a forced smile. "Yes, I think I saw you outside my neighbor's house this morning," she replied. "I met her, too."

"Oh?" Mischa asked, raising one eyebrow quizzically. "Poe introduced herself? That's unusual for her. She's normally a little reserved with new people."

"Actually, I introduced myself. I'm Seneca Wolfram. I couldn't help but notice that there was a gathering outside this morning." She didn't say anything else, but Mischa knew what was implied.

"Oh, yeah, that," she said, widening her smile forcefully. "We totally hoped to catch you and ask if you wanted to stop by this evening at my place," Mischa lied. "I was thinking that we could have some snacks and drinks, you know, get to know each other? Mine's the tan and yellow two-story with the red mailbox."

Mischa never stopped smiling, hoping that Seneca would believe that she was being truthful. Mischa's grandmother had always warned her about the dangers of gossiping and now here she stood, facing the consequences of a potentially angry new neighbor. All because she and her coven couldn't keep their gossipy tongues from wagging right in front of Seneca's house. Her jaw was beginning to ache from the effort of maintaining her smile.

Seneca thought about the invitation for just a moment. "I'm sorry, Mischa, but I have plans this evening. I'm still unpacking everything and, honestly, I just want to relax after work. I haven't slept properly in days and I'm afraid I wouldn't be good company," she added.

Mischa nodded sympathetically. "Oh, I can totally understand how you feel. And I'm sure the police have been bothering you nonstop since what happened to Edith."

Seneca rolled her eyes. "Oh, god, don't get me started." She shook her head, then sighed. "I don't want to talk ill of the woman because she obviously had mental issues," Seneca began. "But I can't but help feel I dodged a bullet with that woman."

Mischa's eyes widened. "What do you mean?"

Seneca glanced around the lobby of the bank nervously. "She assaulted me the first day I moved in."

"What? Edith hit you? What did you do?" Mischa's eyes felt as wide as her smile. She forced both to relax.

"I didn't do anything to her," Seneca assured her. "I only waved at her when I was going out to my car to get some of my things. The crazy old woman ran up and threw a shovelful of dog crap at my front door and then waved the shovel in my face like a lunatic." Seneca took a deep breath, then continued. "She was rambling on about my dog pooping on her lawn, but I can assure you that Alistair does not go poop on other people's properties."

"Alistair? Is that your dog's name?" Mischa asked.

Seneca nodded quickly. "He's house trained to use those doggy pads while I'm at work and then he has his own outdoor area behind the house for other times. And I never let him go out front because I don't want him near the road, so whoever's dog left her that particularly disgusting gift, it wasn't mine."

Mischa thought about this for a moment. She could definitely imagine Edith doing such a disgusting thing--the woman had been crazier than a loon--but was Seneca the type of person to tolerate such an action and not retaliate, even a little?

"What did you do?" Mischa asked. "After she left, why didn't you call someone?"

Seneca laughed a stilted, manic chuckle. "Who was I supposed to call? I don't know anyone here yet. And I'm not calling the cops on my neighbor five minutes after I've moved in. I felt helpless, and I cannot stand feeling helpless." She shifted on her feet and pushed a strand of blonde hair behind one ear. "At least now I know I won't be having anymore run ins with that woman."

Mischa struggled to find a response to Seneca's icy demeanor. A woman had died. She may have been an awful woman who threw poop at people with a shovel, but she was dead and surely the appropriate response to her death shouldn't be relief. Thankfully, a call from the teller sliced through the tension that had developed between Mischa and her new neighbor.

"Mrs. Henley, here's your receipt," the teller chirped.

Mischa crossed the lobby and took the receipt while the teller offered Seneca one of Mischa's apple muffins.

"You really need to try one of these, Seneca, they are delicious!"

Seneca smiled politely. "Maybe some other time," she replied. "It was a pleasure meeting you, Mischa, but I'm afraid I've lost my appetite after our little conversation." She smiled, but it was a plastic one, something she probably learned in customer service training.

"Some other time, then," Mischa replied before hurrying back to her car with her deposit receipt.

CHAPTER THREE

E leanor "Ellie" Watkins stuck her head inside the walk-in freezer and did a quick count of the boxes of fries she had on the storage shelf. She did some mental calculations, then jotted a number down on her order form. The nagging thought that she really ought to train one her morning staff to do orders flitted through her mind, but she pushed it away. Ellie knew she couldn't trust any of the employees to handle such an important job, not because they were incompetent, but because they were super-incompetent.

She sighed as she passed the handful of workers she had in today. All but one were high school students who were less than thrilled that they'd been asked to work so close to their Christmas break. The one employee who wasn't a pimply teenager was Berneice, a seventy-year-old with bunions who moved at a snail's pace except when it was time to go home.

She peered out into a fairly empty lobby, which wasn't unusual. Eattaburger's drive thru did exponentially more business than its interior, at least throughout the week. She could hear Sam, the drive through operator, talking to a customer. Ellie sighed as he repeated the order back but got half of it wrong. Sam was usually far more interested in playing on his phone than he was in actually getting orders correct, but he was also one of the only kids who showed up consistently and didn't complain when he had to work extra hours.

A shriek of laughter told her that her daughter was goofing off again. Holly Watkins had begged her mother for a job at the fast food restaurant but she was hardly what Ellie would call a great employee.

It wasn't that Holly was lazy or disrespectful. Well, maybe she was disrespectful, but that's because her manager was also her mother and no self-respecting teen could be seen showing respect to her parent all the time. Ellie told herself that Holly was just going through a phase, an awful one that would end soon and leave Ellie with only memories and a daughter who wanted to actually spend time with her mother instead of avoid her at all costs, even when they were working together.

And Holly seemed to have terrible luck, which translated itself into an extreme clumsiness that only seemed to bother those around her. In the few months since she'd begun working at the Eattaburger, Holly had broken the doorknob to the ladies' bathroom, spilled countless drinks, and burned several batches of fries. Ellie had moved her daughter to the salad station in the hopes that she'd be safer there, but Holly had still managed to cut herself and bleed all over someone's chicken salad.

Now Ellie handled the slicing herself and Holly merely assembled salads. Ellie hoped that her daughter would tire of working at the burger restaurant soon, but the way her daughter was laughing at that moment, it didn't seem like an imminent possibility.

"Excuse me," a voice said, pulling Ellie's attention back to the lobby. It came from a very angry looking blonde woman in a skirt suit. "Can I speak to a manager?"

Ellie's jaw clenched involuntarily. She forced her biggest smile and stepped up behind the counter. "I'm the manager. How can I help?"

Ellie and the woman both registered a sense of recognition at the same time. It was Ellie who acknowledged it first.

"You live on my street." It was a simple statement, but it came out like an accusation. Ellie cringed. "Sorry, I just recognized you. What seems to be the problem Miss..."

"Wolfram. You can call me Seneca. And the problem is that my order is all wrong. I ordered a chicken salad with a small side of fries and I got a plain salad with burned fries and something that looks like an uncooked hamburger in a box." She slid a bag with the Eattaburger logo on it across the counter to Ellie. "I don't think the person at the drive through understood me when I placed my order," she suggested.

Ellie peered inside the bag and groaned. "I'm so sorry, Seneca. Let me replace this for you on the house, you know, to welcome you to the neighborhood." She disappeared into the back of the restaurant before Seneca could reply and replaced the incorrect order with the right one in under a minute.

"Here you go. And I've thrown in an apple pie as well. Now, let me see how much that was so I can refund you the price of the meal." She began pushing buttons on the cash register but Seneca stopped her.

"Honestly, don't worry about it. Thank you so much for handling this so efficiently. I was beginning to think I'd made a terrible mistake in moving here to Kensleigh Landing East. I've had nothing but friction from everyone on our street, well, except for that Mischa woman. Is she always so darned friendly?" she asked.

Ellie nodded. "Uh-huh. And Poe really isn't as bristly as she seems. Well, at least not all the time. Actually, our biggest pain in the rear bought the farm just after you moved in, so I think you're safe," she added with a grin. "Oh, I know I shouldn't speak ill of the dead, but Edith wasn't really that nice of a person. I'm sorry she was killed the way that she was, but still, I can't say too many people will be wailing at her funeral."

Seneca looked confused. "Killed? I thought she just died, you know, of old age and acrimony."

Ellie leaned across the counter conspiratorially. "No, it looks like she was murdered. At least, that's what I hear." Truthfully, Ellie had heard nothing of the sort, but she wanted to see how the snooty blonde reacted to such a horrific proclamation.

The reaction she got wasn't quite what she expected. Seneca's face turned two shades paler than a vanilla milkshake. She picked up her bag of food and thanked Ellie again, then mumbled something about being tired and wanting to put her feet up. Ellie watched the woman hurry from the restaurant, nearly knocking Berneice over in the process.

"What was her problem?" Berneice asked, wiping the soda machine down for the twentieth time that day.

Ellie shook her head. "I guess maybe I said something she didn't want to hear," Ellie replied. "Why don't you go ahead and leave early tonight, Berneice? It's slow and I can finish up by myself up here."

Berneice had already begun removing her apron when she hurried around the counter to clock out. "See you tomorrow, Ellie," she cooed before walking out the door.

Ellie glanced at her watch. Ten more minutes and her assistant manager should arrive and Ellie could go home for the evening. She could wait ten minutes to call Mischa and tell her that she'd be able to meet with her and Poe. She just didn't know if she could wait until she saw them to tell Mischa about their new neighbor's bizarre behavior at the restaurant.

CHAPTER FOUR

"I can't believe you told her Edith had been murdered. I bet she freaked out." Poe pulled her feet in more tightly beneath her on the worn out sofa. She shoved a cracker topped with sharp cheddar into her mouth and chewed noisily.

Ellie swallowed her own mouthful of food and nodded enthusiastically. "Oh, yeah, she practically ran out of the place. I bet she's over there now destroying the evidence now that she knows we're on to her." She was perched on the opposite end of the sofa.

Between the women, Raven lounged, sprawled across the width of the sofa cushion. Ellie tossed him the occasional piece of cheddar and the odd chunk of cubed ham. Cheese, crackers, fruit, and wine was the usual Wednesday evening fare. Tonight there was also sausage balls leftover from a school function and provided by Mischa, who sat across from her friends in a large easy chair.

"What evidence could she be destroying?" Mischa mused. "The police have already been around Edith's house and looked around. I'm sure they must have been pretty thorough in their investigation."

"Yeah, but did they know that Edith and Seneca had their little run-in just before Edith died?" Ellie asked. "I still can't believe that crazy old bat threw poop at Blondie." She shook her head and chuck-led. "She was completely bonkers, wasn't she?"

"And Seneca is totally hiding something," Poe said, not for the first time that evening. "I spent all morning Googling her. There was nothing online about her at all, not even a Facebook profile."

"Maybe she's just a really private person," Mischa suggested.

"Or maybe she's in the witness protection program," Ellie offered. "Or maybe she's a spy."

"Or, maybe she's a cold-blooded killer who pushed a little old woman down some icy stairs in broad daylight and who's now getting away with it." Poe tipped her wine glass back to her lips, forgetting it was empty. She frowned at the empty vessel. "I just don't get what she stood to gain from it, though."

"Maybe Edith had something that Seneca wanted," Ellie suggested. "I mean, have you seen the inside of her house? It's full of all kinds of weird, expensive stuff."

"Like what?" Poe asked.

"Like a huge flat screen TV, for starters," Raven interjected. The cat glanced at the women's surprised expressions. "What? So I went over there a few times. She may have hated dogs, but she loved cats. And she gave me kippers," he sighed.

"She had a lot of money, actually." Mischa's statement pulled every-one's attention to her. "One of the moms in the PTA said that her husband had drawn up Edith's will for her last year. She said that he told her that Edith was worth a fortune and was leaving it all to the local cat shelters."

"How is that even possible?" Ellie asked. "I mean, we all saw how Edith lived. She never wore nice clothes, had an old clunker for a car, and she was always using a million coupons at the grocery store. Does that sound like a rich person to you?"

"Actually, that's probably why she had money," Mischa pointed out. "If she never spent anything, she could have been saving it all up."

"Actually," Poe said, glancing up from her iPhone, "it says here on the local news website that they're auctioning off her stuff next week and there's a really expensive painting listed. I'll bet that's what made up the bulk of her worth." She powered down the device and dropped it onto the table at the end of the couch. "Don't you just love technology?" she asked, a grin spreading across her face.

"Did it say how much the painting was worth?" Mischa asked.

"It said that they estimated it to be around a quarter of a million dollars," Poe replied, refilling her wine glass. "It was some sort of weird painting of cats."

"Sounds about right," grumbled Ellie. "I mean, no offense to you, Raven, but she was one truly eccentric cat lady who didn't even own a cat. How weird can you get?"

"Well," he purred, "you could be a young, eccentric cat lady who casts a spell on her cats so she'll have someone to talk to," he replied, eyeing Poe through bright green eyes.

"I can reverse that spell any time, chatterbox," Poe replied, running a finger from the top of the cat's head down his spine. He shivered and rolled over to allow her to stroke his tummy.

"Does anybody else just really want to see this so-called quarter of a million dollar painting?" Ellie asked suddenly.

For a moment, no one answered. Finally, Poe spoke up. "Well, yeah, but we can't just go sneaking into the woman's house."

"We don't have to," Ellie replied. "I have a key." She grabbed her purse from its spot on the floor and fished around inside it. After a minute she pulled out a single silver key from its depths. "Edith gave this to me last month when she went away to her sister's place for a week. She made me go inside and turn on different lights at different times of the day so people wouldn't think the house was empty."

Mischa raised one eyebrow. "She must have actually liked you," she said to Ellie.

"Nah. She just knew I wasn't going to steal anything. And I did bring her burgers now and then when the weather was bad and she couldn't get out to the store." She blushed when she realized her friends were staring at her in amazement. "What? It was just the decent thing to do. Besides, I kind of thought maybe she wouldn't be so hateful to everybody if someone was nice to her."

"Yeah, that didn't work too well, did it?" Poe asked. "I mean, she was still pretty irritable from what I saw."

"Ellie was right. We should have been nicer to her," Mischa said. "I feel awful about it now. I mean, she lived all by herself. It's not like she had anyone to help her out with stuff. Maybe if we'd have been nicer to her she wouldn't have ended up dying all alone like that." She sniffed back a tear.

"Okay, no more wine for you," Poe said, wagging one bony finger at Mischa. "Have you forgotten how she used to yell at your kids any time they walked too close to the edge of her yard? And what about the time she threatened the mailman for delivering my mail to her accidentally? The poor guy nearly crashed his truck trying to get away from the woman."

"Okay, okay--she was no saint. But Ellie has a point. Edith was probably only hateful because no one took the time to get to know her and appreciate her." Mischa sighed. "Not even her own sister visited her, apparently."

"I visited her," Raven reminded them. "And don't worry, I kept my mouth shut. I'd like to think that my sacrifice was a worthy one," the cat yawned. "I mean, I did put up with her craziness more than anyone else."

"Yeah, but she was feeding your furry little face," Poe reminded him. "So it wasn't completely selfless, was it?"

"So should we go over to Edith's house and take a look at this painting?" Ellie asked, waving the key in the air once again.

"Isn't that breaking and entering?" Mischa's eyes widened. "I can't get arrested. I have a PTA meeting in the morning and lunches to pack."

Poe stood. She was only a little wobbly from the wine. "Nobody's getting arrested. We'll just sneak in the back door--"

"I only have a front door key," Ellie advised her. "So everybody act sober and non-suspicious."

Mischa crossed her arms. "I am sober. But I don't think this is a good idea. What if someone sees us?"

"We'll just tell them that we were feeding her cat," Poe declared.

"She didn't have a cat," Mischa replied pointedly.

"Didn't she?" Poe returned, glaring at Raven.

"Don't use me in your emotional tug of war, people," he mewled before proceeding to clean one paw. "Wait," he said, mid-lick. "Do I have to come with you?"

"Well, to make our cover story more convincing," Ellie began, but the cat's groan drowned her out.

"The things I do for you witches! I swear, you never ask Cleo to do these things."

"That's because we're afraid of her," Ellie whispered loudly. "Where is she, anyway?"

"Oh, you know her. She's probably off eating the souls of the damned or something," Raven replied. "Now, are we gonna do this thing or not?"

Poe eyed her cat suspiciously. "You've changed your tune pretty quickly. Why are you suddenly willing to help us?"

"Uh, hellooo! Didn't you hear what I said about kippers? We can grab some while we're there. It will totally make your cover story more authentic," he assured her, stretching his slightly overweight body across the couch cushion.

"I'm not sure about this," Mischa began, but Ellie cut her off.

"We'll be fine. We'll be in and out in five minutes. I just have a strong feeling we need to go take a look inside that house. Call it a hunch, but something tells me that there's a clue to Edith's death somewhere in there."

Mischa pulled her cardigan around herself more tightly and followed her friends, pausing only long enough to pick up Raven from the couch. "Come on, Raven. I guess we're all in this together," she sighed and slipped out into the cold December evening.

CHAPTER FIVE

E dith Whitlow's house was fully dark. The electricity worked--the clock on the microwave told them that much--but the witches argued over whether or not they should turn on a light.

"If we're feeding her cat, we'd need to be able to see to do it, right?" Ellie reasoned. "Besides, you guys won't be able to see that painting in the dark. It's pretty awful, actually. I mean, who values a picture of two cats smoking cigars and playing cards at a quarter of a million dollars?" She shook her head. "Crazy."

"But if someone sees a light on, they're going to know we're in here snooping around," Mischa pointed out.

"That's why we brought the cat, though--he's our alibi." Poe snapped her fingers and a tiny flame appeared at the end of her finger-tip. Raven's eyes reflected the flames like two tiny mirrors.

"I say leave the light off," said the cat. "I can see just fine without it."

Reluctantly, Mischa and Ellie produced their own finger-flames. "Just don't forget and touch anything," Mischa reminded them. "The last thing we need is to become accidental arsonists."

"That sounds like a great band name," Poe murmured, spinning around with her finger held aloft.

The house was fairly drab in its decor, with walls the color of eggshell and carpet the color of sand. They were standing at the bottom of a set of stairs leading off a hallway that led to what Ellie informed them was bedrooms and a bathroom. Opposite the stairs was the kitchen, which itself opened onto a small dining area. The living room could just be glimpsed beyond the dining area.

"This is a lot of house for a single old woman," Mischa commented. "I wonder why she wanted so much space when she lived alone?"

"She probably didn't plan on being alone. Nobody does, but life just happens, I guess." Poe spoke with certainty and sadness.

No one spoke for a few moments as they peered through the darkness at the remnants of a lonely woman's life. There were numerous bookcases and shelves filled to the brim with bricabrac and collectible figurines in the dining room. The kitchen was spotless and the floors were bare, save for a small plastic bowl that still had some kibble in it. Raven scurried over to it and began nibbling at the food.

The witches made their way to the living room. "The painting's in here," Ellie told them. "I had to turn the lamp in the living room on every morning before I left for work when I house sat," she explained.

The flames on Mischa's and Poe's fingers illuminated the look of confusion that settled on Ellie's face. "Well, it *was* in here. But it's not here anymore."

A rectangular mark on the wall, lighter than the rest of the wall, marked the spot where the painting had hung. "Do you think it's already been boxed up for auction?" Poe asked.

"I'm not sure," Ellie admitted. "I would have thought that they would have taken everything at once, though, and nothing else seems to be missing."

The three women were too focused on trying to figure out what had happened to the missing painting to hear the footsteps on the laminate flooring behind them.

"Well, now," said a voice that each of them recognized but didn't immediately place. "Isn't this delightfully awkward?"

Seneca Wolfram stood in the doorway with her arms crossed. A flashlight dangled from her wrist, but they didn't need any light to see her face illuminated by the moon shining in the window.

She smiled at them in the darkness. "Hello, ladies. Do you mind if I ask what you're doing in here?"

CHAPTER SIX

There was a quick scuffling of feet and hands as each witch quickly extinguished her flames. Mischa gasped in horror as Poe held her still flaming hand aloft and gave a little wave to Seneca. Poe blew her fingertip, extinguishing the flame.

Seneca disappeared in the darkness for a moment, then her flashlight beam flooded the room with light. "Are you smoking in here?" she asked, pointing the light in Poe's eyes.

"No," Poe replied, sheepishly brandishing a cigarette lighter that she'd managed to pull seemingly from thin air. "Just didn't want to turn on all the lights. We're here to feed Edith's cat," she added quickly.

"I wasn't aware of a cat," Seneca replied, shining her flashlight around the room quickly. Its beam landed on Raven, who had followed Poe into the living room after finishing off his kibble.

"I told Edith I'd take care of him if anything ever happened to her," Poe lied, scooping the hefty black cat up in her arms. He struggled a little and opened his mouth as if to say something, but Poe clamped her hand over it. "We were looking all over for him," she added. "Guess we'll be going now."

"Why did all of you have to come over here?" Seneca asked, narrowing her eyes. "Maybe I'd better call those nice police officers back out here. I really don't think it's appropriate for you to be sneaking around in the dark inside someone else's house."

"Well, we could say the same thing about you," Mischa pointed out quietly. "What are you doing here?"

Seneca reached for the light switch and flipped it on. The living room was flooded with light, making the three witches blink quickly as they tried to adjust their eyes. "I'm here for work. Apparently Edith was very specific in her will--the bank is to sell off all property of any value and distribute the proceeds as Edith wished."

"Oh," Mischa replied, "you're here representing the bank."

"After hours?" Poe asked, skepticism coloring her voice. "Isn't that a bit weird?"

"Not really," Seneca replied. "I'm the new girl, so I have to pull more hours to prove myself. Plus, I've done this sort of thing before." She crossed her arms once again. "Now, if you'll excuse me, I'd like to get started taking inventory in here. I expect you can find your own way to the front door?"

Mischa, Poe, and Ellie nodded. Raven mewled beneath Poe's hand so she loosened her grip. The trio of witches and the cat started towards the door but stopped when Seneca called out to them.

"Wait--how did you get in here in the first place?" she asked.

Ellie looked sheepish. "I have a key. I used to house sit for Edith," she explained.

Seneca held her hand out, palm turned upwards. "I'm going to need to keep that," she stated. "I'm sure you understand why."

Ellie fished the key out of her coat pocket and dropped it into Seneca's hand. "Don't work too hard," she said, fighting the urge to scowl.

Seneca didn't respond. Instead, she watched the women make their way back out into the cold and watched them cross over into Poe's driveway. When she was sure that they were all inside Poe's house, she turned and gave the room her full attention.

CHAPTER SEVEN

"I told you guys she's fishy!" Poe moved to drop her coat onto a chair as she breezed past it. It missed and slid to the floor.

Mischa picked it up and hung it carefully on an empty coat rack by the front door. "Actually, her story makes sense. The bank will probably want to know exactly what they're putting up for auction and someone has to take inventory. Why wouldn't that someone be Seneca?"

"Maybe because she killed the woman who lived there?" Poe argued.

"We still don't know that for sure," Mischa countered.

"Who else could it be?" Ellie said, taking Poe's side. "And now a stone cold killer knows we were snooping around the scene of the crime. She's probably a trained assassin who had to take Edith out for some corrupt entity. You watch--she'll just disappear in a few days like nothing ever happened at all."

Mischa rolled her eyes. "Listen to you two. You're beginning to sound like those crazies who call into the public radio station to report UFO sightings." She took in a deep breath and let out a long sigh. "Let's just hope she doesn't think we had something to do with that missing painting and then give her the benefit of the doubt. I'm sure she's really nice if we take the chance to get to know her."

"Isn't that what you said about Edith?" Poe replied. "And then she tried to have your kids arrested for trespassing when their soccer ball landed in her yard."

Ellie wandered over to the fireplace in Poe's living room. A black and silver snowglobe sat on the mantel. Instead of a snowman inside, it had a dancing skeleton with an electric guitar. Ellie gave the snowglobe a shake and the skeleton began dancing merrily to the tune of Jingle Bells.

"What if she does think we stole that painting?" Ellie asked, turning suddenly to face her friends. "We could all be arrested."

Mischa's face paled. "I can't be arrested," she gasped. "I'm helping out with Daisy's third grade Christmas party and I still haven't baked enough cookies."

Poe let out a short, sharp laugh. "Ha! She can't have us arrested. She has no proof whatsoever that we took the painting because we didn't do it. Besides, I know she's hiding something. I can just feel it."

"Should we go back over there?" Mischa asked.

"And do what? Put a forgetting spell on Seneca to make her forget that we were ever there?" Poe suggested.

"Ooh, we could try a locating spell and try to find the painting," Ellie offered. "But we'd need to be in the house long enough to cast it. I have no idea how long Miss Kensleigh Landing East Bank & Trust is going to be in there taking inventory."

"Well, we certainly aren't going to be using any more magic near her. Poe nearly got us all in trouble with that lighter trick." Mischa shook her head. "No, I guess we shouldn't bother Seneca after all. We can't be sure how she'd react if she knew that her entire street was filled with actual witches."

"Maybe it would make her move away," Poe said hopefully.

No one spoke for a moment, then Mischa piped up once again. "Of course she won't think we took the painting!" Ellie and Poe looked at each other, then at their friend.

"Huh?"

"Seneca saw all of us. She had her flashlight, she could see all of us and clearly none of us was carrying a painting when we left. She has to know that none of us took the painting."

"Um, yeah, except I admitted to having a key to the house," Ellie reminded her. "Which means you may be off the hook, but I'm not."

"Well, who else would have had access to Edith's house?" Mischa asked. "Maybe someone else had a key."

"Besides Edith, maybe her sister. But probably not," Ellie replied, turning the idea over in her head. "Edith wasn't very close to her sister. In fact, the last time I looked after the house for her, Edith came back and told me that she was writing her sister out of her will. I thought she was joking, but I guess she was serious."

"Yeah, dead serious," Poe deadpanned. "I'd say that makes the sister a suspect, at least a person of interest, but my money's still on Seneca for the murder. If she worked for the bank, she could have known about the painting before Edith died."

"How? People generally don't keep lists of their valuables at their bank," Mischa protested. "That's kind of a stretch, isn't it?"

"They do if their homeowners insurance is through their bank," Ellie countered. "And Edith did bank with KLEBT. I saw a letter from the insurance department of the bank in her mail when I looked after her house. It's not unreasonable to think she might have had her home inventoried for insurance purposes."

Poe shook her head in disbelief. "I still can't believe the old bat was worth over a quarter of a million bucks. She asked me to pick her up a gallon of milk once and refused to pay me back for it. She was the ultimate tightwad."

"So, if the bank—and Seneca—knew about the painting's value, and Edith's sister knew, then that means either Seneca or the sister could have taken the painting." Ellie turned this over in her head. "But who killed Edith?"

"I haven't seen anyone coming or going from Edith's place except for Edith. And us," Poe added. "And Seneca, well, tonight at least."

"Maybe the painting was stolen a while ago. Or maybe Edith had it in storage?" Mischa asked hopefully.

"It was on the wall last week when I dropped some cheeseburgers off for Edith," Ellie replied. "It just all feels so weird to think that I saw her alive and well just a week ago."

"Joe says we're crazy," Mischa admitted. "I told him what Seneca said about Edith and the dog poop incident. He says that Edith was crazy and she probably slipped and fell. He thinks that's how she died. Maybe he's right--maybe she *did* just die accidentally."

"I don't think she died accidentally," said Raven. He was sitting on the coffee table, licking butter off a cracker. "Mmm...she...she was talking to someone the night she died. I was outside that night, the night she took her little trip," he explained.

"I heard her talking to herself and I thought she was just being her usual, crazy self. Or maybe she was on the telephone," the cat added before scooping up a piece of cheddar with one paw. The witches waited as he popped the cheese into his mouth and chewed enthusiastically. He didn't speak again, but instead reached for a chunk of ham.

"Well?" Poe asked impatiently. "Why do you think her death wasn't an accident? Maybe she was on the phone when she slipped and fell."

"Nuh-uh," Raven countered. "The phone was on the counter in the kitchen when we went over there. If she'd have been using it, it would have been found with her, not in the kitchen." He sat back on his haunches and smiled smugly. "I think someone pushed her down the steps outside her house, then she died. Do you have any more of this cheese?"

Poe tossed him a chunk of cheese from her own plate. No one spoke for a long moment, but finally Ellie piped up.

"Fat cat's got a good point about the phone. And the steps were icy, but Edith kept them salted. Didn't you all notice the salt outside her place? It was crunching under my shoes." She lifted her foot and looked at the bottom of her sneaker. A large chunk of salt was wedged between the ridges of the sole. "See?"

Raven looked offended. "I'm not fat. It's all fur," he purred.

No one acknowledged him. Instead, they stared at the salt on Ellie's shoe. "So who pushed Edith down the stairs?" Mischa asked finally.

"I still say that Seneca could have done it," Poe maintained, "but I'm open to other suggestions. Ellie, what do you know about Edith's sister?"

Ellie shrugged. "Not much. I have a first and last name--Margie Smaulder--and I know she lives in Kentucky."

Poe grinned and reached for her phone. "Perfect. Give me ten minutes and another glass of wine. I'll tell you everything you ever wanted to know about Edith's sister."

Ellie laughed, but Mischa frowned. "Poe, you really need to get out of the house more often."

Poe shrugged. "What can I say—Google is my boyfriend." She tapped away at her phone furiously, pausing only long enough to sip from the refilled wine glass that Ellie handed her.

It took her longer than ten minutes, but Poe managed to find Margie Smaulder's pertinent details online in a relatively short amount of time. "Give me until the morning and I can tell you everything about this Margie woman, even what side of the bed this chick sleeps on," Poe assured them. "But I'll need my laptop for that."

Mischa glanced nervously at the clock above Poe's fireplace. "I'd better get home. I promised I'd help Simon with a school project and Daisy needs her hair braided before bedtime or it will be a hot mess tomorrow."

Ellie gave her a wicked side-eye. "Can't Joe take care of that? I mean, I know he's not magical, but he is a pretty amazing guy. Are you telling me that he can't handle a six-year-old's braids so you can hang out with your coven?"

Mischa blushed. "Well, I was hoping to spend some time alone with him after the kids go to bed," she replied sheepishly.

Ellie held up one hand. "Say no more. At least one of us still has a love life. Too bad it's the married chick," she laughed. "I guess I'd better go, too. Holly will not do her homework if I don't stand over her and threaten bodily harm."

Poe glanced over at Raven. "Well, one of my kids is out walking the streets and the other is licking himself on the sofa. I guess I'm as cozy as I'm going to get, so see you guys tomorrow, right?"

Ellie and Mischa wrapped themselves up for the short walk back to each of their own houses. They gave Poe a little wave each and darted out into the cold, dark evening. Poe kicked off her shoes and grabbed her laptop from her desk. Noticing a slight breeze in the air, she raised her hand and snapped her fingers three times, chanting a summoning spell under her breath. Moments later, a fuzzy afghan blanket zipped through the air and settled itself on her lap. With a contented sigh, the witch began tapping away at the keys of her computer, determined to find out all she could about her late neighbor's mysterious sister.

CHAPTER EIGHT

"You're not going to believe this. Well, maybe you will, but it took me awhile to get over what I found." Poe's teeth chattered in the cold morning air. She longed to cast a heat spell, but she couldn't be sure that Seneca wouldn't see. It was strictly against the Council of Magic's rules to perform magic in front of non-magical beings, except in a few rare cases.

Mischa placed a piping hot mug of coffee in Poe's icy hands. "Where are your gloves? And you're not even wearing a hat–do you want to freeze to death before my Christmas party?"

Poe sipped the coffee eagerly, then wrinkled up her nose in disgust. "There's no alcohol in this."

"There's not supposed to be any," Mischa replied, rolling her eyes.

"And there's not enough sugar," Poe continued.

"Sugar gives you zits," Ellie scolded her. "Now, what did you find out about Margie?"

Poe cleared her throat. "Margie Smaulders lives in Bluebucket, Kentucky, with her forty-year-old son and a bunch of chickens. She is widowed, plays Bingo every Wednesday, and owes a crap-ton of money to some credit card companies. She recently tried to take out a life insurance policy on her sister, but apparently was not successful because Edith refused to take a physical."

"Wow. How did you find all that out?" Ellie asked. "That's not Google-type information."

Poe flashed a crooked grin. "I had to go a little dark for some of this, but it was worth it. The internet is a very useful weapon if you know how to wield it. So now we know that Margie clearly had a motive to kill her sister," she added.

"Yeah, but not the means," Ellie pointed out. "Didn't Edith ever tell you the reason why her sister never visited her?"

Poe shook her head. "I just assumed she didn't like Edith."

"No, Edith told me that Margie was in a wheelchair. She hurt herself pretty badly a few years back and could barely even stand up, let alone walk. She couldn't get up Edith's stairs, so Edith just went to visit her instead."

Poe's smile evaporated. "Oh. Well, then, maybe Seneca did do it." She sighed loudly. "Ugh. We know nothing more than we did yesterday. This is just great."

"What about the son? The forty-year-old? Isn't that a little too old to be living at home?" Mischa asked.

"I guess if his mom's in a wheelchair, he probably lives there to help her out," Poe suggested.

Mischa glanced towards Seneca's house. "Ssshhh, ixnay on the urdermay alktay," she whispered. "Morning, Seneca," she called out, waving to the blonde as she put her purse in her car and prepared to climb in.

Seneca looked puzzled for a moment, then lifted her hand stiffly to return the wave. She climbed into her car and reversed it down her driveway, carefully turning to exit the street.

The three witches watched her with great interest, but there was nothing to see. Seneca's car disappeared as she turned the corner leading onto the main road that led out of the subdivision.

"I guess I'd better be going, too," Ellie told them. "Not that I want to. I am so sick of work right now. But I like to keep a roof over my head," she moaned, "so hi-ho, hi-ho and all that jazz."

Poe turned to Mischa. "You too? Can't you just let the kids play hooky for the day and hang out at with me for a bit? I swear I think we're this close to figuring out what happened to Edith."

Mischa smiled gently at Poe. "Go and rest your brain for a while. The kids go today and tomorrow, then they're out for nearly three weeks. I can't wait," she said sarcastically. "And I'm sending them to stay with Aunt Poe for at least a few days," she added with a grin.

Poe's lips twitched into a smile. "Oh, I almost forgot! Edith's funeral is tomorrow at noon. I saw the announcement online when I was digging around for dirt on Margie. I know she wasn't that nice to us, but maybe Ellie would like to go."

Mischa nodded. "Yeah, alright. I'll have Joe pick the kids up from school for me. You and Ellie and I can all go pay our last respects to Edith." She started to turn towards her house, but stopped. "Make sure you bundle up, though. That coat isn't nearly warm enough," she scolded Poe, whose leather bomber was getting a little threadbare in places. "And no booze," she added before scurrying back towards her house.

"But it's medicinal!" Poe called out, chuckling to herself before retreating into the warmth of her own abode.

CHAPTER NINE

"There's something so weird about having a funeral on a Friday," Ellie pointed out. "I mean, I know Edith probably didn't plan it this way, but it really starts the weekend off with a fizzle."

Mischa elbowed her friend in the ribs. "Don't be disrespectful. You shouldn't joke around at a funeral."

Poe leaned over and rapped her knuckles gently on the end of Edith's casket. "I guess I should save my knock knock joke then, huh?"

Ellie tittered as Mischa pulled them both away. The small church hall was practically empty save for the pastor who would be conducting the funeral services. Mischa thought she recognized a woman at the back of the church, but she wasn't sure from where.

"It's quite a low turnout, isn't it?" Poe pointed out. "I mean, you would have thought that maybe some of her family would have come, or someone from the animal shelter."

"That's it!" Mischa murmured. "The woman at the back of the church works at the animal shelter. I think her name's Marilyn something-or-other. We were thinking of getting the kids a pet," she explained. "I thought she looked familiar."

"Wait, look." Ellie pointed discreetly at a couple walking through the door at the far end of the church. A dark-haired man who looked to be in his late thirties or maybe early forties pushed an elderly, white-haired woman in a wheelchair down the middle of the room. They stopped at Edith's casket and bowed their heads. The woman sniffed loudly and wiped her nose on a handkerchief.

"I'm sure that must be Margie Smaulder and her son—what was his name?" Mischa whispered loud enough for her friends to hear.

"Derek," Poe replied. "Wow, they are even creepier than I imagined them being."

"Should we introduce ourselves, you know, pay our respects?" Ellie was already making her way over to the couple, not waiting for her friends.

Poe and Mischa hung back, watching as Ellie made her introductions to the grieving visitors. "I was Edith's neighbor," she explained.

Margie looked Ellie up and down. "She never mentioned you. Well, unless you're the one with the brats who wouldn't stay out of her yard," she grumbled.

Ellie blushed. Mischa stepped forward. "No, that would be me," she admitted, offering her hand to Margie. "My name is Mischa Henley. We all knew Edith, though admittedly not that well. I'm sorry for your loss," she added.

Margie stared at Mischa's hand as though it might bite her. "Don't be sorry," she replied gruffly. "Edith couldn't stand anybody and I reckon that just about everybody I know couldn't stand her, either. Still, she was family." Margie trailed off, staring across the room at something no one else could see.

Ellie, Mischa, and Poe watched as Derek pushed his mother silently across the room. They took a seat near Marilyn from the animal shelter. Poe steered her friends across the room to the opposite side of the seating area, away from everyone else.

"Well, that wasn't weird or extremely awkward," she grumbled. "Ellie, you are way too friendly for your own good."

Ellie shrugged. "What can I say, I'm a people person. Unlike some people," she added, nodding towards Margie and Derek. "She was really rude to you, Mischa. And your kids are not brats."

Mischa shrugged her shoulders. "She's old. My grandma always says that old people are allowed to be rude when they reach a certain age."

She looked as though she wanted to say something more, but she stopped suddenly. Her eyes widened and both Ellie and Poe turned to see what had grabbed her attention.

"What's she doing here?" Poe hissed. Seneca glided into the room silently, her blonde hair pulled into a neat bun and her usual business suit replaced with a somber black dress. She stopped long enough to say a quick word to the pastor, then she made a beeline for Ellie.

"Seneca," Ellie said, nudging Poe with a stealthy elbow to keep her from speaking. She paused, trying to think of an appropriate greeting for a woman who might have killed the lady in the casket at the front of the room. Seneca didn't give her a chance.

"Ellie, Mischa," she said, pasting a quick smile on her face. She glanced at Poe, a hint of a sneer playing at her lips. "Poe. How are you all?"

Poe stepped out of Ellie's elbow range. "We're alive. Unlike some people. Didn't you like totally hate Edith? It's kind of a surprise seeing you here," she said plainly.

Seneca's mouth made a tight line, then she relaxed slightly. "Well, I'm here on behalf of Kensleigh Landing East Bank and Trust, but I also felt really bad about how things went down between Edith and myself that first day we met." She put one finger to her lips as though she was carefully considering her next words. "I wanted to make my peace with Edith by giving my condolences to her friends and family."

"Well, we weren't exactly her friends," Ellie replied.

"But you had a key to her house," Seneca countered. "Surely you knew her fairly well?"

"As well as anyone, I guess, but that's still pretty little. I mean, Edith wasn't the kind of person who wanted friends." Ellie eyed Seneca suspiciously. "You're not just here to give your condolences, are you? You said you were here on behalf of the bank, so is it something to do with Edith's estate?"

Seneca pasted on her best bank employee smile, the plastic one reserved for handling tricky customer service issues. "As you know, I was tasked with taking inventory of Edith's personal belongings for insurance reasons and to facilitate the swift auction of the estate so that Edith's last wishes can be carried out."

"You mean you have to help sell her stuff so the cat shelter can have the money?" Poe interjected.

Seneca looked surprised. "I wasn't aware that her will was common knowledge. She did leave the majority of her money to several animal-related charities, mostly to the local animal shelter," she admitted. "Most of her listed possessions have been accounted for, however, there is one particular item that's quite valuable that I simply cannot locate."

Mischa and Ellie shared a nervous glance. Poe shifted her weight and scratched at her silver cuff on her earlobe. Finally, Ellie spoke up.

"Are you talking about the painting? The one with the cats on it?"

Seneca shook her head. "No, though I did notice that it wasn't in the house either. I'm assuming that Edith had that put in storage after it was appraised several months ago. What I'm looking for is worth considerably more money than the painting," Seneca continued.

Seneca glanced around the room quickly, then leaned towards Ellie and the other witches. "Listen, this is embarrassing and I'm not quite sure how to ask this, but I need a favor. I have to go back to the bank in just a few minutes. I'm meeting with a very important client or I would take care of this myself. Edith listed a priceless Faberge egg in her home contents. Here's a photo," she said, pausing to retrieve a picture from her tiny handbag.

"I'm confuse," Ellie said, taking the photo from Seneca. "What does this have to do with us?"

Seneca squared her shoulders. "I'm going to be blunt. My job is on the line. If I can't locate this egg, my boss is going to fire me. It's a complicated situation, but I'm the new girl and let's just say that I'm expendable as far as my employer is concerned."

Mischa frowned. "Oh, gosh, well, of course we'll help."

"What?" Poe asked incredulously. "Why should we?"

"Because it's the right thing to do," Mischa asked.

"And because Seneca could have called the police when she found us in Edith's house the other night," Ellie grumbled. "Okay, we'll help. But I'm just going to tell you upfront that I've never seen this in Edith's house," she said, holding up the photo. "And I don't have a key to get in there anymore," she reminded Seneca.

Seneca flashed a dazzling white smile. "You are a hero, Ellie." She reached into her purse once again and retrieved the key she'd taken from Ellie just days before. "Here you go. And if you can find that egg, I'll personally cater your next ladies' night. Do you like sushi?"

Poe stared at her like she'd just asked if she liked to dine on the entrails of small children. "Pizza's fine."

Seneca glanced at her watch. "I really do need to run. If you need to reach me, here's my number." She passed a business card to Ellie. "That's my cell phone number. You can reach me anytime on that."

Ellie nodded and passed the card to Mischa, who added the number to her own cell phone. "We'll call you if we find it. I'm off all afternoon, so I guess we can head over to Edith's place after the funeral."

Seneca smiled once again. "You're a lifesaver." Then she turned and headed out of the church without so much as a backward glance.

CHAPTER TEN

E dith's house seemed lonelier in the daytime. Its front door was bare, a gaping maw of isolation that practically shouted *get off my property*. There were no holiday lights or potted plants, just scattered remnants of salt crystals that hadn't fully dissolved yet.

Cleo sauntered across the lawn, her feline form contrasting against the patches of snow that had yet to melt. She glanced around to make sure that no one unexpected was around, then she spoke.

"Are you all going in there?"

Poe knelt to stroke her cat on its back. "Yeah, you want to come in and see if the old bat left any kitty treats behind?"

Cleo stiffened. "No, and you shouldn't go in there, either. I've got a bad feeling about this place. Something bad is going to happen, I can feel it."

"Something bad already happened," Mischa reminded her. "Now we're trying to help the new neighbor keep her job and hopefully help the animal shelter get some money."

Cleo growled. "Animal shelter? You mean animal prison. They should shut that place down. Any self-respecting cat can take care of itself, you know." She sniffed the air. "Be careful, humans. I smell danger."

"Go home, Cleo. I'll be there soon," Poe promised. The cat sauntered off, her tail swishing stiffly in the breeze.

"She hates to be told what to do," Poe sighed.

"Typical cat," Ellie agreed. "Right, let's go find this egg so we can put this whole thing behind us." She skipped up the steps and inserted her key into the door. Moments later, the three women were all inside.

"Let's start in the living room. If I had a fancy egg, I'd want people to see it, so that's where I'd put it," Poe suggested. They went straight to the living room and were shocked by what they saw. Dozens of tiny yellow sticky notes fluttered beneath the air of the heating vent. Some said *trash*, others *donate*, and the rest simply said *auction*.

"Wow. I guess Seneca is even more OCD than you, Mischa." Ellie let out a low whistle. "I'm guessing we can skip this room," she said. "How about we go upstairs? I know Edith had at least one junk room. Knowing her, the egg's probably stuffed in a box in there."

"How about you just stop right there?" A voice carried in from the hallway, surprising the women. They turned to the doorway to find Derek Smauthers. He was followed by Marilyn, from the animal shelter.

"Oh, Mr. Smauthers, I'm sorry, I should have told you we'd be stopping by here," Ellie began. "We were asked to help the bank with your aunt's things." She narrowed her eyes. "Wait, why are you here?"

"And why's the animal lady here?" Mischa added, peering around to see if anyone else was behind Marilyn.

"Well," Derek began, pulling something from behind his back. "I'm here to help myself. I honestly could care less why you're here, but I'm afraid you're doing the wrong thing by helping the bank."

He raised his hand, which now held a gun, and pointed at Ellie. "You seem to know a lot about aunt Edith. More than me, that's for sure. I had no idea the old bat had a real Faberge in the house. I wouldn't have bothered with that crappy painting if I'd have known that."

Mischa gasped, but Ellie scowled. "Get that thing out of my face, man-child, before I make you regret it." She took a step forward. "I've been robbed before. I know how to handle guys like you."

Marilyn stepped forward, putting herself between Derek and Ellie. "We don't really want to hurt you. But we need that egg."

"Wait," said Poe. "I thought the animal shelter is getting most of the money from whatever gets sold. You'll be getting the money from the egg either way--why do you want it so badly now?"

Marilyn shook her head. "No, the shelter gets the money, not me. Not Derek, not his mother, just the shelter and a couple of pet foster organizations." She paused, looking at each woman for a moment before speaking again. "Edith knew that her sister was in financial trouble, but she didn't care. I met Derek when he was visiting his aunt last year and since I've got to know him, well, I realize how unfair Edith was by writing him and his mother out of her will."

"So you killed her and stole the painting?" Poe asked, nodding towards Derek. "I'm sure you were a great nephew," she finished, rolling her eyes.

"My mother has some problems with debt. She can't work, she can hardly make ends meet. And aunt Edith was willing to give a bunch of cats and dogs all of her money instead of helping us out. I'd say she was hardly a fantastic aunt," he replied.

"So what, you're just going to push all of us down the stairs, too? It's going to be pretty hard to make that look like an accident." Poe crossed her arms over her chest defiantly.

"I guess I'll just have to make it look like a murder-suicide instead," Derek growled and raised his gun. "Now, who's feeling suicidal?"

"Oh, for goodness sake, give me that." Seneca appeared behind Derek. He jumped, nearly dropping the gun. Seneca snaked an arm around him and held her hand open. The gun leapt from Derek's grasp and landed in her palm.

Marilyn shrieked. "Why did you give her the gun? And who is she?"

Derek's face contorted in both anger and confusion. "I didn't give it to her! It just jumped out of my hand!" He spun to face the woman who'd just disarmed him. "Who or what are you?" he demanded.

Seneca sighed. "I'm the new neighbor," she replied simply.

"And a witch," noted Ellie with some surprise.

"Well, slap me silly," Poe said drily. "Didn't see that plot twist coming."

CHAPTER ELEVEN

Seneca wrapped Derek's gun in a sheet of newspaper. "I'll make sure this gets put away properly later," she explained before turning back to Derek and Marilyn. They squirmed and wiggled, held against each other as though they were bound with an invisible rope, with their mouths moving but with no sound coming out.

"You do know you're not supposed to use magic on non-magical beings, right?" Poe asked.

Seneca smiled and fished out a sheet of paper from her impossibly small purse. "Of course. But, the law says that we can in exceptional circumstances, and I'd say that this was an exceptional circumstance, wouldn't you?"

"How did you know?" Ellie asked her. "How did you know about Derek and Marilyn? And how did you know that we wouldn't be freaked out when we saw what you did?"

Seneca sighed. "I've known you were witches since that night I found you in here," she said. "The fingertip flames, the smell of magic in the air–how did you not know I was one?"

Ellie shrugged, her cheeks flushing slightly. "I don't know. I guess we weren't looking for a witch. We just wanted to make sure that Edith's murder didn't go unsolved."

Seneca nodded. "And it won't. Derek here is going to write out a nice, long confession letter that will be delivered to the police station. Then, he and Marilyn are going to forget all about our little meeting today, isn't that right?"

Marilyn shook her head violently back and forth. Derek glared and clenched his fist. Seneca waved her hand over his fist and a pen appeared in his hand. He watched with wide eyes as his arm moved on its own, sliding the pen across the paper and producing the confession that Seneca had mentioned.

"Wow," Poe acknowledged, "Impressive."

Seneca beamed. "Thank you. You don't want to know how many boring magical transcription classes I had to take to learn that little trick."

"But the confession is his own, right?" Mischa asked. "You're not telling him what to say, right?"

Seneca retrieved the note from Derek. "You can see for yourself. It's pretty much verbatim what he told you. I just made him add something about a guilty conscience, though I seriously doubt he has one of those. Oh, and I may have added something about him wanting to run away with Marilyn here. I'm kind of a big softie when it comes to romantic stories," she cooed.

After Mischa, Ellie, and Poe read the letter, Seneca folded it neatly and tucked it into her purse. "I'll get this to the police station anonymously. You two go and drive yourselves to the Eattaburger parking lot and wait for the police to come and get you."

Without a word of protest, Derek and Marilyn walked out the front door and climbed into Derek's car.

"How do you know they won't just run?" Ellie asked.

"Oh, that spell should last for a few hours. I combined an obedience spell with the binding spell. They won't have any choice but obey me, at least until it wears off. You can call your restaurant and ask someone to make sure they arrive there safely, if you want." Seneca smoothed her skirt and took a look around. "Nobody touched anything in here, did they?" she asked. "I had those sticky notes just the way I wanted them."

Poe dropped the stack of yellow paper squares she'd been fiddling with discreetly behind her. "Was there even a Faberge egg?"

Seneca laughed. "No. I just needed something to lure Edith's killer out. I knew that whoever stole that painting would just die to get their hands on a real Faberge."

Poe frowned. "I Googled you. I even searched the dark web, but why didn't I find anything about you? Who are you?"

Seneca's smile faded. "Wolfram is my mother's maiden name. Until recently, I was known as Seneca Voltare."

"Holy crap. As in Viktor Voltare?" Ellie shook her head. "Wow."

"Viktor who?" Mischa asked, perplexed by Ellie's reaction.

"He's sort of a famous warlock," Ellie explained. "My parents used to talk about him all the time. Didn't he get into some trouble with the Magical Council?" she asked, turning back to Seneca.

Seneca nodded. "It's all very embarrassing. I'd rather not talk about it just now, especially since I have to get back to work. Besides, I'm sure Poe can find all the newspaper articles online." She raised one eyebrow. Poe already had her phone in hand, search engine open.

Seneca turned to leave, but Mischa stopped her. "Come to my Christmas party. It's at my house on Christmas Eve. We'd all love it if you came."

Seneca looked surprised. "I'm not sure," she began. "I wouldn't want to impose."

Ellie put her hand on Seneca's shoulder. "You don't want to miss Mischa's Christmas party. This girl can *cook*," she added seriously.

Seneca smiled a shy, genuine smile. "Okay. I'll be there."

Ellie, Mischa, and Poe watched Seneca get into her car and drive away.

"Blondie's not so bad, eh?" Mischa asked, nudging Poe with her elbow.

"I don't know. Wait until you see what I found out about her father," Poe replied, hefting her smartphone in her hand like a brick.

Mischa's house was warm and chaotic. It smelled of mulled wine, peppermint, and something savory that Seneca couldn't quite identify. In the living room, Poe battled Mischa's son, Simon, at a video game featuring dinosaurs and machine guns. Ellie's daughter Holly sat in a corner, patiently braiding Daisy's hair the 'cool' way while Ellie carried trays of snacks from the kitchen to a table that was already covered with food.

Mischa's husband, Joe sat in a chair flanked by Raven and Cleo. The cats were arguing about something while Mischa's non-magical husband looked on in amusement.

"I'm so glad you decided to come," Mischa beamed, taking Seneca's coat and hanging it neatly on an oversized coat rack. She noted Seneca's fascination with the domestic scene spread out before them. "We sort of do Christmas big time," Mischa explained. "Friends, family, food--my favorite things!"

Joe rose from his chair and joined his wife. "Seneca, welcome to our home," he said, offering his hand and a smile. She shook it and returned a smile of her own.

"Thank you for having me," she replied.

She followed the married couple into the living room where she was greeted with a chorus of hellos.

"Can I get you something to eat?" Mischa asked, pushing her dark hair away from her face. She started filling a plate with food before Seneca could answer, and Joe laughed.

"I married a feeder," he moaned playfully. He wrapped his tan arms around his wife's waist, making her jump. She pulled back in surprise, but he simply pointed above them. "Mistletoe," he explained. "Gotta kiss you."

Seneca took her plate from Mischa and nodded her head. "He's right. I'm sure there's something in the Magical Council rules about that," she laughed.

Ellie steered Seneca to an empty sofa and sat down, motioning for her to do the same. Seneca sat, looking at the witches and their families, and she felt a pang of sadness.

"Hey," Ellie said. "We haven't had a chance to say it yet, but welcome to the neighborhood." She handed Seneca a glass of wine and raised her own. "More importantly, welcome to the coven."

Seneca's face lit up. "Are you sure? What do the others think?"

"We think we'd love to have you," Mischa said, scooting onto the sofa beside Ellie.

"Yeah," called Poe from across the room, "and we think you'd better teach us that magical transcription spell," she added before returning to her dinosaur battle.

"So, what do you say?" Ellie asked, sipping her wine.

"I guess I'd have to say yes," Seneca beamed. "Merry Christmas, witches!"

Want to know more about the wonderful witches of the Country Acres Coven? Visit www.rubyblaylock.com today and sign up for updates on future Suburban Witch books!

ABOUT THE AUTHOR

Ruby Blaylock grew up in a small, southern town surrounded by colorful characters and lots of food. She loves a good helping of gossip and great food, not necessarily in that order. She is a country girl at heart and can often be found sitting on the back porch, sipping sweet tea and watching her fat hound dogs chase bugs.

If she's not reading a book, she's writing one, or reading one to her kids, who can always help her think up new ways to kill off annoying characters. Despite what her husband thinks, she's not actually a witch, though she does get very angry if you mess with her broom.

Follow Ruby Blaylock online:
    Facebook
    Twitter
    Website

WHEN SPELL FREEZES OVER

REGINA WELLING AND ERIN LYNN

SUMMARY

When Mag and Clara Balefire leave home to take over the coven in Harmony, they didn't count on the added complication of having to deal with former leader, Hagatha Crow's antics. Or with finding a dead Christmas elf.

CHAPTER ONE

"There's a dead elf in the snowbank out front." Hagatha Crow announced to no one in particular. It was the third time in a week she'd slipped away and pointed her tennis ball-footed walker toward her former residence.

Deep in a discussion, let's just call it what it was—a feud—over the name and makeup of their new business, sisters Clara and Mag Balefire ignored both Hagatha and her outrageous statement.

"Soaps and lotions. That's what we agreed on." Clara tapped the sturdy toe of one pointed shoe on the floor with impatience.

A large sign leaned up against the front counter of their new storefront. Even with opening day weeks away, the finer details, like what wares to sell and what to call their new venture, might doom their fledgling business before it ever had a chance.

"I like antiques. Old stuff sells."

"So do toiletries." Clara flicked her wand toward the ecru-colored surface of the blank sign, and the words Lotions and Potions appeared there by magic.

"When, in our hundreds of years of history, have I ever declared a love for soap?" Mag pulled out her own wand with a flair and the sign

269

shifted to read: Knicks and Knacks. "I didn't mean that the way it sounded and you know it," she clarified when her sister snorted.

"Probably at about the same time I developed a fondness for dusty old notions." Another flick and the sign changed again. This went on for some time until old Hagatha decided she'd had enough.

"Stubborn fools."

A witch of advanced years—so many of them it was speculated they could be counted in millenniums rather than centuries—Hagatha required no tools to work her magic. She merely looked at the sign, and the letters arranged themselves to read: Lotions and Notions.

"You," Hagatha pointed a bony finger at Mag, "can stock the place with antiques, use some of the furniture as a showcase, for her," the gnarled digit turned toward Clara, "soaps and unguents. Best of both worlds, everybody wins. Now stop acting like children and do something about that dead elf before it rots and stinks up the town."

Shown the possibilities of combining their two passions, the sister witches dropped the competition and began brainstorming. They ignored any mention of the elf; old Haggie must be imagining things.

"She's right. We could take out all this sterile shelving, bring in some elegance. I'm seeing amber and blue glass bottles with our logo on them, all lined up on polished wood with strategic lighting to make them shine."

"Well, I hate that name, though." Mag balanced Clara's enthusiasm with a touch of her typical grumpiness. "Lotions and Notions. Might as well call it Gunk and Junk." A twitch of the eyebrow showed the grouchy only went surface deep. "It could work, though. With the right pieces."

"Snowbank. Elf. Dead." Booming with enhanced magical strength, Hagatha finally got the attention of both sisters and stomped off toward the door as quickly as the walker, and her spindly legs would allow.

"We'd better go see what the old bat is going on about before she freaks out the entire neighborhood again." Clara couldn't decide if Hagatha was in the process of losing her mind—which was the coven's prevailing theory and the whole reason she and Mag had taken over the place. Or, if being older than dirt, Hagatha no longer gave a tin whistle about censoring anything she said or did.

Neither situation would be good for the local witch population, and both meant more headaches for her and for Mag given they'd unofficially taken charge of the coven while letting Hagatha think she still held the reins. Witches had no trouble hiding in plain sight in a city the size of Port Harbor, but here in the boonies, as Mag liked to call the area, magic was harder to conceal.

Harder still when the coven leader had a wild hair up her butt about the need for keeping things under wraps. As far as Hagatha was concerned, witches should be free to lead their lives out in the open, and the rest of humanity could just suck it up. Once determined to follow this course of logic, the old witch made it her mission to use magic as often and as openly as possible.

Toward the middle of November, Hagatha embarked on a one-woman rampage that nearly got the whole town plastered all over the news and triggered a series of increasingly frantic phone calls to the Balefire sisters. Skyclad, grinning maniacally, and holding her broom aloft like a baton, Hagatha had led her version of a Thanksgiving day parade straight through the center of town. A crazy, naked woman could be explained away fairly easily. Twenty enchanted turkeys singing "I Put A Spell on You" could not.

It took a joint effort from six covens worth of witches to craft an effective enough memory charm to wash away the spectacle. Clara and Mag had been offered control of the coven on the spot, and while they would rather not have had to deal with Hagatha, the idea of starting over someplace new appealed to both.

And so, that is how it came to be that Mag and Clara now found themselves staring down at the very dead, red and green clad elf lying in the snowbank in front of their new home.

"See. Dead elf. What'd I tell you? Toss it in the trash before someone sees it. I thought you two cared about appearances, and if anyone else discovers a rotting elf carcass on your lawn, you'll have a bigger mess to clean up than a dead body." Heart of gold, that Hagatha.

The poor creature lay sprawled over the back side of the freshly plowed snow which was the only reason passersby had not yet noticed the tragic figure.

"Yes, well." Clara searched for the appropriate response, while Mag, who had more experience with magical creatures, hunkered down to check for a pulse. Looking up at her sister, Mag frowned and shook her head.

"It's not dead," came the solemn pronouncement. "Close, but not entirely."

"We'd better take it inside before it freezes to death out here." Raised in a traditional witch household, and one of the most powerful witches in a handful of centuries, Clara Balefire had not the first clue how to tend to a sick Christmas elf. Still, her tender heart would only be satisfied once she had made an effort to save the poor thing.

"Cold won't hurt it. Snow is one of the main ingredients when it comes to making Christmas elves."

"Making?" Clara slid gentle hands under fragile shoulders while Mag laid hold of the ankles above the curled tips of bell-laden shoes. A cheery jingle sounded when the sisters heaved the elf's body off the ground.

"It's gonna die and stink up the place. Dead elves smell like candy canes." Hagatha predicted darkly and then cackled out a laugh as she shuffled back inside and let the door slam behind her.

"Thanks for all your help, Haggie," Mag muttered.

"Do you think her parents knew what she'd turn into when they named her?" Clara used a touch of power to turn the knob, and nudged the door open with her butt. "Can you make it up the stairs? Or should we just put him on the floor behind the counter? Away from prying eyes."

Only eight years separated Clara and Mag by the calendar, but to look at them, you'd swear it was ten times that number.

"I can carry it up there by myself and don't you think I can't." Mag blew a fluff of white hair out of snapping dark eyes. "Just because I look like I could have dated Methuselah, doesn't mean I'm decrepit or incapable of doing things." A couple of centuries spent tracking rogue magic had taken its toll on Margaret Balefire's appearance. A choice she'd made knowing the consequences, and for that, Clara respected her sister even if she liked to tease from time to time.

"Pyewacket, Jinx!" Clara called, and two cats immediately jetted into the room with a flurry of fur, took a good look at the elf cradled between their masters, and raced back out of the room with their tails puffed out to three times their normal girth.

Every witch has a feline familiar—a companion with a plethora of knowledge whose life is inextricably linked to his or her charge. Each familiar is blessed with nine lives and nine corresponding witches. Pyewacket belonged to Clara, and Jinx to Mag.

"What's that about? I guess they're not going to be any help to us in this situation. I'll make sure to hide all the smoked salmon before breakfast tomorrow."

"Kitty kibble it is. Can't wait for that argument. If they ever decide to switch back to human form, of course. We don't need them anyway; we got this. Grab its feet."

"Can you tell if it's a boy or a girl?" Calling the elf an it all this time seemed like a form of disrespect to Clara.

"Not by its feet, if that's what you're asking. And I'm not exactly in a position to see anything else at the moment. Besides, I wasn't planning to check and see if it had any jingle bells if you know what I mean."

Clara suppressed a smile as she made an effort to take more of the elf's weight. Despite her sister's assurances that the aged look went only skin-deep, Clara had seen Mag leaning heavily on her cane at times and knew there was more physical damage than her sister wanted to admit. "I wasn't asking you to, and you know it. Let's hurry; one of us needs to go back down and see to Hagatha. I don't like leaving her in the shop by herself."

"She's a keg of dynamite waiting on a fuse," Mag agreed. "Someone ought to tie a bell around her neck, so they know when she's escaping."

"Oh, I'm pretty sure that niece of hers is the one holding the door open. Wouldn't you do the same if you had to deal with her all day?"

"You do have a point."

Hagatha's voice tinkled from below, "You know I can hear you, right? And the elf is a boy, obviously." Clara and Mag shared an eye roll and a wry grin as they made their way up the stairs.

"Saw that too," Hagatha's assurance rose up behind them.

CHAPTER TWO

"Here, in Hargraven's Guide to Mythical Creatures, it says: Christmas elves, a creation of the wizard known as Santa Claus, require a constant supply of Christmas spirit to survive, and rarely venture far from the North Pole, where their source of energy is most potent." Mag paced the upstairs spare bedroom with the helpful volume two inches from her face, deftly sidestepping piles of boxes still waiting to be unpacked without taking her eyes off the page.

Clara's brow furrowed, "I wonder what he was doing so far away from home. Poor little thing." The tenderest of hearts, she couldn't bear to see anyone or anything in pain. "Let's see what we can do to make this room more festive. Maybe that will enhance the elf's Christmas spirit."

"It can't hurt," Mag agreed, tucking Hargraven's into a nightstand drawer and pulling out her wand.

Clara did the same, and with a flick of her wrist an old phonograph wheeled across the floor, the merry notes of Christmas music emitting from its weathered brass horn, "That ought to get us started."

Humming along, and allowing holiday cheer to fuel their magic, the sister witches summoned every Christmas decoration—and anything red, green, silver, or gold that could qualify as such—into the bedroom.

No fewer than four ornament-laden trees filled the room with a riot of color.

"I really like the pink and white lights, but can you kill the blinkers? The flashing gives me a headache," Clara grumbled.

"This one needs more tinsel." Mag gestured, and an absolute avalanche of the stuff fell over the blue spruce clad in red and green plaid ornaments. "Oops, too much." Half the tinsel faded, and she surveyed the results with a tilted head. "That's better." In fact, Clara liked it so much, she made a complicated gesture, and the tree zoomed into the living room where it took up space in the center of the bay window overlooking the street below.

"It looks like a craft store sale two days after New Years in here," she looked around doubtfully, "Shouldn't we at least try to make it less gaudy?"

"I don't think the aesthetic makes much difference, and besides, this is probably what it looks like at the North Pole. Santa's not exactly known for keeping things low-key. You think it's a coincidence that before the Halloween costumes have gone 50% off, you can already buy tinsel and twinkle lights? The gaudier, the better, I'd wager. Now, let's sing."

"Sing?"

"Yes, to activate the magic. Sing, and think about Christmas Eve when we were kids."

Clara closed her eyes and, with the lilting lyrics to "Silent Night" rolling off her tongue, joined in Mag's recollection. Scents of cinnamon, sugar, and butter filled the air as Clara recalled pulling sticky globs of yeasty dough from the tower of homemade monkey bread their mother, Tempest, constructed each year. One portion always ended up tucked into a cache near the chimney, a treat for the reindeer who always managed to avoid detection no matter how hard Clara tried to catch a glimpse.

For Mag, the magic of Yuletide rested in reciting traditional spells and reading the omens for the coming year. Hanging holly and mistletoe over each threshold and above the fireplace for protection made her feel safe. And, of course, there was the Christmas pudding.

Making a wish while she stirred, always clockwise in the direction of the sun.

With each happy memory, magic bubbled and churned and grew into a visible haze of sparkling motes that coalesced into a stream of festive, multicolored glitter. It snaked through the air, and finally made a beeline for the prone elf, shooting into his nostrils with a resounding boom.

The little guy stirred, some of the color returning to his cheeks. His eyelids fluttered once and then stilled again, but a tiny smile remained on his thin lips.

"Well, it sort of worked. We just need more juice." Mag pronounced.

"Look, there," Clara pointed toward the ceiling where a faint glimmer sparkled against the age-darkened paint, "It's another trail of Christmas spirit, and it's headed downstairs. Let's see where it leads us."

"Good catch, little sister." Mag's tone was entirely complimentary, but it still made Clara feel like a child. But there were more important things than a temper tantrum, and giving in to the temptation to throw one wouldn't go far in proving herself otherwise.

On her way by, Clara tossed a blanket over the elf. Sick people, in her experience, tended to do better when cuddled up and comfy.

Reclaimed by her niece during the decorating extravaganza, Hagatha was nowhere to be seen, and for that small mercy, Clara felt thankful. The woman reminded her of a geriatric pit bull. Taking the lead, she trailed the magic essence out the door and down the street with Mag following close behind.

Harmony homeowners apparently viewed decorating for Christmas as a prime competitive sport. That was the only explanation Mag could find for the absolute glee and abandon with which the town had embraced the many manifestations of the twinkle light. They glittered, and flickered, and chased roof, door, and window outlines. They dripped from eaves, blanketed shrubs in glimmering webs, and that was just the start of the madness.

Each house, Clara was happy to note, in the row leading to the single-street shopping district known as downtown, was different from the next. No cookie cutter neighborhood, this. And the houses had some breathing space between them.

"Oh Mag, look at that one." Rigged up on a metal structure, the tableau of Santa's sleigh taking off without him inspired a chuckle. The manikin of the jolly old elf carried an expression of consternation as he reached toward the runaway sled. Gifts spilled from his bag; his hat set askew on his head. "It's so very clever."

"You're already planning something. I can see the wheels turning, but let's not get distracted. The trail is stronger now, do you see it?"

It wouldn't have taken a crystal ball to predict which house the spirit trail would lead to, the sheer magnitude of decorations gave it away. If there were fewer than a thousand strings of lights winding up tree trunks, and along the eaves of the gingerbread trim, Mag would lick a stinkbug.

Plastic candy canes and lollipops festively fenced the property on three sides. Every window sported a wreath, the door was wrapped up like a gift, and the porch held an entire scene made from brightly-painted wooden cutouts. A herd of lighted, wire-framed reindeer frolicked behind a fence wrapped in glittering gold garland on the left half of the lawn. An entire workshop's worth of plastic and wooden elves danced across the right. There was more than the eye could take in all at one go.

All of that showed an unparalleled dedication to the art of decorating for the season, but it was the thick blanket of Christmas spirit that had called Mag and Clara to this place.

"Holy Hecate, would you look at that?"

"The name on the mailbox says Granger, and there's the coven symbol etched into the front door frame. This is Gertrude Granger's house." Clara pulled the details from her steel trap of a memory, having read through the list of coven members prior to accepting the position in Harmony.

"Anything sketchy on her record?" Mag asked.

"Nope, she's older than us—I believe she'll celebrate her quincentennial this year—and not a black mark to speak of. Coven secretary, and once upon a time she was second in command to old Haggie. But, Gertrude stepped down for unrecorded personal reasons about a century ago. Seems an odd thing to do. Maybe there's something to it. She missed the whole Thanksgiving parade debacle, too."

"You know how easy it is to step over to the dark side. It's not out of the question. She had to get all this Christmas spirit from some-where, and I don't believe in coincidences. Put on your high priestess hat and let's find out what's been going on here."

Clara straightened her shoulders and approached the front walk-way, snow crunching beneath her feet. Christmas spirit virtually poured out of the chimney like wood smoke, and when Mag jabbed the doorbell, they could hear Jingle Bells chiming from inside.

The woman who opened the door looked nothing like what either Mag or Clara expected; five hundred years isn't all that long for a witch to live, and Gertrude Granger looked more like a toned-down fifty-something cougar than a grandmotherly old spinster. With less than thirty-six hours to go before midnight on Christmas Eve, she was dressed in a modest yet hip-hugging version of Mrs. Claus' outfit, complete with a cotton-trimmed velvet skirt and matching Santa hat.

"Merry Christmas!" Gertrude boomed as she welcomed the sisters into her cinnamon and balsam-scented foyer. "You're the newest members of our coven, aren't you? Balefire witches?" Her aqua blue eyes sparkled with excitement.

Both women nodded in assent. "I'm Mag, and this is my sister, Clara."

"Nice to finally meet you, would you like a cup of cocoa?" A twirl of her finger conjured three mugs and a doily-lined plate of peppermint-speckled fudge. "Candy cane white chocolate, have a taste."

It might have been all the Christmas spirit zinging around the place, but suddenly white chocolate candy cane fudge and hot cocoa sounded a lot like the nectar of the gods, and it was a full fifteen minutes before the poor, unconscious elf crossed Clara's mind again.

"Thank you for your hospitality, Gertrude, but we didn't come here to eat you out of house and home." Clara began, keeping her tone friendly and non-threatening.

Mag interjected before the poor woman had a chance to answer, brisk and to the point, "Just where did you happen to come across such a high volume of Christmas spirit?"

Clara sighed; this was Mag's way, and probably always would be. A big bulldozer, Mag would raze an entire field trying to pick a single flower.

Gertrude looked between the two as though questioning their sanity and replied, "What do you mean, come across? The holidays are my favorite time of year, and I work quite diligently to spread cheer. In fact, I'd call it a full-time job, considering the state of the world we live in today. Do you know how many children don't believe in Santa Claus nowadays?"

"Well, yes, it's quite sad, really, but..." Clara's response got lost in Gertrude's excitement.

"Just last night, in fact, I managed to make believers out of half a dozen kids, thanks to a gentleman friend of mine, a simple glamour, and a chimney engorgement charm. You should have seen the looks on their faces. I never had any children of my own, you know, but I volunteer at the community center and the children's hospital over in Charleston."

"You sound like a regular good Samaritan," Clara said pointedly, shooting dagger eyes at her sister.

"Yes, she does," Mag agreed, but she returned Clara's glare with a raised eyebrow and exaggerated side-eye motion which pulled Clara's attention to the wall of bookshelves and to the fireplace mantel where a veritable army of Elf On a Shelf dolls cavorted.

Bearing an uncanny resemblance to the elf currently riding their spare bed, the little dolls were arranged into a series of amusing vignettes.

"Do you mind?" Clara crossed the room for a closer look. "However did you come up with all these ideas?"

In one scene, three elves clustered around a half-finished snowman made from marshmallows. Another featured an elf stranded on a beach after a sleigh crash, complete with palm trees and HELP spelled out in tiny sticks and stones. A closer look at the upturned face revealed an expression of fear that was a little too realistic.

"So creative, and such attention to detail. How do you make them look so life-like?" Doing her level best to maintain a curious tone, Clara pried. "It's uncanny."

Could Gertrude be capturing real elves, harvesting their Christmas spirit, and turning them into dolls? The idea was enough to make Clara shiver and reconsider her love of the porcelain-faced beauties. Never mind that the elf on their sofa seemed more likely to melt into the ether than to shrink to doll stature, the notion of him being trapped and forced into one of Gertrude's theatrical displays lodged like a splinter.

"Mag, you have to come look at this, it's the cutest thing." Anyone who knew Clara well would recognize the false cheer in her tone as a warning of some type. Mag certainly did and joined her sister while Gertrude practically beamed.

"Look at those little faces. How did you find dolls with such varied expressions? I'd love to get in touch with the manufacturer, we could carry these in our shop next Christmas," Mag followed Clara's lead and practically gushed, but her hand slid into the pocket where she kept her wand and a few handy defensive potions. Mag might be out of the dark hunting game these days, but some habits never die.

Face reddening under a layer of artfully applied makeup, Gertrude mumbled something about not revealing her source and Mag elbowed Clara in the ribs.

"Ow!" Clara whispered and returned the favor before putting on her most intimidating scowl. "We know you're hiding something, now out with it. There's an elf's life hanging in the balance."

"A real live one?" Gertrude's face registered a series of emotions. Shock followed by shame, and then an avid curiosity.

"Of course it's a live elf. How could it's life be hanging in the balance if it wasn't alive?" Mag's patience for foolish questions could best be measured in fractions of an inch. Her willingness to point out the obvious, though, was at least a mile long.

"Can I meet him? I've always wanted to meet a real, live Christmas elf." When Gertie clapped her hands like a little girl, Mag lost her last ounce of control.

"Have you or have you not been stealing Christmas spirit from elves and then using their husks in your little theater of pain here?"

Every drop of blood drained from Gertrude's face, taking it from a dull flush to a pale mask.

"What is wrong with you? How could you even suggest a thing like that? I love Christmas and elves. I would never...I could never. Oh, Margaret Balefire, you're a horrible person for thinking anything of the sort. You should be ashamed of yourself."

Mag recognized truth when she saw it. She'd been playing the game long enough to identify a dead end when the wall stared her in the face.

"Maybe there's a way Gertrude can help us out with our elf problem." Gently, Clara turned her attention to the older witch, who now sported a guarded expression. "But first, where did you get these?"

"I make them." Eager now, Gertrude spilled the truth out of ruby-painted lips. "I've spent years perfecting the spell for generating Christmas spirit, and I still can't make live elves, only these," a ring-laden hand gestured toward the shelves. "Poppets. It's the best I can do. I've concluded that Santa adds a secret ingredient besides those listed in Hargraven's because I think my Christmas spirit is every bit as strong as his. I use only the purest driven snow and the finest hot chocolate, too."

"I wouldn't be surprised," Mag stated matter-of-factly, "He's gone to quite a lot of trouble ensuring nobody knows too many details about what happens up there, and I doubt he would have given away one of his proprietary methods so easily."

Clara noted the crestfallen look on Gertrude's face and an idea began to take shape in her mind, "You know what, Gertrude, maybe there's a way we can all get what we want. We've got a languishing elf at home, and you've got enough excess Christmas spirit to save him."

"You mean you'd let me see him, talk to him, maybe even ask him a few questions about his, er, constitution?"

"In exchange for enough magic to revive him, absolutely." Clara agreed.

"Let us go back home and see if it works first," Mag cautioned, for once the more conscientious sister, "No sense making promises we can't keep."

Positively giddy, Gertrude left the room for a moment, returning with a gilded potion bottle that sparkled with inner light.

"This is my best stuff. It's from the most potent batch I've ever made. I keep a few bottles handy just in case. You call me, and I'll drop everything to come and meet that elf."

CHAPTER THREE

A cold northerly wind had sucked one side of a set of old lace
curtains through the kitchen window. Clara saw the flutter of
white as soon as she and Mag turned the corner.

"I thought this was a safe, quiet town," Mag grumbled. "Looks like
we've been robbed."

"I don't think so." Hagatha's walker stood next to the front steps.
"But it is a home invasion of sorts."

"Don't know why she bothered to move out if she's going to be
here every ding-dong day." Ding-dong had not been the phrase
Margaret meant to say, Clara could tell by the look on her sister's face.
Hagatha had left a few handy charms on the old place, and an anti-
cussing spell was among the more annoying ones.

That old Haggie had chosen to substitute her own phrases for
those spoken within the confines of the property made Mag's verbal
gaffes even more hilarious to her sister. In a fine fit of pique, Mag
stomped up the steps, tried the door, and found it still locked.

"I don't care if I have to wallow through snow up to my
badonkadonk," Clara hooted until she nearly cried at the idea of
Hagatha even knowing that word, much less preferring it over whatever Mag had been trying to say. Eyes slitted and sparkling with barely

contained ire, Mag continued, "I'm doing a cleansing ritual to rid the place of her influence if it takes fifty pounds of salt and a garden full of sage."

"Okay." The giggles still coming, Clara agreed. "I'll help." Keeping the peace might be less amusing, but was probably the best course of action.

The rooms at the top of the stairs felt even colder than the air outside because Hagatha had turned off the heat and conjured an industrial-sized fan to blow on the elf.

"What were you thinking putting a blanket over a Christmas elf? Don't you know anything about the species? They're made of snow and magic. He was practically transparent by the time I got here."

Clara looked and felt chagrined, unused to being in the proximity of a witch with so much more knowledge and experience at her disposal. "Oops. I didn't even think…"

"No matter, he looks much better now. And we've managed to get our hands on some concentrated Christmas spirit, so let's see if we can revive him enough to get him back to the North Pole." Mag thundered across the bedroom and perched herself on the edge of the bed. "Down the hatch," She placed one thumb against the little guy's chin and not-so-gently pulled his bottom lip open far enough to deposit the swirling mist directly into his mouth.

With a cough and sputter, the elf stirred. His eyes fluttered open, and his gaze darted back and forth for a moment before he hit panic mode, "Where am I? Who are you? What happened?"

"We'll be the ones asking the questions. What were you doing down here anyway? I thought Christmas elves stayed in the North Pole." Mag got straight to the point, making no effort to comfort the creature and causing Clara to sigh and push her sister aside with a harder-than-necessary shove.

"I'm Clara, this is my sister Mag, and this is Hagatha," Clara gestured to the senior witch who, for once completely silent, watched with amusement. "We're not going to hurt you; we're trying to help." She added with a gentle smile.

"Yes, yes, I can see that. I'm sorry. I came here because someone has been stealing elve's Christmas spirit. I need to find whoever it is and return the culprit to the North Pole before...before it's too late. It's almost Christmas Eve, and there's important work to do."

"Tell us exactly what happened. We're witches; maybe we can help."

The elf held up a tiny hand in the gesture that means stop. While Clara and Mag waited, he took a moment to compose himself, and then rolled his eyes up and to the right as though accessing his memory bank.

"Clara and Margaret Balefire; daughters of Tempest, mother and aunt to Sylvana, grandmother and great-aunt to Alexis. Correct? Yes, I believe you are trustworthy. I permit you to help me."

Mag and Clara exchanged a look of annoyance, "Is there some sort of hobknocking briefing about the Balefire clan circling around? Why does everyone and their grandmother seem to know who we are?" Mag grumbled and ignored the fact that her words had once again been censored.

"Well, if it makes you more comfortable, my name is Evergreen Goldensparkles, and I happen to be Santa's right-hand man. It's my job to compile the naughty and nice lists every year, and neither of you has been on the naughty list since you were children." He shot a pointed look at Mag.

"It's nice to meet you, Evergreen. Now, please, explain what we can do to help."

"Didn't you just hear him, or do you have cotton balls stuffed between your ears?" Hagatha piped up from the corner, "Obviously, someone hijacked his connection to the Christmas spirit, and if he doesn't get it back he'll fade into nothingness and cease to be."

"Is that all of it?" Clara's eyes burned daggers at Hagatha, who she vehemently hoped would disappear instead. The brief conversation seemed to have taken its toll on Evergreen Goldensparkles, because Clara had to give him a second dose to keep him from fading away on the spot.

"Yes, precisely," Evergreen sighed, "I followed the trail from the North Pole all the way here, but then I was attacked out of nowhere. Must have...tipped off..."

As he talked, Evergreen turned paler by the second. Either

Gertrude's spirit-brewing skills were not as potent as she thought, or she had been right about Santa leaving an ingredient out of the recipe when he'd give it to Hargraven.

"Tipped who off? Tell me who did this so we can help," Clara implored.

He gasped, "Elf. Not like me. Name is Ja...." With that, he lapsed back into an unconscious state leaving the sister witches staring at each other in consternation. Mag dumped another dose into Evergreen, but it wasn't enough to rouse him.

"Haggie, you know more than we do about elves, can you keep an eye on him while we try to track down whoever did this? They couldn't have gone far. Keep the Christmas spirit going and try to keep him alive while we're gone," Gertrude's bottle passed into Hagatha's hands, "it won't be a very fun holiday if we kill an elf before the eggnog's been served." Mag sprang into problem-solving mode and began to delegate. Haggie agreed with a bit more enthusiasm than necessary, leaving Clara wondering what condition the place might be upon their return.

"Yes, of course, he needs to conserve his strength. One thing, before you go." Hagatha held out a hand, and a thermometer appeared in her palm. Into Evergreen's mouth it went, and after a few seconds, she pulled it out, wiped off any moisture on the back of her pants, and handed the fragile glass to Clara.

"It'll measure how much Christmas spirit he has left. Get back here before it's all gone. Now, there is one place someone looking for the holy grail of Christmas spirit might go in this town—The Harmony Holiday Hullabaloo, which takes place tonight at the community center." Hagatha offered.

"Organized by Gertrude Granger, right? She mentioned it was the culmination of her fourteen days of Christmas celebration. Gone a little overboard, hasn't she? Most people do twelve."

"Gertrude Granger doesn't have a lower setting. But she's got a heart of gold, and she's one of the most generous women in town. Mind your manners, little lady." Clara's ears turned candy apple red, and Mag couldn't suppress a grin wondering if they were about to pour steam.

"I'm a couple of hundred years old, I'm hardly a "little lady," she grumbled once Hagatha was out of earshot.

"I heard that, and you're still practically an infant compared to me."

"That woman has ears like a hawk," Clara muttered.

"It's eyes, but I get your point," Mag agreed, "She's going to be a handful."

"Understatement of the year. Now, we need to come up with a plan, and I think I know exactly where to start." Mag followed her sister downstairs to the shop, where Clara searched behind a counter for some paper and a pen. "We're calling in reinforcements. This is Santa's mess; he can come clean it up. I want to be back in Port Harbor by the time Lexi and the faeries start their midnight snack on Christmas eve."

"What are you planning on writing? Dear Santa, if you want to see your elf alive again...?" Mag affected a deep, Italian accented voice in a perfect impression of Don Corleone.

"You really don't want any gifts this year, do you?" Clara chided, but the reproach held no weight considering the gigantic smile on her face. She might be a big, fat, pain in the badonkadonk, but Clara wouldn't change her sister for all the magic in the world.

CHAPTER FOUR

Held at the town hall, the Harmony Holiday Hullabaloo had Gertrude Granger written all over it. In glitter and canned snow. Armed with the enchanted thermometer and very little information about who they were looking for, the Balefire sisters braved the winter wonderland-themed party. The decorating committee had outdone themselves in shades of blue and silver and white.

"Hagatha would have had a field day with this," Mag commented when she got a look around the room. Coven members made up a tiny portion of the attendees with the rest of the throng being townsfolk who weren't supposed to know they lived among the magically inclined. "Good job convincing her we were too stupid to look after the elf without her help."

"Speaking of Evergreen, we have to figure this out fast. Look!" Evergreen's spirit meter showed the barest hint of glimmer at the lower end of the glass. "We're almost out of time." Whispering loudly, Clara poked Mag with her elbow.

"Think I don't know that?" Mag scanned the crowded room with an eagle-sharp gaze. Hopped up on the excess of Christmas spirit thanks to Gertrude's ministrations, several likely suspects sported sparkling auras more dense than the rest of the spirit coloring the air.

She dragged Clara toward the front end of the great hall and through the door where a set of steps led to a curtained stage.

Dust lifted off thick blue velvet when Mag twitched it aside to peer out over the crowd from the elevated platform that gave a better vantage point.

"I count six possibles," she said.

"Same here. We can rule out Gertrude and her familiar, don't you think? That leaves four."

"And I think those two kids are probably okay, too. They're too young to be that diabolical."

Together, Mag and Clara focused their attention on the remaining two people who stood out.

"I'll take the guy dressed up as Santa; you get the other one." Fake Santa's laugh, to Clara's practiced ear, held a note of derision at odds with the amount of Christmas spirit pouring off him. She'd have laid a crisp hundred dollar bill on him being the culprit if anyone had been taking bets.

The other suspect was a twenty-something looking girl with a mane of curly dark hair falling over the collar of a hand-knitted sweater in a white snowflake pattern scattered over an ice-blue background. Shorter than most of the adults, but taller than the children, she flitted in and out of the crowd without speaking to anyone.

"Deal." Mag chortled, and without further ado, the sisters filed back into the main hall to track their quarry. Clara made a beeline for Santa while Mag ambled in the direction snowflake sweater girl had gone.

"Excuse me, might I..."

"Out of the way, lady. I got something I gotta do." Fake Santa dodged past Clara and lurched toward the side door while her heart thundered in her chest. He must be guilty if he was trying to make a break for it, but how had he figured out she was onto him?

"Stop." Power sizzled up from the source of Clara's magic, from the place in her center that owed everything to the mighty Balefire from which she took her name. The command scorched the air between her mouth and where it landed on the cheap fuzzy back of his red coat.

Santa stopped so fast his top half continued on a pace longer than his feet had carried him and he overbalanced to land on in a heap on the floor. People rushed to cluster around the fallen man, but Clara was already on her knees beside him.

"What happened?" The muffled question came out from behind a beard that had been knocked askew in the fall. Wannabe Santa ripped off his stocking cap, yanked the elastic band off over his head, and spit out strands of fluffy white. Annoyed, he tossed the beard and hat away and turned his face toward Clara. Bald and wearing makeup to simulate rosy cheeks, the man didn't seem like much of a threat.

"Why were you leaving in such a hurry?"

"Look, I just need to go to the can. Some kid peed on my leg, and I gotta clean up the suit. It's rented."

Squinting, Clara took stock of the Christmas spirit swirling around him. All of it came from the suit, none from the man. She'd made a mistake. Of course, she had. Hundreds of children speaking their Christmas wishes to the man in the faux fur would imbue the suit with enough spirit to be seen from space.

"Sorry. Here, let me help you." Clara braced herself and yanked fake Santa to his feet before searching for her sister.

Despite Mag's assurances that her advanced age only went skin deep, her slower pace allowed Clara to catch up.

"Not Santa," Clara said as she rocketed around her sister to cannon into the back of the second suspect. No small woman, Clara's tender mercies nearly knocked the poor thing off her feet, and in the ensuing scuffle to get the younger woman righted, exposed the merest hint of a pointed ear lurking under the riot of hair.

"Oh, I am sorry. I didn't see you standing there. Are you all right?" Acting concerned, Clara grasped the woman's arm firmly and leaned down to make eye contact. "My name is Clara, and I'm such a klutz sometimes. This is the second time I've knocked someone over in the last five minutes." While she prattled on, Mag had time to catch up.

"My sister is a hazard to herself and others. Allow me to apologize on her behalf. Are you hurt, Miss..."

"Jackie. Jackie Frost."

The name fit what little the elf had been able to say before he passed out.

"Miss Frost?" Solicitously leading Jackie Frost toward a less populated area, Mag peppered her captive with questions.

"We're new in town. Have you lived here long? Did you help with the party? Everything looks so festive, and the people are so nice. It's nothing like the city where we used to live."

Clara held back a snort when her sister put on a voice to match the doddering exterior she displayed to the world. There's nothing more harmless than a little old lady with a cane. Unless that little old lady was Margaret Balefire, who possessed a keen intellect and a rare gift of magic that had been passed down through the family line. Jackie Frost didn't stand a chance.

"No, I'm not local. I'm just here for the party, and I need to..." Jackie started to turn away.

Fanning her face, Mag declared, "Oh my goodness! I'm feeling faint." She clutched onto Jackie's arm like a limpet. "Be a dear, won't you, and help me outside. It's so warm in here." When Jackie made a move to say no, Mag poured it on even harder, sagged at the knee, and nearly swooned. There was nothing else the young woman could do, she sighed and gave in to the need to help.

Keeping the smirk to herself as much as she could, Clara followed Mag and her unwitting captive toward the door. The second it closed behind them, Clara touched Mag's arm and disappeared the trio into thin air.

Back at the house, Hagatha's eyes widened as three women toppled to the floor at the foot of Evergreen's bed. She sprang into action as Jackie Frost shrieked and lunged for the door—as much as a woman with a walker can spring, that is. Hagatha let out a holler of her own and dropped a magic dampening spell right before two streaks of fur raced up the stairs, whirred into a man and a woman, and blocked Jackie's passage.

"Pye, Jinx! Your timing is exquisite. Get her over to that chair, quickly."

Jinx held Jackie's arms at her sides while Mag patted the woman down quickly and with an air of a police officer simply going about her duties, as though she frisked people for weapons every day.

"Ah ha!" Mag exclaimed, pulling a baseball-sized object from deep within the folds of Jackie's skirt. Crystal clear water magnified the red and green-clad figures encased in the glass ball set into a simple pedestal of polished ebony until a flurry of snow obscured them from view. Elven spirit glittered and glimmered among the flakes.

Panic-stricken, Jackie went wild, struggling against her captors, "Give that back, it's mine!" She shrieked at a pitch that should have shattered the snow globe she was trying so hard to reclaim and lurched with enough gusto to break free of Jinx's hold.

Mag tucked the globe into the crook of her arm like a football, shifted from one foot to the other in a little hop-skip and then waited for Jackie to take the bait before lobbing the thing over her head to her sister. Clara, recalling her monkey-in-the-middle skills from when she and Mag were children, caught it deftly in one hand and prepared for Jackie to change course.

What she wasn't prepared for was a barrel roll of Donkey Kong proportions. Jackie plowed into Clara's knees, knocking her off balance, and the globe went flying into the air. In slow motion, everyone, including old Haggie, leaped to catch the coveted object, but they were all too late. Clara watched as it hit the wood plank floor and shattered into a million pieces.

"No!" Jackie screamed, her face contorted into one of pain rather than anger, and she used the moment of confusion to, with a mournful glance backward, whoosh through the door and down the stairs.

"Look," Clara drew the room's attention back to the floor, where a swirling ball of sparkling motes had begun to zing through the air toward Evergreen's translucent form.

The essence of holiday magic enveloped him in a ball of snow, lifting him off the bed and into the air where he spun around in a miniature blizzard that chilled the room to near-freezing. Pye and Jinx took their leave in a similar fashion to the first time they laid eyes on Evergreen, opting to chase after Jackie instead.

Evergreen's eyes popped open as the full force of his Christmas spirit was restored, and he sprung into action with newfound vigor.

"She's getting away. That wily little minx somehow escaped Santa's workshop. I suspect there's a traitor in our midst because she was locked up tight as a jack-in-the-box."

"I guess someone turned her crank," Hagatha dissolved into giggles of glee. The woman really did have the oddest sense of humor.

"Somewhere, someone is running around with a giant butterfly net, looking for that woman," Mag muttered under her breath to her sister, who nodded in agreement.

"Respect your elders, Margaret, or you'll receive nothing but a bundle of coal in your stocking this year." Evergreen chided. "Jackie Frost must be contained. She was the mastermind behind her twin brother, Jack Frost's plan to steal Christmas. We managed to foil him last year and capture her, and she's been held at the North Pole ever since. We were hoping to use her as bait for her brother, and the clock is ticking. Santa Claus is probably having a conniption right about now."

"Well, now that you're back to your old self, we'll just leave you to take care of things." Santa's problem wasn't coven business, and Mag saw no need to trouble herself further. She'd done her best by the elf and Clara wanted to be back in Port Harbor to spend the holiday with her granddaughter. So did Mag, for that matter.

Evergreen folded slim arms over his chest, tapped his jingle bell-tipped toe, fixed Mag with a withering stare.

"Do you really want to be the witch who stole Christmas?"

"Look here, you little..."

"Mag." Clara cut off what was sure to be an entertaining substitution for a nasty name. "We have to help him. Not just because it's Christmas, but because you know as well as I do where Jackie is going to end up. The party should be over by now, and Gertrude will be home alone. We can't just turn our backs on a coven member."

"I suppose."

"This is just so heartwarming." Clapping her hands together, Hagatha made it hard to tell if she was being sarcastic or not.

With the promise of assistance, Evergreen turned thoughtful, then flitted around the room muttering things like, "Ugh, artificial tinsel. That won't hold her. Plastic. This will never do." He tested most of the decorations and came up with nothing that satisfied his purist's soul. "Too bad the snow globe is broken, it would have worked a treat. I don't suppose you could fix it?" After making the rounds, he ended up back in front of Mag who thought about it for half a minute.

"It would be tricky."

"Pshaw." Scoffing, Hagatha merely directed a glance at the shards of glass littering the floor, and they whizzed back together good as new.

"Useful spell for someone about to open a shop. You mind teaching it to us sometime?" Clara's question earned her a wink from Hagatha. Having the old witch around might not be so bad after all.

"Now to turn it into a trap." This was Mag's field of expertise. "First we need the bait." The steady look she laid on Evergreen told him exactly what she was after.

"Okay, but just a little." Concentrating, he spun a portion of Christmas spirit into a shimmering ball. Mag nodded to Clara who cast the ball into the snow globe with a flick of her wrist.

"And now, we make it sticky." Seeing the direction her sister was going, Clara pulled a piece of fudge out of her pocket. "Gertrude's candy cane and white chocolate. I snagged it while we were at the party. I think I might be addicted; it's so good." Quick as a wink, she stole a nibble off one corner then sent the candy hovering over the glowing globe. A swish of her wand turned the candy into a shower of sticky, clear liquid that coated the glass. "That should do it. It's like flypaper for rogue winter imps."

Clara carried the globe and Mag transported the elf when the two of them skimmed to Gertrude's house where the front door hung askew on its hinges. Crashing and banging noises provided more evidence that something was wrong inside.

"She's here all right." Evergreen's words slurred slightly. "This much spirit in one place is intoxicating."

"You stay out here, then. Can't have you falling down drunk in the middle of a sting operation." Clara shoved Evergreen into the midst of the plastic elves decorating the lawn. "No one will notice you there. I'm going in. Mag, you keep watch out here, if she tries to get away, blast her back inside."

Clara grasped the snow globe and vaulted onto the porch. Mag would only have slowed her down. She sidled along the wall to peer inside, and, happy with what she saw, gave her sister the high sign before disappearing through the door.

Inside, Jackie was rifling Gertrude's cabinets, tossing bottle after bottle of Christmas spirit into a bag. Clara crouched behind the sofa and gently, ever so gently, magicked the snow globe a little closer each time Jackie turned her back. Soon enough, she managed to settle the trap in place. Now it was a matter of waiting until her quarry took the bait.

Scanning the room Jackie's eyes alighted upon the trinket, and her hand closed over the glass globe at the precise instant she realized the object shouldn't have been there in the first place.

She let out a howl and tried to shake it free of her hand, but the fudge-coated exterior refused to budge. A clamor of hooves from the ceiling two stories above preceded the muffled slide of a robust belly rocketing down the chimney, and Jackie spouted a slew of profanities at Santa before being sucked into the globe with a pop and a thud.

"Tisk tisk, Jackie Frost, you've been a naughty girl this year." Santa tucked the globe away in the pocket of his velvet suit and turned to face the group assembled before him.

Evergreen leaped into his creator's arms and explained what had happened in a flurry of excitement.

"Yes, yes, my child, you did a wonderful job," Santa assured the elf kindly and with a wink over his head for Mag and Clara who were rudely shoved aside by a returning Gertrude.

"What happened?" The late arrival scanned the room with mounting surprise as she took in the assembled group. "Oh. An elf. A real live elf." She beamed and clapped her hands, but when she got a look at who owned the arms currently cradling the red and green clad figure.

"Santa," she breathed barely able to take it all in, and then her lips curled into a wicked smile as Mag and Clara sidled toward the freedom waiting outside.

"Oh my Goddess, you're really here!" Gertrude scurried into action, conjuring enough cookies and cocoa to feed the entire staff of Santa's workshop. "Please, have a snack before you go. Try the monkey bread and if you don't mind, I have a few questions."

Thanks for taking the time to read about Mag and Clara Balefire's Christmas adventure.

To learn more about the Fate Weaver series and the related Psychic Seasons series please visit ReGina Welling's website: http://reginawelling.com

Find more information about Erin Lynn at http://erinlynnwrites.com

QUICK AND EASY MONKEY BREAD

3 cans refrigerator biscuits, buttermilk
   1 cup sugar
   2 tbsp cinnamon
   1 stick of butter
   1/2 cup brown sugar
   1/2 cup raisins (optional)
   1/2 cup broken nuts (walnuts or pecans work best)

Add sugar and cinnamon to a gallon sized freezer bag. Cut each biscuit into quarters and add to the sugar and cinnamon a handful at a time, shaking to coat each piece in the sugar and cinnamon mixture. Layer coated biscuits in a Bundt pan, along with raisins and nuts.

Melt butter in a saucepan, add brown sugar and bring to a boil. Pour mixture over the biscuits, raisins, and nuts. Bake at 350 degrees for 30 minutes. Cool before eating.

This is a pull apart bread, great for holidays.

ABOUT THE AUTHOR

Regina Welling and Erin Lynn are the mother/daughter writing team behind the Fate Weaver series as well as the Ponderosa Pines mysteries. They both enjoy small town life in Maine and have been known to finish each other's sentences. Literally.

Follow ReGina online:
  Facebook
  Twitter

Follow Erin online:
  Facebook
  Twitter

THE FRUITCAKE THAT SAVES CHRISTMAS

Moonchuckle Bay Monster Movie Short #3 / MCB #9.5

HEATHER HORROCKS

SUMMARY

Safeguard the Fruitcake of Youth? Say what?!?

When the Oracle of Delphi is the first customer in Elizabeth Lee's new shop, she thinks it's a good omen — until she's given the task of safeguarding the valuable Fruitcake of Youth. And not only is the Oracle dead serious — but somebody's after that fruitcake! Daniel Grant falls under the spell of the owner of Drop of Magic, the most beautiful woman he's ever met. He's either met his lifemate — or he has the flu. When their destinies collide over a piece of fruitcake, almost anything can happen. Danger. Healing. Maybe even love...?

Dedicated to my son, Patrick Fenn

THE WORST FOOD IN THE HISTORY OF THE WORLD

As Elizabeth Lee flipped the sign from CLOSED to OPEN on the door of her new shop, a wave of satisfaction flowed over her. This new venture was both scary and exciting. This would be her best Christmas ever, with her shop having opened three days before.

Her best friend, Chicory Connolly, grinned. "You're really doing it."

"I know." She unlocked the door. "Thanks for helping out. I'm glad your mom was okay with you working here instead of at the Bubbling Cauldron. I hope we have some customers today."

"You will." Chicory wore her usual gypsy garb—a colorful skirt, ruffled blouse, bangles and hoop earrings—and a matching ribbon barely tamed her riotous curls. "You announced the grand opening online and in the *Carpe Noctem News*. You'll have customers."

"I wonder if they'll be magical folk or tourists."

"A little of both, I suspect. You'll get tourists from Town Square and overflow from the café. Plus my new neighbor asked me about the best place to buy potions in town and so he'll be coming in today." She smirked. "Did I mention how handsome he is? Just your type, I think."

"I don't have a type." As Elizabeth looked at her new logo emblazoned on her window, doubts poured in. "Do you really think Drops of Magic is a good name for the shop?"

Chicory put an arm around her shoulder. "Stop worrying. It's a perfect name for the shop of the best elixir mixer in Moonchuckle Bay. You're going to do great."

Through the frosted glass in the top half of the door, they saw someone moving toward the shop, then reaching out for the door handle. They locked eyes and grinned at each other, as they had with every shared adventure since they were kids.

Stepping back, they tried to act nonchalant as the door opened and their first customer walked in. But when she saw who it was, Elizabeth's breath caught. Surely this was a good omen.

Dressed in a flowing Grecian robe with real gold accents, the woman had a commanding presence and a powerful violet aura that spread out around her. The woman gazed at the Christmas tree set up in the seating area and at the rest of the shop.

What on earth was the Oracle doing here? Not just *an* oracle, but *the* Oracle. Of Delphi. As in from ancient times. She looked like a young woman, vibrantly alive—and intimidating as heck.

"Good morning, Ms. Connolly." The woman nodded her head at Chicory, and then at Elizabeth. "Ms. Lee."

"Good morning," they both parroted. Elizabeth's heart was actually doing a nervous little dance in her chest, but since it would be a good thing to have the Oracle as a customer, she gathered herself and smiled. "Welcome to my shop. What may I do for you today?"

"My business with you today is for your eyes and ears only." She looked at Chicory. "Would you please step out and allow us privacy?"

"Of course." Chicory shot Elizabeth a look. "I'll just step into the Cauldron until you're done."

"Thank you." After Chicory left, the Oracle turned the sign from OPEN back to CLOSED. "Lock the door, please."

"Of course." What was going on? Nervous, she did as instructed.

The Oracle moved toward the counter. "I'll get right to the point, Ms. Lee. I have watched you from afar and been impressed with what I've seen and heard."

"Thank you," Elizabeth stammered, unsure of the protocol when being flattered by the Oracle.

310

"I had one of my visions last night," the woman said. "It involved you."

"Me?" Her heart danced a little faster, now doing the cha-cha.

"Yes." The woman looked into her eyes. "I have come bearing something both valuable and precious."

"My area of expertise is potions, though I can do an excellent concealment spell when needed. What did you bring?"

She could sense something powerful, but wasn't sure what.

The Oracle looked down at the small, package wrapped in brown paper she'd set on the counter. She touched it and the paper fell back, revealing ... a piece of fruitcake? A *fruitcake* was precious and valuable? The Oracle had closed her brand-new shop for *this*?

Was this a joke? *Did* the Oracle joke?

"It is your talent for both that brings me here. You're going to need this fruitcake to create a potion."

They both stared at the bits of candied fruit embedded in the two-inch cube of Christmas atrocity. *Seriously?*

Elizabeth hazarded a question. "What type of potion?"

The Oracle looked up and shrugged. "You'll know when it's time. But it is extremely valuable. Can you keep it safe until you need it?"

"If you feel I'm the one to do it," Elizabeth said, unsure.

"I was led here to you."

Elizabeth raised an eyebrow. "Do you want it back? Because if I create a potion, I may use it all."

"I would prefer any unused be returned to me, but I understand if it's used up in the making." The Oracle touched the wrapping with a long red nail and said, pensively, "This was cut from the only fruitcake remaining from the original three. This is all I can spare so use it wisely."

Elizabeth nodded. "I will."

"It's a magical fruitcake." The Oracle looked up and Elizabeth felt like a bug pinned in place. "Do not reveal its presence to anyone. Not even your friend, who is at this moment dying of curiosity in the Bubbling Cauldron."

"Yes, ma'am." She gulped, her palms growing sweaty. The Oracle's auric waves pulsed. "How long until I need it?"

"Within three days, according to my dream. After that, it won't matter." The Oracle shrugged casually. "But that should be enough time to save Christmas."

Save Christmas? Was the woman freaking kidding? Could she be any more vague?

The Oracle gathered her coat about her. "Oh, and you'll need holly to complete the potion."

"Holly," she repeated, looking down at the package as though it were a bomb starting to tick. Three days to save Christmas?

The Grecian beauty waited for her to unlock the door and reached for the handle—then turned back. "You must protect it—and yourself. There are people who would be willing to kill for a scant crumb of the Fruitcake of Youth. Remember, do not let anyone know you have it."

"Yes, ma'am. The Fruitcake of Youth?"

The woman's eyes glazed over and she raised a hand toward Elizabeth, though she didn't answer her. In a voice full of power, the Oracle uttered, "You have been chosen and will be rewarded with your heart's desire if you perform this task well." Then the eyes brightened and the woman actually smiled, throwing her for a loop. "Have a nice day, Ms. Lee. I will expect a report in three days."

A moment after she left, Chicory entered, looking back over her shoulder. "What was that about?"

Oh, I've just been entrusted to safeguard a piece of magical Fruitcake of Youth. Your everyday transaction with the Oracle of Delphi. You know. Three days to save Christmas and all that.

But what she said, with a shrug, was, "She told me not to say anything."

"You know that's just going to drive me crazy."

"Me, too, actually." Oh, boy, did she wish she could share.

Chicory's eyes fell on the wrapped package and narrowed. "And what is that? She left you something?"

Elizabeth picked it up, carefully. "I'll just put this away now."

"This *what?*"

Elizabeth looked at her friend. "I've been sworn to secrecy and I'm sorry because I could really use your perspective on this. Help me out by not prying...?"

Chicory sighed. "You're really going to drive me crazy."

Elizabeth walked into the back room. Where did one hide a valuable piece of magical fruitcake that people would kill to steal?

She had a safe, but was that too obvious?

She walked through her office and stared at the safe in the adjoining workshop. It would have to do for now. She'd cast a concealment spell to hide the entire safe.

As she set the small package next to her important papers and locked the safe, she shook her head.

Were there really people who would come looking for this, willing to harm others to get it? She sighed. Sometime in the next three days, she'd have to make a potion to save Christmas.

What on earth had the Oracle gotten her into?

A WEREWOLF SHE'D BEEN CASUALLY DATING

Daniel Grant adjusted the scarf about his neck. The chilly December wind blew straight through him as he walked the perimeter of Moonchuckle Bay's Town Square. He passed City Hall and crossed Wolfman Walk. The shop he was seeking stood between the werewolves' Blue Moon Sports Bar and the local coven's Bubbling Cauldron.

He hoped the proprietress of Drops of Magic was as good at mixing potions as Chicory, his new neighbor, had claimed.

The storefront was narrower than the two on either side, but cozy. Stained glass pictures of flowers and herbs hung in large frames in each of the two windows, catching the light. One spelled out Drops of Magic.

His mother needed some magic right about now.

Pushing his way inside, he immediately felt the warmth, welcoming him in.

There was no one inside the shop, and his first impression was that it was both quirky and professional. Glass counters lined two walls, along one side and the back, with glass vials standing in supports, both empty and filled.

Something from the back of the store called to him, something he'd never felt before. He had no clue what it was, but he felt … odd. As though he *needed* whatever the item was. Probably some powerful magical artifact they had back there.

He walked toward the seating area set along the third wall. Two bookshelves were filled with spell books and witch movies—*The Wizard of Oz* and *Bewitched* among them—and a curio cabinet loaded with miscellaneous items—a witch's hat, candles, a magic wand which he could feel was not magical at all, and a broomstick. He touched it with a smile. No magic there, either, but the human tourists would love it.

A small painted sign on the wall proclaimed *Resting Witch Face*. Draped over the back of a high-backed chair was a T-shirt with the words *Not Every Witch Lives in Salem*. On a wrought-iron cauldron-shaped jewelry holder hung chains with crystals. Ah, now those did have magic, but nothing a human would notice. He touched the largest one. It was pure magic, enough so he might buy one for his mother. If…

"May I help you?" a melodious voice asked.

He turned—and stopped, frozen in place.

Before him stood the most beautiful creature he'd ever seen in his thirty-five years. Long red hair practically glowed in the light, high-lighting blue eyes and a sweet smile. She glowed. And every nerve in his body felt her presence like a fire rushing through him. Every brush fire, bonfire, and forest fire combined into one, racing through him, burning him.

"Sir?" she asked, worry sparking in her eyes.

He found himself smiling at her. "Are you Elizabeth Lee?"

"I am."

"I moved into the house next to Chicory Connolly, who highly recommends your shop. The word *genius* was bandied about."

She smiled, and his knees actually weakened. "Well, she is a good friend."

He motioned around the shop. "You have a nice place here."

Her face lit up. "Thank you. We just opened earlier today."

"I know. I've been waiting for today so I could come in."

"Do you know what type of potion you need?"

315

That jolted him from the attraction flooding through him. Oh, yes, he'd come in to purchase a potion. He'd forgotten for a moment. He cleared his throat and, hopefully, his brain. He was sure she could sense his magic, just as he could sense hers.

"I need a pain potion."

"Who will it be for and how powerful?" she asked in a wary tone.

"My mother is..." He sighed. "She's dying and in constant pain. I need something powerful and, if you are indeed a genius, something powerful that will not make her too drowsy. I don't have much time left with her."

"I do have healing potions."

"There is only one thing that can heal her, but I appreciate your offering."

"I'm sorry. I can certainly create a pain potion for her. Did you bring in anything belonging to her?"

He nodded, reaching into his pocket and pulling out a paper wrapped around a small lock of his mother's hair.

Elizabeth Lee smiled, taking the lock and closing her eyes, absorbing the magical imprint. When she opened her eyes, they were sympathetic. "She is in a great deal of pain. I can fix that."

"How long will it take to create?"

"I can have it for you by closing time tonight. Eight o'clock."

Relief flooded through him. It had been torture watching his mother suffer. She was only fifty-four but, when she turned fifty-five next week, on Christmas Day, she would die. He couldn't stop the curse, but he could stop her pain. "Thank you. I'll come back for it then."

"Is there anything else I can help you with?" the angel asked, and he knew right then he could be falling in love.

He didn't believe in love at first sight—but there were Lifemates for vampires, werewolves, and, yes, even warlocks.

He definitely felt what was either the Lifemate thing—or the flu. His stomach fluttered, his heart pounded, and warmth flowed through him like a cozy fire. Yes, maybe the flu. But he could actually feel the connection with this woman, could sense their auras touching and meshing. Could she be his Lifemate?

He hadn't been interested in women for a long time, and now, with his mother so ill, was an inconvenient time to realize he wanted this one. But he wasn't one to miss a golden opportunity, and this woman, with her near-glowing red hair and blue eyes, was a golden opportunity if he'd ever seen one.

He smiled at the woman of his dreams. "Would you permit me to take you on a date tomorrow?"

Stunned, Elizabeth stared at the man.

Chicory had been right. He was exceedingly handsome and exactly Elizabeth's type—if, by her type, Chicory had meant he would melt her into a lovestruck puddle on the floor of her shop.

Elizabeth hadn't dated in over a year, not since she'd broken up with a werewolf she'd been casually dating. He'd been more of a friend, anyway.

But this man could be a relationship. They didn't know each other, but she had the feeling she'd known him forever, could trust him.

Surprised, she found herself answering him with a resounding, "Yes."

"May I meet you here at noon, take you to lunch, and then we can spend some time in Town Square?"

She nodded. Chicory could take care of the store for her, though she'd razz her about taking hours off during the second day of her shop's existence. "I'd love that."

He shot her a devilish grin. "I'll see you tomorrow then. Oh, wait, no, I'll see you tonight. To pick up the potion."

And then he'd walked out of the shop, and she'd felt his absence like a physical aura ache.

WHAT DID THIS SNOW PIXIE KNOW?

E lizabeth had barely slept last night because of the anticipation of
    seeing Daniel again. There had been a strong flare of attraction
between them again when he'd come to pick up the Ache-Break potion
she'd created for his mother, who should have finally gotten a good
night's sleep.

Chicory had been delighted to watch the shop—especially so she
could see the two of them together. "I just had a feeling you'd
like him."

"Let's see how today goes. Yesterday might have been a fluke."

But she knew it wasn't. When he'd walked into the shop promptly
at noon, she'd started melting again.

"Have fun, you two," Chicory sing-songed as he helped her on with
her coat.

Blushing, Elizabeth waved and shot a look at her friend, who
smirked.

He'd taken her to A Bite to Eat Café, where they'd both ordered
the Halloween Lunch Special. The Christmas Special wasn't served
until dinner.

It was amazing, but she was able to chat with him as though they
were old friends. Even the silences felt companionable.

The owner, Ilene, carried over their Halloween Specials—stuffed bright-orange peppers carved into jack-o-lanterns, green beans, and long skinny bread*bones* with marinara "blood" dipping sauce.

After Ilene left, he asked, "How long have you lived in Moonchuckle Bay?"

"My whole life."

"I repeat," he said with a smile. "How long have you lived here?"

"Twenty-eight years."

"You don't look a day over twenty-three."

"Thanks," she said, and his words made her think of the stupid Fruitcake of Youth. "Where did you move from?"

"Roswell, New Mexico." He waited for the standard question. She didn't disappoint.

"Really? So were the aliens real?"

"No," he said, "but the supernaturals living there are, like here."

"Why'd you move?"

Ilene returned to their table with a plate holding one Poison Apple, an apple with black caramel wrapped around it. "Just desserts, kids."

"Looks horrible," Elizabeth said with a laugh. Daniel had suggested they just order one so they could share a snow cone after.

"Thanks." Ilene smiled and moved away.

The apple wasn't poisoned, but was decadently sweet. When only the stick was left, Daniel paid for their meals, and stood, reaching out a hand to her.

She took it, and a jolt of electricity shot up her arm. Her eyes widened and his head tipped, so she thought he must have felt it, too. He let go reluctantly to open the door for her.

Outside, they zipped their jackets against the cold. "Did Chicory tell you about Jingle's snow cones?"

"Chicory and my mom's cousin and about a dozen other townsfolk. I can hardly wait."

"They're good. I think I have a little room left."

"Perfect." He took her hand again.

She intertwined her fingers with his. Surprisingly, it felt right to walk along connected to him like that.

They crossed the street from the café into Town Square and sauntered along, with him pointing out the movie crew shooting a scene in the far end of the park. She nodded. "They film here often and use tourists as extras. It's part of the allure of this *monster movie* town. Tourists hope for a starring role. It actually happened once, back in the 1990s."

They headed first to the gigantic tree set up in the middle of Town Square, complete with normal Christmas ornaments mixed with monster-movie stuff. At the top, instead of an angel or a star, there was a dragon with its wings outstretched. Not the real dragon, of course, just a plastic replica.

After walking around the tree, they kept wandering and, before she knew it, they were standing at the Craved Ice booth. She waved at Jingle, a snow pixie and the maker of magical snow cones—and at Dixie, a garden pixie who was apparently helping her today.

"Hey Elizabeth! How are you?" Jingle asked.

Dixie eyed their linked hands with open curiosity.

Elizabeth laughed. "Ladies, I'd like for you to meet Daniel Grant. He's a newcomer in town and lives next door to Chicory. Daniel, these are my friends, Jingle Belle Noel and Dixie Murphy."

"It is a real pleasure to meet you both," he said with that heart-melting smile.

"So you've come for one of Jingle's famous snow cones," Dixie said.

Elizabeth nodded. "Yes, we have."

Dixie grinned. "Okay, Jingle, work your magic."

As Jingle reached over the counter of the booth to take Daniel's free hand and hold it, reading whatever it was she did to work her magic, Dixie said, "I'm just here for comic relief, I guess, because I definitely don't have the snow magic required for this gig."

Jingle reached out for Elizabeth's hand, and she felt a tingle of magic at the touch. She wasn't sure what Jingle's magic was, exactly, but knew it was unique.

Jingle had escaped from Snowville, close to the North Pole, about seven years before, and her now-husband, Nicholas Noel, had been the bounty hunter sent to return her to her abusive uncle, who was marrying her off to a horrid man. Jingle had only told her the story once, but Elizabeth had been appalled and hoped someday to drive the karma bus up to Snowville.

Jingle went to work, studying the rack of flavorings, then pulled out several bottles and set them down. A few moments later, there were two flashes of light, and she handed them over. The first one went to Elizabeth, and Jingle proclaimed, "Holly and mistletoe for you."

Startled, Elizabeth took the green concoction. *Holly?* The Oracle had said she'd need holly, but surely this wasn't what she'd meant? Was it? Did this mean she didn't have to wait for the holly she'd ordered on Amazon last night?

Then Jingle handed over a light brown snow cone with flecks of color. "And fruitcake for you."

He took it with a laugh. "I hope it's better than actual fruitcake."

Jingle shuddered. "It is."

Fruitcake?

Elizabeth stared at Jingle. What did this snow pixie know? She needed to get together with her and have a chat. Maybe after her date.

Jingle said, "I'm not sure how, but those two flavors go together."

Definitely having a chat with Jingle later.

THIS WAS AN IMPOSSIBLE TASK

"That must have been some date." Chicory stared at her. "You're still daydreaming about it."

When Elizabeth'd returned from her date, the store had been hopping. A group of three tourists had just left, leaving the shop uncharacteristically quiet.

"Spill. Tell me all about it. He's super dreamy looking."

"Oh, Chicory, he is dreamy. He's super nice and I really like him."

"He couldn't take his eyes off you. It was *sooooo* romantic." Chicory sighed dramatically. "Where'd you go for lunch?"

"A Bite to Eat. And then we walked around Town Square, got a snow cone, and held hands."

"Ohhhh. Holding hands on the first date." Chicory smiled. "I haven't had a first date in forever."

"Stop telling men no and you could have one." Elizabeth said, bumping shoulders with her friend.

"You should talk. We're like the two most reclusive witches in history." Chicory sighed. "And it looks like you're about to ruin that. If you get involved with this guy, I'll be left all alone."

"You never minded before."

"I don't mean without a guy, silly. I mean without my best friend." Chicory shrugged. "Oh, well. I've been a third wheel before."

"I've only had one date with the guy."

"Yeah, but I saw how you looked at him, too."

Elizabeth chuckled and glanced at the big wall clock shaped like a black cat. It was 4:30. Chicory'd be here until closing at eight and a little after to straighten up.

She really couldn't put it off any longer. She needed to examine the fruitcake and check its properties magically. Only then would she be able to get a clue about what to do with it in the next two days. Or at least what it even was.

"I guess I'd better go work on the task the Oracle set me to." Elizabeth shot a glance at Chicory, who planted her hands on her hips.

"Oh, sure. You just had to mention that, didn't you? You couldn't just say you had to get to work, could you? You had to add the words *the Oracle* and drive me crazy." She switched tactics, batting her eyelashes like a child. "Please, Mommy, please tell me what you're doing."

Elizabeth patted her shoulder. "Sorry. I won't mention the Oracle again."

Back in her office, she locked the door. She trusted Chicory—but she still felt she needed to do it.

Her eye fell on the green plant in the pot on the windowsill. It looked a little wilty and she felt guilty for neglecting it. She poured some water in from her bottle and could see it starting to perk up immediately. Her mother had given her this plant before she died, so it had special meaning to her.

She turned toward her workshop in the large alcove where the safe was tucked—and invisible to humans and most supernaturals because of the concealment spell.

She undid the spell and, after the safe appeared, she spun the magical tumblers and opened it. Her important papers were sitting there, where they'd been yesterday.

But the Oracle's Fruitcake of Youth was gone.

Panic hit her, and she shuffled things around. Surely it was here. She'd locked it in and put the spell on it herself. Only another witch with similar powers to her own could have opened it, assuming they even knew it was there. But, as far as she knew, there was no other witch in Moonchuckle Bay with similar powers to hers. But someone had taken it. Stolen the fruitcake.

She went through the safe again, then closed the door. No point in putting another concealment spell on it now. The horse was already out of the barn. The fruitcake was on the loose.

She leaned against the wall, head spinning. Holy heck. She was in so much trouble.

Stumbling back into her office on wobbly legs, she sank into her desk chair.

How could the fruitcake possibly be missing when supposedly no one even knew it was here in her shop? The Oracle wouldn't have told anyone, right? Not if she wanted Elizabeth to keep it secret as well.

Was it a customer who'd come into the shop on opening day? Over fifty had come in to check out the shop, half of them tourists excited to buy lotions with witchy names—Eye of Newt cream and Wrinkles Be Gone—bottled in stereotypical Halloween-style bottles. The other half had come in and actually purchased some of the magical items she kept behind the counter.

Which of them could it have been?

She hadn't seen anyone with a malevolent aura, and she would have noticed.

And then she realized. She hadn't been in the shop earlier today. The thief could have come in while she was out with Daniel. Chicory was a strong witch, but she couldn't read auras like Elizabeth could.

Could Daniel have something to do with it?

She needed to talk with Chicory but she didn't want her friend to read the expression on her face. That meant calling her from the back room, which was weird, but not unheard of.

"Hey, girl," Chicory said when she answered. "Do you need me to come back and help with the Oracle's task? Because you know I'd do it in a heartbeat. I'm just that helpful a friend."

Elizabeth fought to keep her voice light, but didn't quite succeed. "Was there anyone who came in while I was gone with Daniel?"

"Heck, yeah. There were probably twelve customers. You're doing a landmark business."

"Did anyone seem ... *off* to you?"

"Off how?"

"With a dark aura, maybe?"

"Not that I noticed, but you know I don't sense them as well as you."

"No one did anything weird?"

"No. We had three people ask to use the bathroom, but that's not really weird. Though, now that you mention it, one lady took long enough in there I was about to ask her if she was okay, but then she came out and left the store without looking at anything else. That's kind of weird, maybe."

Bingo. A lead, at least. Her mouth dry, she asked, "Can you describe her?"

"Maybe thirty-five or forty, though we both know that doesn't mean anything in this town."

Elizabeth didn't even ask if the woman was magical, because a human could never have found the safe, much less gotten inside it without leaving a trace.

Chicory paused, and then said, "She was wearing a Christmas-green shirt and black slacks. Dark hair cut short and spiky."

"Would you recognize her again if you saw her?"

"Sure."

"Thanks." She hung up and pondered. Should she send Chicory out to search for this woman? Or should Elizabeth go out and look and send pictures to Chicory if she saw someone?

No, this was a task the Oracle had given Elizabeth. She'd lost the fruitcake. She had to get it back.

At least she hadn't gotten killed for it—unless the Oracle killed her for losing it.

It was quite the Catch-22—she had to get the fruitcake back because the Oracle didn't mess around, but she couldn't tell anyone about it so she couldn't ask people if they'd seen a missing fruitcake. This was an impossible task.

How could she find it if she couldn't mention it to anyone?

And then she remembered Jingle mentioning both *fruitcake* and *holly* as flavors in their snow cones and saying they went together. Could Jingle possibly already know about the fruitcake somehow? What were her powers, anyway?

Pushing to her feet, she retrieved her jacket and purse.

She'd talk to her. After all, if she already knew about the fruitcake, then Elizabeth wouldn't be breaking her promise to the Oracle if they discussed it.

Right?

CAN SHE KEEP A SECRET?

The breeze picked up as Elizabeth crossed the street into Town Square, past the gigantic Christmas tree where three carolers sang to a few people. The cold and dinner hour had most tourists scurrying off toward restaurants or other warm places.

She couldn't shake a niggling sense of doom—as in she'd be doomed if she couldn't figure this out. And right now, she had two possible leads. Two women—Jingle and the mysterious woman in green. She knew where Jingle likely was, and she watched for the woman in green as she walked.

Today Jingle was alone, and there wasn't the usual line. The snow pixie smiled at her. "Back for another snow cone?"

"No, but thank you." Elizabeth placed a hand on the counter. "Jingle, you gave us some very interesting flavor combinations before. I know you have a ton of people come through here every day, but do you happen to remember what our snow cone flavors were?"

"Sure. Fruitcake and holly."

Wow. What a memory. And that gave her a slight glimmer of hope. "You get impressions about people, right? That's how you do your snow magic?"

Jingle nodded. "Yes."

"Would you be willing to share the impressions you had about me before?" She held out her hand. "Or would you be willing to read me again?"

"What's going on?"

"It's really important and I've been sworn to secrecy, but I really need your help."

"Okay," Jingle said. "I'll help as much as I can. I had a definite sense that the man you were with—Daniel—is connected to you somehow."

Did that mean he might have *stolen* the fruitcake? "Connected how? In a good or bad way?"

Jingle sighed. "Hold out your hand again."

Elizabeth did and Jingle took it and closed her eyes. This time she looked more focused, as if she were going deeper than she had before.

After a couple of minutes, Jingle squeezed her fingers and let go, opening her eyes, which had a light shining in them that wasn't quite normal.

Elizabeth felt a tingling in her hand as she lowered it. She could hardly handle the suspense. "What did you feel?"

"In a good way," Jingle said. "He's connected to you in a positive way. Somehow his destiny is intertwined with yours. And I'm not even sure how to say this because it sounds kind of crazy, but there's a fruit-cake connecting you."

"Does he have the fruitcake?"

Jingle shook her head. "No. I don't think he even knows about it, though there was some sort of connection. It's more that I got the feeling he has the key to finding the holly you need, though I don't know why I know that. And the holly will help you find the fruitcake you seek."

"You're good. I am seeking a fruitcake. But it's supposed to be a secret."

"I'm good at keeping secrets."

Since Jingle had brought up the fruitcake, would it be okay if Elizabeth asked a few more questions about it? She sincerely hoped so—and that the Oracle would agree. "Can you tell where the fruitcake is right now?"

"I got a sense of the Oracle somewhere. Maybe she has it.

Though..." Jingle shook her head. "No, there's another fruitcake, a much smaller one, that you are searching for."

"You're *really* good at this."

Jingle's eyes widened. "Are you involved with the Oracle?"

Elizabeth nodded.

"Oh, frostbite!" she exclaimed. "That can't be good."

"I've got to find that piece of fruitcake. I had it yesterday, but it was stolen from my safe. Maybe by a woman in a green shirt and black slacks."

"I haven't seen a green shirt today, just a lot of coats and jackets."

"What am I going to do?" Elizabeth muttered to herself.

"Maybe you should ask Daniel," Jingle said. "About the holly."

She reached out and took Jingle's hand again. "Thank you so very much. You may have saved my life."

Jingle squeezed her hand again. "Glad I could help. If you need anything else, come back and we'll talk some more. After you talk with Daniel."

"I will. Thanks again."

As she walked back past the tree, she paused. The carolers had disbanded.

She could lose everything if the Oracle learned she'd said anything. Not to Jingle, maybe, because Jingle had told *her* about the fruitcake and the Oracle being involved, not the other way around. But if she told *Daniel*. And she couldn't really talk to Daniel without telling him, could she?

Maybe. If she just asked about the holly and learned what he knew.

Because she couldn't ask the Oracle for help without getting in trouble, which Elizabeth wanted to avoid, plus the Oracle wouldn't give her a straight answer anyway.

The Oracle had given her two tasks and extracted two promises—Elizabeth had to keep the fruitcake and save Christmas with it, and she was also supposed to keep the fruitcake a secret.

But she couldn't keep the first promise now without breaking the second.

She pulled out her phone and dialed Daniel's number.

✳

Thirty minutes later, Elizabeth spotted Daniel through the window of her shop and turned to Chicory. "Thanks for closing up. I'll be back if I can."

"Good luck on your secret mission."

Elizabeth nodded, noting the three customers hadn't been paying attention, but were still chuckling over the witchy signs she'd arranged along the non-countered wall.

She stepped outside, pulling on her coat. The wind had picked up again, and there was a feeling of snow in the air.

Daniel caught up with her. "Where did you want to go?"

"Somewhere we won't be overheard."

"In my car?" he asked.

She nodded.

When he took her hand, she wasn't surprised, but she did experience some melting, which she was beginning to recognize as her normal state around Daniel Grant, the most handsome warlock she'd ever met.

As they walked, he lifted her hand to take it with his other hand, and then wrapped an arm around her shoulder to keep her more shielded from the wind. "Thanks."

They crossed the street, walked past city hall, the library, and the council office, the sheriff's department, and into the parking lot.

He opened the passenger door of his gleaming, metallic-blue sports car and got her seated, then jogged around and climbed in himself. He turned the key and the engine gave a throaty purr, and he turned up the heater.

"A Trans Am?"

He grinned. "Not just any Trans Am. This one has 1,000 hp. Magically enhanced."

"You like speed?"

"Let's just say I like being able to pass when I need to. It makes things safer."

She chuckled. "I bet it does."

He took her hand again. "What did you need to ask me about?"

She sighed, not sure how to begin. The Oracle's warning to say nothing kept her silent for a long minute, but she had to talk. She didn't have any other choice. "Remember the two flavors of snow cones we had yesterday?"

"Of course. I remembered because they were so unique. Fruitcake and holly."

"Do those two words mean anything to you?"

"You mean besides my mother?"

Not sure she'd heard him correctly, she blinked.

"And no, my mother's not a fruitcake." He smiled at her. "But her name is Holly."

The Oracle had said she'd need holly to save Christmas with the fruitcake. She'd assumed the *flower*, but maybe it was Daniel's mother. Maybe the Oracle had meant she'd need *Holly*, with a capital H. Cautiously, she said, "I may need to talk with your mother. Does fruitcake mean anything to you?"

"It does, actually. The legend of the fruitcake. It was gone long before I was born, and I only know part of it, so I really need to let her tell you. It's why she's sick."

"Fruitcake made your mother sick?"

"The *lack* of fruitcake, but not just any fruitcake."

She cocked a brow. "A 1000-hp fruitcake, by any chance?"

"Sort of." He laughed. "A magical fruitcake. Again, I'll let her tell you."

"I definitely need to talk with your mother. Can she keep a secret?"

"Sure." He raised an eyebrow. "And so can I."

"Good. That might be what keeps me alive a little longer."

SOMEONE WITH A GOOD FORTUNE-TELLING ABILITY

Daniel led Elizabeth into his house. In the family room, his mother sat in a large, comfy-looking recliner, wrapped in blankets. She seemed to be cold all the time but refused to turn up the thermostat because she didn't want him to be too warm.

As he walked past, he bumped it up a couple of degrees.

"I saw that, Daniel. You put it right back."

"I will, Mom. After you've warmed up."

He also turned up the space heater next to her recliner.

"Who is this beautiful lady?" His mother smiled. She was still pretty, but the curse had taken its toll — her dark hair was full of gray and she was far too thin. She'd been vibrant before, but now she was frail.

"Mom, this is my new friend, Elizabeth Lee. Elizabeth, this is my mother, Holly Grant."

His mother put out her frail hand. "I'm glad to meet you, Ms. Lee."

"Oh, please," Elizabeth said, taking her hand gently. "Call me Elizabeth. And I'm glad to meet you, as well. Did the pain potion help?"

"Was that your potion?" His mother sighed. "It has made everything much more bearable. Thank you, dear."

"Elizabeth owns the shop where I bought the potion, Mom. Drops of Magic."

"It helped the instant I took it. You're a gifted potion maker."

"Thank you," Elizabeth said, still holding his mother's hand, and the sight made him like her even more.

"Here," he said, motioning toward the couch. "Let's sit here."

He and Elizabeth sat close together, and his mother looked from one to the other, and gave a faint smile. Could she feel the Lifemate thing he felt? That almost embarrassed him.

"Mom, Elizabeth has some questions I told her you could answer."

"Of course," his mother said.

"It has to do with fruitcake," he said, meaningfully. "And the family legend."

"Oh. The legend." His mother sighed and slumped back in the recliner. "I haven't talked about the legend for a long time."

"You hardly mentioned it to me, and I'm your son."

His mother studied Elizabeth. "I don't tell this story lightly."

"I don't ask lightly."

After a moment, his mother nodded. "All right. What harm is there in telling? The Fruitcake of Youth has been gone for years now. The starter is gone and so is the actual fruitcake. Our family had one of the original three."

"That's what—" Elizabeth paused. "That's what I was told—that there were three originals. What does that mean?"

"Back in the year 700 BC, a misguided housewife kitchen witch named Aquilina made three fruitcakes of youth. They were meant to last forever, and have healing, regenerative powers."

"But no one actually eats fruitcake," Daniel said, lightly teasing, "so she needn't have bothered."

His mother frowned at him. He shut up. She went on.

"It is rumored that only one of the three may still be in existence, but I have nothing to back that up. It's just a rumor and a wish, I believe."

Elizabeth flicked her eyes down to her hands. Interesting.

His mother said, "We wouldn't need the fruitcake as much if our family had not also experienced a curse. An evil warlock wanted to heal his sick wife, but Aquilina refused to share the fruitcakes. She knew what he could do with that kind of power. He cursed our women to die at the age of fifty-five — the age his wife was when she died — unless they didn't have the fruitcake."

"Mom turns fifty-five on Christmas Day," Daniel told Elizabeth, no longer feeling light-hearted.

She raised her eyes to his and then to his mother. "Isn't there a way for you to find the fruitcake?"

"Yes. We have the ability to sense it when it's near, but since they no longer exist, that's not helpful."

"We can feel it?" Daniel asked. "Why wasn't I ever told about this?"

His mother sighed. "With no fruitcake left to sense, there was no need to tell you."

"But it does exist," Elizabeth said solemnly.

"What?" his mother gasped, her hand to her heart. "How is that possible?"

A shiver race up Daniel's spine. So he could sense the fruitcake if it existed—and a piece *did* exist? "Where is it now?"

Straightening her spine, Elizabeth said, "A small cube of it was entrusted to me. It was in the safe of my shop overnight. It was there when you first came in to order the potion for your mother, but after our date..." She trailed off.

His mother perked up. "Date?"

He smiled. "Yes, Mom. A date."

"Praise all the gods and Oprah, too!"

Elizabeth smiled. "You don't date much?"

He shifted uncomfortably. "I'd rather talk about fruitcake. Mom, what should I be able to sense about the fruitcake? I ask because when I first went in her shop, when the fruitcake was there, I felt an odd sensation, a feeling of *need*. At the time, I thought it was just, well, it got all tangled up in the—" Lifemate feeling, he wanted to say. "Anyway, I thought it was something else, but could I have been sensing it then?"

"Yes. That's exactly how I felt when my father showed me the last crumb we had. It's like a craving."

He studied his ailing mother, who was so close to death. Two days away. "So where is the fruitcake now? We can use it to save my mother."

Elizabeth shook her head. "It was stolen. Out of my bespelled and locked safe. While we were on our date."

"So you need to find it?" he asked.

"I most definitely need to find it. The person who gave it to me is very powerful and I fear what might happen if I don't."

His mother said, "Talk with your cousin, Daniel. Maybe Lorraine can help you because she's really the family expert on this legend. In fact, she's believed for years that it still exists and has been determined to find it. She'll be thrilled to hear she was right."

"You can't tell her that," Elizabeth said, sounding alarmed. "This can't go anywhere but right here or my life could be in danger."

"Who would harm you?" his mother asked.

She sighed. "The Oracle. She's the one who entrusted me with the fruitcake, and I've lost it."

"Can you go talk with her? Ask her for her help?"

"No! I'm not about to tell the Oracle I lost her magical fruitcake."

"Call Lorraine," insisted his mother, "and just ask what she knows about the existence of the fruitcake. Maybe she can help you."

Elizabeth heard Daniel's phone ringing on speakerphone.

She counted the rings. When they reached six, she was afraid they'd have to try again, but then a brisk voice said, "Hello, Daniel. What kind of trouble are you up to now?"

"Hi, Lorraine. No trouble. Ever."

"More like *what*ever."

"I have a question. Mom just told me about the legend of the fruitcake, and she said you could give me more information about it. She even bandied around the word *expert*."

"I have spent a long time researching the fruitcakes."

"Three of them, right?" he asked Lorraine, while looking at Elizabeth. "And all three were used up?"

Did his cousin really have the answers they needed? Feeling childish yet hopeful, she crossed her fingers.

"There *were* three of them," Lorraine explained, "and two of them are used up."

Daniel's lips quirked up in a slight smile. "What about the third?"

"Can you keep a secret, Daniel? Even from your mother?"

Daniel looked right into his mother's eyes and said, "I promise I will never tell her what you are about to share with me."

"You can't tell anyone."

"All right." He shrugged at Elizabeth, as if to say *I know it's a little white lie, but it's for a good cause.*

"Have you heard of the Oracle of Delphi?"

"Sure," Daniel said. "In 1400 BC, the Oracle of Delphi was two things—the most important shrine in Greece, considered to be the center of the world, and an actual person."

"Are you aware the Oracle resides in Moonchuckle Bay?"

"I'd heard that. Yes."

"I'm pretty sure she has the last fruitcake. It's why I moved here a year ago. I've been tracking it all these years and I'm so close to it. But the Oracle is watchful and I haven't been able to get to it."

"Wow," he said. "Are you sure?"

"Yes." Lorraine's voice grew quieter. "Seriously, Daniel, secrecy is of the utmost importance. I only tell you because perhaps you can help me get in to see the Oracle and ask for a piece of fruitcake. We don't need the entire thing."

"I don't know how to get an audience with her. She's pretty reclusive."

Elizabeth felt a little light-headed. She pulled out a tiny notebook she carried for jotting down shop- and spell-related notes, and wrote: *What if someone has already gotten a piece of the fruitcake from the Oracle? Could you help track that person?* She handed it to Daniel. He scanned the note and nodded, then asked the questions of his cousin.

"Well, I don't see how that could happen, with her security, but if they did, it should be easier to obtain a piece from them. Do you know who might have it?"

"No. I just learned about the legend and our ability today."

"Why'd your mother tell you today?"

"I asked her. I actually felt something weird in a shop yesterday but didn't know what it could be. Mom said maybe there's a piece of fruit-cake still left."

"Your mom is smarter than she looks."

Elizabeth shot a glance at his mother, who shrugged and smiled. She liked his mother and really wanted to help her. Another reason to find that fruitcake! And only two days left!

"Yes, she is. Mom says our family can sense the fruitcake. What can you tell me about that?"

"It's both a blessing and a curse. If you're close enough to feel it but you can't get to it, it's torture, like with the Oracle. She's one stubborn supernatural."

"So if I wanted to help you search for the fruitcake, what could I do to help?"

There was silence for a moment, a silence laden with anticipation. Then Lorraine said, "The pixies have the kind of magic that could figure this out. So talk with the pixies, get some pixie dust from them, and do an enchantment."

"Okay. Thanks, Lorraine."

"Any time. If you have any leads, be sure to let me know."

"Will do."

He hung up and looked at the two women.

Elizabeth said, "Well, she had a little more info than we do."

"Yes, we know now that my mother is smarter than she looks." He smiled gently at his mother. "Though I think you look plenty smart."

"Thanks, son."

Daniel patted his mother's hand and looked at Elizabeth. "Jingle's the only pixie I know in town. How about you?"

"I know Dixie. And she's actually one of the two princesses of the pixie court. She could get us an audience with the king, if we needed."

"Not necessary. But someone with a good fortune-telling ability and some pixie dust is."

LET'S DO THIS THING

Three the next afternoon was the soonest Dixie could arrange to safely take them—non-pixie folk—into the Pixielands. A whole day lost.

So it was the afternoon of Christmas Eve when Daniel drove her to Moonchuckle Bay Studios where they parked and waited. When Amber pulled up in her minivan, Dixie in the passenger seat, they climbed into the back seat.

Amber had offered to drive — begged, even — because she really wanted to catch a glimpse of the Pixielands. She called back over her shoulder, "Please excuse the mess. Wolf was chewing on the upholstery and we haven't had a chance to get it fixed yet."

"Wolf?" Daniel asked, sounding confused.

Amber took pity on him and turned around, extending her hand. "I'm Amber Winston. I'm married to Samuel Winston, the town sheriff. We adopted a little freckle-faced boy named Caleb who happens to morph into a wolf that looks a lot like a little white dog. He wants us to call his dog-wolf-self, ridiculously enough, Wolf. Since he's seven and we adore him, we indulge him. Even when he chews upholstery in his wolf form, though we're trying to discourage that."

Dixie laughed. "Did you try some rolled-up newspaper?"

"Very funny," Amber said, but smiled at her pixie friend, then started driving out of the studio parking lot and toward the pixie court. They were both west of town, with the Pixielands north of the studio and west of Troll Knoll.

Amber had come to Moonchuckle Bay a year before, hiding from a stalker. She'd been human when she met Samuel, but after they were married, she'd chosen to become a werewolf. And her stalker was imprisoned so she felt safe now.

"I'd like to meet little Caleb Wolf." He smiled and Elizabeth felt all warm. She had to admit it to herself—she really liked Daniel Grant. *Really* liked him. Maybe was even starting to fall a little in love with the handsome warlock!

"Wolf is running with his father tonight, but we'll invite you both to dinner soon."

"I'd like that," Daniel said. "Thank you."

Dixie grinned at him. "I'm Dixie Murphy and my husband is an attorney, Michael Murphy. I'm a pixie."

"Pleased to meet you, Dixie. I'm Daniel Grant and I moved here with my mother two months ago because our cousin convinced us this climate would be better for my mother's failing health."

"And don't let Dixie fool you. She's not just a pixie," Amber said. "She's one of the two princesses."

Dixie rolled her eyes. "You really have to add that? Every. Single. Time?"

Amber beamed. "I love being friends with a real, live princess."

Dixie looked at Daniel. "Whatever she says, please call me Dixie."

"Yes, your highness," Daniel teased.

Amber laughed. "You're going to fit right into our group."

"It took some arranging, even being the daughter of the king." Dixie sighed. "There's an excellent fortune teller at the Nightshade Hotel in Vegas," Dixie said. "But my twin sister happens to be even better. Princess Pixie. She was raised in the court so sometimes she does like being called Princess."

"Good to know," Daniel said.

"Okay, we're entering the enchanted forest, which is where the glamour of the pixie court begins. We don't want humans accidentally driving into the court."

Elizabeth had never entered the Pixielands and her heart raced with excitement.

Amber said, "So I follow this road into the trees?"

"Yes." Dixie pointed.

Amber pulled forward. After maybe a hundred yards, the trees seemed impenetrable. It appeared as though the road stopped, so Amber stopped. "What now?"

Dixie smiled. "I just learned how to do this a few months ago. It's so cool." She rolled down her window, letting in the chilly air, pointed her hands toward the trees and waggled them. Sparkly motes of pastel light—*pixie dust...?*—floated from her fingertips and moved sideways out the window. They blew straight for the trees, which parted, revealing the road.

"Wow!" Amber said, driving forward.

"That was really cool," Elizabeth said.

"I know, right?" Dixie said. "My sister is meeting us in a small home close to here. We felt it would be safest for everyone involved if we don't take you to the palace."

Elizabeth looked back and saw the trees move back into place, blocking the road again. She felt a little apprehensive moving into this unknown realm. Though she had magic of her own, she didn't understand the pixie magic and so didn't trust it.

Dixie pointed ahead. "There."

Elizabeth peered out the window at a small cottage, quaint and cozy. Even though it was December in Moonchuckle Bay, there were flowers growing here riotously—beautiful, healthy bursts of color everywhere. There was an otherworldly beauty about it, and she felt another skitter of apprehension.

Daniel took her hand, smiled at her reassuringly, and squeezed her hand, as if he knew how worried she was.

She squeezed back, feeling better. "Let's do this thing."

SOMETIMES I HAVE AFTERFLASHES

Elizabeth clutched Daniel's hand like a lifeline as they walked up the winding path toward the cottage.

The temperature was a pleasant seventy degrees, at least fifteen degrees warmer than two miles away in Moonchuckle Bay. The fairy court had its own unique ecosystem.

"Pixie, we're here," Dixie called as she walked up the three steps to the porch and knocked on the door.

It was opened by a woman with a face identical to Dixie's—but her hair had a definite blue undertone rather than Dixie's pinkish-red.

Dixie pulled her sister in for a hug. They were strikingly, ethereally beautiful, especially when standing side by side. She could sense the magic in them, even if she didn't fully understand it.

Pixie's smile was not as open as Dixie's, though, when she spoke to them. "Welcome to this humble abode."

Dixie went inside first, then Elizabeth, Daniel, and Amber, who shot a glance over her shoulder. Perhaps she was nervous, too.

Amber closed the door and the princess led the way into the living room. "I usually take people to the kitchen for something tasty, but that's because it freaks them out when they think I'm giving them food to trick them. Stupid incorrect human myths."

She stopped and motioned around the room. "My servants set it up as a fortune-teller's room, a touch I thought you'd appreciate."

The room had long, dark, dusty drapes which had been pulled closed, so the room was dark, lit only by two lamps. A draped round table stood in the center of the room with two wrought-iron chairs pulled up to it. There was even a crystal ball on the table. A crystal ball that looked suspiciously like a large snow globe.

Could she say *ambiance*? The princess knew how to set a mood.

Dixie introduced everybody, and they all tipped their heads and called her "Princess."

She accepted the title and didn't tell them to call her Pixie. Instead, she said, "Call me Madame Zelena during the reading."

Dixie smiled and gave her sister a nudge. "Are you taking this seriously? This is important."

Princess Pixie smiled and nodded and motioned Elizabeth toward the table.

When she sat, her pulse picked up speed. The princess took the other seat and the other three sat in fancy folding chairs around the table but away from it.

The princess held out her hand and took hold of Elizabeth's, closing her eyes much as Jingle had when she was determining their snow cone flavor.

Elizabeth could feel the pixie's magic reaching out as if tickling her own, probing and feeling. It didn't feel malevolent, so she relaxed a little.

Then Pixie opened her eyes and released Elizabeth's hand, which tingled. The princess said, "Your magic is strong. You're a healer?"

"Yes. I create potions that heal and sometimes I cast healing spells."

"I'll remember that." Pixie drew in a breath. "What is it you need from me?"

"Discretion."

"Of course. I already promised Dixie and a pixie cannot break a promise." The princess shrugged. "What knowledge are you seeking?"

Elizabeth paused, hesitant to break her promise to the Oracle yet again, but she had to find the fruitcake.

The princess raised an eyebrow, wondering what was taking so long.

"The Oracle of Delphi gave me a valuable item for safekeeping. It was stolen from my office by a supernatural the next day. I have only one day left to ... well, to heal Daniel's mother. So we both seek it."

Daniel said, "My mother's birth came at five p.m. so we have until five tomorrow, Christmas Day."

The princess raised her hands and placed them, fingers slightly curved, about an inch from the crystal ball. There were actual swirls of light and color moving about in the glass orb, and some white pieces looking like the snow in a snow globe. After studying the orb, she looked up, puzzled. "Does a *fruitcake* mean anything to you?"

"Unfortunately, yes." Elizabeth nodded. "It's the Fruitcake of Youth."

Nobody snickered.

"I've never heard of this fruitcake, but the Oracle is known for her caginess and secrecy—so neither am I surprised." The princess moved her hands away, but still studied the crystal ball, tipping her head as she gazed. "I see two mothers. They're holding out their hands, and they're both holding keys. I sense these keys are important, something passed from generation to generation."

Elizabeth appreciated the princess doing a reading, but were all fortune tellers this vague? First the Oracle and now Princess Pixie? She'd hoped she could get something more specific. Maybe she'd have to drive to Vegas and try the Nightshade psychic.

The princess looked into Elizabeth's eyes. "Do you know what information your mother holds in her hands?"

"She taught me everything I know about being a witch," Elizabeth said. "But I can't think of any information that would help me now."

The princess studied the ball. "One mother is dressed in green and the other in red."

"Christmas colors," Elizabeth said.

"Yes. I don't understand what the colors signify, but they've got to mean something." The princess sat back in her chair and raised an eyebrow. "You have a great task ahead of you. I wish I could give you more to go on."

Dixie put a hand on her sister's shoulder. "Thanks for doing this."

Pixie patted her sister's hand. "If anything comes to me in the next day, I'll let you know. Sometimes I have after-flashes."

Elizabeth was so disappointed she didn't think she could stand it. Another lead that didn't actually help because it was too vague.

She needed a psychic who could just say, "The fruitcake is in a suitcase in a White Honda being gassed up at the Phillips 666 station. The driver stole it. Go get her and the fruitcake will be yours once more."

Instead, there were red and green dresses. Keys. Mothers. What did any of those have to do with finding the missing fruitcake?

I THINK IT'S TIME TO PAY HER A VISIT

After Dixie worked her magic with the trees again, Amber drove through and headed back to the studio.

Daniel wished the reading had been more specific. He glanced at Elizabeth, who was pensive.

Amber pulled under the Moonchuckle Bay Studios arch and took an empty spot several cars down from Daniel's to park. She turned around. "I don't know how much help that will actually be."

"Thank you both anyway. I appreciate it so much." Elizabeth was gracious, though Daniel sensed her disappointment.

It matched his own. "Yes, thank you."

Dixie turned around and sighed. "The frustrating thing is that after you solve the puzzle, you'll be able to look back at what she said and see that it matches, but it doesn't necessarily bring you any closer to solving it. I'm sorry."

"Hey, you tried. At the very least, I can say I was in the Fairy Court. How many non-pixies can say that?"

Dixie laughed. "You can't ever say it, either, witchling."

"Right."

They said their goodbyes and climbed out, shifting to Daniel's car. The two women waved as the minivan disappeared.

Daniel started his car and cranked up the heater. As he turned back toward town, he said, "I was hoping for more."

"Me, too. If I had just had cameras installed, we could see who came into the store while we were on our date. I can sense auras, but I have to be present to do so, but a camera could show us their thieving face."

Why hadn't he thought of that earlier? "That's it!"

"What?"

"I have the ability to sense people's energy signatures."

She was silent and he glanced over to see her watching him intently. Then she smiled at him. "How long after someone came in my store would you be able to read their signature?"

"Days, though the signals grow weaker. I built a shield to tune them out because otherwise I'm bombarded with them, but if I drop it, I should be able to tell who came in your store while we were gone."

A few minutes later, they entered Drops of Magic, where Chicory Connolly stood behind the counter ringing up a sale while four other customers milled about the shop.

Elizabeth took his sleeve and leaned close to whisper, "Can you do it while people are here or should I close the shop?"

"No. Leave them in here. I can do it. I'll walk around and sort through signatures until I've been through the whole store."

She looked up into his eyes and he saw admiration there, even affection.

And then she stood on tiptoe and kissed him! Lightly, quickly, and she was gone. But the kiss rocked him.

She smiled up at him impishly.

When he looked over at Chicory, she was smiling and shot him a thumb's up. He grinned back.

Then Elizabeth tapped his chest lightly. "Go do your thing, Warlock Grant."

He nodded at her and lifted a chain from around his neck. From it hung the crystal that helped him hold the shield that kept the impressions away. He handed it to her. "Keep this for me, please."

"Can I wear it?"

He smiled and nodded, and she slipped it around her own neck, her eyes widening. He didn't know what she felt, but he'd ask her later.

She approached a customer and asked if she could help them find something.

He stepped to the left and stopped, closing his eyes and opening his senses, bracing himself for the bombardment. Sensations slammed into him, making him take a step back. He held his ground. It was always extra overwhelming when he'd had it quieted for a while, and it would take a few minutes to slip into the state where he could begin to read the signatures.

For that first minute, colors and faces flashed past his thoughts, swirling in a dizzying way. Finally, the chaos began to fade.

He sent out his magic in a circle, expanding it to three feet away. He caught a glimpse of a human family and two witches, but the impressions were too fresh. He pushed and saw other faces. He'd remember and use his talent to draw those faces to show Chicory, who'd been in the store while they were gone.

He opened his eyes. Elizabeth was watching him from behind the counter. He smiled and took several steps forward, closed his eyes, and repeated the procedure.

As he moved again toward the back, he caught a presence he hadn't expected. Surprised, he thought surely she'd been here just as a customer—but he had a bad feeling about this.

He opened his eyes and motioned to Elizabeth. "I need you to take me to the room with the safe. We should have started there anyway."

"You're right." She led the way through a door into the back rooms, into an office. She motioned toward an alcove that obviously served as her workshop. "The safe is here. It was spelled to conceal it from any humans and most supernaturals. I thought it was perfectly concealed."

He stepped within two feet of the safe where the thief would have had to stand to open it, and opened his senses again.

Yes. She'd been here and not just as a customer. His stomach sank. Why had she been in this back room?

He pulled out his phone and searched for the two pictures he'd taken of the woman after a dinner with his mother. "Have you seen this woman in the store?"

She studied the phone and shook her head. "But we can ask Chicory."

"Let's do that."

The store was filled with customers, a group of tourists and several shifters in human form.

Daniel waited until Chicory had handled a transaction and then held out his phone. "Did this woman come in the store while we were gone yesterday?"

Chicory took the phone and studied it, then nodded. "Yes. The younger one. She's the one who spent a long time in the bathroom."

He took his phone back and Elizabeth asked, "Who is she?"

"My cousin Lorraine. I think it's time to pay her a visit."

THAT OUGHT TO COME IN HANDY

E lizabeth clutched the door handle as Daniel squealed around a curve. His lips were tightened into an angry line.

She was angry, too. "So when your cousin said it would be easier to take the fruitcake from another person besides the Oracle, she meant *me*. And she'd already stolen it."

"Yes. She's been lying all along."

He turned into Gremlin Gulch, a new condo development, and parked. By the time he'd circled the car, she was out and heading toward the door. He passed her with his longer strides, and she scurried to keep up.

He pounded on the door. No one answered.

"Maybe she's not home."

"She's home," he said grimly as he pounded again. "I sense her."

A woman yelled, "Go away."

"Open up," Daniel yelled.

The door was thrown open and a woman about ten years older than Elizabeth stood there, a snarl on her face. The woman from the photo, only angrier looking. "Go away. I'm busy."

The woman was about five-five and looked to be thirty pounds overweight, dressed in black leggings and a black T-shirt with a familiar distinctive design and the words *Witch, please!*

Elizabeth pointed at the T-shirt in disbelief. "Did you steal that from my shop?"

Ignoring her, the woman lifted her chin. "I'm not accepting visitors right now."

She started to close the door, but Daniel put a hand up, pushed the door, and stepped inside. "Yes, you are."

"What are you doing?" Lorraine protested.

"What are *you* doing?" he demanded as Elizabeth shut the door. "Where is the fruitcake?"

She opened her eyes in an expression of innocence. "The Oracle has it, remember?"

Fake innocence.

Daniel loomed over his cousin, his face inches from her face. "You stole it from Elizabeth's shop and now you're going to return it to her. She has been entrusted with it by the Oracle, herself. Where is it?"

"Oh, fine." The woman flounced around. "It didn't work anyway. You can have it back. Though it's not in the same form it was before."

"What?" Elizabeth asked, panicked. "What do you mean?"

Lorraine didn't answer, but led them to a small room off the kitchen, probably originally a large pantry, but she used it as a small workshop. There, on a small table, was the brown paper wrapper— with only three minuscule fruitcake crumbs.

"Where's the rest of it?" Elizabeth asked, trying not to hyperventilate.

Lorraine rolled her eyes and pointed at a vial at the end of the table. "I used it to make a potion of youth, but it didn't freaking work. You might as well take it."

Elizabeth stared at the crumbs and then at the vial of liquid. "You used it up?"

"Are you dense or something? Yeah, I used it up. It didn't work. The fruitcake was defective."

"Why don't you think it worked?" Daniel asked.

"It didn't work. Look, I still have wrinkles around my eyes."

"So you tried it on yourself instead of my mother, who is dying?"

His voice was murderous. "I'm going to report you to the Witch Council, cousin."

"Go ahead," she said, though she stepped away from him. "I'm moving out of Moonchuckle Bay tonight. They won't find me."

She flounced out of the room and upstairs, where she was probably packing.

Carefully, Elizabeth gathered up the brown paper wrapping to include the tiny specks of crumbs, wrapping them so as not to lose them.

"Is there enough left to start again?"

"I doubt it but we'll find out."

He lifted the vial and slipped it carefully into a witch's vial holder—an envelope spelled to hold a glass vial safely, with no breakage or spillage or other damage—and slid it into an inside coat pocket. "Let's get back to your shop so you can begin work."

Elizabeth nodded and followed him outside and into the car.

Think. She couldn't panic. She had to figure out what else the potion Lorraine had made might need to make it effective.

If it wasn't too late already.

On the drive to her shop, Elizabeth called Chicory. "I need you to call an emergency meeting of the Connolly Coven."

Chicory didn't question, didn't complain that it was Christmas Eve, but simply said, "Where do you want us to meet?"

"In my shop in the next hour. That's where my supplies are. I'll need each witch to sense what's missing from a potion that an incompetent witch made." Her voice was harsh with anger at Lorraine, who had likely ruined everything.

She hung up and looked over at Daniel, who drove his sports car expertly toward Town Square.

Sensing her gaze, he said, "I trust your ability to fix this."

"I'm glad you do, because I'm totally overwhelmed at this moment."

"Get into your workshop and you'll know what to do."

A hint of a smile crossed her lips. "Thank you. I'm glad at least one of us can see me succeeding. I needed to hear that." And she did. Daniel seemed to know just what to say to her to make bad things a little better.

Keeping his eyes on the road, he took her hand, and the touch sent calming energy into her limbs and through her body, allowing her mind to focus. And she'd need to focus in order to fix the potion or create a new one from mere crumbs.

He parked behind her shop, where she recognized the vehicles of her witch sisters. Not biological sisters, but sisters of the craft and of the heart. Her family, willing to drop everything at eight o'clock on Christmas Eve to help her.

"Are you all right?" he asked. When she nodded, he kissed her hand, and said, "Then let's go work some magic."

"I never asked if you have other powers besides signature reading."

"I have the same talent as my mother, though hers is much stronger —was, anyway." He grinned. "I'm an Augmentor."

"Really? That's pretty rare, isn't it?"

"Really. I can increase the power of any supernatural I'm working with."

"That ought to come in handy."

YOUR MOTHER IS MORE POWERFUL THAN YOU?

E lizabeth's office was filled with witches and other magic wielders. Chicory and Marigold were there, as well as Dixie and Jingle, along with six other Connolly Coven members. That gave them twelve, a powerful number.

The group had varying aura colors, from blues to purples, to Marigold's gold, and an almost white from Daniel. She hadn't expected that.

The first thing she'd done was take an eye dropper and suck up one drop of Lorraine's potion, then carefully cap and place the full vial back into the protective holder. She squeezed out the single drop into a one-ounce glass jar.

Looking at the others, she said, "I'm going to let each of you examine it magically. After we're done, we'll share conclusions and see what comes up."

Then she lifted the glass jar, sniffed the drop, and used her magic to sense what she could—something was missing, but she couldn't tell what. She hoped the others could.

She handed the jar to Marigold. While it went around the group, Elizabeth set up a burner and pulled out ingredients. She didn't know if she'd have to start from scratch with the crumbs or if they could fix the potion. She had to plan on both.

After the women had examined the glass jar, Chicory handed it to Daniel. He did the same as the others, and when he opened his eyes, he caught Elizabeth's gaze. "Do you want our impressions now?"

She nodded.

He said, "It's missing something."

Several of the others agreed, but no one seemed to know what.

Chicory said, "It seemed like it needed an herb, but I have no clue which one."

That was weird, as Chicory was good with herbs and knowing.

Her mother, Marigold, shrugged. "I got the same impression as my daughter."

Chicory's cousin—Jennie Connolly, who had a light psychic ability —said, "It's a secret herb."

Elizabeth tipped her head. "What do you mean, secret?"

Jennie frowned, still concentrating. "I'm not sure, other than no one else has it. Except you."

All eyes were on Elizabeth. "I do?"

"Yes. It's something your family has had for many years."

"An herb that my family has had for many years?"

Jennie held up a hand and pointed toward the tiny plant on the windowsill. "It looks like that."

Elizabeth's eyes widened. "My mother's plant?"

Jennie walked over and touched a tiny leaf, then nodded excitedly. "Yes. This is it."

"What is it? My mother never told me, except that I needed to keep it alive no matter what and no matter where I went. She said it had been handed down from her mother, who'd gotten it from her grandmother."

"For generations," Marigold said softly.

A chill raced up Elizabeth's spine.

Jennie handed the little potted plant to Elizabeth and she took it with a newfound respect. Setting it on the table, she took a pair of scissors, thanked the little plant, snipped off one stalk that had five little leaves, and handed the pot back to Jennie, who replaced it in the windowsill.

"Normally I'd steep this, but we don't have that luxury." Elizabeth lifted the knife to chop the leaf into tiny pieces onto a piece of parchment paper—but stopped. "I feel as though this needs to go in whole."

Marigold nodded, and touched the brown paper wrapper with the three crumbs. "I'm feeling that we need to add these into the new combination you are creating."

Elizabeth hesitated. "But if this doesn't work, we won't have anything to start over with."

"I know. But if this doesn't work, there's not enough here to create a new potion. Just my opinion," the head of the coven and the most powerful witch in all of Moonchuckle Bay said. "What do the rest of you think?"

The rest of them either agreed with Marigold or weren't sure.

Elizabeth stared at the five-leaved piece of herb passed down through the generations and kept secret, and then at the crumbs of magical fruitcake that had also been passed down through the generations and been kept secret. And now they were coming together in this moment. And only the Oracle knew the connection. And Princess Pixie. Two mothers, two keys. And here they were. Holly's family fruitcake and her own mother's herb.

Elizabeth hoped she was up to the task. It was going to take every bit of magic she possessed and then some.

She lit the flame under the beaker, then lifted the five-leaved herb and slid it carefully in, followed by the last three crumbs of magical fruitcake. She then turned to the shelf and pulled out the vial.

Holding the uncapped vial above the beaker, she looked around again. "Yea or nay?"

"Yea," they all answered in unison.

She nodded—and poured in the potion. This either worked or it failed spectacularly and permanently.

"We seek to create a working Fruitcake of Youth potion," Elizabeth announced their intention to the universe, then turned and took Daniel's hand on her right and Marigold's on her left, and the hand-holding created a circle of witches and their magic.

Elizabeth started by sending her magic into the new concoction, bubbling lightly over the low flame. She saw her aura—a swirling mixture of light green and white—extend out into the room and touch the auras of the others. Daniel's was definitely the strongest connection and when his aura touched hers, it jolted her.

She focused, now sending her magic into the beaker, and the others did the same, as together, they worked to turn the potion into a working Fruitcake of Youth potion.

She could feel everyone's magic and auras mixing in the beaker, fixing little mistakes Lorraine had made. Daniel's cousin was quite the inept witch.

And then she felt the herb, which gave her another jolt. The one her mother had given her and said no one else could grow because it needed her magic.

She felt the other powers fade as she connected with the herb and it gave her its name—Jiaogo, related to the Chinese herb Jiaogulan. It told her the original Jiaogo plant had been found among many others by her male ancestor but, decades later, the plant had become extinct in China. The one she had, the one this herb had come from, was the last one in existence on earth.

"Jiaogo," she whispered, and the others whispered it after her. "Thank you."

She sensed the herb's eagerness to work with her and for a few minutes they seemed to be making progress, but then sweat began to bead on her forehead and it was taking all of her energy to stay connected.

A white light balled around the leaf and wound its way around her aura and magic, strengthening, encouraging, helping. It was Daniel, using his Augmentor power to boost her own magic.

A moment later, the beaker gave off a puff of greenish-white mist, and Elizabeth slumped against the table, exhausted.

Daniel wrapped her in his arms. "Are you all right?"

She looked into his face and knew she had to speak the truth. "You are dear to me."

He clutched her to him. "And you to me."

"Did we succeed?"

Marigold's triumphant voice said, "Yes!"

Thinking back to his words when he was discussing his power, Elizabeth said, "Your mother is more powerful than you? I don't ever want to make her upset with me."

I CAN'T TAKE IT IF THIS DOESN'T WORK

Daniel's magic seemed to have won the support of the local coven. His magic and Elizabeth's meshed and matched perfectly. When they'd been connected magically, he'd felt stronger and happier than he'd ever been. It wasn't until afterward that the fears about his mother had crept back in.

Would the potion heal her? It had definitely sparked and that meant it worked—but as what? Lorraine had been attempting a Fruit-cake of Youth potion, but there'd been so many mistakes in it that who knew what she'd actually created. And had they been able to overcome Lorraine's mistakes to create what his mother needed?

He glanced at the car's clock. Nine o'clock on Christmas Eve.

If this didn't work, the curse would take his mother tomorrow afternoon. She had less than one day left. He would spend every minute with her from now until that happened and, when she dropped into sleep tonight, he'd try to find a solution for the curse.

But he'd been searching for years and found nothing. This was her best and only hope. It had to work.

He helped Elizabeth out of his car. She was still weak, but was able to walk without his help now, so she was recovering. He took her hand, and they felt as right together as their magic had.

She held the magical envelope containing the beaker. She hadn't dared pour from the beaker into a vial, but capped it and placed it into the bespelled envelope. And now she clutched that envelope to her chest as though it held the secret of the ages.

As it did. The secret to whether his mother would live or die today.

He opened the door and gently touched Elizabeth's arm as she walked inside. She looked up at him, dark circles under her eyes from working her magic, but she was beaming up at him. Her smile lit his heart.

"I hope this works," she whispered.

"So do I." He nodded. "Let's go see."

His mother slept in her recliner. He touched her arm and she awakened and smiled. "You're here. I'm so glad." She was growing visibly weaker and could barely raise her hand to welcome them. It dropped back into her lap.

"I think we may have it, Mom." He motioned toward the envelope.

Her eyes opened wide in hope. "The potion?"

Daniel nodded. "We think we've fixed Lorraine's mistakes. The entire coven helped."

Elizabeth sank to her knees by his mother's recliner, and carefully pulled out the beaker. "Get a glass, Daniel?"

He hurried to do so, bringing his mother's favorite little cup, one with Mickey Mouse on it.

Elizabeth oh-so-carefully poured half the potion inside. "Do you think that's enough?"

"It should be plenty." He left unsaid *if it works at all.*

She handed it to his mother and Daniel helped lift the cup to her lips, and helped her while she took little sips.

Finally, the cup was empty, and they waited to see what would happen. Would she grow younger and live? Or would she die?

Nothing seemed to happen, and they continued to sit and wait. And wait.

His mother closed her eyes and fell into a light sleep.

He found Elizabeth's gaze and she took his hand. He pulled her into his arms. "I can't take it if this doesn't work." His voice was rough.

"I know," she said, holding him tightly.

And then she did something unexpected. She leaned forward and kissed him again. Lightly. Sweetly. Comfortingly. And then pulled back.

There was a light tinkle of laughter, and they both turned, surprised.

His mother looked ten years younger as she clasped her hands to her heart. "You're in love!"

"You're better!" he cried out.

"Thank you," his mother told Elizabeth.

The beautiful woman beside him—his Lifemate!—smiled gently. "You're very welcome. I couldn't have done it without your son's powers."

His mother reached out her hand and Elizabeth took it. "You have to spend Christmas with us. Stay here with us tonight, unless you have other plans?"

Elizabeth nodded, pleased. "Thank you. I have no plans."

EPILOGUE: I HAVEN'T EVEN ASKED HER YET

Elizabeth awoke on Christmas Day to the sound of voices and laughter. She glanced at her phone. It was seven. For Christmas Day, that was sleeping in.

Somebody gave a soft knock, and she pulled on a loaned robe, then opened the door.

Holly looked thirty years younger, even younger than her fifty-five years. "Come on down. We're about to open presents."

"I didn't bring any."

"You saved my life. Isn't that enough of a present?" Holly hugged her, then stepped back with a light tinkle of laughter. "Hurry, before Daniel eats all the cookies we left out for Santa."

"I'll get dressed—"

Holly motioned to her own pajamas. "You look great. We're all in our pajamas."

"Okay." Why not? She followed Holly down the stairs, hardly believing that this was the same woman who'd been sitting in a recliner ready to die last night. She had new respect for fruitcake.

"Oh, wait. I forgot to wish you a happy birthday."

Holly smiled. "Thank you for remembering. And I'm still alive. That's awesome. You're some witch being able to break that spell."

"Daniel amplified my powers or I couldn't have done it."

At the bottom of the stairs, Elizabeth caught sight of the lit Christmas tree with an angel on top. Presents were scattered around the base of the tree, more than she remembered. Though she had to admit she'd been so worried about Holly's health, and exhausted from performing the potion magic, that she might just not have noticed.

Marigold, Chicory, and Daniel were there. He held out a hand to her. She wrapped her arms about his waist and he whispered, "Merry Christmas."

"Merry Christmas."

When she pulled away, her friends were smiling. "You're here early."

"We wanted to make sure you and Holly were all right." Chicory grinned. "You did it. You created a youth potion."

"*We* did it," Elizabeth said. "I couldn't have done it without all of you. I'm so glad to be part of this coven."

The doorbell rang. "I'll get it," Holly said, moving spryly. A moment later, she came back in—with the Oracle of Delphi!

Dressed in her Grecian robes, her hair pulled back in luxurious draping braids, gold hanging from her earlobes and around her neck, she looked like a queen. She told Elizabeth, "You did well."

This was huge praise from the Oracle, and Elizabeth's heart warmed. "Thank you."

"Our children are going to be powerful witches," Daniel muttered.

She grinned up at him. "Christmas witches."

The doorbell rang again. This time, Amber and Sheriff Winston and their little boy, Caleb, stood there. The boy was about seven years old and cute as a button, with a mischievous glint in his eyes.

Amber said, "We just wanted to stop by to say hello on our way to my in-law's house to open presents. And see how you are."

"Thank you." Elizabeth ruffled his hair. "Hi, mutt."

Fifteen minutes later, Amber and Caleb walked out to their truck.

Elizabeth put her hand on the sheriff's sleeve. "What happened to Lorraine?"

"She's in custody, to be turned over to the Council office in

London. Apparently it's a big no-no to steal valuable magical fruitcake, especially if it belongs to the Oracle." He turned to the Oracle and nodded his head. "Good morning, ma'am."

The Oracle inclined her head coolly.

The sheriff left and the Oracle turned to Holly. "In return for the Fruitcake of Youth, I need your help in completing a task. Not at this time, but soon."

Holly said, "Gladly."

Then the Oracle shot Elizabeth a hint of a smile. "I suppose I must thank you for saving Christmas!"

"You're welcome." Elizabeth shrugged. "But I still don't understand how I saved Christmas."

The Oracle stretched a hand toward Daniel's mother. "Holly married a Grant, but her maiden name is Christmas. And you saved her."

Elizabeth laughed. "I guess I did."

A present floated through the air toward her and she snagged it. "For me?" she asked, surprised.

Holly said, "There's no point in having magical powers if you can't use them for good."

The Oracle left, and presents began marching toward the three of them, and they commenced opening.

After everything was unwrapped, Holly said. "Thank you again, my dear. And I just want to say, welcome to the family. I am going to love having you for my daughter-in-law."

"Mom, I haven't even asked her yet. We've only had one date."

"Well, hop to it. I've got a lot of years ahead of me and I want some grandchildren to spoil." She walked into the kitchen.

Daniel pulled Elizabeth into his arms on the couch. "You heard my mother, right?"

She nodded, smiling. "I like you, but that seems like skipping a few steps."

"Yeah, like getting to know each other better." He leaned his forehead against her. "Will you date me for a month or two before we talk about marrying and giving my mother some grandchildren to spoil?"

She smiled, joy filling her heart. "Yes."

Now it really was her best Christmas ever.

~ The Happy Ending ~

Want to read more? Click here to find other books by Heather Horrocks (several books are currently free ... *Bah, Humbug!, The Artist Cries Wolf,* and *Pride and Precipitation*).

ABOUT THE AUTHOR

Heather Horrocks is the *USA Today* bestselling author of numerous light-hearted, funny, feel-good books (*Moonchuckle Bay* paranormal romances, *Chick Flick Clique* and *Christmas Street* romantic comedies, *Who-Dun-Him Inn* cozy mysteries), plus the *Women Who Knew* inspirational series. The first book in her *Christmas Street* series, *Bah, Humbug!*, is currently in development as a TV movie.

Follow Heather online at:
    Facebook
    Facebook
    Twitter
    Pinterest

GIFTS AND GHOSTS: A CHRISTMAS CAROL

A Ghost Story of Christmas

AMANDA A. ALLEN

SUMMARY

A Mystic Cove Short Story

Harper Oaken is a former foster child whose life is haunted by what she's experienced. Her past effects everything—even her newfound love. Which is when a ghost appears...

CHAPTER ONE

Bridget was dead. There was never any doubt about that, for Harper had seen Bridget's body, her blank staring eyes, and the crime that had been wrought. Bridget had been murdered, her life stolen, and the tragedy bothered Harper still. Maeve, Bridget's sister, had clutched Harper's arm through the funeral, fingers digging in tightly.

Harper wasn't sure why the dead girl was in Harper's thoughts so much lately. Maybe because Harper had snagged Maeve's favorite picture of her first family and had an artist turn it into a painting. Since Maeve had become Harper's adopted sister, they'd had a bond based off of having a rough start.

You needed to own where you'd come from. Maeve had come from a loving mother—lost too soon—and a sister who'd kept Maeve out of foster care and spent every moment caring for her until Bridget had been murdered protecting her sister.

Harper had to wonder...was she being a good enough sister to Maeve? After all, Bridget had died for her kid sister. Did Maeve feel the loss even more because Harper couldn't fill those shoes?

Harper—who had lost her first family too—knew all too well how conflicting it was to love two families and have two histories. She knew what it felt like to love your current life and regret what had been lost...that was hard. But Harper wasn't so sure Maeve loved her current life all that much. Harper took a deep, shuddering breath and shook off the melancholy thoughts.

Today wasn't a day for people. Not for Harper. Today was a day for moving, for avoiding, for...not messing everything up. Her phone had buzzed again. She already knew it was Quinton, her...whatever he was. She just couldn't. Not then.

Harper glanced over her shoulder and then hurried down the street faster. Her scarf was knotted tight around her throat, and her jacket collar was turned up, but the cold was still sinking through. Her quick breaths made puffs of white air in the darkening sky.

She glanced at her store as she passed it, but she didn't go in. She didn't want those who might be looking for her to find her. Not then. She wanted to visit a grove and *think*. She didn't act like a druid very often, but her soul was craving the solace of the trees and the soothing effect of the roots wound together, united, and whole.

"Well if it isn't Harper Oaken," one of Mystic Cove's crones said.

Harper raised a hand and tried to keep going, but Old Mrs. Lovejoy said, "Wait, girl."

Harper paused, turning slowly. Harper had never liked the woman, and she nearly the last person that Harper wanted to see right then.

"You need to let that boy go," Mrs. Lovejoy said without preamble. Her wrinkled face was sour, narrowed eyes, pursed lips, chin pressed to her neck.

Harper considered and then said, "What do you know about it?"

Quinton, "that boy" was, she supposed... her boyfriend. Maybe. Thinking it made her feel itchy. He was her something. They spent parts of every day together. She texted him as soon as she woke up and he was the last person she talked to at night. She missed him when he wasn't around, and she didn't know what to do about that. It felt...very, very suffocating.

"I know that despite how the Oaken women took you in, you aren't one of them. They're kind. They think of others. They do things like adopt no-good brats."

Harper had long since learned to hide her emotions, but internally she was stupefied. Who said these things? Well...besides Harper and Gram. Was this karma? She had to admit it probably was.

"That boy Quinton deserves someone like your sister, Scarlett. Not like *you*. You gonna light him on fire the next time he upsets you? You gonna steal his cats like you did to the librarian? You're trash, girl. You don't deserve him. There are girls in this town who do."

Harper spun on her heel and left before she did something her mother would regret. She breathed in deeply and tried hooting it out, striving for calm. It didn't work.

"Run away," Mrs. Lovejoy called after Harper and anyone within a half mile, "Coward."

Harper had been intending to hit the tiny grove in the Central Park of Mystic Cove but she veered back to her car. It was down the street from her shop, a black Dodge Charger, and she jumped in before she got trapped by her sister, her nieces, or...that *boy* she should dump.

She'd been in a foul mood before, but Mrs. Lovejoy spreading her poison around...now...now Harper couldn't be trusted around other humans or...for that matter...anywhere that *her* humans might try to find her.

She had been antsy for days, and working on her feet all day in her shop hadn't helped. She'd changed her window dressing three times since Thanksgiving, but it wasn't changing how she felt; both watched and alone at the same time.

She'd gone out to the Oaken Family House and chopped wood last weekend, but it hadn't helped. You'd think that being a druid and near the family grove, she'd have been soothed, but no. She had actually gone for a run—which had been a terrible mistake—and that hadn't helped. It was like her flesh was crawling with the *knowing*, her talents wouldn't leave her be, but she couldn't read what her abilities were trying to tell her. She just knew something was up. Something was off.

She had thought meditating in a grove—where her family couldn't see—would help. Harper wasn't one for wandering the trees alone, let alone assuming the lotus position and melding her energies with their beloved trees. The Central Park Grove was out now that Mrs. Lovejoy ruined Harper's mood.

Where to go? Her mind considered the Circle's massive grove, but it was too possible that other druids from the Circle would be there. She could imagine how that would roll out. No matter the druid, they'd see her, they'd know something was off, and her mother would get as many texts as there were druids in the Grove.

She could just imagine the rest of the response. Her family, goodness, they would assume she was dying if they heard she'd gone to the town grove. The way they'd check on her for weeks—just the idea of it —made her flesh crawl. The antsy feeling seemed to explode inside her.

Surely there was somewhere that she could...attempt to...find some sort of internal balance before she scratched off her own skin? She considered for a few minutes but the memory of Maeve's present gave Harper an idea—Bridget's trees. Maeve's dead sister had accidentally awoken a long strip of trees near the bird reserve. Untrained druidic magic was more powerful than people realized. The trees weren't quite a grove, but they were very, very isolated. Perfect.

Harper avoided her neighbors until she was able to slide into her car. The tires squealed as she pulled away, but it wasn't so fast, she couldn't see Quinton's shadow rise in his bookshop and look her way as she sped away.

She wondered if he'd been messaging her. She'd left her phone in her apartment when she'd decided she couldn't sit still any longer. It took her at least 20 minutes to reach the bird reserve. The whole time the image of Quinton's shadow looking after her car was emblazoned on her mind to the soundtrack of the Lovejoy crone telling Harper to shake Quinton loose.

She parked at the end of the trail and hopped out. The cold was *intense* as if she'd left traditional Maine and ended up in Siberia. She didn't let the chill slow her down, trailing her fingers along the path, hoping for some peace. Maybe some guidance. Maybe she *should* break up with Quinton? Of course, he'd been messaging her. Leaving her phone had been on purpose. It was the easy excuse to say she hadn't been aware he'd been trying to contact her. She'd been side-stepping him too much lately, and she wasn't blind, so she knew it was bothering him. Maybe among the trees, she'd find a path and perhaps some solace.

She wandered for a while and realized there wasn't any solace to be found. She just might have to *actually* connect with the trees. She dropped to the ground and leaned against the first tree, opening herself to nature magic. She pressed the back of her head into the trunk, closing her eyes to breathe in the nature around her. It was chilly and the cold made her snuggle deeper into the tree. For others— it might have been uncomfortable but snuggling with a tree for a druid was rather like lying in the sun on a sandy beach for anyone else.

She said, "Hello," and listened to the life in the tree. It didn't thump-thump like her heart, but the swish-swish seemed to echo her all the same.

Harper didn't so much curl into a nap as drop off into sleep entirely unexpectedly. When she woke, the moon was high and her feet were *freezing*. It had been cold, so she shouldn't be surprised to see her breath making puffy clouds in the air, but she was. It was different somehow as if it had dropped 30 degrees cooler which was saying *something*. The cold didn't just reach to her toes or her fingertips, it seemed to reach into her very heart and make her feel as though she'd turned into a block of ice.

"Hello," someone said in a soft voice.

Harper jumped and then turned slowly, a little terrified, but she only found a girl standing over her. The girl was wearing a thin hoodie, t-shirt, and jeans but she seemed unaffected by the weather.

"Are you insane?" Harper asked, shoving her hands under her armpits. She bounced up and down, trying for some warmth and failing.

The girl simply smiled. Her long red hair and freckled nose struck Harper as incredibly familiar, but she was sure she'd never met this girl before.

Harper wiggled her feet, trying to shake feeling back into them and said, "What are you doing here?"

This kid needed to stop staring at Harper, or she was going to have to flip out.

"Normally it's just me around here," the girl said. Her glance wasn't unkind, but she did seem to almost melt into the trees like a tree sprite.

"That's what I was going to say," Harper said, adjusting her scarf and wishing she could breathe fire into it. She was just so *cold*. "Usually there isn't anyone else around here."

The girl smiled and said, "It's pretty late."

"Yeah," Harper agreed, thinking, yes obviously. "I suppose—"

"But not too late."

Harper paused, confused. "What?"

"It's not too late."

"Ok," Harper said. This one was a weird one, Harper thought. She shrugged and tried pulling her coat closer. If anything, it seemed to have gotten colder. She needed to get going. Make some tea, light the fire in her apartment, and face the messages on her phone.

"You need to let him in, Harper."

That was too clear. And too en pointe. Harper was officially spooked. She asked, "How do you know about him? How do you know about me?"

"I know all about you," the girl said. "I know that you like your coffee extra sweet. I know that you're like a dragon for the few people you love. I know that you like sparkly shoes and cat-eye makeup. I know that you eat oatmeal nearly every morning for breakfast because that's what you got in your foster homes and even though you hated it then, it's comfortable now."

Harper backed up several steps. Not even her sister, Scarlett, knew about the oatmeal. But the girl drifted closer, and Harper wasn't able to put any distance between them. It seemed that for every step back she was that much closer.

"Are you stalking me?" Harper wasn't proud of the quaver in her voice, but it was very late, very dark, and she was very alone with someone who knew far too much about her.

"No. You just matter to Maeve, so you matter to me. It's time to change, Harper. You had it bad. We both did. But...I didn't get a second chance."

Harper suddenly realized why she knew that face, those eyes, that hair. She could feel her heart freeze and then stutter to a slow, terrified start again. It wasn't *possible*. "Oh...my....starry...shi..."

She cut herself off to lean over her knees, breathing in and out through her mouth with hooting noises. She needed whiskey. And maybe a cross. She wasn't Christian, but ghosts seemed to be a good reason to carry a cross. Puffy cloud thoughts were *not* going to work for a haunting.

"Bridget?" Harper's voice was the croak of a sick toad.

The girl laughed and then said, "Boo!"

Harper screamed and backed up. She tried reaching for her magic, but what could you do against a ghost? Even if she could calm down enough to use it...nothing. Probably. Harper had no idea.

"I'm not here to hurt you, Harper. I'm here to *help* you." The humor in Bridget's voice did *not* make Harper feel better.

Harper took a shaky breath, hooted it out, and told herself to think the quiet stream thoughts Scarlett preferred. Nope. That didn't work, so Harper thought maybe she'd think fiery thoughts. Campfire thoughts. Marshmallows. Oh Hades, ghosts!

She stepped away but Bridget just followed. Now that Harper knew she was talking to a ghost, she saw how you couldn't quite make out Bridget's feet. They faded into nothing. And the hollows of her cheek-bones were too dark. It was as if she'd contoured her face with black powder. The closer Harper looked, the more she realized that it was *obvious* that she was talking to a ghost. Her eyes were dark holes, her voice seemed to echo as though it were a whisper from a distance.

"Harper Leah Hyacinth Willow Marie Patience Oaken," the ghost said, voice nearly fading away into ghostly howls with each name.

Harper's true name demanded her attention infused as it was with ghostly power. "I didn't get to love. Not really. But you can. Take off the chains that bind you, Harper. Take them off and love fiercely."

Harper swallowed and said, "Just because you didn't..."

"It'll never be anyone but him, Harper. His soul is tied to yours with the red thread, but you *can* ruin it."

Harper took another step back, this time leaving the path of trees for the road. Red threads were fairy tales. They weren't *real*. Harper turned and ran. Bridget rushed after, but she stopped at the edge of the trees. Harper adjusted her keys in her pocket and darted to the car door. She'd thought Bridget had somehow been stopped by the line of trees but that had been stupid thinking. Bridget was leaning on the car opposite Harper, grinning over in the most ghastly of ways. Harper clicked the lock on the door of her car, but it wouldn't open.

"This is the only night I'll look over you, Harper. I'm not your guardian, I'm Maeve's. You remember what has happened between us —what *will* happen between us. Take *off* the chains."

Harper bit her bottom lip and yanked on the car door. It opened and she jumped into the seat, pushing the start button and fleeing towards her apartment. Bridget did not accompany Harper. It didn't matter, she *flew* down the road. You'd have thought the hounds of hell were after her. She was haunted by the words, *What will happen between us.* What did that mean?

Harper swallowed and wondered just what was going on. Was this a hex? A spell of some kind? Had Mrs. Lovejoy done something when she'd stopped Harper before? Harper slowed the car when she reached the downtown area of Mystic Cove and decided to park a few blocks from her building. She didn't want the loud muscle car to awaken Scarlett, the girls, or alert Quinton if he was still around.

She just couldn't...not then. She walked through the alleys behind the buildings to avoid anyone who might be out late walking. As she reached her apartment, she looked both ways before darting to the door and through it. She did not want to run into anyone. Whatever it took.

Not after...she stopped to think and realized.

"It was a dream. Of course, it was."

Something skittered along her spine, but Harper avoided it. She'd fallen asleep among Bridget's trees—it made perfect sense that the location and what Mrs. Lovejoy had said to Harper would cause a dream like the one she'd had.

Of course.

CHAPTER TWO

W hen Harper awoke, it was so dark, that looking across her bedroom, she could scarcely distinguish the window. The lights of the street weren't showing through the window as they usually did, but the howling at the window proclaimed a winter storm. One hadn't been forecast, but the weather had been so odd lately.

Or maybe it had been forecast and she hadn't been paying attention. She fished around for her phone, finding it under the pillow and saw that Quinton had sent her 13 messages. She didn't read them, but just focused long enough to make out the time. It was midnight.

She sniffed and sat up and then looked at her phone again. Midnight didn't make sense. She'd gotten back from her creepy dream in the woods after 2:00 am. Perhaps the satellites for the phone service were somehow blocked by the storm?

And yet...that didn't quite make sense either. She frowned. There was no way she'd have slept through the night and the following day. Scarlett would have shown up, banging on the door. Or Quinton. At the thought of him...she rose and crossed to the window, guilt striking her for avoiding him the previous evening and not answering his messages.

Perhaps it was as simple as her phone being broken. She gazed down on the street and saw that fog had settled between the buildings. She felt as though she were looking down on some ethereal, mystic version of her hometown. Perhaps a night like this one was the reason Mystic Cove earned its name?

There was no sign of life outside her window. Not so unusual for this time of night. Mystic Cove was a very small town, so there was nothing unusual about it being deserted on a cold winter's night, but she still felt a chill. Harper went back to bed, curling into her covers and pillow and the dream of the previous evening returned to her.

Bridget's face had been so haunting and creepy. Harper didn't want to think of Maeve's sister as something so dead. Harper knew, of course, that Bridget was dead, but Harper wanted to think of her like she was in Maeve's photo.

The promise of Quinton being Harper's red thread was bounding around in her mind. A soulmate for someone like her? If only...but... no...not for *her*. Harper couldn't help but hear what Mrs. Lovejoy said about leaving Quinton echoing through Harper's thoughts. There was no doubt that the old woman was a nasty piece of work these days. But she might not be wrong. Quinton was a nice man. A good one.

Surely, he could do better than her? He could do better than someone who avoided him when she was feeling antsy and didn't answer his messages for days before appearing in his life again like nothing had happened.

She knew what it was, of course. There was even an official diagnosis. Harper was on the attachment spectrum. Which meant she'd been kicked around so much as a kid that she'd learned people were untrustworthy. Even with the grove, magic, and the healing power of druids for the spirit it had taken a long time for Harper to trust the Oaken women. She doubted she'd have ever trusted anyone without magic helping her. Which meant she and Quinton might be doomed.

Her mind flew back to meeting him. A baffled man trying to find out what he was and what to do with it. He'd been a librarian. Of course, he had been. Even now he always seemed to smell of books and ink as though the scent had infused into his skin from his bookshop.

By the stars and the root, how she loved that shop. He sold ancient magic texts and histories. But he was nerdy enough to carry comic books and board games. And he sold romances, mysteries, Sci-Fi, and fantasy simply because the people of Mystic Cove had been so excited for a bookshop and he couldn't disappoint them.

She loved the way he had a list of romance authors to recommend based off of interviewing reader after reader. She loved how he'd collected the full works of Georgette Heyer when some sweet little lady had talked him into trying them. She loved how his obsession was history and how that had changed with the discovery of the supernatural.

She had it bad. But sometimes, when she was with him, she felt like just needed to run away. Bridget's ghost bothered Harper. Massively. It bothered her that she'd dreamt up Maeve's sister. That Harper's subconscious had given Bridget the order to do what...maybe...to do what Harper desperately wanted?

She did desperately want Quinton to be tied to her. She didn't need a ghost to tell her that. Maybe if a mystical thread linked them, he would never leave her. Unlike nearly everyone else.

She picked up her phone, checking the time again. It felt as though hours had passed. She frowned—only 45 minutes had gone by? Really? She dropped her phone and flopped her head back on her pillow. This was going to be the longest night. She was sick of it already.

Maybe she should message Quinton back? Maybe he was up late reading? But, of course, he was. What could she say? I'm sorry that I didn't message you and ran away? I'm just so damaged.

She rose, if she could no more sleep than visit the moon, she might as well enjoy a long hot bath. She filled the tub, lit candles in her bathroom, and added some witchy salts that her sister, Scarlett, had given Harper for her birthday. They smelled like trees and spring and nature, and Harper loved them.

She laid back in the tub, letting the salts work on her muscles and work away the cold. She removed her nail polish and put on a face mask, lingering until long after it was cracked and dry before rinsing it off and getting out of the water. Her fingers were wrinkled with the time she'd spent in the tub and her muscles had relaxed. She dressed in pajamas, put on her robe, slid her feet into puffy slippers, and figured a cup of sleepy tea and she'd be able to drift off again. Hopefully dreamlessly this time.

Harper grabbed her phone, telling herself to leave Quinton alone. As she did, her breath puffed a white cloud. She frowned, glancing at the screen and saw it was 12:00 am. That couldn't be right. It had been that time when she'd woken up. Her phone *was* broken. She'd have to get a new one. Oh, man, she hated having to make those choices.

She shivered and felt a rush of cool air. The steamed-over mirror seemed to be altering in front of her. Instead of steam, clouding the glass, it was ice. She reached out a shaking hand and touched the glass.

It was cold as ice. Her damp fingers stuck, and she had to yank them free.

She took a step back.

"Careful now," Bridget said, "I hate it when people walk through me. It makes me feel so very dead."

Harper spun, tripping on her bathroom rug, and fell into the counter. "Oh, my." Harper choked and struggled upright. "What the... holy....oh my....*are* you *here?*"

"I said I'd be looking over you. Somehow, I don't think my warning by the trees sunk in. Why haven't you texted him?

"I..."

"You were abandoned so often. I know. You don't have to explain."

Harper didn't answer. She didn't *want* to answer.

"Your past wasn't easy."

Harper pressed her fingers to her lips. She didn't like to think about those days. "Why are you doing this to me?"

"Your welfare," Bridget said. She didn't breathe, and her feet faded into a blackness so only the top 2/3 of her body was visible. The rest floated ambiguously above Harper's bathroom floor. "Your chance for happiness."

Harper shook her head. She wasn't sure true happiness was in her future. It certainly hadn't been in her past.

"Come," Bridget said. "Walk with me."

Bridget took Harper's hand, and somehow it was like holding hands with one of her nieces. The hand seemed to fit so naturally. The link between them made it so pleasant.

"I..."

"Come," Bridget said, and she stepped forward. Harper followed almost thoughtlessly and as she did, she was no longer in her apartment.

Institutional walls rolled out before her, a stained and old carpet was under her fluffy slippers. Harper's breath started coming faster. A woman was crying near the green wall. Her fingers were dirty, her hair was matted, and black mascara rolled down her face. She sniffled and Harper stepped sideways. This was a place of heartbreak and madness, and Harper did *not* want to revisit.

"Oh," Harper said. "No. Not here." She tried tugging her hand free, she wanted to go back. She wanted her apartment with the red leather couch and the birdcage with the stuffed teddy bear and the afghan her friend, Henna, had knitted. Harper could not break free.

"Come," Bridget said, tugging Harper down the hall without a struggle. Down the hall and into a waiting room with blue plastic chairs. On one of them, a younger Harper sat. Her arms were folded over her chest, her beat-up backpack lying against her feet. Next to her was her foster brother, Jemmie. His jagged bangs hung over his eyes, and she flinched at the sight of him. She'd promised to always be his friend. She yanked a breath in and tried hooting it out. *Nothing* was working.

"I don't..."

"Come," Bridget said, moving Harper past her younger self, bypassing Jemmie as if he didn't haunt Harper far more than Bridget ever could. "You know this part. Let's see the rest."

Bridget walked ahead of Harper, almost dragging her behind. She tried again to pull free, but that ghostly grasp was unbreakable.

"Here," Bridget said brightly.

Harper shook her head as she saw familiar faces. Ones she'd tried to block out.

A harried looking woman with dyed red hair, gray roots, and fading makeup sat with a file in front of her. An elderly woman with a white bun. An official-looking man with a wrinkled suit that needed to be dry-cleaned.

"What about her father?" The man asked. He was leaning his forehead on his hand, hunched over the table.

"He's in jail," said the harried looking woman. The social worker, Harper knew, trying to avoid her name. "He said he'd sign, so she could be adopted."

Harper paused, walking around them, waving her hand in front of their faces. They were so familiar. The lawyer, the social worker, and the advocate. Those who were supposed to take her from what was bad and give her something better. They had failed.

Harper had gotten better but through a fluke.

"Please," the social worker said. Harper had *hated* the social worker. Still did. "No one is going to adopt that one."

"We have to try," the lawyer said. He sounded tired, but he wasn't putting up much of a fight. Back then, he hadn't met Harper's eyes very often. Now she knew why. He hadn't fought for her.

Harper leaned down, sticking her face right into his. She hadn't liked him either. But she couldn't spook him as much as she wanted.

"They can't see you," Bridget said with a hint of a laugh.

"Jared," the social worker said, sighing and shuffling paperwork. "No one is going to want her. She's been arrested. She's run away 4 times. She won't even get into a foster home. Who would take her? This girl is pure group home material. I have other kids who might actually get adopted that I need to focus on."

"Hey now..." The advocate was speaking now. She was the grandmotherly type complete with knitting needles and white bun. "We *aren't* giving up on her."

"We are," the social worker said. "We don't have the man-hours or ability to do anything else. Even if we had time to work her case...she's still unadoptable."

What was her name? Kristen? Linda? Perhaps Harper had blocked it out.

"I don't want to be here," Harper told Bridget. "It's time to go."

"Look at them," Bridget said. "How many kids do you think they were trying to help? 20? 30? Just at this moment in time? Look at that stack of files. How many kids do you think they found homes for?"

"What does it matter?" Harper asked. She tried to open the door, but her hand flew right through the handle as if *she* were the ghost. "They didn't find one for me. I already know this. Can we leave?"

Harper tried again to open the door. She didn't want to see this. She didn't want to hear how worthless she had been. As if Harper didn't know. The girl out there in that waiting room full well knew how her mom had kept using drugs rather than getting Harper back. Her dad had spent his life in and out of jail and signed her away within seconds of being asked. She...none of them wanted her.

"I'm ready to go," Harper said. The tense hack of her voice sounded foreign, but Bridget just shook her head brightly.

"We haven't seen enough," she said.

"I *will* not give up on the child," the advocate said. She put down her knitting needles and said, "We can do better than this. We can do better than a group home and shuffling onto the next child."

"No offense, Pearl, but I don't think you're being very reasonable either," the social worker replied in an irritated tone that said they'd had this argument too many times. "I have talked and begged that girl to behave. To stop running away. To stop, for the love of god, setting things on fire. She's stone-hearted and stone-headed."

"Wouldn't you be?"

"It's not that I don't get it," the social worker said, "I do. I can see it. I can see everything that led up to where the girl is. The system failed her. We were too late. But we aren't too late for the other kids. The one is unadoptable. Others aren't. A group home is the best we can do. Even then, she'll be lucky to keep out of juvie."

Harper hadn't kept out of juvie. She hadn't even tried. If anything, she'd dared herself to get there faster and with a bigger bang.

"We can do better," Harper's advocate repeated. "We *must* do better. She's a child, Linda. Just a child."

"Then do it, Pearl. Have it be your fruitless project. Now about Jemmie...I think he'll be ending up in that group home too. He's almost as bad as Harper but even stupider."

The lawyer sighed and said, "His mom isn't going to sign the release paperwork. We'll have to terminate rights...that'll take forever. Until then...the case is at a stand-still. Not that it matters. No one wants him."

Bridget took Harper's hand and said, "This is why you have a hard time connecting with people. Too many people who should have helped you and didn't."

Harper didn't say anything. She wasn't stupid. She knew. Family after family had found her unworthy of love. Including her first one.

"Pearl found your mom, you know...she searched and searched and told people about you. She even visited your dad in prison time after time. He was the one who got word out about you. To the supernatural community. Where it got to your mom," Bridget said. "Not everyone abandoned you. Pearl and your dad made your life possible. They didn't abandon you. Not everyone will abandon you. Qui—"

"That's not true," Harper said. Her heart had frozen. "My dad and Pearl didn't do that."

She did not want to hear about Quinton.

"It is true," Bridget affirmed. "They did."

"My dad didn't help me. He just signed me away. And yeah, I know that I'm not alone," Harper said, "My mom, Maeve, Scarlett, my nieces, they're all with me."

"Quinton would be too, if you'd let him."

Harper said nothing.

Bridget, very gently, said, "He's your red thread. He's tied to you by the magic thread from your soul to his. He is a soulmate."

"Please," Harper said, ensuring she infused her voice was as much sarcasm and doubt as it was possible for one word to convey.

"Yes," Bridget snapped, and the sympathy was gone from her voice.

Harper shook her head. In the middle of it, Bridget placed her hand on Harper's and yanked. She stumbled forward, through a mist and appeared in the very institutional prison visiting room. Her heart ached in her chest, and her hands clenched. This room and this moment had been emblazoned on her mind, and she couldn't forget it even though she wanted to. "No. Not here."

"Face it," Bridget said gently, placing a very cold hand on Harper's back. "Own it. *This* is your story. Even though it sucks."

Harper shook her head as her young self walked into the room with the advocate, Pearl. Harper's dirty blond hair was hanging in her face, and her too-thin body made Harper wince. She'd forgotten how she hadn't liked to eat then. She'd forgotten how the only thing she felt was the feel of her favorite razor blade against her arm.

She glanced at Bridget for mercy, but Harper only got a sympathetic gaze in that traitor's face.

A tall, thin man stood as her young self approached his table. His jaw was stubbled with hair, his eyes were sunken. His skin was yellowed. He'd lived hard. She hadn't seen that then. She'd just seen the man who'd left her mom before she was more than a few days old and she'd never seen again. Not until this day.

"Harper," he said, his voice a croak. "I..."

She looked at him, and Harper was amazed to see the hatred in her young face. She remembered how she felt that day. She hadn't felt hate. She'd felt hollowed out. Nothing. A snow globe that had been cracked open and lost all its glitter and water. Ruined.

"I..."

Young Harper didn't look at him. She set her hands on the table across from him and stared down at them. You couldn't see it, but she was biting the inside of her cheek bloody.

"I've done what I can for you."

Young Harper still refused to look at him. But adult Harper heard the plea in his voice. Neither of the Harper versions were moved by it.

"I'm sorry," he said.

Her young self snorted and shifted but did not look at him.

"I shouldn't have left your mom like that. I should have told her."

Modern Harper froze at that. Oh Hades, she thought. Suddenly remembering what he had said, suddenly understanding it now that she had the context of the rest of her life.

"I should have explained what was happening, but it was all too much for me. You. Her. Everything. I should have..."

Modern Harper pounded her fist down on the table between her young self and her birth father.

Young Harper did not look up, and Harper's father didn't notice.

"They can't see you," Bridget said softly.

"No," Modern Harper said. "No, it's not true. They were just both addicts. They were stupid. They made bad choices. He didn't..."

"I'm afraid that's not quite true," Bridget said gently. "He knew what he was. What you were. He had a pretty good idea what your mom was. He was a warlock, Harper. Just like you. He had seen enough of your mom to guess her for a druid. Supernaturals are drawn to each other even in groups of hundreds of normal humans."

"Oh," Harper needed to vomit. She stood up, grabbing Bridget by the shoulders and said, "I don't care." What a lie.

Bridget didn't argue it.

"Take me home. Right now. Remove me from this place."

CHAPTER THREE

W aking in the middle of a gasp and sitting up in bed to get her thoughts together, Harper had to get up or go mad. The antsy feeling was back but a thousand times worse. It was as though snakes had infested the place between her skin and her muscles. She rose and paced.

Back and forth, back and forth, so sick to her stomach, she was surprised she wasn't bent over the toilet, vomiting.

She took a sharp look around for Bridget, but of course, the ghost wasn't there. It had all been a dream. Finally she stumbled into her kitchen and took a long drink of water. Her stomach marveled at the water, but she didn't quite puke it up. With shaking hands, she splashed water on her face and then laid on her couch.

She glanced around, her gaze catching the pictures on the mantle. They called to her as if someone were shining a light on them, and she crossed to them. The first was of her and Scarlett. It had been taken only a few months after Harper had been adopted. She was still awkwardly thin, and she'd already begun dying her hair black. Anything to block out things that could remind her of her biological parents.

Scarlett's arm was wrapped around Harper, and Scarlett was grinning right into the camera. Scarlett had been Harper's salvation, the first person Harper had been able to trust. The first person who just took Harper as she was and accepted it.

The next picture was of Maeve, Bridget's sister. Harper and Maeve only been family for a few months, but something between them clicked. Maybe it was because if you could focus just right, it seemed possible to see all the way their lives echoed each other with trauma and loss.

Harper swallowed and picked up the next picture. It was of her and her mother, Maye. Harper reached out with a shaking hand and touched that face. She had to move or die.

She slipped on running pants and shoes and fled. She ran through Mystic Cove, up the streets and down them. The lights were out, everyone was sleeping, but the fog was thick making Harper feel as though she were in the middle of a true haunting instead of a series of terrible dreams. She ran past Quinton's bed and breakfast and noted one single light. His light. It seemed to chase her all the way home, to her apartment. Not even a run could leave her in peace. She wanted to go to him. She couldn't. She couldn't let him leave her too. Better for her to leave first.

Outside her outer apartment door, she pressed her head against the doorjamb and wondered why she had to be so very damaged? Why hadn't she just gone up those stairs and into his room? He'd have opened his arms and wrapped her up. He had every other time she'd freaked out on him.

Would he this time? Or was he so angry with her, so upset, that he would shut the door in her face? Maybe he was sick of all the drama with her?

She opened the door and hoped she could somehow escape these dark thoughts. As she stepped into her entryway, she stumbled. She was in her niece's room instead.

"They're so sweet," Bridget said from behind Harper. "I'm so glad Maeve has them."

Harper gasped and spun. "But I wasn't asleep."

"Oh Harper," Bridget said, laughing. "You never have been."

Harper took a deep breath and then heard her name.

"...she'll take us."

Harper turned slowly to find her beloved nieces, Scarlett's daughters, Ella and Luna.

"But, Mommy will be mad," Ella said. Her little voice was concerned. She was showing none of the disdain she would have if Harper or Scarlett were in the room. Ella needed to be grown up around them, but with Luna, Ella could be herself.

"Auntie Harper isn't afraid of Mommy," Luna scoffed in her piping little voice. She curled onto her side to face Ella. They were both in Ella's bunk, with their blankets tented over them, a flashlight between them that Scarlett hid away to end these late nights.

Harper had to laugh. She crawled onto the bed, and the girls didn't even notice. If anything could make her feel better, it was these two.

"Auntie Harper is the only one who will take us," Ella admitted. "I bet she'll bring Quinton. Do you think they'll get married and have babies? Then we could be the big girls who take the babies places. I would be the best cousin ever."

Luna sniffed and then shrugged. She said, "Auntie Harper is scared."

Harper winced. Luna was *far too* insightful for a 5-year-old, and she was ruling all of them because of it.

Ella gasped and said, "She's not scared of anything."

"She's scared that Quinton doesn't love her," Luna said, sniffing sadly for Harper. "Cause all those people didn't love her when she was little. She doesn't see it had to be that way."

"Why wouldn't they love her? Why did it have to be that way?"

Harper felt her heart and her throat choke at the same time, and she felt something burning at the back of her eyes.

"Cause they were dumb, du-uuh. Besides, if they loved Harper like they should have," Luna said, "She wouldn't have been ours. They had to be stupid, so we could have her."

"Like fate?" Ella asked. "I'm glad fate made her outs."

"Like fate," Luna repeated. "She was always ours. She just had to come a really, really stupid way."

Harper bit down on the inside of her mouth so hard, she drew blood. She rose and walked to the door, imagining for a moment if her foster family, the Walkers, had adopted her or the Michelson's. She knew the Walkers, at least, had thought of it. Starry skies, her entire body rejected that idea of being a Walker instead of an Oaken. Thank goodness she'd lit their shed on fire.

Harper opened the door, surprised it let her escape, and found herself stepping into the room where Scarlett slept. That was not how this apartment worked. She should have been in the entry way across from the kitchen and near the living room. Harper flinched, not sure she could take whatever the next painful revelation would be. But there Scarlett was, lying back in her bed, talking on the phone.

"Harper will take them," Scarlett said and yawned. "I feel like I take advantage of her though. She let me sleep in three weekends in a row but every time she offers sleep, I just can't say no. What would I do without her?"

There was a murmured reply and Harper didn't want to hear the answer. She took a step back and found herself standing in her Gram's room. Mr. Jueavas, shirtless, had his arms wrapped around Gram.

"Oh no," Harper said, immediately squeezing her eyes closed, but knowing she'd never get over the sight of those wrinkled biceps wrapped around a distinctly naked Gram. "No."

Harper hadn't plugged her ears though, so she heard Mr. Jueavas say, "It's not fair. Santiago had everything, and he's a monster. Sometimes I look at Harper and shake my fist at the heavens."

"It's not your fault," Gram said, and her voice held none of its usual meanness.

"And yet your Harper, she's been through *everything*, and she's great. She got kicked around, we catered to Santiago."

"She's damaged," Gram said. "Don't be blind. She's all scarred up on her soul. She might never find happiness."

"Life damages us all," Mr. Jueavas said, "But she bears it so well. She's a shining star to me. A shining star."

Harper turned and fled only to find her Mom talking to Maeve in the attic bedroom room of the Oaken House.

"I love your mom," Bridget said. She stepped closer, rubbing her hand over Maeve's forehead. Their sister seemed to almost sense it. To lean into that ghostly pressure as though their souls were wise enough to sense each other even though Maeve's gaze never turned to where her dead sister stood.

Mom was brushing Maeve's hair. The girl's backpack was on the bed next to them. She was ready to go. Of course she was, but Mom didn't care. She combed back that hair and hummed under her breath. Maeve rarely let her go-bag out of her sight. Of course, if Harper had as much cash in her bag as Maeve was carrying around, Harper would have kept a close eye on it as well.

"Do you think when I grow up Harper and Scarlett will…"

"Yes," Mom said without hearing the rest of the question, "They'll love you as much as they love each other. But you'll be a friend instead of a little sister. They *already* love you the same."

"But they're so close."

"You will be too. You just need time. They need you to be old enough they don't feel responsible for you. Right now, they adore you. But like mama bears. Before long you'll just be another of the grizzly gals."

Harper spun and found herself in Quinton's room. Books were stacked everywhere. She shook her head, she didn't want to know what was happening with him, how she'd hurt or infuriated him. She didn't want to see him loving her *or* hating her. She couldn't take any of it.

"Remove me from this place," Harper said to Bridget. "Now."

CHAPTER FOUR

Harper spun and found herself in her bed. She closed her eyes and covered her head with her arms. By the stars, she felt like a wrung out washrag that wasn't worth throwing in the washing machine. Just throw her away and get a new one.

"Come on, now," Bridget said and her voice was far eerier than before. She sounded rather like she was calling from a long distance and she was very, very tired.

Harper opened her eyes, lifted her arm, and saw that Bridget slowly, gravely, silently approached. She seemed darker somehow. Maybe she was tired? Perhaps she'd expended rather a lot of energy tormenting Harper? For Bridget seemed almost shrouded in a deep black garment, which concealed her head, her face, her form, and left nothing of her visible save one hand.

"No," Harper said. "I'm done. I hurt. I'm done. I'm done. I'm done. Go away."

The hand pointed.

"No," Harper almost shouted.

The hand pointed, and there was something so forceful in it that Harper flinched.

"Please," Harper said and then flinched again at the pleading in her voice.

The hand pointed, more forceful still, and Harper decided to get it over with. She rose and her legs trembled beneath her. She could hardly stand when she prepared to follow this new, darker version of Bridget.

"Where are we going now?" Harper asked, not sure if she could face more emotions that night. More painful revelations. She preferred to try to keep herself in some sort of tenuous balance. This whirlwind of feelings might just take her down forever.

Bridget gave her no reply. The hand was pointed straight before them, and Harper took a deep breath and stepped forward. The side of the bed faded into a long dark road, and she walked ahead of Bridget for quite some time. Harper walked barefoot and felt the crunch of snow beneath her feet but not the chill of it. She could hear the wind howling, but it never touched her skin. She could feel the presence of trees and wolves, perhaps, but could not connect with a single creature.

She was truly a ghost in this world that Bridget was dragging Harper through. When they reached the end of the road, she found a much older Quinton sitting behind a desk.

"Do you have children, Mr. Foxe?" A young girl asked. She wasn't so young, really. Perhaps early adulthood, but she seemed like a baby compared to Quinton as he was then.

"I'm afraid it's just me," he said. His voice sounded tired as though he were grieving. His face was creased with lines, but the laugh lines she'd enjoyed caressing had faded into frown lines. There was a furrow between his brows. There were a few age spots on his forehead. His books were too-neatly put away as though he didn't sink into them like he was wont to do.

"Really? You never fell in love?" The girl was wearing a leather skirt, a t-shirt, and had awesome black hair. She should go away. Harper heard the tinge of a crush even though decades separated the girl's age and Quinton's.

"Oh, I loved," the older Quinton said, "I just wasn't loved in return."

"I can't imagine that," the girl gushed, tucking her hair behind her ear.

Neither could Harper. She loved Quinton so much it *hurt*.

"Well," he said, smiling his polite business smile that never reached his eyes. "I can imagine it rather perfectly. I'd have thought she was my perfect half, but she didn't feel the same. Now about your paper."

He leaned forward business like and Harper turned to shake her head at Bridget. She didn't want him to end up like this. She wanted him to be happy. He'd be happier *without* her and her madness. He'd be better off. Wouldn't he?

Of course, he would be.

"No," Bridget said. "The other half of your red thread isn't something you can leave and leave happy. Not ever. You *must* break the chains that bind you."

"But," Harper started. Life with her was *not* happiness. Not for anyone. It didn't matter what dream-Mr. Jueavas said, she did not shine. She was nothing.

"No," Bridget said flatly. Her voice echoed and it turned into a howl. A shrieking howl that dropped Harper to her knees and as she fell, she found time slowed from seconds to millennia and in those passing ages, she saw a thousand images.

Quinton standing next to the sea alone. He was broken inside, Harper didn't need to know what had happened to see he had been crushed. Something terrible had happened, and he was all alone.

Another flash and then another, and then Harper saw her sister, Scarlett, crying, bent over her knees, shaking with the force of those tears. She was crying so hard her whole body shook.

Another flash. Harper's head spun. And she saw Maeve running, looking behind her, face terrified.

"No!" Harper found the breath to shout, but she could do nothing and then there was another flash, another, another, another. She held her head as if she could somehow stop the barrage of visions.

But she couldn't. Another. Stars, make it stop! Make it stop. The baby Mom was carrying, alone in a cradle where no one was rocking her. She needed help and no one was there. Tears were rolling down her face, her skin was flushed in the fury of it, and the voice of that child was something Harper had never heard and yet instantly recognized it as if she'd always known it.

She whimpered with the next flash, trying to just squeeze her eyes tight and not see. But no. A flash. Another image. Another moment. Another horror. Ella and Luna holding hands and looking at something Harper couldn't see. Their eyes were wide, a tear was rolling down Ella's face while Luna was shouting. Harper needed to be there. To help them. To...anything.

She didn't just see the images though she felt the feelings. And the feelings, all at once. Too much. Harper was already on her knees, but she ended up face on the ground, in the snow that wasn't cold, hearing the howl of both the wind she couldn't feel, and the emotions that weren't hers.

"They need you," Bridget said, somehow her howling ghost voice sliding between the sounds of Harper's screams and the emotions ricocheting through her body. "They need you in these moments. They need you to *break the chains that bind you.*"

Harper clawed herself back to her knees, pounded by feelings she couldn't identify as hers or theirs. They needed her. They need *her* to help them. She pushed herself up to shaking feet. And as she did, she stepped forward and found herself facing her bedroom window. The sun hadn't risen yet, but as she looked outside she found fresh snow on the streets. There had been so many faces that had needed her, but there was one *she* needed the most.

She put on her jacket and her running shoes, realizing she was still wearing her running pants from the night before. She was grateful for small blessings because she was *not* waiting to change. She darted through the streets, where people were starting to move. She bypassed faces she knew, faces that nodded and called hello.

Harper avoided Mrs. Lovejoy who called after. As if she would stop for that old biddy. Harper bypassed Henna who Harper loved, but it didn't matter. Another needed her. Or maybe she needed another. Either way. She ran past the old-fashioned milkman who still delivered dairy products to half the town. She ran until she reached the bed and breakfast, and then she made her way through the back door, up the steps, and to his door.

Normally she had to gear up her courage to knock but not this time. She knocked and a mere moment later, Quinton opened the door.

"Hello," he said. His gaze was clouded. Or perhaps that was hers. She couldn't be sure.

"I'm sorry," she said.

He opened his arms to her and she threw herself into them.

"I'm so sorry," she whispered into his neck, wrapping herself around his body and hoping that he'd somehow burn away the chill that the ghost had left.

"Ok, he replied. "It's ok. I got you. Don't you know? I love you."

It hurt to say it for so many, many reasons. Because her fears weren't gone. Because she'd never said it to anyone who wasn't Scarlett or their mother. Because life had taught Harper that to love was to hurt, but she said it, "I love you."

She pulled back to see his face, to make sure he heard her, to try to see if he forgave her. She saw that he had but before she could say anything else, he was kissing her.

The End

Want to read more? This story is set in the world of the Mystic Cove Mysteries. You can read more of Harper and her family by checking out Bedtimes and Broomsticks.

ABOUT THE AUTHOR

Amanda A. Allen writes paranormal cozy mysteries including the Rue Hallow Mysteries, the Inept Witches Mysteries, and the Mystic Cove Mysteries. She also writes historical mysteries set in the 1950s with the Zinnia West Mysteries. She also has a new series coming out under the pen name, Beth Byers.

Amanda can be found in the Pacific Northwest with her four children, her sweet, tortured dog, and mounds of novels.

Follow Amanda Allen online:
Website
Facebook
Amazon
Newsletter

BREWING CHEER

SARA BOURGEOIS

SUMMARY

Brewing Cheer is story five in the Tree's Hollow Witches Series. Come along as Lenny and Jezebel find out what happened to their missing ghost roommate, Abby, and save Christmas for children all over the world.

CHAPTER ONE

The basement at Aunt Kara's bed-and-breakfast looked like something ripped from the pages of a horror movie, but I'd been assured that I would find everything I needed to decorate for the holiday down there. She said I could have anything I wanted for free, on the condition that I hauled her Christmas tree and the decorations for the inn upstairs before I left.

After an hour of searching, I found the holiday boxes. Fifteen minutes after that, I had ten boxes of Christmas decorations opened so I could root around in them.

"Which boxes can you take, and which ones do you have to haul upstairs for Kara?" Jezebel asked as she swished her tail back and forth impatiently. "I'm bored. Are we almost done here?"

"You know, you didn't have to come along," I said and pulled an eight-foot strand of gold garland from one of the boxes. "The ones over there are the ones she wants," I said and pointed toward a stack of boxes separate from the ones I was going through.

"Are you seriously going to take all of these home?" Jez asked.

"I don't know. That's why I'm going through them. If you're so bored, why don't you teleport home?"

"Nathan is trying to make a traditional Yule log cake because he lost some sort of bet at work, and the whole house smells like burnt flour," she said.

"Oh jeez. It's too bad we still haven't seen Abby. I'm sure she'd be willing to help," I said and looked through a stack of wall hangings. They looked like something that Aunt Kara used to hang on the walls when I was little. They probably were the exact same decorations.

"I know," Jezebel replied. "But what are you supposed to do when you have a missing ghost? It's not like we can file a missing person's report with Sheriff Stick-up-his-Butt Brad."

"We probably could, and don't be so hard on Brad. Esme told him again that she was a witch, and he seems to be taking it well this time around. But a fat lot of good it will do because he can't exactly use law enforcement techniques to find a missing ghost."

"There has to be something we can do," Jezebel said and jumped into a box that was only half full. I gave her the side eye. "What, lady? I'm a cat. We like boxes."

"Maybe if we just let Nate keep making horrible baked goods, it will draw her back from wherever she's gone off to," I said.

"Oh no. I can't deal with the house smelling of burnt food."

"You could go stay with Esme and the goat," I teased.

"Lady, you're pushing it."

"What about Calinda? I'm sure she'd let you hang out for a few days," I offered.

"She snores."

"I think I am going to take all of these. Whatever I don't use at home, I can take to work."

"I'm not helping you carry them to the car," Jezebel said, without leaving the box she was curled up in.

"I was hoping you'd teleport them," I said. "I can push them all together so they're touching and then you could zap them back to the house without even having to get out of that one."

"Fine," Jezebel said with a huff. "Just be careful. I'm comfortable in here. Don't jostle me."

I pushed the boxes together while Jez thoroughly cleaned her ears and whiskers. When I was done, she said, "Bon voyage, bit—" But she was gone before the rest came out.

There were five boxes I needed to carry up to the utility room for Aunt Kara. I hoped that she didn't need me to stick around and help put them up, but there was a new maintenance man hanging about. I assumed it would be his job.

"Where's my aunt?" I asked Lacey at the front desk.

"She had to go into town to get something from the hardware store."

"Okay, well, I'm going to take off then. The boxes she wanted are in the utility room."

"What about the ones you're taking?" Lacey asked.

I hadn't thought about the fact that someone might ask about the boxes when I'd had Jezebel poof them out for me. "I took them out through the cellar door. They're already loaded up in my Jeep," I said with a smile and then left before she could inquire further.

Back at home, Nathan was still in the kitchen, working on his seventh attempt at a Yule log cake. At least the house smelled slightly less like burnt food. Perhaps the sixth attempt had gone a little better.

"You should really just let me fix this one," I said. "A little magic never hurt anyone."

"Nope. Not going to do that. I can do this, Lenny. I'm not going to let a cake beat me."

"You mean the way Norma beat you at that bet?" I teased.

"Hush you," he said with a broad smile.

"You know, I'm still unclear as to what that bet was all about."

"It had something to do with old sofa cushions, plastic cups, and a semi-raging stream. That's all you need to know," he said. "But this cake is my way of redeeming my honor."

"Would you let Abby help you if she were here?" I asked.

"Hey, babe, I'm sorry she's gone AWOL on you. I know you guys miss her, and I wish we knew what happened, too," he said and turned to kiss my nose as I stood next to him at the counter.

"Well, if I can't help you bake, I'm at least going to start cleaning some of this up," I said and looked around at the disaster that was our kitchen.

"You don't have to do that," Nathan said. "It's my mess."

"Yeah, but my cleaning methods will be far less painful than you having to police this calamity by hand."

"Okay, Lenny. Thank you," he said and went back to his mixing bowl.

A few waves of my hands and the dishes were spotless. Once I'd floated them back into the cabinets, I danced around in circles while humming a toon, and the broom and mop waltzed with me.

"You are the cheesiest witch who ever lived," Jezebel said as she sashayed into the kitchen. "Seriously, how do you tolerate yourself?"

Instead of answering her, I swooped down and picked her up into my arms.

"Hey, lady, put me down," she groused as I held her against my chest, but I could feel her begin to purr.

I closed my eyes and snuggled her fur. When I opened them, we weren't in the house anymore.

"Hey, lady, what gives?" Jezebel asked, but she'd stopped trying to escape me.

"I don't know. Where are we?" I asked and hugged her tighter.

"We're not in Tree's Hollow anymore, Dorothy. That's for sure."

I looked around and had to blink when soft snowflakes hit my nose and eyelashes.

CHAPTER TWO

"What do we do?" Jezebel asked.

"I have no idea. I was hoping you had some idea," I said.

We were standing in the dark, but I could see lights from what looked like a village up ahead.

"Use magic. Cast a spell or something. That's what you do, right?" Jez said.

So I tried a transport spell. All it did is make it snow harder.

"What is that?" I asked.

"It's Christmas music."

"That's what I thought. I think I see a town ahead. Let's walk there."

"Ugh. Seriously?" Jezebel groused.

"Well, can you teleport us to it?" I asked.

Jezebel closed her eyes for a moment. She concentrated as hard as she could. Totally farted. "That wasn't me."

"Of course it wasn't," I said and began walking toward the warm glow of the mystery village.

"You should say excuse me," Jez said as she sprinted to catch up with me.

"You're working too hard to sell it," I said, so we walked a mile or so in silence.

"Have you noticed something?" Jezebel asked.

"Did you toot again?" I chuckled. I couldn't help myself.

"Ugh, you humans and your juvenile sense of humor. No. I'm talking about the weather."

"It's snowing," I said.

"Yeah, but look at how you're dressed."

"It's snowing, but it's not that cold. I'm definitely not dressed for winter weather, but I don't feel chilled."

"My feet aren't cold, either. This snow isn't snow temperature."

"Let's just keep going. We're almost to the town. I'm sure someone there can tell us what's going on," I said hopefully.

The closer we got to the village, the more I realized we were walking uphill. Jezebel seemed to handle it fine, but I was huffing and puffing by the time we stepped foot into the little town's square.

"There's nobody around," Jezebel said. "Where is everyone? This place looks like a ghost town, but the lights are all on."

"And that Christmas music is still playing," I said. "Maybe everyone is still eating dinner, or they are asleep. We don't have any idea what time it is."

"Oh hey, do you have your phone?" Jez asked hopefully.

"Right! I completely forgot to check."

I pulled my phone out of my pocket, and my shoulders immediately fell in defeat.

"What is it? What does it say? Can you call?" Jezebel's questions prodded me as I tried to make sense of what I was seeing.

"It says the time is purple," I said and turned the phone toward my familiar.

"I'm a cat, lady. I can't see in two dimensions."

"You can also teleport, so I thought maybe you could see phone screens."

"Well, I can't teleport here."

"Yeah, I know. Sorry. We should stop bickering and figure something out,' I said.

"The bakery looks like it might be open. Let's try going in there," Jezebel said.

The building with a bakery sign was catty-corner to where we stood on the far edge of the square. Since the snow wasn't cold, I decided to cut through the center.

About halfway across, the snow began to shake and something started to rise up out of it. I watched in morbid fascination as a fully formed snowman took shape before us.

The childish delight I felt took a frightening turn when the snowman's smile revealed a row of jagged, icy teeth. "You guys stumbled into the wrong village," it snarled at me.

The snow creature began to glide toward us on its round bottom.

"A freaking killer snowman. You've got to be kidding me!" Jezebel said, and to my surprise, she pounced on it.

"Jezebel, no." I called out and lunged at the thing.

When I tackled it, the snowman poofed apart and fell into a pile of snow on the ground. I took a few steps back, and to my dismay, the abominable snowman began to reform.

"Oh jeez. This could go on all night," Jezebel said.

"Well, what do we do?"

"Run," she called, and I did.

I couldn't help but ruminate on what he'd said about us picking the wrong town. It caused me to hesitate outside of the bakery's door.

The scent of fresh cinnamon rolls permeated the air outside. I turned around, and Frosty the Killer Snowman was still making his way toward us. Only this time, his ice teeth were twice as big as before.

"Open the door!" Jezebel shouted.

So I did.

CHAPTER THREE

I nside the bakery, the sounds of the Christmas music outside faded away, but they was replaced by the sound of a woman humming "Silent Night".

I turned around and saw the snowman standing at the door, staring at me. My eyes scanned the room, looking for something I could use as a weapon against a rabid snowman.

"Don't mind Larry." A woman's voice pricked my ears. "He's just a weirdo, but I'm sure he's harmless.

I watched as a large, older woman emerged from the back room of the bakery. She waved her hand at Larry, and his stick shoulders slumped as he turned and slid away.

"Come in. Come in." The woman said. Her voice was warm like honey, and the sound of it was soothing.

"We should go," Jezebel said flatly. "This place is wrong somehow.

I could see what she meant. The cards in front of the rows of baked goods were written in a strange, angular text. It didn't look like any modern language, and yet the woman behind the counter spoke English.

"Oh, a talking kitty. May I hold her?" the woman said and reached her hands out across the counter. "Would you like a sugar cookie, sweet kitty?"

The sound of her voice was too saccharine. I finally noticed that her smile didn't reach her eyes, and that her eyes looked less than human.

Until that moment, I'd wanted to stay. Even with the weird cards, I wanted to be there. The scent of cinnamon had needled its way inside of me, and I felt like melted butter.

"I think she's skittish because of the thing outside," I said and held Jezebel tighter. "I'm sorry, I'm going to hold her."

"Well now; that won't do," the woman said and leaped onto the counter.

She sat there, crouched on the counter over us, looking down. It looked as though she was ready to pounce at any moment.

As a low growled emanated from the baker woman, the bakery door flung open behind me. I spun around and a woman stepped through the door. It took me a moment to figure out who she was because the woman was no longer a ghost.

"Abby!!" I exclaimed and almost dropped Jezebel.

"Come on. Get out of here before she catches you," she said and held the door open.

When I turned around to look at the woman, she'd become a massive spider. But she wasn't just any spider. Her head was red, her body was green fuzz, and her legs were long and silver, like tree tinsel.

After letting out a loud yelp, I ran out the door and into the street. My head swiveled around as I furiously searched for the ravenous snow man.

"He's not here. The snowman. I tricked him into following me into a nearby stream. He can't reform. It will take him hours to figure it out," she said and motioned for us to follow her.

"Abby, you're alive," I said, stunned.

"Here, I am alive. I'm not sure exactly what is going on, but as long as I've been here, I've been a living person again."

"What is this place?"

"I'm not sure yet," Abby said. "I've only been here for a few days. I know it's not good though. Everything looks warm and inviting, but there is something very wrong bubbling under the surface."

"A few days? You've been gone at home for a lot longer than that. We had no idea what happened to you," I said. "You just disappeared one day and didn't come back."

"I don't remember exactly when it was, but one day while everyone was gone, there was a knock at the door," Abby said. "Usually I hide when that happens, just in case someone peeks in the windows. But for some reason, the curiosity about that visitor was overwhelming."

"What happened after that?" Jezebel asked.

"Well, I looked out the window and saw an old woman standing on the porch. She was wearing a tattered charcoal-colored coat and carried an old leather suitcase. Something about her drew me in, and when she looked at me and smiled, I went right out the window to her. The only problem was, when I passed through the glass, I was here."

"You were home alone? Where was Jezebel?" I asked and looked at the cat.

"Hey, lady, sometimes I like to go out for a walk. I'm an interdimensional being that's capable of teleportation; you can't expect me to stay in the house licking my butt all day."

I just stood there and stared down at her for a moment. Sometimes the things Jezebel said caught me so off guard that I didn't know how to respond. Abby began to laugh and so did I.

"So, none of us knows what this place is or how to get out," I said once we all quieted down.

"I've been exploring and watching as much as I could while I've been here. I think this is a magical village near the North Pole or something, but it's been corrupted. I haven't figured out by what. I think there is probably someone here who could send us back, but I can't find them," Abby said.

CHAPTER FOUR

"Do you have any idea where we should look first?" Jezebel asked.

"There's a hair salon a couple of doors down from the bakery. I think I saw a pair of scissors laying on the stylist's work bench that had a strange glow. We should get them," Abby said.

"Why?" Jezebel asked.

"I've seen a few items around town that have that same weird glow. For some reason, it feels like they are the key," Abby said.

"Okay. Are you sure you want to do this, Abby?" I asked. "You're alive. How many people get the chance to be alive again?"

"What choice do we have, Lenny?" Abby asked bravely, but I could pick up the hint of sadness in her voice. "At least if we get out of here, I can go home. I'll be with you guys again."

"Let's do this," Jezebel said and wiggled so that I'd put her down.

My familiar took the lead and Abby and I followed her two doors down to the salon. "How do we get in?" I asked no one in particular.

"Just try the door," Abby said. "This place is a small town too. I doubt too many people lock their doors, and I seriously doubt the creatures that have taken over this place thought to lock up."

I tried the knob, and sure enough, the door opened with a quiet pop. When I stepped inside, the air around me felt cold for the first time since we'd arrived in the strange place.

The three of us stepped into the dark salon in a single file line with Jezebel still in the lead. "It's cold in here," Jez said.

"You guys stay by the door. I'll grab the scissors. Don't let the door close," Abby said, and I wished we had time for me to ask her why we couldn't close the door.

As soon as Abby picked up the shears from the bench, the temperature in the empty salon dropped even more. I could see my breath and felt my teeth begin to chatter.

"Oh no," Jezebel said, and I looked up in time to see what had set her off.

It started with the salon chair in the back. Then, one at a time, all of the chairs began to spin in unison as if someone invisible stood behind each one and gave them a push.

The song "Here Comes Santa Claus" began to play, but there was something off about the music. It was too slow and the voice singing was low and had a strange metallic ting.

A huge, transparent penguin in a scarf and Santa hat emerged from the salon's back room. I started to smile and my spirits lifted because, for a brief moment, I thought we'd stumbled across an ally. That was until I saw the huge kitchen knife in the friendly penguin's hand.

I'm not sure how a ghost penguin could hold onto a real knife, but it had one. I wasn't in a position to ask questions.

"Abby, we've got to get out of here," I called, and she bolted toward the door.

We spilled out into the street and ran. I could hear the *plop whoosh* sound of the penguin waddle-chasing us. It would have been hilarious if not for the prospect of being stabbed to death in the world's spookiest Christmas village.

CHAPTER FIVE

"**F**ollow me," Abby called. "I know where we can hide, and it's the same place where can find the next object."

I had my serious doubts about whether there was any place we could actually hide, but if we needed another object, I was on-board.

"A cemetery," Jezebel snarked. "Really, Abby? After everything we've seen, you want us to go into a cemetery?"

"Well, there's a wreath in there. It has that same glow. We need it," she said as we all stood huddled at the graveyard entrance.

"A wreath in a cemetery? What?" I asked, mostly because I really didn't want to go in.

"Yeah, it's hanging on one of the graves. We have to get it. Try to stay as quiet as possible once we cross into the cemetery. Keep your eyes on that," she said and pointed at a lone mausoleum at the back end of the graveyard.

I took a step onto the road in front of me. Once I was on the other side of the gates, the silence was oppressive. I'd moved no more than six inches, but the Christmas music you could hear throughout the town had disappeared.

There must have been a layer of leaves on the ground under the snow because when Abby stepped off the road, there was a slight crunching sound that reverberated through the air. With that one tiny sound, fog began to roll across the snow toward us. It came from somewhere behind the mausoleum, but at the same time, it seemed to come from nowhere.

"We have to stick to the road until we're almost there," Abby whispered as quietly as she could.

The sound of her voice brought the fog faster and heavier. It was understood at that point that silence was the only way for us to stay safe.

I'd say that the most disturbing thing about the fog was that parts of it sparkled and it smelled of sugar cookies. Well, it almost smelled of cookies. Something about it was too sweet. It was sickly.

We tiptoed to the middle of the cemetery. Abby pointed down a row of head stones, and I could see a small wreath hanging on one of those shepherd's crooks next to a large black headstone. From our angle, I couldn't see what was written on the stone, but I could tell it was written in those same weird scratches I'd seen on the cards in the bakery.

In fact, when I looked around, all of the headstones had that same strange writing. Some of the stones had circles etched in them, and inside of the circles were carvings of what looked like they could have been humanoid form.

I tried to use silencing magic to keep my footsteps quiet as I crossed the snow to gather the wreath. It appeared that none of my magic worked. I pointed and indicated that Abby and Jezebel should wait on the road. The fewer of us walking on the snow, the quieter it would be.

The first tendrils of the fog were about to reach me as I crept to my target. The sickeningly sweet smell was almost overpowering. I held my nose with one hand, but then I could taste the slimy flavor on my tongue when I breathed through my mouth. It helped a little when I pulled my shirt up over the lower half of my face.

We were halfway back to the cemetery gates, after I'd acquired the wreath, when I heard the voice. "Leaving so soon?"

I didn't want to turn around, but I did. Behind us on the road was a large white bear with a razorback of longer white fur. Instead of speaking again, it opened its mouth and let out a deafening roar. The bear's gaping maw was filled with several rows of shark-like teeth.

"That's my wreath, little girls. Give it back and I'll bake you into some cookies." The bear chucked sinisterly when it realized its mistake. "Ooops. I mean, I'll bake you some cookies. Christmas cheer all around. If. You'll. Just. Give. Back. The. Wreath," it snarled.

"Run," I cried out and we crossed the threshold of the cemetery just before the bear caught us. I felt the puff of breeze its paw made when it took a swipe at the back of my head.

The bear sat down and watched us. Thankfully, it appeared to be trapped inside the confines of the graveyard. It waved at me when I turned around to look at it one last time.

"Can't wait for you to meet Clarence," it said. "He'll have a good time with the likes of you three."

CHAPTER SIX

"We need one more item," Abby said. "I saw one more thing glowing."

"Are you sure there's only one more?" Jezebel asked.

"I hope so," Abby said, but she wasn't confident.

"Well, where is it?" I asked. "Take us there. We've made it this far, and I'm ready to go home."

"A few streets over, there's an old mill. I saw the glow coming from inside, but I'm not sure what it is. You'll see it from the window."

As we made our way across the town, I began to get the feeling that hundreds of eyes were on us. Sometimes when I would look up at the windows, I thought I'd catch a flash of someone moving quickly away.

Whatever it was we were doing, we'd attracted the attention of the town. Yet none of them came out to offer us assistance. At first, I'd thought that everyone was evil, but in the quiet, I could sense their fear. The evil things we'd encountered were not the residents of the tiny village; they were the captors.

At the mill, we all lined up along one of the windows on the side of the building away from the road. I held Jezebel in my arms so she could peer inside as well.

It was easy to see that something deep inside the massive structure glowed, but I couldn't tell what it was either.

"I guess we should just go in. What else can we do?" I asked. "Let's find a door."

We walked halfway around the building and found a rusted metal door that banged against the frame in the breeze. "What are these items going to do anyway?" Jezebel asked.

"I have no idea," Abby said. "But they glow. I figured that had to be important. Plus, I've been here for days and it's the only sign I have that we can do anything to get out of here."

When we stepped inside, hundreds of strands of bright white Christmas lights switched on. They were strung everywhere from the ceiling and the walls. It was beautiful, but the light drowned out the glow from the object. My stomach churned with unease.

"We can't see the glow anymore.," I said with dismay. "How do we find it now?"

"I've just been sitting here," Jezebel said. "I haven't moved an inch. Follow me."

"Are you sure?" Abby asked, and I winced.

"Look, ghost lady, I said I haven't moved. What other options do we have?"

"You're right. Sorry, *kitty*." Abby enjoyed her little snark and I had to stifle a giggle. "Lead the way."

Jezebel led us through a doorway into a large room with a giant wooden spool in the center. The spool was turned on its side and functioned as a table. Our feet made a swishing sound against the dirty, dusty concrete floor.

The room had windows lining its outside walls, but they were all up near the ceiling. You couldn't see anything but tree limbs through them.

"Stay there," a woman's voice cried out from behind us.

I whirled around and saw an older woman wearing a red velvet dress and matching hat. Both the dress and hat were trimmed in white fur.

"That's her," Abby said. "That's the woman that rang the doorbell. She's dressed differently, but I know it's her."

"I'm sorry, dear. I shouldn't have taken you the way I did, but we needed a witch. I couldn't take a witch without Tinkerton noticing, so I took you. We needed your friend's help."

"Did someone say my name?" A tiny voice emerged from the center of the room.

"You're done," the woman in red said. "We've got a witch to help us."

"Oh, Mrs. Claus, that's sweet. But you see, I knew what you were up to. That witch can't do anything to help you. But she and her little friends can be your newest companions." An elf stepped forward. In his hand was a snow globe with a green glow.

"That's it. The elf has the last object," Abby said hopefully.

"Haha. Silly ghost. This globe is the only object. The others were just to keep you busy. Well, it was actually more for my amusement. I had fun watching you guys run all over town collecting things. Unfortunately, none of that junk can help you."

"Does he have any magic other than that globe?" Jezebel asked.

"Why?" Mrs. Claus looked perplexed.

"Just go with me here, Lady Santa," Jezebel said.

"Well, he can create toys, but that's about it."

Jezebel crouched down. She stared at the elf before us, and I watched as her pupils dilatated. Jez waggled her butt just before yelling, "Attack!"

She sprinted at the elf and jumped onto his head. Abby and I ran over to him, but we stayed back as Tinkerton thrashed and hollered. He could not get Jezebel off of his head and keep hold of the snow globe.

It crashed to the floor.

CHAPTER SEVEN

S uddenly, we were all standing in the living room. Nathan stood there with a Yule log cake in his hands and his mouth agape.

"Well, dears. If I'd known that all we had to do was break that little twerp's snow globe, I'd have pounded his little self right into a shelf days ago," Mrs. Claus said.

"I got the cake right," Nathan said, and it was obvious he was in shock.

"Well, that explains why you guys finally showed up. Something quite magical about getting one of those things right," Mrs. Claus said with a wink.

"Who are you?" Nathan asked, still dumbfounded. "Abby?"

"I'm Mrs. Claus. I had to borrow your friends for a while. A rogue elf imprisoned everyone in North Pole Village when he didn't get the promotion he thought he deserved. It's a long story. Suffice to say that your friends are heroes to all of the little boys and girls who will get their Christmas gifts on time this year."

"Abby looks funny," Nate said.

We turned around and looked, and sure enough, Abby was still alive. I couldn't believe my eyes.

"Oh yes," Mrs. Claus began. "About that. I have a little magic of my own now that I'm not trapped in that wretched globe. I thought as a reward for you saving us all, we'd give your friend the greatest gift of all."

"Life?" I asked.

"Well, that too," Mrs. Claus said with a chuckle. "Most importantly, I've given her a second chance."

Want to read more? Click <u>here</u> to find other books by Sara Bourgeois.

ABOUT THE AUTHOR

Sara Bourgeois is a Midwesterner through and through. She spends her time writing, reading, and herding cats.

Follow Sara Bourgeois online:
    Facebook
    Newsletter
    Start the Tree's Hollow Witches series from the beginning here: www.amazon.com/dp/B074J9B2CN

FELIZ NAVIDEAD

PEARL GOODFELLOW

SUMMARY

Christmas week 1957. It's Santa week in Gothic Harbor, and Chimera Opal and her back-chatting cats should be having fun. But a case of a local missing man, **his** dead wife, and **her** grieving sister soon put an end to the festivities. Tasked with finding the dead woman's husband, Chimera and the Infiniti uncover dark family secrets that are best taken to the grave. Because someone is up to SnoW good.

Can the crew unravel this triangular mystery and make it back to Glessie Isle on time for the cat's Christmas salmon dinner? The kitties are praying for a Christmas miracle.

CHAPTER ONE

"**B**ut why are we picking them if they're illegal?" Gloom asked from her woolly spot on the passenger seat. My female cat had won the 'Shotgun' contest as soon as I had mentioned to my furry gang of eight that we were traveling to Bonemark Isle.

I turned to my kitty. I could just make out the inky-blackness of her nose amid the jumble of the hat, scarf, and mittens I'd tossed on the seat earlier.

"We have the permit, honey. We're golden," I said, waving the official document in the air between us. "Talisman approved," I added, hoping I'd hear no more on the matter. Gloom's something of a naysayer. But she couldn't help being *her* any more than I could help being *me* so I mostly ignored her grumblings.

"But, why so close to Christmas?" My kitty pressed. "How are we going to get back to Glessie Isle in time for you to prepare the salmon?" She pulled her head back into the tangle of cashmere, and muttered: "We're gonna end up eating cat food, I know it."

"I heard that," I said, giving Gloom a sideward glance. "And, let's not forget, immortal and ...uh....talkative or not, you are, in fact, a *cat*."

"No salmon?" Shade's head appeared between the two front seats.

431

He flattened his ears. "Did I hear that right? We're not getting our Christmas fish for Christmas dinner on Christmas day?"

I glimpsed his crestfallen face in the rearview, and my hands gripped the steering wheel until my knuckles paled. I knew what was coming next. Shade would wake the others. And, for the purposes of this story, I really had no intention of unleashing my animals on you in one overwhelming torrent.

Apologies, and strap yourselves in.

"Nope, nope, nope. Who says we're not getting salmon for Christmas dinner? That right? Is it, yep?" Jet's staccato vocals ricocheted around the small car. His black face squeezed into the gap between the driver and passenger seat next to Shade. Jet's eyes expanded, and he swerved his pupils out to the side of each of his eyeballs so he could pin both Gloom and me with an accusing glare.

"Guys, there's been no mention of you *not* getting—" I started.

"You're giving us c-cat food? For *Christmas*? Isn't that like animal cruelty or something?" Fraidy popped up directly behind me. My cat's bottom jaw fell so low it came to rest on top of my head. His horrified face was submerged under the red cyclone of my curls almost immediately.

"If you'd let me fin —" I tried again.

"I feel like I've awoken to a Dickensian nightmare," Eclipse said, his chin plopping onto Shade's head. The most cryptic of my eight cats, Eclipse's expression was passive. He returned my mirrored stare with a pair of neutral black and golden eyes. "Please, ma'am, may I have some more cat-gruel?" He finished.

Whether he was being flippant or highly intuitive was anyone's guess.

"See what you've started?" I said, turning to the lump-in-the-scarf next to me. I noticed Gloom's lips curl into a crafty smile just before she pulled my hat over her head.

Checking the rearview again, I only counted four heads. Good. Onyx, Carbon and Midnight were still sleeping. Maybe I could contain the situation while I had just five of the Infiniti to deal with.

"I'm cold," Carbon's disembodied voice declared.

My shoulders slumped.

We'd just left the Glessie-to-Bonemark ferry and were now road-tripping along Bonemark Isle's southern shores, about to head north-ward. Not toward Femur, the capital, though, but, instead, toward a snug little coastal town where we were to hole-up for a couple of days.

Ordinarily, I'd have flown us across from Glessie by broom, but the skies over the Sea of Mages in December weren't exactly a cozy thor-oughfare. Besides, there's no way I'd have exposed Carbon to these wintery elements. I'd never hear the last of it. On top of that, Bone-mark had a strict 'no travel magic' policy. Even though the isle was inhabited entirely by folks from both the paranormal and magical communities, Bonemark's entry requirements were wholly pedestrian.

It was supposed to be a fun weekend getaway; a pre-Christmas break in a cozy cottage by the sea, on the most northerly of our island chain. This 'chain' is our home, and our little 'plot' lies at the southern end of the archipelago: Glessie Isle.

Snowflakes with the size and grace of monarch butterflies fluttered silently around the car as I rounded into the northbound road. Like so many intricate petals, the flakes of snow danced along the black serpentine highway before us. The scene was so beautiful as to be almost magical.

The sparkly spectacle momentarily silenced the cats.

"Neat, neat. Yep. We're gonna catch us some of those, right boss? Yep, yep." Jet's paws pummeled the window in a mock exercise for some upcoming snowflake-hunting.

"Why'd you think I brought you guys out here, buster?" I asked, grinning at my cat via the rear view. "Snow's one of the only things you'll leave the house for, Jetpack."

Jet was an agoraphobe. He left the house rarely, and only if he was under the influence of a good dose of catnip. Catnip gave my zippy kitty confidence.

I swept a glance at my backseat passengers and felt my heart squeeze a little. The thought of them bouncing, leaping, pouncing and tearing through the snow brought me more than a little warmth. The Infiniti LOVED snow.

Which is why I brought them on this trip. A two-for-one deal in that I'd get to harvest the Stillbreath, and my moggies would get to cavort in mounds of the cold powdery stuff. It was a win-win. They just didn't realize it yet.

Gloom spoke: "Snow's peachy, I'll admit. And I've no doubt I'll look swell against this white background." To the window, she swept a paw across the snow-covered fields to our right and then busied herself with re-forming her bed of scarf and hat. She stopped in mid arrangement. "But, we're risking losing our dinner for dirty old mushrooms?" Gloom wrinkled her nose and went to work washing a glossy patch of resplendent fur. *Must be the fish oils.*

"My dear sister, Chimera has brought us to Bonemark so we can assist her with the harvest of a rather incredible specimen of fungus. The Stillbreath toadstool is one of the most talked about mushrooms among mycology enthusiasts today. Originating in the Precambrian ..."

Onyx was awake.

Shade's ears rotated. "I feel a nap comin' on," he said through a gaping yawn.

Unaware and unperturbed, Onyx, the self-appointed president and scholar of my clatch of kitties, continued. "... so, of course, the Stillbreath has many diverse applications. However, its high toxicity level, and, well, let us say, its more *unsavory* uses, has led to strict regulation of both its application and distribution. These days the toadstool is mostly used for --"

"*Death Magic?*" Eclipse interrupted, piercing Onyx with his unreadable gaze. Other than the sound of Fraidy's chattering teeth, a heavy silence fell over the car.

"'Clipsy! Enough of that now," I cautioned.

"W-what is death magic?" Fraidy squeaked.

"It's a spell the Warlocks used on innocent witches and wizards in WWI," Eclipse said. "The Warlocks cast Death Magic over no fewer than two-hundred and eighty-four souls."

"S-so it ... " Fraidy gulped. "...killed them? This D-Death Magic made these people dead?"

"No, it was far dirtier than that," Gloom said, her voice taking on a low pitch. "The Warlocks didn't *kill* them. Death Magic makes it *look* like someone's dead. But, all the hex really does, is slow down the victim's metabolism to an unreadable level." Gloom stared at her timid brother. "It's not hard to pronounce someone dead if they have no vital signs."

"But.. but... what's so dirty about that? Making people *look* dead seems much friendlier than making them dead." Fraidy pressed.

Onyx sighed. "I regret to further your agitation, dear brother, but the Warlocks were never charged for the murder of these poor souls. The Wizard Council for Burials, on the other hand, was charged with manslaughter."

Fraidy's eyes widened, then bulged, then squeezed shut. "Please don't tell me that the good guys buried their own good guys ....a-alive?"

Onyx placed a paw on Fraidy's shoulders. "As our beloved sister just said: The Warlocks pulled a lascivious and dirty move."

Fraidy started to sway.

"Ice it, guys," I said. "Death Magic has been outlawed for over a century now. The crime you're talking about was the last known case, in fact. Besides, no warlock or Big Daddy wizard can just waltz into a Sillbreath field and start picking. These toadstools are stringently regulated these days." I grabbed the consent form once more, and this time shook it in front of my cat's faces. "The 'go-ahead' is right here. A medicinal application permit. We're allowed to harvest twelve grams of the fungus so I can formulate a compound for anxiety and stress. No Death Magic in sight, capiche?"

Carbon's sleepy face popped up in the mirror. "If this car gets any colder then we won't *need* Death Magic to kill us off," he grumbled. "Think you can crank the heat a little, Chimera?"

I pretended to turn the heating dial. The car already felt like a toaster oven, but my fire-loving cat needed to see that I was taking action on his behalf.

"Who are these 'shrooms for, anyway, boss-lady?" Shade asked, headbutting Carbon's face away from the center position.

"I'm preparing a formula for Portia Fearwyn. *Saint John's Wort* isn't cutting it, so I need something stronger." I raised the permit for the third time. "Hence the *Stillbreath*. Because these toadstools aren't just used for evil deeds. They can also help slow down respiration and most other metabolic bodily processes. Portia's panic attacks will almost certainly reduce in frequency and intensity with a little help from these 'stools."

I might be a witch -- a proficient one, at that -- with eight talking cats, but I'm also a practicing herbalist. And I took my work at The Angel, my apothecary, with compassionate seriousness. I'm not kidding...my clients' well-being is at the top of my business plan. The 'spiky' Portia Fearwyn might be an at-arm's-length-friend, but she was suffering. By preparing this formula using Stillbreath's, I fully intended to help cushion the Witch Fearwyn's strife somewhat.

I turned the car left, this time onto a gravel road. The snow continued to fall, covering the lane in a snuggly blanket of bedazzling white.

"Guys?" I said. "Can we stop with all this death talk now? Can't we just all try to have a happy couple of days?" I couldn't keep the pleading out of my voice.

My cats said nothing, but I got a silent nod of furry heads from the seven conscious ones.

A small hand-painted sign came into view. Through the plump snowflakes, I could just make out the words. In black painted Gothic styled script: Gothic Harbor 12 miles. Our destination, and where Foxley Cottage, our rented home for the next two nights awaited us.

CHAPTER TWO

"Huh?" Gloom said, raising her paws to the window and swiveling her head. "There isn't a mountain in sight, so why would there be a risk of...."

My front-seat kitty peered at the curious 'warning' sign as we rounded the last bend. I shrugged at the crude depiction of snow tumbling helter-skelter down a mountain. I looked around at the low lying landscape.

"Weird," I whispered.

Without notice, and out of nowhere. And, I mean *nowhere*, the fields on our right gave way to a stand of perilously high peaks. Four giant sentinels of sheer rock face loomed over our passage. We gawped at the drifts of snow, fathoms deep, as it overflowed from the mountains' geographical scars and gullies. And then we noticed the flashing red and blue lights through the curtain of windblown snow. The cruiser's door opened, and a man with the bulk and gait of a mainland moose lumbered to the middle of the road and presented a giant palm to us.

I understood the man's implied 'stop' signal and brought the car to a somewhat sliding standstill before the uniformed man.

"Keep quiet, guys," I cautioned my kitties. I rolled down the window just as Officer Moose ducked down to parlay with me.

"Going somewhere, ma'am?"

Strange question.

"Yes, I am, officer," I offered. "We're heading to Gothic Harbor right now. Is there a problem?"

The man chewed gum the way I imagined a moose would chew on a water-reed.

"Sergeant, ma'am," he said, flashing his badge. "Sergeant Donkerton at your service." He squinted at me and poked his head inside the window. "These your cats?"

This one's sharp.

"They are indeed."

"I have one myself. Piece of work."

"I empathize. Sergeant Donkerton, is there a reason you stopped me?"

He stopped chewing, pulled a folder from underneath his arm. He rustled through the contents and plucked something from the file.

"Seen this man, ma'am?" Donkerton thrust a photo in my face. It was one of those *magi-motion* images, taken from a camera that snapped not just the split-second moment, but also the following three seconds after shooting. The *magi-motion* was Warlock tech, and there was currently nothing else like it on the market in the Wizarding community. I gazed at the image in motion. A man with silvery blond hair stood next to a conservatively dressed woman with pinned up hair and a stern face. I noticed the chilly looking gap between the pair immediately. The man was wearing a forced smile as the photographer captured the moment. Then the following three seconds played out. The man in the image turned his head to look behind him. Only two other people were clearly visible in the background of the photo. One was a woman in a satin cerulean blue dress that I'd have cheerfully killed for. Her chestnut hair fell in glossy waves over her right shoulder. Her head was thrown back in laughter. I imagined her laugh to sound rich and infectious.

"Nice rags," Gloom breathed, studying the woman's beautiful gown. I nodded and then moved my attention to the other person in the background. A man. He was squinting in the direction of the missing man and his dour-faced companion. Once the picture had been snapped, and the missing man turned his head. However, the background man turned on his heel rather sharpish and left through a back exit. *Interesting.*

Donkerton cleared his throat, reached into the car and tapped the man in the foreground of the image. "This is the missing person, ma'am," he explained. "Leland Clavelle."

I passed the photo back shaking my head at the same time. "Sorry, officer, I don't know this man, and I haven't seen him. This is my first visit to Gothic Harbor, so I've no idea how I could be any help to you."

"What brings you to our town?"

"I'm picking mushrooms," I replied, beginning to feel a little impatient.

"Mushrooms? Stillbreath toadstools?" Donkerton asked, his eyes narrowing.

"The very ones," I said.

"You work with the deceased?" *The deceased?*

"I beg your pardon, Sergeant?"

Donkerton produced the image again, this time tapping his finger above the face of the scowling woman in the foreground.

"The deceased," he repeated, offering nothing more.

"N .. no, I don't even know who this wom—"

"You have a permit for the Stillbreath's ma'am?" He asked, whisking away the image once more. Gloom pawed the permit onto my lap and I handed it to the sergeant. He scanned the document and handed it back almost immediately.

"Thanks for your time, ma'am. I won't take any more of it. I hope you enjoy your stay in G.H. It's Santa Week, so I'm sure you'll have a whole lotta fun. The kids love it." Placing his hands on his hips, he added. "If you spot Mr. Clavelle in your travels, please give the local station a call. I'll be back in town once my officer takes over for me here."

I nodded. "How long has Mr. Clavelle been missing, Sergeant?"

"Three days now, as it happens," Donkerton replied, turning back toward me.

"Well, that doesn't seem like a terribly long time for --"

"Didn't show up for his wife's funeral three days ago, ma'am. Believe me, there's a cause for concern, considering Lelan was seen readyin' himself for the burial just the day before, 'n' all."

"Readying?"

"Yep, drowning his sorrows at the pub just the night before his wife's funeral. Plus, Clavelle had been spendin' heaps for fancy floral arrangements at Nosegay's -- that's the florist in town, ma'am -- for Stella's service. Now, what kind of man would just up an' vanish after takin' care to get his wife the most expensive wreaths this side of the Mainland?"

"Oh. Quite."

"We'll find him, don't you worry about that. Nobody goes missing under Donkerton's nose and get's away with it," he said, pushing his hips forward.

"His wife .... That's the woman standing next to him in the--"

"Stella Blazier," the Sergeant confirmed. "Found in a snow drift just outside her estate five days ago. Came off her filly and damned well froze to death. Looked like this when we found her:" Donkerton's face contorted into a sudden and grotesque mask of terror; eyes like saucers, mouth cranked open in a mute scream. He snapped his jaw shut. "Terrible thing. Terrible." The sergeant shook his head. "Well, I'll let you get on. Careful of the Four Horsemen there. They look about ready to drop their load," he said nodding to the rock giants before us. "There's no way in and no way out if they do."

"Thank you, Sergeant," I said. "I'll be careful." I moved to roll up my window, but couldn't resist calling out to the officer. "Sergeant Donkerton, if you don't mind me asking, how long do you intend to lay in wait here?"

"Been a man here since the funeral, ma'am. Nobody's crossed here from inside or outside since then, at least. Course, Mr. Clavelle could have wandered out of town the night before his wife's service, but unlikely. Anyway, I reckon I'll keep it up until the Horsemen do their work. Like I said before; ain't nobody getting in or out of G.H once those boys drop their cargo." Donkerton squinted at the Four Horsemen, turned on his heel and lurched back to the comfort of his cruiser.

I wound up the window. Seven cats stared at me, their mouths ajar.

I shrugged. "Well, that was weird," I said with practiced nonchalance. My stomach, however, erupted into its very own bee-bop-hop. A mystery! I LOVED puzzles!

The cats continued to stare.

"What?" I asked.

"Why are you pretending that you are a person who isn't about to go snooping?" Eclipse said.

A reasonable question, I guess.

"You *do* love the mysteries, boss-lady," Shade said. " You thinkin' about pullin' an Agatha?" while we're here?"

"Missing cats and missing persons are hardly in the same league," Gloom opined.

She had a point. My mystery-solving career, thus far, was limited to reuniting lost pets with their distraught owners. But, still, I had had to unravel a host of clues before finding the wandering animals. I did it for fun, and because I didn't like the idea of a lost and confused domesticated pet. But there was something more. It was the act of *connecting* the puzzle pieces that thrilled my soul. I felt that familiar tingle now.

"Well, I ...well, what would it hurt to help out the Sergeant by asking a few well-placed, and discreet questions, right?"

"It would appear there's a good possibility that you'll be working alone on this missing person's case, Chimera," Onyx said.

I raised a reflected pair of questioning brows at my sage cat.

"Sergeant Donkerton is co-ordinating his surveillance efforts on entirely the wrong side of the mountain pass. If there's an avalanche, the sergeant will be trapped on the other side." Onyx concluded.

"Yep, yep, ol' sargie there wasn't too bright, nope?" Jet babbled.

I thought of turning back. To share this pertinent factoid with the sergeant. But, I didn't. I pressed the gas pedal and crept slowly forward instead. We started our journey past the Four Horsemen.

Fraidy pointed to a cornice of whipped snow the size of an oil tanker. It was nothing more than a cantilevered snow-shelf, held in place on just one side of its bulk.

"H-how does it stay up there?" My timid cat asked.

"It doesn't," Gloom said. "Or, I should say: it *won't*."

"Yeah, I don't trust 'em, either," Shade said, peering at the icy arrangements. "These drifts look like they're about to start a cascade-crusade to ruin our parade." Midnight tapped my shoulder. "Time to agitate the gravel, boss," I nodded and accelerated. Thank the Goddess I had the snow-chains put on before we left.

The car sped up; nothing crazy, just a little *zip* so we could get out of Avalanche Alley as soon as possible.

"What's going on?" I heard rather than saw the last of my eight cats show up to the party. Midnight squeezed his face between Carbon's and Shade's. "Where are we? Was I napping?"

I smiled in the rearview at Midnight. "Hi, handsome," I said. "Sleep well?"

"Out like a light," Middie confessed. "Where are we?" He leaned over and pressed his fuzzy face to the window.

"Just about to escape Death Row," Gloom quipped, flicking her tail toward the mountains with their loads of icy murder.

We held our collective breath as we crept past the outer edge of the last Horseman. We then shared a group sigh just as an avalanche worthy of the history books made its tumultuous descent down the mountain. The car shook as the weight of the falling snow gained power. We must have really been on one another's wavelength because this time we let out a communal gasp as we watched the white stuff land in an immense pile not thirty feet behind the car. Midnight was the first to the back window. His ears twitched, and his tail snaked in twisty excitement as he surveyed the scene. "Woah! That's gotta be the size of an oil tanker!"

I cringed. The questions would come now.

"So, is this *really* the only way in and out of town?" Gloom stared at me, her jaw square.

"I ...I don't know, honey. The sergeant seemed to think so. And, we can't use magic to get out of here..." My words trailed off. I ran my fingers through my hair. "It wasn't something I looked for when I booked this place. It just wasn't."

"I can melt it away," Carbon said, sitting up taller. "Don't worry, sis, we'll have salmon in our bellies, for sure." My fire-starting kitty looked pretty satisfied with himself.

"Carbs," I said. "You can't use your fire, honey. It's considered magic. Not only is it not permitted, but the protective wards at the town's exit points will make it impossible, anyway. Nobody's magicked their way in or out of Bonemark for at least a century."

"Oh .... Oh, swell," Shade whispered. He sounded on the brink of tears. "So, we're having cat food for Christmas dinner, then."

"Shade, sweetness. It's too early to say --"

"Yeah, sure. Merry freakin' CAT FOOD, and goodwill to all m..." It was too much for him. My Romeo cat's voice cracked, and he retreated to the back seat completely beaten. I watched him topple under the weight of his cruel and hopeless life.

Gloom turned her rear to me, pushed her head under my scarf until her whole face was obscured.

"Aw, c'mon, guys, Whatever we eat or don't eat for dinner, isn't the whole point of Christmas that we have one another?" I swiveled my head toward my backseat cats. They sat like loaves of bread in a row; mute and unimpressed. "We're with each other, and that's what counts, right? We're here *with* each other and *for* each other. What could be more meaningful?"

My cats said nothing, but if they thought I couldn't hear their low rumbling purrs over the engine, the gravelly road, and the squishy sound of the snow tires, they were mistaken.

CHAPTER THREE

W e pulled up in front of Foxley Cottage just as the day's light folded into dusk. Deep blues and purples, like violent bruises, unfurled and stretched into ever-darkening realms. We still had to pick up the keys from the landlady of this slum: Iris Crimple. Iris owned the only pub in Gothic Harbor, but seeing as we had to pass our cottage first, I thought it'd be the perfect diversion for getting the cats excited about our stay. I checked the map to make sure we were in the right place. And swallowed. Hard.

"You have to be kidding me," Gloom said, standing on two paws on my lap, her face pressed against the window to better analyze the dilapidated dwelling. I have to say, on first glance, Foxley Cottage didn't seem to live up to its description in the brochure. The filthy windows did little to cover the even dirtier net curtains hanging askew inside the peeling frames. The roof, sagging in the middle, was a patch-work of mismatched shingles and seemed to be attracting a lot of the local wildlife. Namely, pigeons who were busy settling in for the night.

Yuk.

My stomach knotted.

"Boss, we stayin' *here?*" Shade asked. His tone told me that he didn't really believe it.

I glanced at the brochure again, scanning for something charming; something to lift this place from the apparent flea-pit it was. I could see a sliver of the harbor at the rear of the house; liquid moonlight kissing its velvety surface. A beam of warm light swept across the scene.

"Look! We have views of the harbor and the lighthouse over there on Codders point," I said, getting out of the car. The cats followed me, while I tried to find any other delightful aspects of the house in the brochure.

"Oh, and, wait, it says here there are also splendid views over Silent Meadows. Sounds nice, right?" I didn't wait for an answer; I was already trudging through the snow to the back of the cabin so I could see Silent Meadows in the 'flesh.'

The cats kept quiet and tailed me, leaping through the snow, sure, but not really seeming to enjoy it as much as they normally did.

"Looks like where we were born," Eclipse muttered as we passed the side of the dwelling.

"Aww, see?" I turned to 'Clipsy, smiling. "That's nice, yes? That it reminds you of your birthplace?" My pace picked up, and I started whistling. Maybe my kitties wouldn't be too difficult about this situation, after all.

"We were born eight hundred years ago, though." Carbon warned me. "Home comfort wasn't a concern back then. It was more about cold and dirty dwellings infused with plague, cholera and blackwater fever." His caution delivered, Carbie trotted ahead of me. The other kitties followed him.

I walked on, rounding the corner of the house. My cats, all in a row, stood in the snow staring forward. I followed their gaze.

Oh, please, Goddess, no.

"Well, ain't this special?" Midnight quipped. "Ladies and gents, I present to you: *Silent Meadows*," he said, offering a deep bow while flinging one paw out toward the cemetery in front of us.

"Nope, nope, nope." Jet said. "And, nope, nope again." He paced on the spot.

"Chimera, do you think there's perhaps been an oversight?" Onyx asked with his usual politeness. "Could this be the groundsman's abode?"

"I don't think so, O. I booked 'Foxley Cottage.' And, *this* is Foxley Cottage."

"Great," Shade said, his voice cracking again. "A Christmas of cat food and corpses."

Fraidy buried his face into his two front paws and swung his head left and right in a flagrant display of a cat who feels he is doomed.

"Fresh dead too," Gloom said, pointing to a recently shoveled mound of earth sitting in between a couple of cracked tombstones.

"What an exquisite nightmare," Onyx muttered.

"C'mon guys, let's go and pick up the keys," I said. What else could I do? I'd already booked and paid for this horror show, and despite my reluctance to get inside, it had to be better than standing in the snow looking at the *outside*. I turned and began the short journey back to the car.

"W-wait!" Fraidy's voice was so high-pitched so as to be nearly inaudible. "I think I just saw something," he said, his head cocked toward the graveyard. I peered over Fraidy's head, training my eyes over the assortment of haphazard headstones. Too dark. I saw nothing and was about to turn again when the beam from Codders Point lighthouse made its sweep and bathed the area in a brief burst of light.

"There!" Midnight shrieked, pointing to the fresh mound of dirt.

I trained my eyes to the spot Middie was indicating and saw a flash of movement. It was low to the ground. Strike that, it appeared to be *on* the ground. I saw what looked like an arm fly up from the pile of earth, and then dive down again. The beam of light passed, plunging the scene into darkness once more. I blinked, unsure of what I'd just witnessed.

"We're all going to die here," Fraidy rasped. "Eaten by zombies."

"Oh, hush, now, honey," I whispered, picking my scaredy-cat up and tiptoeing closer to the cemetery to see if I could spot any more movement. Fraidy forced his small head into the pit of my arm.

"Say, boss, you think that's the grave of the deceased? Stella Blazier?" Shade asked, moving to my side.

"I don't know, chum," I said. "Let's get a closer look." Fraidy stiffened in my arms, but he remained quiet.

The lighthouse beam came in for another orbit.

"Yep. Zombie on the move, yep, yep," Jet jabbered.

I cast my head right, and just caught a glimpse of something or someone hurdling the low wall of the graveyard. A breeze picked up, and in the distance, what seemed like a veil of hair, as long as your arm, fluttered in the wind for a moment before disappearing over the wall. A glimmer of unearthly blue was the last thing I glimpsed before the beam of light retreated once more.

Arms swinging, I trudged toward the cemetery.

"And, she's off," Gloom said, shaking her head.

"Don't you want to find out what's going on?" I said over my shoulder.

My kitties said nothing, but I heard the soft crunch of snow as they followed behind me.

Stepping up to the fresh grave, I instructed Jet and Carbon to look over the wall; the last place we saw movement. I bent down to study the earth. It seemed a little flattened. As if something or someone had been lying on top of it. Maybe a grieving mourner had come to say their last goodbye and had desperately embraced the earth that held their loved one? But, other than that, there was no gaping hole, nor any evidence of a zombie uprising. I was about to stand up when the lighthouse's beacon highlighted a glint in the earth pile at my feet. With one hand, I fumbled in the dirt to excavate the shiny object. "What is it?" Midnight asked, standing on his hind legs for a better view.

"A bracelet." I brushed off the clods of soil from the gilded jewelry piece. "Wait, there are some initials engraved here. I held the bracelet up to the lighthouse, waiting for its glimmer to illuminate the engraving. The inscription was too delicate, and the beam too quick, however.

"Carbie, come over here. I need fire," I instructed my kitty. Carbon ambled over, already clicking his paws together to produce a flame. I bent down to his level so his furry hand could illuminate the jewelry. The initials 'A.B.' Nothing more, nothing less.

"Well, if this is Stella's grave, this isn't Stella's bracelet," I said, showing my furry companions the initials.

"You think someone was trying to get in," Eclipse said, sitting bolt upright on top of a nearby headstone.

"Doubt it, 'Clipsy," I confessed. "Who'd wanna do something like that? What we saw ... it could have been a trick of the light, I guess. And, this soil ..." I said, looking down at the patted-down earth. "Maybe the undertakers just flattened it with their shovels?"

"Doesn't explain the bracelet," Gloom said looking directly at me.

"No, it doesn't ... but there's no other real proof to suggest --"

"I believe I may have found an acceptable quantity of evidence here," Onyx called out from the end of the grave. "Observe." He pointed a furry paw to the snow; to the fresh tracks that lay there. Footprints. Medium sized. Could be male or female. They led to where Midnight stood guard at the wall.

"That's the good thing about snow, huh, boss?" Shade asked, staring, first at the tracks, then me. "It don't hide no dirty-deeds." He finished.

"Also worth noting is the lack of precipitation covering the new grave," Onyx opined. "It's been snowing here since we arrived. It appears there is no evidence of it on this, ahem, resting place."

All heads swerved to the grave. My cat's observation was right. It also made me feel completely stupid. How did I not notice that?

Getting too excited, Chimera. Breathe. Slow down.

"Hrmph, mmmph, harumph!" Fraidy said from under my arm. I understood it to mean "Let's get the hell out of here."

I agreed with my kitty. "Middie, c'mon, let's go," I said, turning to my cat guarding the wall. "We can pick up those tracks later." But, Midnight wasn't there.

"Carbs?" I said, wheeling around to my flame-throwing cat. Carbon had beaten me to it; he had his lit paw aloft, waddling on three legs toward the low stone wall.

In the glow of Carbon's claw, I saw the outline of Middie's head atop the rock fence. He was digging for something amid the stones.

"Midnight, what have you found, honey?" I said, moving toward my night-wandering cat.

Middie's head swiveled toward me. "Just .....*this*," he said, hooking a small piece of fabric with his claw. He held it up to Carbon's fire so we could all see. "Looks like the wall snagged a piece of our grave-loving friend's dress," he said.

Gloom gasped. "Give me that," she demanded, snagging the satiny scrap from Midnight's outstretched paw. My female kitty held up the material against her black fur and twirled in the snow. "How do I look?" she asked, with a coquettish smile on her face. Something about the fabric swatch bothered me, and once Gloom stopped parading on her snowy runway, I noticed what it was. It looked an awful lot like the material of the dress the woman in the background of Sergeant Donkerton's picture wore. I snatched it from Gloom and inspected it. Silk. And if the light wasn't playing tricks, it looked to be a shade of cerulean blue.

"The woman in the picture, boss!" Shade exclaimed.

"That's what I was thinking, Shadester," I admitted. "I wonder what this means," I breathed, tapping my chin.

"We're not getting salmon for Christmas dinner?" Gloom offered. I ignored my snarky kitty.

"Harumph, mmmph, grrmph,"

"Fraidy's right. C'mon, guys. Let's get to the pub for the keys. We can talk about all this later, and take a closer look at the path our visitor took."

I followed our snow-prints back to the car.

"Where are the keys, boss?" Midnight asked.

"I just told you, buster; the local pub," I said. "A three-minute drive from here, apparently."

"What's this pub called? The Slaughtered Lamb?" Gloom scoffed.

Shade chuckled at his sister's black humor. "Or 'The Drafty Barn,'" he chimed in, amused with his entry.

"Yep! 'The Rat's Lair!' Yep, yep!" Jet chirped.

"The M-mummy's T-t-tomb," Fraidy had finally freed his head from my armpit.

"'The Zombie's Entrails,' Midnight roared, holding his jiggling tummy.

A collective "Ew!" at that offering.

The Infiniti threw around their grisly pub names and laughed all the way to the car. At least they'd found their sense of humor.

I keyed the ignition.

"So, boss?" Shade asked, still chuckling.

"What's it *really* called?"

"The Maggoty Apple."

Stony silence.

CHAPTER FOUR

T he Apple was packed to the gills when we arrived. I picked my
way to the bar, the kitties in tow, amid a barrage of drunken
banter, sloshing warm ale and festive spirits. The boozy kind, not the
ghostly variety. A moving tide of reds and whites lifted goblets
of cheer.

Midnight chuckled. "Santa Week! Neat!" He trotted through the St
Nick impersonators, his face turned upward, grinning at each bearded
chin as he passed.

I plopped myself on the one vacant bar stool and instructed the
cats to stay by my feet. They hopped up onto the bar straight away.

A woman, with bleached, bee-hive hair, fuschia lipstick, and
multiple chins greeted us.

"What can I get ya?" Her chins rippled as she spoke, the lowest one
giving a final wobble against the woman's crepey neck.

"I'm Chimera Opal," I said, extending a mittened hand across the
bar. Two Santa's to the left of me chinked their ale-filled goblets
together in merriment. "I'm here to pick up the keys to Foxley
Cottage?"

"Ah, well, by Goddess, you made it!" The woman chortled. "Never thought you'd get through the Four Horsemen. Snow-tumble there this mornin'. Nobody's getting in or out of Gothic Harbor today, or likely for the next few days for that matter." She confirmed.

The cats squeaked their alarm at the news.

"Iris Crimple. Glad to make yer acquaintance." She slapped the key down on the bar with one hand and reached out with her other. Iris pumped my fist in her fleshy palm.

"We just escaped the Avalanche at the Horsemen," Gloom said. "But your Sergeant Donkerton wasn't so lucky."

"Yep, we left him, yep. On the other side of the pass, see?" Jet offered.

"Well, you sweeties must be the Eternity. Heard all about you!" Iris said, ruffling Jet's head. My zippy cat fired up his deranged motor-purr.

"The Infiniti," I corrected, Iris. "That's what the cats are called: The Infiniti."

"Well, Infiniti, course your fame is Isle wide. Been dying to meet you up close an' personal, hafta say." Iris' smile was brighter than the lighthouse beam. She was clearly delighted to have my whole clowder of kitties prowling the length of her bar. The other patrons paid little mind as the cats deftly weaved in and out of glasses of sherry and beer alike, looking for attention.

A crashing sound came from the far end of the bar. I turned to see Jet shaking droplets from his paw, and cringed. Okay, maybe there was one kitty who wasn't quite as deft as his siblings. Jet had knocked over a tray of drinks directly into the handbag of a woman standing next to me, splashing one irritated Santa beside her in the process.

I covered my face and turned the other way, hoping that nobody would link my club-footed cat to me. The landlady chuckled and shook her head. "S'cuse me a moment, hon," Iris said. Her hand reached under the bar, and out came a small nickel bell. Iris shook the bell with such vigor; her chins chimed right along with it. "Hear ye! Hear ye! Donkerton's Foibles number two hundred and thirty-one: He's got himself stuck the wrong side of the Horsemen. Yer in a lawless town now, boys!" She rang the bell again; this time to a blast of "Yeehaws!" From a vast plain of reveling Santas. The landlady shook her head and looked at me.

"Sorry 'bout that," Iris said. "So, what did our Sergeant hafta say?"

"He mentioned he was looking for a missing person," I said, leaning forward on the bar.

"Leland Clavelle, that's right," she said. "Complete mystery. His wife dies just five days ago; freezes to death when she comes off 'er horse, then Leland doesn't show for Stella's funeral. Got the whole town talkin', I tell ya."

"Stella Blazier," I said. "Stella wouldn't happen to be the newest addition to the cemetery in front of our cottage?"

"You saw Silent Meadows already?" Iris' penciled eyebrows shot up to her beehive hairline. "Well, lady, aren't you the lucky one to have the front row view to Stella's resting place?" Crimple slapped the bar as she chortled. I waited for her chins to stop shaking.

I noticed Fraidy, motionless on a beer mat, staring at the landlady's mass of quivering flesh. My timid kitty began hyperventilating. I grabbed him from the bar and tucked him on my lap, giving his head a reassuring rub.

Shade headbutted my arm. "Psst, ask about the bracelet, boss-lady," he urged. I gave my Romeo kitty a barely perceptible 'no.' I wanted to uncover a few facts first before I started spooking the locals.

Sergeant Donkerton's strange question about me being the deceased's colleague popped into my head.

"Say, Stella Blazier didn't happen to be a herbalist, did she?"

"Herbalist?" Crimple batted the air with her pudgy hand. "No, nothin' as humble as that. She headed up the WSA was what she did. She was a figure of import, was our Stella."

"WSA?" Carbon said.

"Yeah, kitty, the WSA: Warlock Space Agency. Stella was the head honcho of WSA's ROP."

"ROP?" Eclipse asked.

Iris rolled her eyes, praying to an unseen Goddess for patience. "Red Orb Program. Get with the program, kitty-cats." Her voice was fierce, but her eyes smiled at my sleuthing moggies.

I waved my hand in the air, "Sorry, Iris, tell us more about the WSA and ROP."

"The Blazier family founded the program best part of ten years ago.

Way ahead of their time, a real tech family, you know? Anyway, Warlocks being mostly from the 'Old Boy' establishment, and the Blazier's bein' at the top of all this brass, well, they piled their money into the space program. In particular, the plan for sending the Warlock race to Mars. Mark my words, they Warlocks will be the first men in space." Iris looked up. She squinted at the imagined cosmos above her head. "Anyways, Stella Blazier took the CEO torch from her daddy, and though their program is hush-hush, we been hearin' whispers that them mages are close to success."

"Wow." Midnight breathed.

"But, the Clavelles .... Leland's family, I mean. They had their own business concerns?" I asked.

"Owns Bonemark outright," Iris confirmed. "And half the countries with *all* the resources on the Mainland."

I whistled through my teeth and changed tack.

"Were Stella and Leland close?" I asked.

Iris sighed, and closed her eyes for a second, revealing an obscene amount of pale blue shadow on her lids.

"Oh, aye, they were close alright. On account of Stella oversaw every movement her man-made." Iris gave me a conspiratorial look. "Control matron, she was. Didn't like Leland making any moves without her. Had schedules drawn up for him, an' every-thin'. Fer his gym classes, fer his social time, hells, even fer the driving route to and from his office. Poor chap couldn't catch a break, I reckon." She shook her head. " And, Goddess help the guy if he was caught 'off schedule,' know what I mean? But it's Stella's sister that needs watchin' right now if you ask me. She's been walkin' around half-crazed since the accident. Now that Leland's gone an' vanished, she's bordering loon territory. Askin' questions of his whereabouts ev'ry ten minutes. And, besides, what sister doesn't show up to her own flesh-and-blood's funeral? Huh, hun? Can you tell me that?" Iris moved to the end of the bar to draw a pint for the Santa Jet had poured drinks on, leaving me to ponder her questions.

Santa lifted his head and grunted, pointing to the closest beer tap. Iris rolled her eyes.

"I know ya got a mouth behind all that beard there, Santy," she scolded. "Feel free to use words next time ya be wantin' a brew, now."

Shade tittered. Drunk Santa made a gruff sound and handed over his tender with a white-gloved hand.

"This is only your second ale, so I'm not sure how much liquor you nipped at before you got here, but don't make me cut you off for ill manners, fella." Iris slammed the pint down and took Santa's money.

"So, I guess Stella and her sister didn't get along too well?" I called to the end of the bar.

"Quite the other way round, hun. They got along same as a house on fire."

"Well, that seems to make little sense." Onyx stood up on his beer towel, peering at Crimple. "If their relationship were affable, it would stand to reason that Stella's sister would attend the latter's funeral."

Iris fixed her eyes on my clever cat. "I don't believe I understood one darn word you said there, kitty."

"What my cat is asking, Mrs. Crimple, is *why* didn't Stella's sister show up for the burial service? If they got along so well, wouldn't that behavior seem a little strange to you?"

Iris Crimple's eyes bulged. Quite unexpectedly, I might add. She guffawed, vibrating her chins and misting the air before her with a shower of spittle.

"What do ya's think I was sayin' earlier?! Adorania Blazier needs to be watched!"

"Adorania? That's Stella's sister's name?"

The initials on the bracelet, Chimera. I looked at Onyx and nodded; a simple thanks for his valued discretion. If it were Jet with Onyx's telepathic ability, a whole bar load of Father Christmas's would be asking questions by now.

"That's right, honey. Adorania Blazier. Stella's younger siblin'."

Fraidy clued into the implications. "I feel sick," he whined from his spot on my lap.

"Iris," I said. "You wouldn't happen to have a photo of Adorania would you?"

"You don't need one, honey," Iris replied. "She's walking up behind ya right now."

I turned on my stool and spotted a willowy woman advancing toward the bar, She had long, slightly wavy chestnut hair, which lay in a disheveled tail over her left shoulder. My eyes went to her face. The woman in the background of the photograph! The woman in the blue dress!

It's the woman in the background of the photo--.

I know, Onyx, I know.

Apart from the tell-tale hair arrangement, and the soft, yet defined, structure of the woman's face, there really wasn't much resemblance between the person who stood before me and the vibrant woman in the picture. She looked haunted.

Adorania moved closer to the bar; her hands balled into fists by her sides. She hadn't noticed me, or even the cats.

"Iris?" Her voice sounded reedy -- not the rich, throaty sound I'd imagined. "Has Leland showed his face in here yet?"

"I told ya I'd call ya if I heard or seen anythin'," Iris said, cooly. She picked up a glass and polished.

"It's been ...three days now. He has to be somewhere, for Goddess' sake!" Adorania's pitch raced to a near-hysterical high point.

"Donkerton's on the case, and I told ya if I heard of anythin' I'd let ya know."

"Sergeant Donkerton is stuck on the *outside* of town!" Adorania exploded, slapping her hands down on the bar to emphasize her point.

Iris stopped her polishing. "Listen, hun. I think a spot of sleep would be the best thing for you right now. Not all this chasin' your tail, looking for the missin'." Iris' face softened with what looked like genuine compassion. "Now, get yerself to your cradle, get some shut-eye, and I'll call ya, like I said I would, if I hear or see anythin'."

Drunk Santa slid from his chair; releasing himself from the awkward moment. Adorania kept her hands on the bar, but she dropped her head and gave a heavy nod.

That's when I felt Fraidy's fur electrify. Static fronds of cat hair shot through my fingers, and I winced when I felt my timid kitten's claws prick my thighs.

I turned toward what my spooked cat had locked eyes on, and the fine hairs on my neck sprang to life.

Adorania dropped her hands from the bar and crept out of the pub.

Uttering a hasty -- and, probably quite rude -- 'thanks' to Iris, I snatched the key, and, cats in tow, rushed out of the Maggoty Apple.

Because I wanted to know why Adorania Blazier had mud under her fingernails.

CHAPTER FIVE

"Whoa! I Don't think those tracks at the cemetery will be visible now, yep, yep!" Jet jumped like a maniacal ferret into and out of a deep drift of snow. It looked like at least a foot of the stuff had fallen while we were asking questions at the bar.

"Ah, humans. They're so smart," Gloom said squinting through a snowflake-covered eye.

"You look so pretty!" I gasped. I know I just confirmed Gloom's (snarky) point with my blurted comment, but it was true. I whirled around to admire all my kitties. All soft, glossy balls of black fur, speckled under plump flakes of tinseled white.

"Uh, boss-lady?" Shade patted my leg to nudge me back to the more real and gritty world. The world where cats needed answers as to why their owner was so dense.

I sighed. "I know, I know. I was stupid, and we should have stopped to look at them right away. A mistake. Okay?"

"*We?*" Gloom arched a snowflake tipped eyebrow at me.

I looked at her. "Me. I meant me." I turned my attention to the snow drifts that surrounded my car. "Looks like we're walking, guys."

"Ahem." Carbon cleared his throat. "There's shriekin' lady if anyone's interested," he said, nodding to a figure standing just a few steps down from the pub. Adorania Blazier stood, head hung, hands stuffed into the pockets of her long coat.

I tiptoed over to the woman. I could hear her sniffling as I approached.

"Ms. Blazier?" I asked, making my voice soft and non-threatening.

Adorania snapped her head up. Her cheeks were damp from fresh tears.

"Yes?"

"Chimera Opal," I said with a confidence I didn't feel. "I'm a herbalist on Glessie Isle. I'm here to harvest some Stillbreath's, but listen, I overheard you in the bar there, and I just wondered if you might permit me to help you find your sister's husband?"

Stella's sister gawked at me.

"I've worked a few jobs in my hometown," I explained. "Nothing serious, by any means, but I've been known to find a few missing *pets* p-people," I lied. "I'd love to help if I could?"

Adorania blinked. "I-I'm not sure how you could help. Leland's been missing for three days now. Nobody has seen hide nor hair of him, so what makes you think you--"

I placed a hand on her forearm. "Please. I can help."

The woman swallowed, and I watched as fresh tears streaked their way through the makeup grime under her eyes.

"It was only me that was supposed to stay away from the funeral." She croaked. "Not, Leland. And he spent so much money on the wreaths, he ... he..." Her voice broke.

"It's alright, it's alright," I said rubbing her arm. "Can you tell me why you had to stay away? Is that something you can share with us?"

Adorania stiffened. She withdrew her arm. "I--I, no. I can't tell you. But it was in the precepts. I had no choice. I *had* to stay away!" Fresh tears.

I kept my voice gentle. "Precepts?"

"Warlock tradition." She waved a dismissive hand. " It didn't apply to Leland, anyway. And it's of no relevance to his disappearance."

I nodded. "May I ask why you'd think that?"

Adorania Blazier's eyes flashed. "Because my sister is dead, Ms.

Opal. And Stella would be the only person I could think of who would want Leland 'gone.'"

"Stella would have liked her husband 'gone?'"

"Leland was nothing more than a scheduling nuisance to Stella." Adorania's words were clipped and harsh. "My sister didn't see Leland for what he was ... *is*. She saw an automaton only. One that she could control."

"Help me understand," I said calmly.

"Stella was a control freak. Her life and Leland's was timed to precision. Stella knew where Leland was every second of every day. She planned his gym time, his games night with friends...his squash lessons." Adorania drew in a deep breath. "Leland Clavelle should have been set free when Stella died, not ... not made invisible!"

I rubbed her arm again. "I'm sure he's not far, Ms. Blazier. I'm positive we'll find him." I paused. "As I understood it, you and your sister got along well. And, yet, talking to you now, it seems --"

"On the surface of it, yes. We're very different people, Stella and I, but somehow we almost always saw eye to eye on things." Adorania sighed. "Most things, anyway. And, thankfully, my sister hadn't yet tried to 'arrange' my life the way she had her husband's. Do you know the first thing Leland did when Stella died?"

I shook my head.

"He went off schedule," Adorania said, her voice triumphant. "Let's see, just this Tuesday evening -- the night before Stella's burial -- Leland, instead of going for his pre-planned six p.m run, he went for drinks at the Apple instead." Stella's sister shook her head. "By Brigid, if Stella had been alive to see such flagrant abuse of her scheduling system, she'd have turned in her grave."

"Was that the last time Mr. Clavelle was seen? At the pub?"

Adorania nodded silently.

"You said 'most things.'" I said. "You and Stella saw eye to eye on most things."

The woman looked at me. Her eyes were clear, centered, even though her eye makeup muddied the look somewhat.

"There was a matter of some land," Adorania said. "It was an old argument, Ms. Opal, and very likely unimportant, but if you must know ..."

"Please," I said.

"Okay, well, short version, then. Included in the Blazier estate is a tract of land, some three hundred acres, that sits at the top of Gothic Wood. That's the name of the estate too, actually: Gothic Wood." Adorania took a breath. "So, this land, it's been sitting there doing nothing for over a century now. My grandfather, the late Modesto Blazier, hadn't even so much as visited the plot in all the time he was alive, and my father didn't break that tradition. It was only Stella who had had an interest in the land. A bizarre fascination, if you will." She looked at me.

"Do you have a manor there? In Gothic Wood?"

"There's no manor or stately home up there, Ms. Opal. But there is a small crofters cottage; more of a ruin, really. The land is boggy, buggy, dark and full of trees. Only the Godmarsh toad flourishes there. Oh, and the coyotes. Tons of coyotes up there. Stella had had some strange affinity with the beasts. Anyway, the land; it's depressingly awful. But Stella always loved the place. Even when we were teenagers, Stella would sneak off there if father had applied too much pressure about her exam results or if Stella and I had argued." Adorania's eyes became hazy as she recaptured some past teenage quarrel. She shook her head. "Anyway, my point is, is that apart from Stella's occasional hermitages up there, the land was ...*is*... never used. For years Leland and I had been trying to convince my sister to sell the land. Do you know of the Dark Elm group?" Adorania asked.

I shook my head.

"It's a Warlock Hotel conglomerate. You'd have heard of some of their properties. The Lantern? The Best Mages?"

"Yes, of course," I said. "I've stayed at both the Lantern and the Best Mages." I nodded toward my kitties. "They both have great pet policies."

Adorania, her mind on bigger things, ignored my cats and continued. "Dark Elm was ... is ... showing interest in the plot. The group builds properties in unique and haunting locations, as I'm sure you're aware, so the hotel chain was asking questions about Gothic Wood.

They came forward with an attractive offer, and one that won't come by again, I'm sure." She shook her head again. "Stella refused to hear of it. We, that is Leland and I, came at my sister in every approach imaginable, but she point-blank refused to part with the land."

Shade headbutted Adorania's shin, startling the woman. "Lady, if you don't mind me askin', how is it you and Leland even got the time to talk in private? Didn't Stella, like, manage all of Leland's time?"

Adorania looked at Shade. "I've heard about you talking cats," she said taking a small step backward. "I'm...I'm not a fan of cats."

"Hey, I got no hard feelin's," Shade said, shrugging a small snowfall from his shoulders. "But, if you could answer this talkin' cat's question?" He grinned a toothy smile at her.

"Squash lessons," Stella's sister said. "I taught Leland's squash lessons ... my sister and Leland's estate has a couple of squash courts on site. We talked while we played."

"Makes sense." I bit my lip before adding: "Was Stella ever around when you and her husband were playing squash?"

"No, lessons were every Thursday at two-thirty-p.m. My sister doesn't normally get home from work until about seven ...." Adorania trailed off. "Wait, last Thursday Stella was home early. Leland had been the first to spot her car in the driveway when we came out from the squash courts. We walked up to the house, and Stella had been there, sitting at the kitchen table with a full glass of brandy in front of her. Unusual for my sister. Not the brandy, just the time of day, you know? Anyway, Leland and I were both more than a little surprised to see my sister there."

"Did she say why she was home so early?" Gloom asked, looking up at the woman.

Adorania shook her head. "No, she didn't. She just gave us this weird smile, you know? Said that there was a lot of pressure at work and she had to work on a solution. Um, what else..." Stella's sister pursed her lips. "Oh, yeah, she asked how the lesson was, and if Leland's drive had improved, and then she mumbled some apology, took her drink to her study, and closed the door. It was strange ... I thought maybe she'd heard us..." Adorania stopped and released a deep breath. "Anyway, it's probably nothing. I'm sure it was just my sister's workload that had her looking so strained."

"Lady, are there any other unusual dynamics that you can think of between either you and your sister or your sister and Leland?" Midnight, not one for respecting a human's personal space, sat on Adorania's foot as he posed his questions.

"No, kitty, there's isn't." She shook Midnight from her foot and took another step backward.

"Ms. Blazier, if you don't mind me asking, why are you so interested in finding Mr. Clavelle?"

Adorania stiffened. "Leland Clavelle is family, Ms. Opal. Now that Stella's gone, and I'm the only living Blazier left, Leland Clavelle is the closest person in my life right now." She brought her hands to her face and rubbed her eyes.

I eyed the woman's fingers. "Enjoying some late-season gardening?"

Adorania pulled her hands from her face and stuffed them under her arms, nodding. She looked at her feet and kicked some snow from her boots. "I have a greenhouse," she said. "It calms my mind. Listen, it's late, and I need to—"

"Of course," I said. "I think Iris was right. You need a good night's sleep. Is there any chance we can resume this conversation? Tomorrow, perhaps? At the Apple?"

"I'm not sure what else I can tell you, really. But, yes, I'll meet you. Five p.m?"

"Well, you never know what you can uncover from seemingly irrelevant pieces of information," I offered. "All I need is for you to be honest with your answers, and I'm quite convinced we can get to the bottom of all this." I smiled at the woman. Adorania gave me a brief nod and walked away.

Leaving the cats and I to face the horrors of Foxley Cottage. In silence, we trudged the rest of the way to our horrendous house with its first-rate view of Silent Meadows.

CHAPTER SIX

"So, like, boss-lady, what do you think is goin' on around here?" Shade said, flopping on my chest and tucking his head under my chin. Seven black heads pushed their way into the conversation.

We were on a lumpy bed, under damp sheets and musty blankets, in a drafty room of a crumbling cottage. The wind howled its agonized passage through the cracks, holes, and gaps of the dwelling.

"I'll tell you what's going on," Carbon said, looking over his shoulder to check on his recently lit fire in the hearth. His eyes took on the glow of the flames. "Adorania is the one in the photograph behind Stella and Leland Clavelle."

"She's got grave-dirt under her nails!" Fraidy choked.

"Yep, right. I nearly blurted it at the bar, but I didn't, nope. The initials on the bracelet, the A, and the B, which is Adorania Blazier, yeppers."

"Thanks for not blurting, buster," I said, reaching down the bed to tussle Jet's head. I looked at my kitties. "And, we don't know if that's grave-dirt, Fraidy. You heard her; she said she'd been in her greenhouse."

"She was lying!" Fraidy screeched. He hurtled sideward on the bed, back arched, like a furry crab. "Adorania and Stella's husband were plotting to take that land, that Gothic Wood, and sell it." My timid cat continued his crab walk. "Stella comes home early one day and overhears her sister and her husband discussing it while they play squash. Hence Stella's behavior when they found her sitting at the kitchen table afterward. Stella Blazier knew her sister and her husband were plotting to sell the land to the hotel chain, and she acted strangely in the kitchen because she was ... Stella, I mean ... well, she was .... plotting revenge!"

Fraidy dropped from his crab posture to a cowering, flat slab of fur on top of the covers. We stared at him.

"Wow, that cat might have just said something almost plausible," Gloom said, eyeing her brother.

"Only one problem with the revenge angle, though," Shade said, scratching behind his ear. "The person who wanted to 'do' the revenge died before she could dish it out.

I held my hands up. "Alright, alright, so let's leave the conjecture out of it for now," I said. "We can revisit the revenge angle when we have some basic answers first. So let's put our vivid imaginations aside for now, and focus on the facts, agreed?"

My cats bobbed their heads in visibly reluctant agreement.

"Thank you," I said. "Okay, what do we have so far?"

"Leaving the 'revenge' angle well alone," Onyx began. "It does, perhaps, sound likely that Stella overheard one of Adorania and Leland's conversations about the land, does it not?"

"It does," I admitted. "But, as I said, let's talk about what we do know first, okay, buster?"

Onyx dipped his head in a bow so regal that only he could pull it off.

"The fabric," Gloom said. "In the photo, Adorania was wearing a dress that looked very much like the divine duds we snagged from the wall by the boneyard. And, why didn't you challenge Adorania on it, human?"

"I want to ask some more questions first, Gloom," I said. "If Adorania was at her sister's grave this evening, that's not exactly illegal now, is it? Besides, if she was kept away from the burial, for some as yet unknown reason, then maybe she just needed to show her last respects ... in her own way."

"Grave-hugging is a weird way to show your respect," Carbon said.

"Show some compassion for those that grieve, brother," Onyx warned. "Grief isn't a one-size-fits-all experience. It hits how it hits, and if hugging a mound of earth brings some relief to a human, then I would say we should not pour scorn on their suffering."

"Yeah," Shade said. "So what if it's weird. All humans do weird stuff, right?"

Jet's expression looked thoughtful."Yep, yep, like they stay awake ALL day, never nappin', nope."

"And they mysteriously ignore boxes," Eclipse said.

Gloom shuddered. "Ugh, it gives me the creeps. The way they walk past boxes as if they're not even there."

"Freaky, for sure," Midnight said. "But, what about the newspaper thing? Now *that's* chilling."

Against my better judgment, I questioned my kitty. "The newspaper thing?"

"Yeah, boss. Humans. They *look* at newspapers. You've gotta admit, that's weird, right?" Midnight puffed his cheeks and blew out air. "You know, I once spent a whole day with your mother when she had come down with the flu. One of your mother's neighbors had brought a stack of newspapers over so that Glendonite would have some 'entertainment.'" Midnight puffed again. "So, I watched. I watched Glendonite and what she 'did' with those papers. I watched for a full day, I swear. It was stomach-churning."

"What happened?" Gloom said, holding her two front paws together in front of her.

Midnight gave his sister a grave look. "It's what *didn't* happen that got me worried." He paused, shook his head. "Not once. Honestly, not one time did Glendonite lay or roll on the paper. She just looked at it. All day."

"Not one cat-nap?" Shade asked.

"Like I said, bro. She just looked at it. When she leafed through, I kept expecting her to flop down on the newly turned page, but, nope."

Eclipse looked thoughtful "Didn't you show Glendonite what you're supposed to do with newspapers?"

Midnight leveled his gaze at his brother. "'Bro, what do you take me for?" He said. "Of course I showed her what to do. I sat squarely on each page she turned. I stretched, I rolled, I played, I napped on nearly every page of those papers. Not only did Glendonite not get the hint, but she also kept pushing me off. Here I was giving her lessons, and she was disrespectin' my teaching's, you know?"

"Makes you wonder what's going on in their minds," Carbon suggested.

"Um, I'm right here, guys," I said, pulling my hands from the covers again and waving them in the air. "If we could just bring our focus back? Hmm?" I leaned back on the pillow and closed my eyes. I picked through the clues that danced behind my closed lids.

"If I might be so bold as to point out that unless Adorania was incredibly distraught, to the point of losing her senses, a satin evening gown isn't exactly the most tactical choice of attire for one who is about to claw at a muddy grave on a wintery night."

"It *is* a strange choice of clothing, Onyx," I said, not opening my eyes. "Anyone notice what she was wearing under that long coat of hers?"

I felt the cats shake their heads.

"I'm still wondering why Adorania didn't attend Stella's funeral," I said. "And, why is she obsessively hunting for Leland Clavelle, anyway?"

"Dunno, but I get the feeling that all three are connected, some-how," Shade said from under my chin. "Stella's death, Adorania not showing for the funeral, and Clavelle's vanishing act."

"But, you heard Iris say...as far as everyone knew, Adorania and Stella were the best of friends," I said.

A clattering noise joined the sound of the wailing wind.

"What was that?" Fraidy sprinted the length of the bed and plopped himself on my head, his claws at the ready in case he really had to latch on. My eyes flew open. "Sounded like it came from a way aways," I said. "Probably this infernal wind knocking over some trash cans."

Midnight trotted to the far side of the bed. He put his two front paws up to the window and chuckled.

"Well, trash cans have fallen, you're right," he said. "But it was a drunk Santa, maybe THE drunk Santa, that toppled 'em."

I smiled and closed my eyes again. "Hope he doesn't get stuck in a chimney tonight," I murmured.

"Well, then, it seems clear that the sisters had had a meltdown at some point," Gloom said, bringing our attention back to the case. The case. I felt my body flood with adrenaline. *Chimera, calm down. You're not a detective.*

"Yeah, but even so, an old Warlock family like the Blazier's?" Midnight said. "They'd definitely have to follow the precepts. There ain't no way that a first-circle family member's stayin' away from the burial unless the precept states it for some grim reason or other."

I lifted my head and stared at my cat. "You know about these precepts, Middie?"

Midnight's eyes widened. "You've really not heard of them?" He asked. "Not even you, O?"

Onyx shook his head, his eyes filled with regret. Which was Midnight's cue to take the stage.

My night-wandering kitty puffed out his chest and paraded the length of the bed. He couldn't have been more delighted. Midnight considered himself an 'intelligence gatherer.' The rest of the cats and I gave him the more informal title of 'gossip,' however. Middie prowled the night collecting data from creatures that only existed in the dead-of-night realms. My explorer of the dark gathered this intelligence for unspecified future use, but I suspected one of those purposes was for inflating his self-importance.

"So, all Warlocks ... well, most Warlocks, anyway ... they have these familial laws written up, you with me?"

We nodded.

"Precepts, they're called. Written to govern all aspects of Warlock living, dying and death situations. The practice is pretty much dead these days, though. Too rigid, not enough leeway, the young Warlocks don't like these old ways. But ... the real old families tend to keep them in place. Families like the Blazier's, I mean." Midnight beamed. He was enjoying this.

"So, what like? Say if Adorania and Leland had somehow gone behind Stella's back and sold the land. Would something like that be written into the orders?" Gloom said.

"I ain't a Blazier, sis, so I dunno," Midnight confessed. "But, for example, it could be a clause like ...stay away if you stole something from the deceased. Or, like, if you were about to bring shame on the family, or something, then you'd be forced to steer clear of the burial for something like that too."

"Good examples, Middie, thanks," I said.

Midnight swiped the air with a casual paw. "Aw, it's nothing, boss," he said. "Just one tiny piece of information in the huge pile I store up here." He tapped the side of his head with a paw.

"Still," I said. "Interesting about the precepts. I'd never heard of such a thing until now."

Middie's grin widened. "Yeah, and there are other kinds of precepts too," he said. "Like, one of my buddies told me that the Blackbugler's ... you know the Blackbugler's, right?"

"The old Warlock family originally from Nanker Isle, you mean?" I asked.

"Yeah, those cats. I think they have some family here too, but anyway ... one of their precepts is that they have a closed casket. Know why?"

We shook our heads.

"'Cos they refuse to have their organs drained before burial. The Blackbugler's believe that by allowing their vital fluids from their organs to drain into the earth, they have once again returned to the darkness from which they were born. For the Blackbugler's this precept completes the circle of life for them."

"That's disgusting," Gloom said, holding her nose high.

"Great shock value, Middie," I said, "But, let's keep on track here, okay?"

The sparkle left Midnight's eyes. "Well, anyway, the precepts are only written for biological families. It wouldn't extend to in-laws, just the immediate family."

"I want to know why Donkerton asked if you and Stella Blazier were colleagues," Eclipse said.

"Me too, 'Clipsy. But I'm pretty sure the Warlock Space Program isn't much like running a herbalist apothecary."

"Right," Gloom said. "Because that would be like comparing a rocket scientist to a common gardener."

"Thanks for that, missy," I said. "But, let's get back to why Adorania didn't show for Stella's service. So, a falling out? As Fraidy posited, maybe a row over selling Gothic Wood to the Black Elm group? And what if Gloom is right? What if Leland and Adorania somehow sold the land under Stella's nose? Maybe they didn't get a chance to explain their actions before Stella died, and so maybe the result of their scheming counted as theft? A transgression that would already be written into the precepts?"

Was I getting drawn into Fraidy and Gloom's mountain of hastily constructed speculations? It was tempting, I'll admit.

"Let's tell it like a story!" Shade shrieked; his excitement making us all jump. "You know, like, a story has a beginnin', a middle, and an end. It runs in sequins, right?"

"'Sequence,' but, yeah, I know what you're getting at, honey," I said.

"Yeah, so, it's like we speak the bits of story we have already, and we speak them in the order they happened. Maybe a storyline will make more sense?"

I nodded. "Sure, buddy. As long as we don't all try and fill the missing pieces with speculation."

"Yep, yep, I'll start," Jet said. "Stella Blazier falls from her horse and dies five days ago." He swiveled his head to look at us all. "Yep." He finished.

"Woah, let's back up," I said. "We have data that *precedes* Stella's death." Jet's eyelids twitched at me. I sighed. "The fact that Gothic Wood was a bone of contention between the the two Blazier's and one Clavelle."

"Yep, well, sure, yep, but —"

"Also, the possibility that Stella overheard Leland and Adorania discussing the estate when she came home early from work," Gloom said.

"Okay, yep, but, well, *then* Stella falls from her horse, yep." Jet bounced on the spot, happy to have had neatly slotted in his piece of the puzzle.

"Right," I said. "She's buried three days, ago, but Leland and Adorania don't show for the funeral."

Shade hummed."Roll on to now, and we've still got a dead Stella, and we've still got a missing Leland. Only new thing now is our worrying-wanderer, Adorania."

We each fell into our own thoughts for a second.

"The stress on an astronaut's body is extreme, to say the least," Onyx piped up.

Where did that come from?

"Could the Stillbreath's be a reasonable application for space travel? To bring an astronaut's body into resting state while he's hurled out of orbit?" He asked.

My pulse quickened. "Interesting, O," I said, pulling the blankets up around my chin. "Donkerton certainly knows something about Stella that we don't, anyway. Or else why would he have asked that question? Maybe Stillbreath's are being used in the Red Orb Program?"

"And, maybe our snow-bound sergeant has a file on her back at the station? A file that might just tell us what the connection is." Carbon suggested.

"Yeah, and as he's not here right now, maybe he wouldn't mind us taking a peek at his notes?" Shade said.

"I think he would mind, buster," I said to my good-natured tom. "But, what he doesn't know, can't hurt him, right?"

"We're gonna break into the police station?" Fraidy said, his voice a high-pitched squeak.

"Relax, honey." I swept my cat from my head and into my arms. Shade rolled, without protest, to the side of me, while I covered his cowardly brother's cheeks with kisses. "We'll take a look tomorrow. If there's nobody around, we'll just have a little snoop and see if we can see anything. His officer might be there, so there's a chance we won't get close, anyway."

"Yeah, and if Donkerton's got a file on Stella, then maybe there's something in there about the Blazier Death Precepts too. Might shed some light on some things 'n' stuff." Shade grinned at me. I blew him a kiss.

"So, we need to formulate a plan. I'm slated for ten a.m tomorrow for Stillbreath picking time, and I can't miss that window or else it'll take another month for me to re-apply. That leaves us the rest of the afternoon and evening. We don't have much time. We leave the day after tomorrow, remember?"

"Uh, boss-lady, are you forgetting the avalanche?" Shade reminded me.

"No. I'm not, buster. But I'm still hopeful we can get home by Christmas Eve." I wasn't lying. I just had a feeling that a Christmas Miracle was heading our way. Don't ask me why I felt that, but my witch-senses were twitching.

"Before we start this 'plan,'" Gloom said. "What, exactly, are we investigating? Clavelle's disappearance? Why Adorania didn't show up to her sister's funeral? The relationship between Leland and Adorania? What?"

Shade groaned. "I get your drift, sis. My brain hurts." My cat raised both of his front paws to the sides of his head. "Boss-lady? What should we be focusin' on here?"

I didn't answer my cat.

"Chimera?" Onyx tiptoed up the bed until he was beside my head.

I said nothing.

A few moments passed, and I could feel the kitties get fidgety around me.

"Okay, I've got it," I blurted, bolting upright to look at my crew. "This is what we've gotta do..."

CHAPTER SEVEN

"So you're all clear on what you need to do?" I fussed over my kitties, smoothing their fur, removing sleep from their bleary eyes while ushering them through the door. The Infiniti made no objections; just grunted and allowed themselves to be coaxed, like a litter of obedient zombie-cats.

We had slept poorly on our first night at Foxley. Carbon had maintained a roaring fire in the hearth, so at least we didn't freeze to death. But the icy drafts that whipped through the disintegrating house screamed like so many love-sick banshees that we all got very little sleep. And my (exactly seven inch) share of the bed didn't help my slumber much either.

The kitties didn't care for the military grade woolen blankets; said they made them itchy, and they were too much like 'Bones,' a wiry-haired mangey mutt that lived at the end of our street on Glessie.

When we were outside, I lined up my three cats chosen for today's investigations. Onyx, Carbon and Midnight looked up at me with dull, sleep-deprived eyes.

"Sure you guys are clear on everything?" I grilled, giving them a suspicious arch of my brow. "What time and where are we meeting?"

Onyx yawned. "Four p.m."

"Maggoty Apple," Carbon and Middie said in unison. I gave each of them a kiss on the forehead and shooed them toward their respective targets.

Gloom, Eclipse, Jet, Fraidy, and Shade followed me to the car.

"Why wasn't I chosen to go out in the 'field?'" Eclipse said.

"Honey, I told you already. I need you with me. Who else is going to *mind-wipe* the registrations clerk?"

The plan I'd made last night had been hasty, to say the least. But, hopefully, with what I had in mind, it would at least answer a few questions.

I sent Carbon to the police station to see if he could find any report on Stella that would tell us why the Sergeant had asked me if I was the deceased's colleague. We were also hoping to uncover the Blazier's Death Precepts, if any, to find out the reason for Adorania's inexplicable absence from her sister's funeral.

I chose Carbie for this mission because, as well as lighting fires, my heat-seeking cat could also behave like smoke; wisping and curling himself into the smallest of gaps, such as keyholes or minor cracks in window sills. Carbon could gain entry into Gothic Harbor P.D without attracting attention.

Onyx, I sent to Spleener & Sons, the local funeral director's place of business. My learned cat was to use his love of science as a ruse for obtaining information regarding the after-death processes Spleener took to ready Stella Blazier's body for burial.

"Remember, tell him you're writing a crime book," I advised my kitty. "Tell him you want to respect the accuracy of what happens to a dead body before its interned," I said, scratching O's ear. "Stella was likely Spleener's last ... um...client, so he might divulge some specifics on our Ms. Blazier." *Kind of a long shot, Chimera.*

I sent Midnight to check out Gothic Wood. There probably wasn't much point to this endeavor, but as Adorania had brought up the property, I thought it was worth checking out.

I brought 'Clipsy with me to the Stillbreath patch, because my enigmatic kitty could wipe minds of temporarily. This power came in useful from time to time. Mostly -- and, on my behalf -- Eclipse used his *Obliviscatur* spell on Mrs.Chitterlong; a gibbering neighbor whose unsolicited company I sometimes found hard to escape. Eclipse, with one mentally constructed charm, invariably brought Mrs.Chitterlong's gossipy ramblings to a sharp stop. It was during my neighbors confused after-moments that I generally made my escape.

Anyway, my hope was Obliviscatur would come in handy when I signed in with the registrations agent. If Stella Blazier *had* been picking Stillbreath's, then her name may well just show up on the registrant's list. I'd have to scan that record, however, so I needed 'Clipsy to distract the agent with a mind-wipe while I inspected the column of names.

I kept the windows open for the drive to the fungus patch. The cats could barely keep their eyes open, so I thought the fresh air might help combat their drowsiness.

Gloom, Shade, and Fraidy sat huddled together in the back seat, their faces like thunder. I knew I'd pay for this inhumane treatment later. Gloom had already accused me of degrading her, given that I'd capped each of my kittie's paws with balloons. My grumpy cat's balloon covered feet didn't match, and she was still sulking about it.

Eclipse sat right where I wanted him in the passenger seat, ready to spring into memory-erasing action.

We rolled up to the first gate; manned, but the agent there showed no interest in our arrival. He had his feet crossed on the table in front of him. He had a freshly shaken snow globe in his hand, and he gazed, entranced, at the myriad of falling flakes within the dome. I drove on.

A rusty-brown streak of fur raced through the snow to my right. A squirrel or other small rodent.

The registration office was just ahead. I could make out the outline of the agent as he paced the length of his small room.

"Okay, 'Clipsy, you ready?" I said turning to my cat.

But my cat wasn't there. Because Eclipse had seen the racing furry-thing too.

The kitties in the back laughed as they watched their brother bound after the small creature in the snow.

I banged my forehead on the steering wheel a couple of times before closing the final few yards to the office.

I leaned out the window to the man who bent out of his window.

"Hello, I'm --"

"Is that your cat?" He asked, nodding toward a galloping Eclipse.

"It is."

"You're going to have to put him on a leash, ma'am."

"I will, yes, of course, he--"

"Name," the clerk said, not looking up from his papers.

"Yes, I'm Chimera Opal, I'm here--"

"Permit."

I reached for the license and presented it to the officer. He traced his pencil down a column until he found what he was looking for and then put a clipboard in front of my face.

"Sign here," he said, tapping an empty box with his finger. His other hand held the top of the clipboard so firmly that his thumb outstretched until it rested over three last names at the top of the form.

I grabbed the pen secured to the top of the board, and hovered for a few seconds, my eyes darting to the list of names on the left.

"Right in the box there." His finger tapped again.

I made a squiggle and looked at the man. He didn't return my gaze. He merely reached under his desk and depressed the secret button that would allow us access to 'Facility 3522,' the only operating Still-breath patch on Bonemark Isle.

"Park your car on the left," the man called after us as we passed through the electronic gates.

"Okay, so I got Boris, Astrid, and Polonia for the top three names," Shade said. "Buddy there had his thumb over the last names, but I think I saw the letter "B" after Polonia."

"Good work, honey," I said.

"I got Yevgeny Asimov, Gertrude Hahn, and somebody Eaglespeak-er," I said of the three names listed under the one's Shade had just mentioned.

"Rainbird," Gloom said. "Rainbird Eaglespeaker."

I slumped in my seat. "No, Stella, then," I said, motorboating my lips.

"Not unless Polonia's last name is Blazier, and Stella's real name is Polonia," Shade offered.

I pulled into the parking spot and drummed my fingers on the steering wheel, not sure what to make of the dead-end.

I sighed. "Come on guys. Let's get your deranged brother and pick these mushrooms."

Gloom pulled her ears back and thumped her tail. "I'm not going anywhere in mismatching shoes," she stated. "Why am I wearing these anyway?" She wiped her paws on the backseat for the umpteenth time, trying to dislodge the offending pieces of rubber.

"They're protection, honey," I begged. "A barrier for your fine paws, so you don't absorb the toxins in the Stillbreath."

"Protection or not, they should at least match." My grumpy cat crossed her paws in front of her and sat down. I eyed the one green and one red balloon that adorned Gloom's front feet and groaned.

"Exactly," Gloom said. "It's hideous." She pointed a green rubbered paw to where her brother was leaping through the snow. "HE has the other red one."

"Honey, you can't expect me to catch Eclipse just so you can have matching shoes," I said through gritted teeth. My kitty turned her head away from me.

So, then, of course, I proceeded to chase Eclipse through a field of deep snow.

But every time I caught up to my rodent-hunting moggie, he sprang, unpredictably, in an entirely different direction. After ten minutes or so of chasing I finally gave up and swaggered back to the car, winded, my chest lurching for air.

"I c-can't ... catch...him," I breathed.

Gloom refused to make eye contact with me.

"Can we make a matching set between us?" Shade said, his eyes brightening. He flopped on his side on the back seat and offered his paws for perusal. Two blue, one green, one purple. Fraidy rolled onto his side. Two purple, one green, one blue.

Argh! Eclipse was bouncing around out there in no less than four colors then.

"Gloom, honey," I pleaded. Actually, I prayed to her. Kneeling in the snow by the side of the car, my hands pressed together in meditation; I whined "Please. Please don't do this."

My sulking cat turned her head toward me at last. She sighed. "I'll take two purple for the front and two blue for the back, I guess."

"Thank you, oh merciful one, thank you," I said, already snapping Gloom's color choices into place over her paws.

Eclipse decided to turn himself in, and trotted to the car with his multi-colored paws. He shook a flurry of flakes from his fur. "We ready to pick mushrooms, then?" He said, acting like he hadn't just made me run around a field.

"Come on, guys, let's get picking."

My cats followed me, FINALLY, to Fungal Area 31, and, even after Gloom's wardrobe meltdown, we managed to have a surprisingly calm, restful, and without-further-incident kind of morning. In a broad green field of mist and sunlight, we harvested the Stillbreath's in silence.

I won't pretend to know what was going on in my cats minds as they helped me pick, but for me? My mind was straining to stay focused on the task at hand. Because my curiosity for what my mission-cats might have found eclipsed every other thought.

CHAPTER EIGHT

"Nothing?" The uttered word carried the full weight of my disappointment. I asked Carbon again. "Really? Nothing?"

"It doesn't mean it doesn't exist," Carbon explained, his voice rising. "It just means it wasn't there at the police station." The noise level at the Maggoty Apple had reached uproarious levels. The carpeted area in front of the bar had turned into a mini Santa dance floor. Two Father Christmas's were twirling one another around; both were holding the other's drunken stupor in a festive embrace. A few different Santa's danced into the scene to join the two hugging Papa Noel's.

Fraidy's head popped up from my lap. He placed his two front paws on the table. "Donkerton was carrying a file. The photo he showed us. He pulled it from a file, remember?"

Onyx nodded. "Brother, it makes sense. The Sergeant pulled hardcopied evidence from that folder, so it would be more than a little uncanny if the subject of that file *weren't* Stella Blazier."

I ran a hand through my hair. "Okay, so we know as much about Stella as we did when we got here yesterday, I said. How frustrating. We had nothing. Exactly nothing. I reached for the leader of my

479

kitties and put a gentle finger under his chin. "O? What did you find out?"

"I regret to inform, not a great deal," Onyx said, sitting tall next to his sister. "But I will share with you what I discovered, anyway. It is a truth that big mysteries have been instantly unraveled by the presence and accumulation of delicate threads of seemingly insignificant details."

Shade scratched his head. "Is that, like, one of those philofossicle wisdom sayings?"

"No, it's pomposity," Gloom said, glaring at her wordsmith brother. "Start again, Shakespeare. This time drop the Elizabethan English."

Onyx peered down his nose at his bolshy sister and began. "Mr. Spleener wasn't very helpful, to be frank. He was happy to discuss his field but in general terms only. Nothing pertaining to Ms. Blazier specifically. Casual banter with Mr. Spleener's wife and office manager, turned over a tidbit of data, however. Mrs. Spleener was keen to show what kind of satin was chosen for Mrs. Blazier's coffin, for instance."

"Go on," I said to Onyx. I glanced at my watch. Adorania would be here in fifteen minutes. We needed to unfurl what we had so far, so I could ask the woman some reasonable and intelligent questions.

"Red satin," he said. "A rare color option in this day and age." Onyx paused. "Although, I'm not sure what that could possibly tell us."

"Anything about those ..." Fraidy swallowed and brought his paws to his ears, preparing himself for blocking out the answer. "....Death Precepts?"

Onyx shook his head. "You're safe, dear brother," he said. "Nothing was revealed with regards to the Blazier precepts. I did find the intake form for Ms.Blazier's body, however. Enclosed was a copy of the autopsy report, complete with a signature from Medical Examiner, Stan Derminall."

"So it said she froze to death?" I asked.

"Indeed," Onyx said. "Were you expecting something different, Chimera?"

I smiled sheepishly at my cat and waved a hand in the air. "No...no, I guess not."

What's on your mind, Chimera?

It's ..it's nothing, O. Go on with your findings, please.

Why did I feel like something was screaming for my attention? And that this something felt like it was partying just out of sight?

Onyx nodded. "There was also a break-in," he said.

My eyes widened. "A break-in? What do you mean? Anything taken?" I pictured an empty coffin, all billowing red satin and nothing else.

My mind-reading cat saw my imagination running away with me.

"No, Chimera, Stella's body wasn't taken," he said. "Mrs. Spleener even checked the coffin the morning of the funeral to make sure of that." Onyx paused. "No, our dear funeral director's wife assured me it was just kids. A sound woke her in the very early hours of the morning of Stella's service. It was still dark, and Mrs. Spleener went downstairs to the workshop to investigate."

"What did she find?" I asked.

"Just a spilled jar of formaldehyde," Onyx said. "Mrs. Spleener suggests that the kids knocked it over in their haste to get out. They were probably spooked by the presence of Mrs.Blazier's corpse. Mrs. Spleener said that it wasn't the first time kids had broken in and it wouldn't be the last, either. She said the kids have their own ways, morbid or not, to discover the truths about death."

"You're sure the kids didn't take anything?" I said. "Mrs. Spleener checked --"

"Yes. She did, Chimera. Stella and the items she was buried with were all still there." Onyx narrowed his eyes. "Although, Mrs. Spleener said she thinks the kids had messed with Stella's hair."

"What made her say that?" Eclipse said.

"I know nothing of the specifics, dear brother," Onyx replied. "But, Mrs. Spleener suggested that the corpse's previously styled hair-do looked a little disheveled to her eyes."

"Okay," I said, drumming the table with impatient fingers. "Did Mrs. Spleener let on what Stella was wearing? What artifacts were in the coffin with her?"

"Regrettably, no," Onyx said. "She just indicated that everything in the coffin was as it should be."

"So what else?" Gloom huffed.

"Dear, sister, you are now apprised of all I know. The red satin, I feel, has a significance in some --"

"Oh, man, are you being serious?" Midnight interrupted. "That's it?"

"As I mentioned before, dear brother, it is sometimes the little det--"

"Guys, enough," I said, clapping my hands together. "Thanks for the report, O, but I don't think your red satin is going to be the thread that holds this case together."

"Talking about threads," Eclipse said. "Are you going to bring that to the table in your discussion with Adorania?"

I pinched the blue silk in my pocket and nodded.

"When I show her the bracelet and the fabric, guys," I said. "It's important that you're watching for her reaction, okay?"

"You kidding me?" Gloom said. "Human guilt's as easy to catch as SALMON swimming upstream."

Shade bobbed his head. "Yeah, if Adorania's guilty of grave-worship we'll know right away, I reckon."

"Wanna know what I found, boss?" Midnight jumped onto the table. On an impulse, I leaned over and kissed my handsome cat between the eyes. Middie gave a purr-burst and headbutted my cheek.

"Go on, honey," I said.

"Well, I found the cabin. It was pretty well hidden in the pines up there," he said, nodding to some indeterminate place far beyond the walls of the Apple. "But, you know me, I won't drop the scent until I've sniffed things out." Midnight stuck his chest out, fully preparing himself for his self-aggrandizing session. "So there's nothing much up there except a pack of scruffy coyotes and a whole bunch of those Godmarsh toads. The cabin looked empty when I first got there; no smoke coming from the chimney or anything like that. No lights on or sounds from the television." My night-prowling cat paused, making sure he had everyone's attention.

"There's a point to this story, right?" Carbon said.

"Yeah, yeah, brother, chill," Midnight replied holding up his paws. "So, I was about to walk away, thinking there was nobody home, that it was just an empty cabin, you know? So, I turn to leave, when I hear a noise behind me. I pop a squat behind a conifer, and I look back at the house. And, guess who's coming out the door?" Midnight's black eyes moved from face to captive face.

"Drunk Santa!" He said, and fell on the table laughing.

I screwed up my face. "Wait, what? Drunk Santa?"

"Yep, plain as day," Midnight said, wiping a mirthful tear from his eye. "He probably thought he was gonna get some milk and cookies." The cats fell about in various states of laughter. I pushed back from the table, motor-boating my lips. Cat humor. So bizarre. Something a human can never hope to understand. As mysterious as those spine-tingling moments when your cat suddenly turns his head to a point in the room and stares. Stares like there's something there.

"Yeah, that's sidesplitting funny," I said. "But, Middie, how could you have known that it was drunk Santa if he was in costume?"

Midnight twitched his ears. "Easy," he said. "He had a red wine stain on his fur trim. The wine Jet poured over him yesterday."

Jet tittered. "Bullseye! Yep!" he gushed. My zippy kitty was clearly quite proud that his bar-demolition had made its mark in the world.

Gloom wrinkled her nose. "Ew, what animal doesn't wash after he gets something on his fur?"

I clenched my jaw. "Guys, do you want to eat salmon for Christmas dinner, or not?"

The laughter stopped. Gloom squinted at me, bringing her paws to her side in a slow, smooth, downward slide. If my embittered cat had been allowed to carry firearms, I'd have been ducking for cover right about now. "You know we can't get out of this burg," she said. "Why taunt us with your spiteful salmon jokes when you know we can't get through the avalanche?"

"Nope, nope, not nice, nope," Jet said, swinging his head from side to side.

Iris Crimple came over. "Get you lovelies anythin' else?" She asked, nodding to my glass and the eight empty saucers. I smiled at the land-lady. "We're good for now, Iris, thanks so much." But, Iris noticed the Infiniti's glum expressions.

"You honies not happy with the cream I gave ya?"

The Infiniti looked at her. Jowls long, lips trembling, eyes brimming with self-pity; my kitties shook their heads in unison. It was an award-worthy performance. Their best yet, I'd say.

"Oh, please," I muttered.

But Iris remained concerned. "My darlin's, whatever's wrong?" She bent over the table until her chins swung just over the cats heads. Shade gave a few playful swats of the landlady's pendulous bits but otherwise kept up his Oliver Twist act.

I sighed. "They want to get back to Glessie, Iris. A salmon is waiting for them there. It's a tradition," I said, rolling my eyes.

"But yer scared because you don't think the avalanche will be cleared in time?"

Iris didn't wait for an answer. She nodded, more to herself than to us, and wandered back to the bar through a sea of partying Santa's.

"At least Iris understands," Fraidy said.

I shook my head. "Listen, guys; I wasn't taunting you about the salmon. Honestly, I wasn't. It's just ... don't ask me why, but I have this feeling. I think we're gonna make it home."

My cats swiveled their eyes to my face. It was clear to me: They saw only a mad woman.

"Ms. Opal?" A thin voice interrupted. I stood up to greet Adorania Blazier. I pumped her hand with both of mine.

"Thanks so much for coming, Adorania. May I call you that?" I said, sitting back down.

Stella's sister blew an errant strand of hair from her face and nodded. Her eyes searched the room as she sat down.

"Well, I'm not sure what I can offer you, Ms. Opal, that will help you find Leland," she said, her eyes still darting in all directions.

I gave a theatrically 'casual' shrug and leaned back in my chair smiling. "Well, as they say, it's only the finest threads that are left dangling in the big cases."

Gloom slapped a paw to her forehead and rolled her eyes.

I cleared my throat. "Adorania," I said, leaning in and tenting my fingers on the table in front of me. "I'd like you to think very carefully. Back to the day your sister came home from work early. The day you and Leland were playing squash, can you do that?"

Adorania gave me a curt nod. She drew her elbows close to her side, no doubt trying to create some distance between her and my cats.

"Do you think there's any chance that your sister may have overheard yours and Leland's conversation about the land deal? While you were playing squash?"

She shook her head but said nothing.

I tried again. "We have reason to believe your sister may have overheard her husband and you conspiring behind her back. We also believe that this might well be the reason you didn't attend your sister's funeral." I didn't pose my speculations as questions. I had to break through to this woman somehow, so I figured if she needed to defend herself she would.

Adorania shook her head again and bit her bottom lip. I could see tears building under her thick eyelashes. She let one fall, and then looked at me.

"If Stella heard anything at all, it was her husband and me...." she wrung her hands on the table. "Leland and I were ...." More tears fell.

Shade placed a paw on Adorania's arm. His voice was all tenderness when he said: "Lady, were you and Stella's husband doing a bit of matin' on the side, like?"

"Shade!" I shrieked. My cat's mouth hung open, his eyes wide with kitty-innocence.

"Adorania, please, forgive my cat," I said, giving Shade a stern look. "He's like a bull in a china--"

"He's right." She said. "Leland and I ... we were ... lovers." The woman's head dropped forward, her shame temporarily hidden.

I didn't know what to say. To be honest, I wasn't really thinking of this woman's predicament. But I was certainly jolted by the fact that our case had just taken a sharp and unforeseen turn. My every nerve began to vibrate.

A small team of Santa's staggered from the bar, all jostling to get out of the door, while another walked in. I watched as the lone Santa walked to a recently vacated table to the left of us, only to be beaten by two young lovebirds. He grunted and sauntered over to the bar instead. The sea of red and white in the bar had dwindled down to erratic waves. Maybe all the Saint Nick's had gone out to make deliveries. Or, even more likely, back to their wives and families. Only a few of the more inebriated Father Christmas's remained. I turned my head back to Adorania.

"I'm sure that couldn't have been an easy situation to be in," I empathized. "And, I've no doubt that having to stay away from your sister's funeral was even harder." I paused. "Adorania, were you forced to stay away from the service because of one of the Blazier Precepts?"

"The Blazier Death Precepts," she whispered; more to herself than to us. She looked up. "Do you know how archaic these death orders are?" She asked. "Do you know that one of the Blazier precepts is that only red satin may be used as a coffin liner? Know why that is?"

I shook my head.

"Because the mighty Blazier's believe that our blood will run from our bodies into the soil we are buried in. An arrogant statement to let the world know that, we, the Blazier's, will one day inherit the earth." She looked at us. "Can you believe that? My family thinks this planet belongs to them. And, now we're spearheading the Red Orb Program, because, apparently, one planet isn't enough." She shook her head and her eyes filled with fresh tears.

"Wait, so you're saying your sister wasn't embalmed?" I asked.

Stella's sister nodded. She pulled a handkerchief from her sleeve and blew her nose.

Something flashed from under the woman's sleeve. "Blazier funerals are closed casket. Always," Adorania confirmed. "And, as for what kept me away from Stella's burial ...I cheated on my sister. And, yes, it was one of the precepts. Infidelity is, and always has been, a big no-no in my family." She wiped at her tears with the handkerchief, revealing another glint of metal from beneath her sleeve.

I pointed to her wrist. "Your bracelet," I said. "Mind if I take a look?"

Adorania looked puzzled but lifted her sleeve. A gold bracelet. She turned the engraving plate toward us to show us the initials engraved there: A.B

"Nice jewelry," I said, smiling. "I'm guessing those are your initials?"

She nodded dumbly. "It has ... sentimental value."

"Enough sentimental value to have two copies made?" Midnight piped up.

Adorania turned to my kitty. "I-I don't understand."

"Is there another bracelet like this in existence, he means," I said.

Adorania looked blank. "No. Well, I mean, yes, my sister. Stella, she has the matching one to this," she said. "What are you getting at?"

"But, if your sister has the matching bracelet, wouldn't it -- presumably, I mean -- have Stella's initials on it? S.B?"

"Correct, Ms. Opal." Adorania's voice was cool with a newfound impatience. "Only my sister's initials are also: A.B."

"I beg your pardon?" *Well, this is an exciting turn.*

"Astrid," Adorania said. "My sister's real name was Astrid; not Stella. Of course, she always hated the name, Astrid. She defied father by switching it in her mid-teens to 'Stella.' It wasn't a legal transition, though. She was a rebel like that, Stella. Always playing at the boundaries of any written rules."

"Star," Gloom whispered. "They both mean 'star.'"

"That's right, kitty cat. But I fail to see how this has anything to do with anything. Seeing as my sister and her bracelet are buried six feet under right now." Adorania sighed. "Along with my favorite dress."

The hairs on my neck stood on end. "Can you repeat that last part, please?"

"My dress, you mean?" Adorania blinked at me. "It's of no importance, Ms. Opal, and shame on me for even mentioning something as insignificant as fabric, but, well, Stella was buried in my favorite frock. A blue, silk number I'd picked up on the mainland. Leland suggested I hand it over because we all knew how much Stella loved that dress. She had borrowed it on countless occasions ...." Adorania's words trailed off. "What?" She asked. "Why are you all looking at me like that?"

I leaned over to Fraidy and cupped a shaking hand to his ear. I whispered instructions to my anxious kitty.

"Why me?" Fraidy hissed. "I'm not exactly the best man for the job here."

"Carbon, you go with him," I said.

"Huh? Go where?"

"Fraidy will tell you, just go with him."

Carbon stared at me. "Now!" I said.

My two cats slinked their way to the front door of the Maggoty Apple, keeping to the shadows the whole way. Adorania spun around in her seat to see what my cats were up to. "Wha—what's going on?"

I held my downturned palm over the table and looked at Stella's sister. "I am about to lay some items on the table," I said. "But, you must promise me, when you see them you won't react. Okay? Is that clear, Adorania? I need you to remain passive." The woman bobbed her head.

I lay the fabric down, but covered it from outside view with the palm of my hand.

Adorania stiffened, her eyes flew open in visible alarm. "Where did you find these things?" She whispered.

"Please remain calm," I said. "But, I think I know where to find Leland Clavelle."

She slapped a hand to her chest. "You know where he is? Leland's alive?"

The certainty I felt over Leland's fate kicked in then. I gave an almost imperceptible shake of my head, and cupped my hand over Adorania's and squeezed. "Leland's gone, sweetie," I whispered. "And, there's something else you need to know ..."

CHAPTER NINE

"Stella Blazier!" I bellowed, standing up from my seat and whirling toward the Santa who sat at the bar. He spun around, his mouth hanging open.

"Drunk Santa!" Midnight gasped, staring at the red wine stain on Santa's fur-trimmed jacket.

The Claus impersonator bolted toward the door.

"Fraidy, Carbon, now!" I shouted over to my guard-cats.

Fraidy, more in reflex from my command than from bravery, leaped at Father Christmas' face, hooking his claws into the bewildered Santa's beard. He swung there, left and right, grunting with the effort of trying to unmask our killer. Santa grappled with my terrified cat, trying to pull Fraidy from his face while trying to hold his beard in place and his identity covered.

Fraidy swung, his lips curled back in a manic grimace, his tail swishing for added momentum.

"Get off me, you flea-bitten animal!" Stella Blazier swatted at my dangling cat, lost her footing, and fell to the floor. Fraidy didn't let go and tumbled with the woman. I think my scaredy-cat was pretty much in the grip of paralyzed terror. He just lay there, like a mute sphynx, on top of Stella's chest, staring into the undead woman's face with a glaze to his eyes.

"Stella?" Adorania took a tentative step toward the fallen Santa. Stella looked at her sister and yanked the beard clear of her face.

"What's the matter, Addie?" she spat, pushing Fraidy to the side. The latter fell to the floor, as petrified as a dead oak tree, eyes like glass, and sipping shallow breaths. *This is going to cost you a lifetime's supply of salmon, Chimera.*

"Looks like you've seen a ghost." Stella's smile bordered on the barbaric.

"No," Adorania choked. "No, I don't ... I don't believe this is happening." She rocked on her feet.

Stella rose to her feet, pulling off both the curly white wig and the Santa hat in one fluid motion. A wave of chestnut hair fanned out behind her.

"You can believe your eyes, dear sister." She unbuttoned her red jacket, tugging at the gold-buckled belt. A pillow, or Santa's stomach, fell to the floor. "Because this is really happening." Stella offered her sister another demonic smile.

"What ... why would you ... where is Leland?" Adorania fell to her knees, her face registering the full shock of what was unfolding. She folded her hands together in front of her and beseeched her sister. "Please, Stella," she said. "Please tell me you haven't hurt Leland?"

Stella's chilly laugh sounded like she had swallowed a grave-full of soil. "*Hurt* him?" She said. "No, Addie, I didn't *hurt* Leland. I *killed* him." Stella laughed again. This time in the style of a storied maniacal killer.

Adorania's body shook. Her hands flew from their prayer position to her face. Tears poured freely down the woman's face. "No," she said, her head swaying from side to side. "No, I don't believe you .... You're ... you're dead!"

I stepped in between the two women, but said nothing. Adorania needed a lifetime to digest what she was seeing and hearing, but I figured I could give her a few seconds at least.

I looked at my petrified cat laying still next to Stella and then nodded to Gloom. "Go and take care of your brother, honey."

Gloom, unhappy that she was about to be taken out of the circle of excitement and put to pasture as a caregiver, rolled her eyes at me and sauntered over to Fraidy.

She sat on him.

Because Gloom deems this a suitable way of giving comfort.

I waved to Iris Crimple who stood motionless at the bar, watching the spectacle unfold. Even her chins remained still. "Iris," I shouted. "Is Donkerton's officer still in town?" The landlady nodded mutely.

"Call him," I said. "Now."

Iris sprung into action and dived for the phone, knocking over an opened bottle of gin in the process. I turned back to the sisters. "Stella .... Astrid, I mean, maybe it's time you start talking," I said, looking directly at Stella Blazier. I knew enough to know what had happened, but I didn't know *how* stuff had happened. My kitties gathered round, and folded their legs under them, as curious as I was about how all the bizarre events might have unfolded. Gloom sat upright on Fraidy's head, her ears twitching.

The sobbing Adorania swiped at her tears and faced her sister. She left her right hand clutching at her heart.

"Well, I'd like to know who the hell you are, first," Stella said. "And, why have you been asking questions about my family and me?"

"I'm a private investigator, Mrs. Blazier, and I --" Gloom's gales of laughter interrupted my discourse. I glared at my kitty until she settled down on top of Fraidy's head once more.

"As I was saying, I'm investigating Leland Clavelle's disappearance. I'm helping your sister."

Leland Clavelle's 'late' wife snuck a glance at her overwhelmed sister.

"I guess it's no secret that I didn't die last week," she said.

"Courtesy of the Stillbreath's, I believe," Onyx said.

Stella frowned. "Ugh, I hate talking cats." She looked down the length of her nose at Onyx.

"But, yes, cat, the Stillbreath's are superb for faking death," she said. "And so easy to obtain, given my position at the WSA." Stella sighed. "I guess the top-secret designator doesn't really count now, so

I'd might as well share with you that the WSA was conducting Still-breath research for our astronauts in the ROP."

I looked toward Adorania. "Your sister's talking about the Warlock Space Agency and the Red Orb Program. Stella had a permit to harvest the fungus. We saw her name: Astrid, on the registration form." Adorania gave me a vacant stare

"The astronauts in the program, " I said. "Their bodies are subjected to all kinds of gravitational stress, not to mention a host of psychological stressors ... Stillbreath brings down the rate of respiration, heart-rate, you name it. It limits cortisol and adrenaline production too. In carefully measured doses, it's a boon for anxiety, but in heavy-handed doses .... well..." I waved a hand toward Stella to illustrate to Adorania what a heavy-handed dose of the fungus could do.

"A Stillbreath death can only work if your family is governed by a list of Death Precepts, however," I said. "A precept that doesn't permit embalming, for example." I looked at Stella.

She threw her hands to her face and gasped in mock surprise."Oh, no! Has my sister been sharing our family secrets? You know about our penchant for red satin? Oh, dear, oh dear."

"B-but why? Why would you do this, Stella? Why?"

"Oh, sister, you really need to ask why?" Stella said. "Did you honestly think I'd let you run off with my husband and live the rest of your life in the happily-ever-after? Seriously?"

"Y-you knew?" Adorania said. "You knew Leland and I were having an affair?"

"If I hadn't come home from work early, then I'd have likely never have known," Stella confessed. "I mean, who'd have thought my own flesh and blood would cavort with my husband behind my back?" She paused. "I thought I had Leland's life scheduled enough to mitigate any such philanderings, but I guess you used my scheduling against me, Addie. You used Leland's Goddamned squash lessons to get at my husband." Stella's eyes flashed.

"We .. we're in love," Adorania mumbled. "Leland and I are in love."

"Were," Stella spat. "You *were* in love."

"Oh, my Goddess, what have you done?" Adorania got to her feet, and stared at her sister through a veil of tears.

"What have *I* done?" Stella screeched. "*You* did this. If you hadn't been trying to steal my husband from me, Leland would still be alive and on schedule right now!" She pulled back her lips and let her breath seethe through her barred teeth.

"We were going to tell you!" Adorania blared. "We were in love, and wanted to do things right! We were planning on telling you, Stella! Where is he? Where is Leland? Tell me!"

Stella offered her sister a sly grin. "Why, he's in Silent Meadows, of course. Only, he's *in* my grave now; not *visiting* it."

Adorania lunged. I stepped in just before she reached her sister, and held the grieving woman at arm's length. Her grief-induced strength was incredible. I fumbled in my pocket for my wand while I wrestled Adorania with my one free hand. Pulling out the cherrywood stick I flicked my wrist toward Stella's sister. "*Pluma Gravitas!*" I shouted my 'feather-light' spell, and Adorania's force weakened to that of a newborn kitten. The woman flailed her arms in futile circles as she tried to overcome me. I could have held her back with my little finger. I drew in a deep breath and turned to Stella. "But, you were buried," I said. "How did you do it? How, and when did you kill your husband?"

"Well, I had to make it realistic, didn't I?" Stella thrust her chin at me. "I had to make sure that old lady Spleener saw me in my coffin on the morning of my burial. I needed to make sure that I wouldn't be held under suspicion."

Shade scratched his head. "I don't get it," he said. "So when did you off Leland?"

"Before I was buried," said Stella.

"Before?" We all chimed in unison.

"No thanks to Leland," Stella said. "He positively blew off his schedule. He had me working all damned night. I was lucky to get back to my coffin before morning broke. That's when I made a ruckus so that Mrs. Spleener would hear and check up on me before finally sealing my casket."

"You were the one who knocked over the formaldehyde?" Onyx

asked. Stella nodded. "I created a little disturbance, yes," she said. "Didn't have much time to fix my hair, though," she added.

"Sorry, I'm still confused," I said. "We *saw* you. On top of your own grave at Silent Meadows just two days ago."

"Whoever the hell you are, you are correct," Stella said squinting at me. She looked like an angry snake. "I was burying Leland when you and your never-stop-talking cats came snooping, not crawling out of my grave."

"She talkin' about me, yep, yep?" Jet chittered.

Stella pulled a chair from a nearby table and sat down. She wiped a hand over her face. "If you'll shut up and listen, I'll lay it out for you." She eyed us all with her reptilian gaze. "Clear?"

We nodded.

"I planned to wait at home for Leland. This was the night before the funeral. Leland was supposed to be running at six p.m, as per his schedule. But my spineless husband came here to drown his sorrows instead." She pointed to the bar where Iris Crimple stood rapt. Stella cleared her throat. "The Spleener's shut up shop at five p.m. The Still-breath serum had worn off about an hour beforehand. I felt groggy, and my head ached." She looked at us. "Fungal hangover. The worst. Anyway, I waited for the Spleener's to go upstairs and back to their humdrum lives of early evening tv shows, and then I crept out. I took the path through the woods back to the house. I had to. I was wearing a ballgown for Pete's sake. I needed to get back to the estate to put on some comfy clothes for my mission ahead. My first task was to spike Leland's sport's drink before he took off on his run. I knew my husband would arrive home from work at five-forty-five p.m, so I had to act quickly."

"You spiked Leland's sports drink with Stillbreath?" I said.

"No, no. Simple cyanide. Faster acting than the mushrooms. Plus, cyanide kills. Outright."

I couldn't get over this woman's apparent glee. A sparkle of the darkest kind of humor danced in her eyes. "Anyway, I had to wait for Leland to stagger home from the pub," Stella said. "Which put me three hours behind schedule. I thought my plan was ruined when he stumbled his drunken ass through the door," she said. "But, luckily for me, my husband's boozing session had made him very thirsty. It took him no more than thirty seconds to reach for the drink. And he guzzled the whole damned lot."

"D-did Leland see you?" Adorania asked.

"Oh, I made sure of it, Addie," Stella sneered. "Cyanide is very fast acting, as I mentioned, but, yes, I made sure to step into Leland's last glimpse of the world."

"No, no, no." Adorania shook her head in disbelief.

"Aww, Addie, you'll get over it," Stella hissed. "You've still got your beloved greenhouse, right? I hear gardening can be beneficial for grief, so I'm sure you'll be okay in no time."

My mind flashed back to Adorania's dirty fingernails. *I guess that explains that.*

"So let me get this straight," I said, pulling on my lip. "You're pronounced dead by the coroner, shipped to Spleener's for prettying up and prep ... stop me if I get it wrong," I said. Stella gave me an acid smile and a nod of her head.

"Because of the Blazier precepts, you're not embalmed, just washed, made up a little, hair styled, dressed up and whatnot, correct?"

"So far so good."

"So because of the Blazier embalming ban you knew you weren't going to have your system flooded with formaldehyde," Onyx said.

"'Yep, yep, 'cos the embalming process, like, would kill you for sure, yep."

"Yes, and because I wasn't embalmed, it afforded me a little freedom to move around, as it were," Stella said.

"So you zombie-walked to your house, took out your hubby, and then what? You went back to your coffin to be buried? Lady, I'm not gonna lie, that just doesn't make any sense," Midnight said, his arms out to his side in question.

"That's exactly what happened, cat," Stella said. "I already told you, I didn't want my involvement with Leland's disappearance to come into question. I wanted my death to look authentic. And final."

Adorania fell to her knees. I was thankful because even though she was made light by my charm, my arm was getting tired. Stella's sister uttered a low moan.

"You were buried for ... what ... two days?" I asked. "How did you get out?"

Stella's leer morphed into something a little more sincere looking. There was real warmth in her smile. "My coyote friends," she said. "They came when they were needed. We share a language. We understand one another, and they came. They came at the exact time I requested of them."

"That's nuts," Shade said.

"Where was Leland when you were in the ground?" Adorania stared at her sister. "Where was your MURDERED HUSBAND while you lay around biding your time?"

"I hid him in the Blackbugler's mausoleum," Stella said. "The only living Blackbugler today lives on the mainland. Nobody ever visits that crumbling crypt." She ran a hand through her hair. "It was easy, I performed a spell much like our unknown snooper here," Stella said, flicking her head toward me. "I made Leland as light as a feather, and I carried his sorry bones from the house back to the crypt in preparation for burying in a couple of days time. I made the mistake of forgetting to bring a change of clothes, though." She paused and looked at my cats. "But, anyway, this lot spotted me while I was attempting to cover my husband wearing nothing but Addie's ballgown."

I shook my head. "I still don't understand," I said. "So your canine buddies dug you out, okay. I got that. But, how did you unlatch the coffin from the inside? I thought you said that Mrs. Spleener had sealed it."

Stella stroked her chin. "Remember I told you I had had to work all night? Well, after Leland had put me three hours behind schedule, I then spent another six hours looking for my wand. My husband, you see, in his haste to rid me from his memory, I guess, packed up all my stuff and had stuffed it all in the attic. You have no idea how many boxes I had to go through to find it. As I told you, it was nearly dawn by the time I got back to Spleener's. I simply charmed the latch and hid my wand underneath the folds of my dress. I used it to charm the air in the coffin too. I squeezed out double the amount of oxygen from the interior. It kept me breathing for the two days I was in the ground.

By the time my coyote friends arrived for their digging work, all I had to do was flick my wand to re-release the coffin's latch."

I was surprised to see a solitary tear streaking down Stella's cheek. She wiped at it furiously. "My good husband had packed me away even before I was in the ground," she muttered.

"Stella, did you know there's a roadblock at the Horsemen? Donkerton's there; he's looking for your husband. How did you expect to get out of town? You know you can't use magic, so what were you thinking?" I asked.

Stella looked at Midnight. "If your stupid snooping cat here thought to look on the *inside* of the cabin, then he'd have noticed the stockpile of food. I planned to wait it out up there. Until the search lost steam. I'm a patient woman."

"No kidding," Shade said. "Anyone who can spend two days underground without losing their marbles gets the Zen award, I'd say."

The door to the Maggoty Apple opened, and Gothic Harbor's one and only remaining officer walked in. He walked to the bar, where he engaged in a lively debate with Iris. The landlady pointed over to us, and the officer strode over, already unclipping a pair of handcuffs from his belt.

He cuffed Stella's wrists and guided her silently toward the exit.

"Wait!" I yelled. I groped inside my pocket for the bracelet, and handed it to Stella. "Here," I said. "It's your family heirloom." The scrap of cerulean blue silk had wedged itself between one of the bracelets links. Stella smoothed it between her thumb and forefinger.

"Sorry, about the dress, Addie," she whispered before she was led away.

CHAPTER TEN

The Christmas Miracle happened shortly after we had solved the case. It took a while to calm Adorania down, but after Iris' generous offerings of free brandy, Adorania's wracking sobs became muted sniffles. We had her neighbor, Agnes Carp, sit with her before she escorted her to the police station for questioning.

"Boss-lady, we gonna have to stay here another night?" Midnight asked. He looked agitated.

"I-I don't know, buddy. I *still* have a feeling --"

"Forget it, human," Gloom sniffed. It's Christmas Eve tomorrow. We're never getting out of here on time. The salmon's a goner."

I sighed. I guess I had to admit we were running out of time.

"Okay, I'm sorry guys. I really am. I still have this feeling, but ... well, do you want me to ask Iris if the place is free for another night?"

"No need of that, lovey." The landlady beamed from ear to ear. "I think you should probably take your kitties and head to the pass. You'll find a way through, I'm sure." She winked at me.

"What? Iris, what do you mean?" I said, already grabbing my coat and bag.

"Merry Christmas, Chimera and beautiful cats," she said. "Go. Go now."

I ran over to her and gave her a big squeeze. I felt her chins shift a little under my shoulder. "I don't know what you've done, or what you did, or what you're doing, Iris, but thank you. From the bottom of my heart, thank you."

"Aw, get away with ya! Get going now, while the roads are clear. The snow melted fast, but there's more on the way." She patted my back and turned away. The Infiniti and I walked out of the Maggoty Apple to the car. Well, I had to carry Fraidy. He wasn't walking anywhere in his present CATatonic state. I massaged his head with one hand until I heard him offer a low purr.

"You think Iris put some magic on the avalanche?" Eclipse asked, taking his place on the back seat.

"I don't know, 'Clipsy,'" I said. "But, I wouldn't think so. I'm pretty sure it wouldn't work anyway, would it?"

"Well, what else could it be?" Gloom snapped. Iris' news had my cat excited. Which meant she was more than a little grumpy as a consequence of her excitement. "Because I'm telling you now, only magic will get us out of here. There will be no Christmas without it, so deal with it."

"Oh, will you zip it, Ebenezer?" Carbon said. "Have a little faith this Christmas season, won't you?"

"Let's talk about faith when your breath is stinking of cheap cat food on Boxing day," Gloom scoffed.

"Are we, like, gonna actually get any boxes this Boxing day?" Midnight asked. "I mean, it sounds like the best holiday ever, but I dunno, it always comes up short for me. I mean, no new boxes ever turn up. It's like we have to make do with the wrappings of Christmas day."

"That's true, bro, that's true," Shade empathized. "I mean, Christmas wrappings are fun and all, but they're kinda old news by Boxing day."

Gloom rolled her eyes. "You guys are a pair of plankton. You don't ...."

I didn't even hear my cats bickering as I drove to the Four Horsemen pass. I was too busy vibrating with a sense of hope and excitement I hadn't felt since the Christmas mornings of my childhood days.

I rounded the last bend into the pass and brought the car to a stop. We stared, in silent wonder, at the Christmas Miracle playing out before us. An army of whistling Santa's, hundreds in number, digging away at the mound of fallen snow, shipping truckloads of it out to parts unknown. A huge tunnel had already been carved through the ice. I wondered how far they were from the 'other side.' My heart hammered in my chest; not through excitement this time, but from the beating grace of gratitude and love I felt for these people working so hard on our behalf.

Here we were trying to get home to Glessie for Christmas, and, yet, before us was a brightly-shining example of the true meaning of Christmas. A community coming together to help a stranger (and her cats) in need. Gloom had suggested that we'd need magic to get out of Gothic Harbor. Well, if this play of human generosity on the other side of my windshield wasn't magic, then I'd eat the magician's hat. Shade was also bowled over by a wave of emotion. He hugged each of his siblings first, and then came to embrace me just as the first Santa waved us through the tunnel. I could see the flashing lights of Donkerton's cruiser on the other side.

Shade rubbed his cheek against mine, placing both of his paws either side of my neck. "I love you, boss," he said. "Merry Salmon."

I kissed him on the head. "Merry Salmon, honey."

THE END.

Want to read more? Dive into The Infiniti Chronicles

ABOUT THE AUTHOR

Pearl lives in the beautiful province of Nova Scotia, Canada. She's a cat lady, a loner, and maybe even a little bit of a weirdo. But perhaps this helps when writing stories about talking cats?

Follow Pearl Goodfellow online:
  Website
  Facebook

HOLLY-LOCKED

In a Town Called Christmas Cove Mystery

AVA MALLORY

SUMMARY

Welcome to Christmas Cove, a town celebrated for its magic and its mysteries.

When Holly Belle said goodbye to Christmas Cove in search of fame and fortune in Hollywood, she knew she'd one-day find herself in the limelight. But she never imagined a murder in her hometown would be her first brush with fame. Her precocious grandmother, a witch with an eye for trouble, stands accused of a doozy of crime. Will Holly's grand return save her grandmother, or will it open the door to more drama?

CHAPTER ONE

Holly Belle rushed into the nondescript concrete structure and slammed into the guard's desk with full force.

The guard, a redheaded woman with dark eyes and a harsh brow line stiffened her back as she took in the harried thirty-something-year-old woman, who hadn't dressed for the weather. With her thick, false eyelashes, and short red, leather skirt with matching stilettos on her tattooed feet, two things were obvious: She didn't belong here and wasn't afraid of catching pneumonia.

"Can I help you?" Maxine, a twenty-year veteran of the Christmas Cove sheriff's office, asked.

Holly pushed her curls off her face and said in a thick Midwestern accent, "I can't believe I'm about to say this, but I'm here to bail my grandmother out of jail." She gulped back a giggle because it didn't seem like the proper thing to do in this situation.

Nothing about the last twelve hours of her life seemed appropriate. One minute she's standing in front of a camera, getting ready to say her first official line for her new acting gig and the next, she's scraping coins out of her sofa cushions because she's forty-dollars shy of the full fee for a plane ticket back to the place she'd hoped to never see again:

Christmas Cove, the tiny town who celebrated the holidays all year round, whether any of the local residents wanted to or not.

Maxine hoisted her pants over her thick middle, a sneer on her face. "Well, isn't that sweet? Your grandmother doesn't happen to have a name, does she? Or would you like me to cut all the inmates loose for you? Your wish is my command."

Unappreciative of Maxine's mocking tone, Holly arched a newly-perfected brow at her and lodged what she thought was the appropriate response, "That depends. Do many feeble elderly women get locked up on a regular night? I'm sure the streets of this Podunk town are safer now that my grandmother is in a steel cage."

Maxine wasn't amused often, but she'd made an exception for the spunky misfit. "Let me guess. Calliope Belle is your grandmother?"

Holly gulped. The guard's tone conveyed what most people in Christmas Cove thought about her family. The tales they'd tell about their mysterious past were enough to make her want to leave town for good. Back then, The Cove, as it's known by the locals, was nothing more than a near-defunct eyesore stuck between acres of feedlots.

When a developer from southern California accidentally found himself and his young family stranded on the side of the road a mile south of town, he and his hotel decorator wife, decided it would be the ideal location for their high-concept tourist destination. Before anyone knew what was happening, the town - population: 402 at the time - was turned into a scene from The Nightmare Before Christmas permanently. Soon after that, she packed her bags and headed for Hollywood in search of a real acting job, instead of the reluctant witch thing she had going on at home.

"Yes, she is. I'm here to bail her out," she answered.

Maxine leaned forward, elbows on the desk, and whispered, "What if I told you there's no bail for murderers?"

Holly gasped.

In all the confusion, she hadn't written down the details. Her daily diaries were her lifeline. Ever since a spell gone wrong had taken her ability to remember anything she didn't write down, she filled reams of paper with her notes to make sure she didn't forget the important things, like to brush her teeth or wear pants.

While her condition made it excruciatingly difficult to concentrate when she was a student, it has fed her creative side. She'd become quite the artist, often turning in assignments with elaborate drawings instead of the mundane information like actual answers to the questions asked. Since the Christmas Cove school district frowned upon letting students use their notes on tests, she had to channel her energy into the arts. Drawing and scrapbooking replaced Algebra, Economics, and Social Studies until her grandmother convinced her mother to homeschool her. Not that it went any better, but it did at least make for interesting dinner conversations, though.

"I'm sorry. Did you say murder?" She reached for her diary to check her notes. "No, that can't be right. I have it right here. It says she was mistakenly picked up in a raid at Santa's Workshop. One of the elves kicked an officer and she intervened and accidentally scratched him. How is that murder?"

Sarcasm laced through her words, Maxine answered, "It became murder when the elf died. That's how." She snickered. "Look, darling, I don't know where you're from, but you might want to consider checking into the Solstice Suites for a while. The courthouse is closed until after the new year. Merry Christmas. Happy New Year and all that jazz."

"What? No. That can't be right. The elf died? How?" She had so many questions.

"How am I supposed to know? I just work here. Why don't you take your mini skirt and those ridiculous shoes and get out of here? There's nothing you can do to help her. It was bound to happen anyway. No offense, but your family isn't exactly known for keeping their hands to themselves. You're lucky you don't live here."

"Lucky? What's lucky about any of this? I have to see her. This must be some kind of mistake." She fought back tears as the guard busied herself with paperwork, oblivious to her concerns.

The double doors opened behind her.

Holly begged the guard, "Isn't there someone I can talk to? Can I at least see her? I need to know she's okay."

Maxine glanced up at the door and plastered a smile on her face. "Oh, I didn't hear you come in. Nice to see you again, Henry." She smoothed her hands over her wrinkled uniform. "If I'd known you were stopping by, I would have ironed this morning."

"Hello, ladies," the handsome man with dark locks, the sculptured face of a Roman god, and sea blue colored eyes greeted them. "How is everything?" He eyed Holly, taking in her shapely tanned legs. "I don't believe we've met before, have we?"

She hadn't expected to find herself face to face with someone as handsome as Henry. When she turned to face him, her smeared make-up startled him.

He stifled a laugh as he offered his hand. "I'm Henry Castle, the city manager."

Wishing she'd had the presence of mind to fix her face before addressing him, she stared at her feet to avoid making eye contact. "Hello. Did you say city manager? What is that? Like the mayor? I thought Eugene Bottles was the mayor?"

He gave her hand a gentle squeeze. "Eugene is still the mayor. There's no getting rid of him. Is there something I can help you with?" He glanced over her shoulder at Maxine. "Could you get her a tissue, please?"

Unlike when Holly had asked her for help, Maxine readily agreed to help him. She reached into a drawer and pulled out a box of tissues. "This isn't unusual. All the perp's families leave here in tears. It comes with the territory. She'll be fine."

"Perps?" Holly didn't appreciate the statement. "My grandmother isn't a perp."

"Yeah, you know, cons, criminals, thugs? You know what I mean. The inmates," Maxine explained, her eye twitching as she stared at Henry.

"My grandmother is not a criminal, thank you very much," Holly protested. "Whatever happened to innocent until proven guilty?" She was so angry, she could barely get the words out of her mouth.

Henry placed a tender hand on the middle of her back. "Let's just take a breather. I'm sure she didn't mean it that way. Did you, Maxine?" He cocked an eyebrow at her. "Do you think you could rephrase what you just said?"

Blushing, she tried again, "What I mean is when inmate's families stop by, they always leave disappointed. That's the way things go around here. It's nothing I haven't seen before."

"All I want to do is take her home," Holly said, emotion garbling her words. "She isn't a murderer."

"But she's a witch, right?" Maxine pointed out the well-known secret.

Henry gasped. "Are you here for Mrs. Belle?"

"Ms. Belle," I corrected him. "She's divorced."

"Yeah, three times," Maxine chimed in. "The Belle women never could keep a man. I mean, I don't blame the men for leaving. Who would want to be married to anyone from that lot? They're a screw short of a—"

"Could you not?" Holly asked. "What do you know about me and my family? I don't recall ever meeting you before. So what if my grand-mother got divorced a few times? What does that have to do with any of this?"

She held her belly as she laughed. "Everything because the elf she killed happened to be one of your ex-grandfathers."

The information hit Holly like a meteor. Her voice barely above a whisper, she asked, "Which one?"

Her actual grandfather died long before she was born according to her diary entries. From what she'd been told, her grandparents were the perfect couple. Her grandmother's second husband never made it as an entry in her diary, so she had no memory to speak of. Her grand-mother's last husband filled enough pages in her diaries, she could have written a whole book about the years they'd spent together. The last she'd checked - on April 22nd, to be exact - he was alive and well, living in the Florida Keys.

"It's not Fred, is it? Please, tell me it wasn't him," she begged.

Maxine shook her head. "Nope. That old piece of useless man-dom is still in Florida. I heard he got married again, but I can't say for sure."

Holly breathed a sigh of relief. "So, it has to be husband number two. What's his name?" She opened her diary to an empty page.

"What's the book?" Maxine asked. "You're not a reporter, are you?"

She shook her head. "No. This is just something I have to do to keep the facts straight."

Henry interjected, "There's nothing wrong with taking notes. Let her be. Tell her what she needs to know."

"Fine, but I don't want to be quoted," she said. She pulled a newspaper out of a drawer and flopped it on the desk. "Here's the whole story. You can keep it."

The story of the elf's death covered the front page: Joseph "Uncle Joe" Quick Murdered.

"Uncle Joe?" Holly tried to pull an image out of her head but failed. She had no memory of anyone by that name. Frustrated, she skimmed through the pages of her diary. "I'll have to have my roommate send my old diaries. I don't have anything about him in here."

Maxine decided to make a game out of her memory issues. "You can remember you have a roommate, but you can't remember your grandmother's ex-husband. Can you remember your name, or did you forget to write that in your notes?"

Holly flipped to the inside flap of her book, where she had detailed descriptions of her roommate, her dog, and her job. "I keep important information written right here. Is that okay with you?"

"Did you hit your head or something?" Maxine asked.

"No. A long time ago, a spell went wrong. It was an accident." Holly stopped herself, wondering why she had to explain at all. "You know what? It doesn't matter. Right now, I need to focus on my grandmother and this Uncle Joe guy. Tell me what you know about him, so I can verify it with her."

"Nope. Visiting hours are from five to seven on Sundays and Fridays." Maxine pointed to a calendar on the wall. "Today is Monday. Too bad."

Holly's knees wobbled. "Please. I'm begging you."

"You have to wait. You have a cell phone, right? She'll call you if she wants to talk to you," Maxine said, before turning her attention back to Henry. "What can I help you with today, Mr. Castle?"

He walked around Holly. "I have an appointment with the warden about the Christmas parade."

Holly made her way to the door, heartbroken.

"Oh, yeah. You seriously want inmates to help with the parade.

Don't you think they'll be bad for business? How do you know they're any good?" Maxine asked.

He answered, "The artists we hired had to bow out. They were over-committed. Since it's too late to find new artists, the warden suggested we invite some of the non-violent offenders to lend a hand."

Holly didn't mean to eavesdrop, but she couldn't help herself. If Maxine wouldn't let her in for a visit, maybe volunteering to help Henry would help her gain access. "I'm an artist," she volunteered. "I could help."

CHAPTER TWO

"Good morning," Holly offered as Henry's secretary, a girl she'd gone to elementary school with, ushered her into his office. "First, I want to thank you for allowing me to help you with your project. I've never actually been here for the big holiday celebrations. I've lived in California for—"

He held up a hand to stave off a long, drawn-out explanation. "No need for the small talk. I know you didn't do this because you wanted to help. You're using me, and that's fine. As long as the work gets done, I don't have a problem with it. Now, let's get some things straight." He motioned for her to take the seat opposite him at a large conference table, covered in artist's renderings of massive parade floats and a huge balloon-like figure in the shape of a globe. "The concept is simple. One world. We want to celebrate unity and harmony throughout the world. You might not know this, but Christmas Cove is undergoing a bit of a Renaissance. We're transitioning from the old Halloween-ish theme of the past and going with a more all-inclusive theme. Sleigh bells, candles, reindeer, Santas from around the world, tiny figurines made to look like some of our most memorable residents. You know, that kind of thing.

Holly studied the drawings. "Okay. Sounds great. What do you want me to do?" She hoped he'd say he'd get her a visit with her grandmother.

"I need you to convince your grandmother to use a little magic," he said in a matter-of-fact tone.

She checked her notes from their brief conversation the night before. "I'm sorry. What? I don't recall a conversation about magic."

He flashed a winning smile at her. "That's because it didn't happen yesterday. We're having that conversation now."

She swallowed hard. "I'm confused. Maybe no one told you," she started as she flipped open her diary to the first page. "We're forbidden from using magic. The city council came down on us when I was a little kid. No one can use magic within the city limits."

"I know the story. I'm saying to you that I don't care about what you were told then. This is about the here and now." He pulled a folded piece of paper out of his breast pocket. "Here, look at this. Maybe this will help you understand. Feel free to take notes if you need to."

She unfolded the paper, her hands shaking. No one had ever asked her to do anything like this before. It was an unwritten rule not to speak about their magic to anyone.

"What is this?" she asked as she stared at the rudimentary drawing.

"What does it look like?" he asked, a sly smile on his face.

She had to be honest. "It looks like something out of a nightmare. Why are there people in a snow globe?"

He leaned forward, clasping his hands in front of him. "The better question is can your grandmother make that happen?"

She shoved her chair back as she noticed his eyes grow dark. "No. She won't do that. That's not what we do. We use white magic. That's black magic. We don't hurt people and we definitely don't shrink them and stick them in glass globes. I don't know what this is, but I'm afraid, I can't help you. I just volunteered because I thought you'd help me get into the jail."

He unclasped his hands and pushed his seat back, taking on a more jovial tone. "Fine. You don't have to do anything you don't want to. Sit down. Let's discuss how we'll make that visit happen."

Part of her told her to run, but another part - the part that wanted to do whatever she could to help her grandmother – begged her to stay. "Who were those people? Who do you want to trap and why?"

"No one. It was just an idea. Something to entertain the children with at the parade. Nothing to worry about at all. I just thought it'd be fun."

She narrowed her eyes at him, wondering if he could be trusted. Good looks were one thing, but if he truly was an evil person behind the beautiful, chiseled facade, that could ruin everything. She excused herself from the room, so she could make some notes without him noticing. "I'll be right back. Could you point me in the direction of the powder room?"

"I can do better than that. I'll let you use mine," he offered. "The second door on the left. I'll step out while you take care of your business."

Holly thanked him as she watched him walk out the door. With him away, she could have a quick look around to see what he was up to. The drawers in his desk were locked. And from what she could tell, there were no keys in plain sight. A liquor cabinet in the corner was open, but there was nothing in there that seemed unusual. Expensive bottles of champagne. Draft beers. A 2-liter of diet soda. None of which she liked, so she left them untouched.

She checked the time on her cell phone, figuring she had about five minutes before he'd return to check on her. "What are you up to, handsome man, and why do you need my grandmother's help?" She'd almost forgotten about the drawing. He'd left it on the table. She slipped it into her purse, then took a seat.

While she waited for him to return, she wrote as fast as she could, penciling a quick mock-up of the room layout while she was there.

The door swung open. "Are you decent?" he asked, chuckling.

"Yes. Thank you. Can we talk about my grandmother now? I'd really like to see her," she said.

He leaned on the edge of his desk. "I know you do. I'll tell you what. Why don't I visit her for you? I doubt Maxine will let me take you or any of the volunteers inside. Jot down what you want me to tell her and I'll pay her a visit later today. You can leave your phone number with my secretary and I'll give you a call when I get back."

As much as she thought he was a conman, she had no other choice. He didn't seem like the kind of man who could be easily persuaded into doing anything, especially for someone he didn't know well.

"Okay. Give me a minute and I'll get something together for you," she said. She wrote down a list of questions, then, wrote a quick coded message to her grandmother. "Here you go. Thank you for this. You have no idea what this means to me."

He grabbed her hand. "My pleasure. Are you sure I can't persuade you to help me with the parade floats?"

She gulped, wondering if she'd made a deal with the devil by asking him to visit her grandmother. "I really just want to get her out of that place. I don't know that I'd be of any use to you."

He ignored her comments and asked, "So you really have no memory of her second husband?"

She shook her head. "None, but in my defense, I was pretty young when they got married. That I know for sure because I wrote that down. Funny how I didn't write down his name though. I wonder why not."

"Maybe, he wasn't that memorable of a guy back then," he suggested. "I didn't know him well, but I liked him. He was nice enough in an old farmer sort of way. He'd nod or tip his ballcap to me when I saw him. Did you know he didn't even want to be an elf this year? It took a lot of convincing to get him to agree to play the role. Now, I feel bad for asking him to do it. If I had known--" He stopped mid-sentence.

"She didn't kill him," Holly said. "She'd never hurt anyone."

He smiled. "I believe you. The question is will those whose opinions matter?"

She hadn't thought that far ahead. She pulled out her diary and wrote that down. Could an elderly witch with sometimes-wacky ideas get a fair trial in a town that banned her from using magic and refused to admit witches even existed?

"What are you thinking?" he asked.

"I think something isn't right," she answered. "I should go. There's no use sitting around. I have to find a way to help her."

He walked her to the door. "Don't forget to leave your phone number. I'm sure your grandmother will have a message for you too."

She swallowed a lump in her throat. "I will." After leaving her phone number with the secretary, she rushed out the door and found the nearest store to buy a pair of winter boots and a warm coat.

CHAPTER THREE

Tassie and Sassie Rivers were local legends. They were famous for always knowing every else's business but never paying much attention to their own. Being the only heirs to the Rivers' family fortune, they didn't bother with the small details like budgeting, inventory, and aesthetic. If it could be sold, they sold it. If no one bought whatever it was, they gave it away for free. Their non-business acumen was the whole reason why their store housed both fine clothing and pig feed. They simply didn't care.

"Howdy, Rivers Twins!" Holly said as she wiped snow off her bare feet. "Please, tell me you have cute boots here."

Tassie, the brunette sister, jumped out of her seat and ran over to hug her. "You're home? It's about time." When she noticed the tears in Holly's eyes, her tone changed. "Oh, sorry, looks like I need to start taking notes like you. I forgot about what happened to Calliope. It's a shame really. Everyone knows she didn't kill that conniving pipsqueak of a man. Why would she? She hasn't spoken to him in twenty years."

Sassie looked up from her book. "Is that?" She pulled her glasses off. "Well, someone slap me and call me blonde, it is her, isn't it?" She walked over, her blonde bob bouncing, and pulled her sister away from

Holly. "Let me see her. Why, Miss Fancy Pants, aren't you a Hollywood star now? What brings you here?"

Tassie elbowed her. "Uncle Joe."

She cleared her throat. "Oh, that's right. He was one of your grandfathers. So sorry for your loss, but truth be told, not too many people will miss him around here. Ever since he took up with that floozy ex-wife of the city manager, he's been ten times worse than he ever used to be."

Holly's ears perked up. "Excuse me? Did you say the city manager's wife?" She knew there had to be a reason Henry was so interested in seeing her grandmother.

Tassie said, "Pull out your diary. This is going to be a good one."

Holly was a step ahead of her, already taking notes. "Tell me more." She wrote until her hand cramped. When the twins told her all they knew, she thought she had a good handle on how her grandmother had gotten framed for murder.

"I don't care what anyone says, Calliope didn't kill that man, and we can prove it," Sassie said.

"You can?" Holly could barely contain herself. "Would you be willing to testify to that?"

Sassie waved off her words. "Of course, I would, but I won't have to. There won't be a trial. Not in Christmas Cove. They'll have to move to another location. No one in their right mind would convict her here. Boy, could you imagine if they did? She'd forget all about the moratorium on magic and make them pay for what they did. No one would be safe from her, not even us."

Holly found a pair of boots with a Cheetah pattern on them that she liked. "Do you have these in a size six?"

Tassie laughed. "We do, but you'll never get those size eights into them."

Holly blushed.

"Oh, help the girl out, will you?" Sassie said.

"Have you seen Calliope yet?" Tassie asked. "How was she?"

She shook her head. "No. They wouldn't let me see her."

"Who? Maxine? Why not?" Sassie asked. "She doesn't own the jail. She doesn't make the rules. Did she tell you why you couldn't see her?"

"She just said it wasn't a visiting day," Holly answered. "Henry Castle is going to go in for me." As soon as the words left her mouth, she realized what a huge mistake that was. If her grandmother was accused of killing his ex-wife's boyfriend, then, their conversation would look suspicious. "We have to stop him."

A swath of cold air hit Holly in the back as the door flung open. She turned around to see who'd walked in.

"It's about time you got yourself some decent clothes," Maxine said as she unraveled her scarf. "I don't know if anyone told you this, but here in the Midwest, we have this thing called winter."

Tassie snorted. "Maybe you haven't noticed, but no one cares what you have to say."

Maxine smiled, exposing coffee-stained teeth. "That's what you say now, but wait until I tell you what I heard."

Her words got Holly's attention. "What?"

"It appears Calliope didn't kill the elf after all," Maxine said. "Henry, the Hottie, just paid her a visit and said some interesting things. We have it all on tape." She reached for her back pocket, then, realized it was empty. "Wait a minute. What happened to it? Have you seen a VHS tape?" She checked under a display table. "I just had it."

Tassie laughed. "Who still has VHS tapes? Do you have a dinosaur in your back pocket too?"

From the back of the store, a man's sinister voice boomed, "Had it, but I guess you don't have it anymore, do you?"

"Who is that?" Sassie whispered.

Holly said, "It's Henry."

He stepped out of the back room, pulling Calliope with him. "Surprise! Looks like you'll get to see your grandmother after all. Too bad it will be for the last time." He laughed a sinister laugh as he yanked a chain and pulled her handcuffed grandmother closer. "Say hello to your granddaughter. She came all the way from California to bail you out."

Calliope's face lit up when she saw Holly, then, paled when she realized there was nothing she could do about it.

"Are you okay?" Holly asked her.

She nodded. When Henry turned his back on her, she stuck her tongue out at him before signaling for Holly to come closer.

Holly couldn't read her signals. She looked at Tassie and Sassie for help. They were already in movement, each choosing a side as they moved closer to Henry.

"Stop right there, ladies. I'm one step ahead of you. Isn't that right, Maxine?" He glanced in her direction, but she was gone. "Where did she go?"

He didn't notice movement behind him. A giant work boot, attached to a muscular leg, hit him in the back of the head.

"Not on my watch, buddy. Not on my watch." Maxine hogtied him with her belt and threw a key for the handcuffs in Holly's direction. "Cut her loose before this beast wakes up." She lifted his head by his hair and planted a kiss on his forehead. "Why do the cute ones always have to be evil?"

"Cute ones?" Holly asked.

Calliope placed the handcuffs over Henry's wrists. "Like you didn't notice how handsome he was. Even a blind man could see that." She yelled at the twins. "Would you scaredy-cats mind calling the police or do you plan to hang on to each other for dear life forever?"

CHAPTER FOUR

Mayor Bottles spoke over the sheriff. "You mean to tell me he killed Uncle Joe? How? He wasn't even there?"

"But he was," Holly explained. "You're not going to like this, but it turns out, the witches weren't the ones you should have been worried about. Rogue warlocks were the cause of all the problems."

He scratched his head. "I didn't even know we had warlocks here."

Calliope snorted. "That's because you don't know much. If it hadn't been for my nearly-naked granddaughter, I could have been locked up for life for something I didn't do. If you keep inviting strangers to come in and make the rules, you'll end up with more problems than you can handle. Next time, vet these people. Who knows what kind of vermin they'll let in here!" She eyed Maxine.

"I know you're not talking about me," Maxine said.

"If the giant shoe fits, why not?" Calliope challenged her.

"But how did he kill him?" the mayor asked.

Holly checked her notebook and read her notes aloud, "He used black magic to shrink my grandmother down to the size of a pen cap and trapped her in a snow globe, so he could pose as her and poison Uncle Joe with a concoction he mixed up from the fake bottles of champagne he keeps in his liquor cabinet."

Mayor Bottles looked at the sheriff. "Do you believe this nonsense? What am I? A fool?"

The sheriff shrugged. "Coming from the Belle family, I'll believe anything. But I do have one question--okay, maybe two--where's Henry's ex-wife and how did Calliope get out of the globe?"

Calliope snickered. "I can answer those. Henry's ex was in there with me and I may have used a little bit of magic."

Mayor Bottles gasped.

"Oh, get over it. A little good magic never hurt anyone," she said.

"So, the case is solved?" Maxine asked.

Holly wrote one last note and held it up to show her. It read: Winter Solstice 2016: Case Closed. Henry has been charged with the elf's murder.

Want to read more? Click here to find other books by Ava Mallory on her website.

ABOUT THE AUTHOR

Ava Mallory has been a grade school teacher, a psychiatric technician, a dementia unit nurse manager, and a Hospice nurse. She has embarrassed herself in front of handsome celebrities, won vocal contests much to the chagrin of her children, survived a major earthquake, and nearly drowned when she mistakenly thought a YMCA lifeguard asked her to dive into the deep end on her first day of swim lessons. She and her eternally annoyed children share their home with a massive collection of books and a never-ending supply of new book ideas.

If you'd like to sign up for Ava's email newsletter and be the first to learn about new releases, sales, exclusive newsletter reads, and other fun things, copy and paste this link into your browser and sign up here: http://eepurl.com/cLOoK9

Follow Ava Mallory online:
Instagram
Facebook
Pinterest

JINGLE PURRS

SONIA PARIN

SUMMARY

It's days before Christmas, the first one Lexie and Luna will spend together, and Lexie has a missing cat to find and a feline companion to appease. Luna has expectations and dreams of a magical Christmas, and that means shopping for presents... not exactly Lexie's favorite pastime. Without any solid leads to pursue, she unwittingly enlists the help of the elements she has recently connected with, but the breeze assisting her has some strange ideas of how she should go about investigating the case of the missing cat as it leads her to another crime scene and the most unlikable O'Rourke detective she's ever met...

CHAPTER ONE

L exie tapped her small notebook and asked, "When did you last see your cat?"

Mimi Hargreaves shifted and reorganized the cushions on her chintz sofa. "This morning. I fed Frederick his breakfast. He's always been a fastidious eater and refuses to even look at food served by anyone else."

Lexie glanced around the sumptuous living room and caught sight of a maid dressed in a light blue uniform hovering by the door.

Still fidgeting with her cushions, Mimi Hargreaves said, "That's Marcie. She's been with me for over a dozen years." Leaning in, she whispered, "Marcie doesn't like cats. They pick up on it. But she's an angel and I could never think of letting her go."

Lexie introduced herself to the maid and asked when she'd last seen Frederick. Apparently, he'd been sticking to his usual routine of curling up in the terrace garden to soak in the morning sun.

"And you've searched the apartment."

Mimi nodded.

"Would you mind if we look around?"

Luna's little head popped out from within the lush branches of a Christmas tree, golden tinsel falling around her little face. "Frederick didn't leave of his own accord. What cat in their right mind would abandon such a splendid abode? Just look at the luxurious furnishings. The carpet is lusciously thick. I love the feel of sinking my dainty paws into it. It's such a lovely change to the hardwood floors in your apartment."

Lexie gave a small shake of her head and returned her attention to Mimi. "How long have you had Frederick for?"

"Five years."

"Ask her about his breed," Luna suggested.

Lexie waited a few moments to see if Mimi Hargreaves had heard Luna. Mimi Hargreaves had contacted Lexie after hearing about her P.I. services from a friend who'd heard about Crafty Investigations from a friend. She had no way of telling if any one of those people recommending her had affiliations with a coven. Word about Crafty Investigations had been spreading with little effort from Lexie. She'd had business cards printed and had considered taking out an ad but her dear cousin Mirabelle, the High Chair of the British Isles and all Circumferential Domains Pertaining to the Mackenzie Coven, had vetoed it, saying she required more information before making a sound decision.

As the incoming High Chair of the American Continent... Lexie had made the executive decision and had gone ahead and pinned a few business cards around her neighborhood.

"What breed is he?" Lexie asked.

"My Frederick is an Ashera."

Lexie looked at Luna who sniffed. "It's a la-de-la breed."

Lexie wrote the name on her notebook. "I take it Ashera cats are expensive."

"I have never thought of dear Frederick in terms of dollars, but acquiring him was a costly venture," Mimi said.

"How costly?"

"One hundred and fifty thousand."

Dollars? "W-what makes him so expensive?"

Mimi retrieved a framed photo from a side table.

A leopard?

Luna pranced up to her. "It's nothing but a hybrid of genes from several cats, namely the domestic housecat and the Asian leopard cat. Only a handful are bred every year, hence the hefty price tag."

Mimi hugged a cushion against her chest. "Please find my Frederick. The thought of him out there all alone is tearing me apart. He's not accustomed to the outdoors." Mimi glanced at the Christmas tree. "I've been counting down the days to Christmas morning when we can open his gifts. We always have such great fun."

"All these gifts are for him?" Luna sniffed them. "What am I getting for Christmas? Are we getting a tree? Please tell me we're getting a tree." Luna scurried over and sat by Lexie's feet. "I know you think this is not the appropriate time to talk about it, especially as you're the only one who can hear me and any response might be perceived as a sign of mental instability, but a little nod will suffice."

Knowing she'd never hear the end of it, Lexie nodded. "Has there been any suspicious activity in your life lately?" she asked Mimi Hargreaves.

"What do you mean?"

"Strange people hanging around the apartment building."

"You'll have to ask our doorman, Smithers."

Lexie made a note of the name. "Anyone else? Most apartment buildings have at least one resident who tends to notice things." A resident busybody, Lexie thought.

Mimi shifted in her seat. "Mrs. Edgar McAvoy likes to keep herself informed."

"And does she like cats?"

Mimi's pursed lips suggested Mrs. Edgar McAvoy might be a person of interest. Lexie rose to her feet. "With your permission, we'd like to inspect the rest of the apartment."

"We?"

"Oh, my feline companion and I. Luna has a superior sense of smell."

"I see, yes... Of course. Marcie will show you through."

The rest of the apartment didn't yield any clues other than an obsession with snow globes. They were everywhere. Summer scenes. Fall. Winter. Spring. She had them all.

"They're very pretty," Luna said. "Why don't we have snow globes?"

Lexie shrugged. "Because it's something else for me to dust?"

"I would spend endless hours entertained by them," Luna said.

"Only after asking me to shake them for you."

"Of course, that goes without saying." Luna made quick work of inspecting the contents of each room and remarking on the splendor enjoyed by Frederick. "Mimi Hargreaves cherishes her feline companion."

Lexie chuckled. "Yes, she definitely dotes on him to the point of spoiling him."

Lifting her chin, Luna pranced around. "You call it spoiling, I call it appreciative pampering. A little indulgence would go a long way with me."

"Your food has taken up all the available cupboard space in my kitchen. I had a fainting couch custom made for you." Lexie's voice hitched. "What more do you want?"

Luna sighed. "Do you actually require an answer or are you trying to suggest I already have more than enough?" When Lexie didn't answer, Luna said under her breath, "I am still waiting for my hand-made Amish quilt."

Lexie checked the windows. She turned to the maid and asked, "Are these windows ever opened?"

The maid shook her head. "Never. The temperature in the apartment is kept at a moderate level all year round for Frederick's comfort."

Lexie thought she'd picked up a hint of resentment in Marcie's voice but she guessed the maid valued her job too much to risk putting it in peril.

"I enjoy admiring him from a distance," Marcie said, "But I've never touched him. You'd understand if you saw him."

"Ashera cats are rather large," Luna murmured. "And they make a ferocious sound when they eat. Personally, I'd keep my distance."

They checked cupboards and closets, under beds, inside the chimneys, and still saw no sign of Frederick.

"More snow globes," Luna said as they strode into another room. Mimi stood by the fireplace, a snow globe in her hands.

"I'm trying to distract myself," she said.

"We were just admiring your snow globes."

Mimi smiled. "I find them charming. They're my little bubbles of dreams."

The wistfulness in her tone didn't make sense to Lexie. The woman clearly had everything her heart desired.

"We'll keep looking," Lexie told her. As they strode out to the hallway, she turned to Luna and said, "Come on, let's go check out the rooftop garden."

Luna took a backward step. "You go out first. He might be hiding out there."

With no adjoining buildings, there could only be one way out of there, Lexie thought as she peered down at the street below. A long way to go from the 5th Avenue tenth floor penthouse apartment.

Luna purred. "Frederick would have to have been pushed. Or..."

"Or he might have jumped of his own accord," Lexie suggested, "How much mollycoddling can one cat take?"

Luna lifted her chin. "If you are calling on my personal experience being coddled, I'm afraid I have only scant knowledge. Sorry, I can't help you."

"Okay. We're not going to find anything here. Let's try the doorman, Smithers. I'm guessing Mrs. Edgar McAvoy will make an appearance at some point. Otherwise, we'll have to hunt her down."

"You could try willing her to step out," Luna suggested as they made their way down to the lobby.

Could she? "Are you encouraging me to acquire a new skill and force someone into doing something that will possibly go against their will?"

Luna scratched her ear. "Being a witch has been a steep learning curve for you. I suspect you might still be in the throes of denial."

"The throes of... Never mind. Please get to the point."

"There is an easier way," Luna offered, "Clearly state your intention. Focus on her. You can nudge her into stepping out. Have you ever thought of someone and soon after they call you or you bump into them?"

Far too often.

Lexie sighed. Recently, an Oracle had told her to embrace change.

"As you've often said, practice makes perfect but I really don't want to overburden myself." Eventually, she'd graduate from the baby steps she'd been taking and it would all become second nature. Meditating into a state of clarity had helped close in on an evil presence. She'd also been able to connect with the elements. Earth, wind, fire and water. Belatedly, Lexie looked around her to see if merely thinking about the elements had conjured something...

Luna tilted her little head in thought. "I'm glad to see your powers haven't gone to your head."

Smithers held the front entrance door open for them and, to Lexie's surprise, tipped his hat.

"I had no idea Mimi Hargreaves had a cat," he said, "All the other pet owning residents go for daily walks, but I've never seen Mimi stepping out with her cat."

Mimi had said Frederick was strictly an indoor cat. Lexie had assumed that only meant Frederick didn't roam around freely. How did he get his exercise?

"Here comes Mrs. Edgar McAvoy. If there has been any unusual activity here, she'll be the one to know," Smithers said.

Right on cue, Mrs. Edgar McAvoy emerged from the elevator and strode toward them, giving both Lexie and Luna a head to toe sweep. Twig thin, her snow-white hair sat in a neat bob around her shoulders. Dressed in an elegant powder blue suit, she fiddled with a strand of pearls as she said, "I've heard Mimi's cat has gone missing. What a dreadful state of affairs this is. Smithers, you do a fine job keeping the undesirables out, but someone must have slipped through. How is that possible? Are we to be murdered in our beds now?"

Unfortunately, Mrs. Edgar McAvoy didn't have any useful information.

Lexie stepped out of the building and looked around her. "Keep your eyes peeled for anything unusual," she told Luna.

"Such as?"

"Some criminals enjoy revisiting the scene of their crimes. If someone took Frederick by force, they might be hovering nearby."

"Okay," Luna said, "I see an elderly woman pushing a stroller."

"And why did that catch your attention?"

"There's a tail sticking out of the stroller," Luna said.

Lexie looked down the street and spotted the woman dressed in a bright purple coat. "It's a stuffed toy." Nevertheless, she strode toward her. Tuffs of gray hair stuck out from beneath a purple hat. The woman looked ancient, with gnarled fingers and a stooped posture.

When the woman turned down the street, Lexie hurried her steps and called out to her, "Wait."

Hearing Lexie, she flung her arm out almost as if to strike her. "What do you think you're doing?" the woman demanded.

"Sorry, wrong person," Lexie said as she had a closer look inside the stroller to make sure the tail she'd seen belonged to a stuffed toy. Peering in, she saw a collection of junk. The stuffed toy, a snow globe, an old newspaper and some other items she couldn't identify.

"What are you doing?" The woman put herself between her stash of goodies and Lexie. "This is all mine."

Lexie didn't want to judge the woman by appearances, but she felt compelled to dig inside her pocket and give her all the money she had. She sure looked as if she needed it.

Apologizing, she turned back. "Like I said," she told Luna, "A stuffed toy."

"If you say so. Can we go to the park?" Luna asked as they strode along 5th Avenue. "You could commune with nature. The Coven will like that. Please, can we go? I've never been. As you know, my previous companion spent her days drunk as a skunk. We rarely stepped out."

"Where did she live?"

Luna looked over her shoulder. "A couple of blocks back that way."

"You were a 5th Avenue cat? It's no wonder you constantly grumble about your current living situation. How did she afford a place here?"

"Like you, she was an heiress, unlike you, she enjoyed spending money."

"Hey, I'm on a budget. It's not my fault if my great aunt placed restrictions on how much money I'm allowed to have."

"Perhaps you could renegotiate. After all, you've proven yourself to be quite frugal, living well below your means and any other acceptable standard of living."

"Give it up, Luna. Even with full access to my inheritance, I'm not moving out of the Village. I like it there."

"How can you be sure you won't like living here unless you try it first?"

Lexie scooped Luna up and crossed the street. "Okay, go forth and romp to your heart's content. But don't stray too far. There might be a cat burglar on the prowl."

Luna strayed off the path only to scurry back onto it. "The grass is cold and wet. Perhaps we should return in the springtime."

"Hang on. I'm sensing something."

Luna shivered. "Yes, a cold snap."

Lexie looked around. "Maybe it was just the wind. Okay, let's head back." Without any leads, she had no idea how she'd find Mimi Hargreaves' cat.

"Frederick has only been missing for a few hours," Luna said, "Someone might be holding him for ransom and they are now waiting for the appropriate moment to send a ransom note. Also, you could look into her husband's financials. Maybe the Hargreaves are experiencing difficulties and he decided to sell Frederick." Luna shivered again and danced on the spot. "I can't feel my paws. Pick me up."

Lexie unbuttoned her overcoat. "Curl up inside and don't show yourself. I'll try and hail a cab."

Lexie had to agree with Luna. A cat used to the comfort of a warm home wouldn't stray. If someone hoped to extort money out of Mimi Hargreaves, they would probably wait another day to make contact. But what if someone had simply stolen Frederick? Or... left the door open for him to escape...

When they managed to hail a cab, they headed for O'Connor's Bar. "Maybe Jonathan can help us out."

"Are you prepared to hear him grumbling because you're no longer bothering to turn up for work?"

"I'll risk it," Lexie murmured. Besides, she didn't think Jonathan had much of a choice. As her guardian, his duties included being available to help her out... She hoped.

Lexie crinkled her nose.

"What is it?" Luna asked.

Something in the air, Lexie thought as she tried to define the sensation. Not a smell. More of a feeling. The same feeling she'd had in the park.

"The one you couldn't define?" Luna asked taking full advantage of the fact she could talk to her heart's content because only Lexie could hear her. "Have you been practicing your daily meditation?"

Not as often as she should. She'd become a lapsed practitioner...

Who had time to hum?

A breeze swept inside the cab and swirled around Lexie.

"Whoa! I felt that," Luna said, peering out from within the comfort and warmth of Lexie's coat. "Are you all right?"

The breeze continued to swirl around her, delivering a message. The soft whispers—

"Stop the cab." Lexie paid the driver and jumped out.

Luna shivered. "Why did you do that? We're not there yet."

"Did you hear that?"

Luna's head emerged. "I think I need ear muffs. Those would be a nice Christmas gift, but then, they wouldn't be a surprise. And no, I didn't hear anything. Not even with my superior feline hearing, which wouldn't be affected by ear muffs."

The breeze and the voice swept around Lexie one more time and then stopped only to tug her along.

"That felt odd," Luna said.

"Something's pulling me."

"You mean, the breeze you said you felt and heard?"

"Yes. I think so."

"Well, talk to it."

"Huh?"

Luna burrowed inside her coat. "You are one with the elements. You can communicate with them."

"What do you want?" Lexie asked.

Luna purred. "Did it answer?"

"Yes. It said to follow it."

"Where? You know I'm not entirely comfortable blindly following you."

"I'll tell you as soon as I find out." Lexie tried to resist the pull, but it was too strong. Crossing the street, she finally felt the invisible force ease up. "I guess I'm supposed to go into this building." Inside the spacious lobby, she studied the business directory. "Oscar Hargreaves is listed."

Luna's little head popped out again. "For the record, I don't like this at all. At least the Coven sends you written commands. How can you argue with the force of nature, especially if it's possessed by an otherworldly force?"

They took the elevator to the twentieth floor and a set of double doors led them through to a resplendent office space.

Luna purred deeply. "I don't know about you, but I'm feeling slightly apprehensive. I wonder if that's a sign of paranoia and the early onset of some dreadful disease?" Luna sniffed the air. "Hang on. False alarm. That's a relief. I'm quite sane."

"Huh?"

"There's a dead body behind the desk."

CHAPTER TWO

"Explain to me again how you happened to be here?" Gunner O'Rourke asked.

Lexie blinked and tried to speak but no words came out. She'd met several detectives associated with the O'Rourke Group. Working under cover in plain sight and within all major police departments, both here and abroad, the detectives dealt with supernatural deaths.

I don't like him, Lexie thought.

"Neither do I," Luna agreed.

"Where's Whip O'Rourke? I want to speak with Whip." Lexie had recently met the O'Rourke detective and had become quite familiar with his way of doing things. Gunner looked exactly like him... yet different, and not in a good way. Annoyingly, Lexie couldn't put her finger on it.

Luna had curled up on her lap and now tried to climb back inside Lexie's coat.

"What's wrong with your cat?" Gunner asked.

"My feline companion doesn't care to be referred to as a cat. Where's Whip?"

Giving his gold cufflinks a twist, Gunner said, "He's busy."

"I thought this was his precinct."

"He's the same but different," Luna murmured. "He looks like a stockbroker or a lawyer, and he appears to be looking down his nose at us."

Lexie recalled the other O'Rourke detectives she'd met. They'd all been replicas of each other but they'd each had their own individual personalities and styles. None had dressed like Gunner. Who wore vests? His three-piece dark blue suit and pristine white shirt with a navy blue tie and caramel colored brogues definitely set him apart.

When he folded his arms, Lexie caught sight of his watch.

Elegant. Sleek. Expensive.

"I called for Whip O'Rourke," Lexie insisted, "Why did we get you?"

He gave a casual shrug. "I drew the short straw."

"Huh?"

"I think he's trying to push your buttons." Luna made another attempt to climb inside her coat but Lexie held her down. If she had to deal with Gunner O'Rourke, she wouldn't do it alone. "In answer to your question, we were guided here."

Gunner drew out a small leather bound notebook and fancy pen. "By whom."

"A breeze."

"How do you spell that?" he asked.

Lexie exchanged a look with Luna who said, "I think you need to speak slower. He might have a hearing impairment."

"A breeze, as in a gentle gust of wind," Lexie explained.

"And how do you know the victim?" he asked.

"His wife engaged our services. I'm a P.I." Lexie handed him one of her business cards. "Crafty Investigations."

He surprised her by accepting the card and putting it in his pocket.

"Why do you think a breeze brought you to see Oscar Hargreaves?" Gunner O'Rourke asked.

"I'm not sure. The words sounded garbled."

He lifted an eyebrow. "The breeze spoke to you?"

"Yes," Lexie shrugged. "Anyway, we were at the corner of a busy intersection. I couldn't concentrate properly." Her attention strayed to a bookcase and the snow globes taking up all the top shelf space.

"Perhaps you should try meditation," Luna suggested. "The message might come back to you. Your brain is a sponge, storing information. It's all in there. You only need to tap into it."

Gunner put his notebook down and, a moment later, said, "Yes, that's a very good idea. You could meditate now."

"Huh?"

"He can't possibly have heard me," Luna said, "I blocked him from my mind."

Lexie searched for a reaction. Some sort of sign he'd heard Luna.

"I heard you." He shrugged. "You can try to block me, but you're too intimidated by me for it to work."

"He's insufferable." Luna hissed. "I really don't like him."

Seconds later, Gunner said, "You'll get used to me."

"Argh!" Luna screeched. "This has never happened to me before. If I'd known this could happen, I would have devised a secret language. How are we going to communicate with him eavesdropping on everything we think?"

Gunner leaned against a massive oak desk and crossed his feet at the ankles. "What do you think triggered that gust of wind? What were you doing or thinking before it happened?"

"I can't remember," Lexie said and tried to clear her mind of all thoughts.

"Well then, let's get to it."

"Huh?"

"Meditate," he said, "Clear your mind. Everything you heard is still stored in your mind. Sift through and you'll find it."

"Right now?"

"Yes."

I can't function properly under these conditions, Lexie thought.

A few seconds later, Gunner said, "Try."

Luna complained. "You don't need to take orders from him. You're the incoming High Chair. Put him in his place."

Lexie wished she could.

Could she?

Several seconds later, Gunner gave her another raised eyebrow look that appeared to challenge her. "Your cat is not being very helpful."

"Is nothing sacred?" Luna leaped out of Lexie's arms and, taking a giant leap, grabbed hold of his lapels. "Get out of my head," she screeched.

Gunner yelped. "What is wrong with your cat?"

Lexie sprung to her feet and tried to pull Luna off him but she'd dug her claws into his lapels.

"Get out of my head," Luna shrieked.

"Get her off me," Gunner growled.

Luna, feel free to bite him, Lexie thought. Regretting it, she rushed to erase the thought from her mind.

"Interesting," Luna said as she withdrew her claws.

"What?" Lexie settled back down on the chair and cradled Luna in her arms.

"Try thinking a thought and quickly erasing it."

I'm going to wipe the smugness of his face by turning him into a frog, Lexie thought and quickly erased the thought. She studied him closely and looked for a reaction.

Nothing.

"Think and erase," Luna purred, "There's a time delay between us thinking and him hearing us. We're bonded and hear each other on real time. So, think and erase. Oh, and I had a close look at his watch. Erase. It's a Patek Phillipe. Erase."

Gunner gave his sleeves a tug and said, "Whatever you two are doing is not going to work. You don't have the discipline for it." He looked at Lexie. "Your reputation for landing in closets precedes you."

"For your information, I land in closets by choice." Having the power to travel from one place to another by merely thinking about it, Lexie knew she should be able to hold an image in her mind of where she wanted to be, and go there. For some reason, she always landed in closets. Although, recently she'd had a few successes...

"I've liked all the O'Rourke detectives we've met. Erase," Luna said, "This one is dreadful. You should do something. Erase."

What do you suggest I do? Erase, Lexie thought.

Luna purred deeply and then sprung up. "I got it. Erase. Recently, you changed the color of your outfit with nothing but your thoughts. Erase. Can you do it to him too? Erase."

Gunner frowned. His eyes bounced between Lexie and Luna.

Lexie smiled. "I can do one better than that." Looking at his suit, she pictured a purple tuxedo with velvet trim. His suit changed instantly.

Seeing it, Luna rolled onto her back and laughed.

"What's going on between you two?" Gunner asked.

"Nothing." Lexie tried to hold back her smile but failed.

Luna looked up at Lexie and said, "Do something about his fancy watch. Erase."

Mickey Mouse watch coming right up. Erase. Lexie leaned forward. Yep. It worked.

"What worked?" Gunner asked.

"You forgot to erase the thought. Erase," Luna said.

"I remembered something the breeze said."

"About time." Gunner checked his watch. His eyes widened. Then he noticed his sleeve... and the rest of his suit. Looking up, he said, "You did this."

"I don't know what you're talking about."

"Change it back. Right now," he growled.

"You need to get your priorities straight." Lexie lifted her chin. "You're supposed to be here investigating a suspicious death. By the way, how did Oscar Hargreaves die?"

Frowning at his purple suit, Gunner snapped, "Blow to the head."

Lexie asked, "The front? The back?"

"The back of his head."

"So someone caught him by surprise. Do you have the security footage for his office?"

"Are you going to turn my clothes and watch back to normal?"

"He seems to be rather cross with you. Erase," Luna purred. "Keep up the good work. Erase."

"What about his office staff?" Lexie asked.

"They were all out to lunch," Gunner said through gritted teeth. "One of the staff is going on maternity leave. Oscar Hargreaves stayed behind to deal with a business call and had planned on joining them later. Now, change my suit and watch back."

Lexie looked around. "Is there a rest room I can use? I feel an emergency coming on."

Gunner frowned and pointed her in the right direction.

"I'll be back shortly."

"Are we making a getaway? Erase." Luna asked.

Lexie waited until they were out of sight to nod. They couldn't use the elevator because he'd see them. She'd have to blink them out of there.

There's nowhere like home, Lexie thought, and clicked her heels.

"If Mirabelle hears you, she'll growl. Your powers are not to be taken lightly." Luna leaped off Lexie and pressed her paw against the closet door. "Home sweet home."

"Do you think it's safe to talk?" Lexie asked as she crawled out of her closet and straightened.

"I doubt Gunner O'Rourke can hear us all the way from the Upper East Side."

Lexie followed Luna into the living room and slumped down on the couch. "This is odd."

"What?"

"I feel dreadful about taking such an instant dislike to Gunner O'Rourke. I can't make sense of it. He looks exactly like all the other O'Rourke detectives we've met and yet, I just don't like him. When did I become that type of person? I've never been so quick to judge someone."

"I'm comfortable with my feline instincts," Luna said, "You can't go against nature."

"Yes, but... It's never happened before. I always give people the benefit of the doubt and assume they're going to be, if not nice, then decent. It's not as if Gunner did or said anything wrong."

"He might be hiding something and you picked up on it. Don't beat yourself up about it. I'm sure there are people who take an instant dislike to you."

"Ditto."

Luna curled up on her lap. Lexie automatically gave her a scratch behind the ears. "I suppose we now have to combine our search and look for a killer."

Luna looked up. "Mimi Hargreaves only engaged your services to find Frederick."

"She must be beside herself. Two loses in one day." Lexie sat up.

"Ouch. Can you give me some warning before you do that? I curled up on your lap assuming I'd get some peace and quiet."

"Sorry, I'm still feeling guilty about Gunner. I should change his clothes back." She closed her eyes and pictured his pristine gray suit. Or had it been blue?

"And don't forget the watch," Luna said.

"Done. Come on. Let's go."

"Where? We've only just returned?"

"To O'Connor's. Jonathan might be able to help us. I have no idea where to start looking for Frederick."

"What are you talking about? You haven't even scratched the surface."

"I'm trying a new tactic," Lexie said. "Let someone else do the thinking for me. It might save us some time."

"Do you know what else will save us time and spare me the ordeal of walking on a cold pavement?" Luna asked.

"Are you suggesting I buy you kitty boots?"

"I'm suggesting you do everything in your power to ensure I don't come down with a cold. I'd rather not spend Christmas nursing a cold."

"Fine. But you know how I feel about excessive use of my powers."

"Actually, no I don't. How do you feel about it?"

Undecided...

Lexie closed her eyes and pictured the inside of O'Connor's Bar. She mentally strolled to the back room and focused on getting them there.

She sensed them shifting. Lexie had never bothered to delve into the inner workings of whisking herself from place to place. She probably didn't even need to close her eyes, but at this point, the less she knew, the better.

When she opened her eyes, Jonathan stood in front of her, glaring and growling at her. "What do you think you're doing?"

Lexie smiled at him. "I'm employing my skills." She looked around her.

Oops. She'd landed right in the middle of the bar during its busy time. "Sorry, I actually aimed for the storeroom."

Jonathan swept his hand in front of him. Everyone around them stilled for a moment and then snapped out of whatever had compelled them into silence.

Lexie's mouth gaped open. "Did you... Did you just use..." She leaned in and whispered, "Magical powers?" She'd had no idea he had any.

"In case anyone is the slightest bit concerned about me, I'm fine," Luna said. "Why is Jonathan scowling at you?"

"I nearly exposed us to the wider world, or at least, to the patrons at the bar. I think Jonathan wiped everyone's memory."

Jonathan leaned in and growled, "Do you realize how dangerous that is? I could have erased something important."

"Such as?"

"Someone could have been thinking about an appointment they needed to keep. Or a birthday they had to remember. I only wiped that split second you appeared away, but who knows what thoughts they were entertaining."

"Sorry." Lexie lifted her chin. "I'll make sure it doesn't happen again."

Still scowling at her, Jonathan reached down behind the counter and produced a red Santa hat. "Everyone wears one. 'Tis the season to be jolly," he muttered.

Whether she liked it or not? "You're not wearing one. Hats flatten my hair. That's why I could never be a princess."

Both Luna and Jonathan looked at her.

"What? It's true. Check out any magazine and you'll see them all dressed up and wearing stylish hats."

Luna purred. "We're actually mystified over the idea that you might consider the possibility of ever becoming a princess."

"Hey. I'm good enough."

"You seem to be flying high in your delusional state," Luna said, "And I really don't wish to be the one to clip your wings, but the closest you could ever come to royalty is if you played the role of a wicked, evil witch enchantress. You'll just have to settle for being an incoming High Chair, which in itself, carries a great deal of prestige."

"I don't recall discouraging you when you wanted to become a feline companion to a princess."

"My apologies," Luna purred. "As I said, I can't go against my nature and I suppose part of my job is to keep you grounded."

Jonathan sighed and wiped the counter in front of her. "Aren't you supposed to be busy hunting down a killer?"

"You heard about that?" Lexie asked.

He nodded.

"I've actually been hired to find a missing cat." Lexie grinned. "But as the two appear to be connected, we might have to multi-task. Have you heard anything about an Ashera cat? Someone could be trying to sell it."

"Are you suggesting I fence stolen goods at O'Connor's?"

Luna's little head tilted in thought as she studied Jonathan. "Let's give him a few moments to deny it and defend his integrity with fervor."

"I thought you might be in the know." Lexie leaned over the counter and reached for a basket of peanuts.

"Shouldn't you focus on the dead man you found and, specifically, on how you were lured to his office?" Jonathan asked.

"You know about that too? Is it any wonder I come to you for answers. You know everything. Would you care to tell me exactly how you do that?"

"I think you have bigger problems to deal with right now," Jonathan said.

A hand clamped on her shoulder. Lexie slanted her gaze and caught sight of a Mickey Mouse watch.

CHAPTER THREE

"One out of two," Lexie mused. "That's quite good." She hadn't managed to change Gunner's watch back, but his purple suit had changed back to... something else.

In her defense, she hadn't been able to remember if his suit had been blue or gray. He had both. A gray sleeve and a blue sleeve. As for his trousers...

They had blue polka dots on a gray background.

"I rather like it," Luna said. "It makes him less rigid."

"Whatever you do," Jonathan warned, "Do it out of sight." He nudged his head toward the back room.

Lexie hopped off the barstool. "Okay, follow me. At a discreet distance, please." She needed to figure out how to undo whatever she'd done. Being new at something didn't excuse her ineptitude. She had skills and the more she practiced, the better she'd get at using them, or so everyone kept telling her. Now, if only she could remember the color of his suit.

"Dark blue," Luna said. "And he wore a fancy Patek Phillipe watch."

"Thank you." Although, she had no idea how that information would help.

"Would you like me to walk you through your meditation?" Luna asked, "It might help to clear your mind first. Lately, it's been rather cluttered."

"Thank you, Luna. I'll let you know if I need help." Lexie spoke without really having a plan of action. In fact, she had no idea where her confidence had come from. Yes, from somewhere deep within her —the part of her that had been born a witch. It all remained a mystery to her. Shrugging the thought away, Lexie closed her eyes. As soon as she did, a thought swept through her mind.

Restore all that was to exactly how it was. Leave no trace of fun and games and make this man... dull again.

That sort of rhymed.

Had it worked?

"Why do you still have your eyes closed?" Luna asked.

Lexie nibbled her lip. "Is it safe to open them?"

"It depends on what you were hoping to achieve."

Lexie had a peek and smiled. "Happy now?" she asked Gunner.

He tugged the sleeve of his dark blue suit and adjusted his tie, his dark blue eyes delivering a silent warning.

"That's it," Lexie exclaimed. She'd always managed to give the other O'Rourke detectives reason to be annoyed with her, but they'd remained good humored about it. "He doesn't have a sense of humor."

Gunner crossed his arms. "You have a problem with that?"

"You actually take yourself seriously." Lexie laughed and strode back to the bar.

"I guess that went well for you," Jonathan said.

"Yeah, better than expected. I now have ammunition to use against him."

Jonathan leaned across the counter. "In your place, I'd tread with care. He doesn't have a sense of humor."

"Now you tell me." Lexie growled and sat down at the bar again.

"What are you doing?" Gunner asked, his tone hard.

"I'm trying to find a cat and you are supposed to be solving a murder. Off you go." She waved. "Bye, bye."

Annoyingly, Gunner O'Rourke didn't move.

"Okay, if you won't leave, I will." She strode off thinking she'd walk around the block and come back later when the coast was clear.

"Sorry to be the bearer of bad news," Luna said as they turned a corner. "He's behind us."

Lexie crossed the street.

"He's still tailing us."

Swinging around, she pointed her finger at him. Gunner stopped abruptly.

"Oh, that's interesting. I think he's afraid of your finger. Try turning him into a monkey."

Lexie frowned at him. "Stop following us. I've told you everything I know."

Gunner slipped his hands inside his pockets and shrugged. "You're going to help me solve the crime."

That's not what Lexie had expected him to say. "In what universe do you see us working together?"

"You must give him some credit for even considering it," Luna said.

A light breeze swept around Lexie. Instead of making her shiver, it reminded her of the strange sensation she'd felt in the park.

Recently, she'd made a tentative effort to connect to the elements and had managed to conjure enough power to battle an evil presence. If she'd known the elements could turn on her and control her, she might have left well enough alone.

Luna purred deeply. "I suspect it is give and take."

"Silly me. I assumed they were at my disposal to do with as I pleased. I wonder if they'd be willing to give a little in return for me being under their control?" She called on the breeze to ruffle Gunner's perfectly combed hair. "I guess the answer is yes," Lexie murmured as she watched Gunner struggling to keep his hair in place.

"It's a mini tornado." Luna snickered. "Well done."

"Okay, enough fun. He has a murder to solve and I have an expensive cat to find." She took a step only to find herself pulled back and toward Gunner. "Hey. Stop," she told the breeze, but the breeze refused to listen.

"Have you changed your mind?" he asked.

Lexie tried to turn but she was being compelled to walk toward him. "What did you do?" she demanded. Again, she tried to swing around and stride off, to no avail.

Luna purred. "I think that breeze of yours is trying to tell you something."

"This is all your doing," Gunner said.

And she had no way of stopping it. "Okay, it seems we have no choice in the matter." When she headed back to O'Connor's, Gunner followed.

"Look what the wind blew in," Jonathan said.

What did he know about it? While she didn't really expect him to break his habit of not divulging any pertinent information about himself, she went ahead and asked. Not surprisingly, Jonathan clammed up. Turning to Gunner, she asked, "How did Mimi Hargreaves take the news about her husband?"

Gunner was still trying to get his hair under control. "Not well. She went into hysterics."

"I guess you have your people looking into the Hargreaves' finances. I need to know if they were having financial problems. What about his business dealings? Did he have any enemies, perhaps someone he outsmarted, someone who held a grudge against him?"

Gunner looked confused.

"Well, if this is going to work, you have to treat me as an equal and you have to share information. It seems we don't have a choice, so we might as well make the best of it. Let's eat something and figure out how to go about solving our crimes." She ordered lunch. "This is a business expense," she told Jonathan. "Gunner is picking up the tab."

While she ordered a burger with the lot, Gunner had a chicken salad with no dressing.

When Jonathan set her burger in front of her, Gunner gave her a lifted eyebrow look that spoke of disapproval.

Lexie said, "My body is my temple and I like to give it offerings."

"I'm sure I didn't say anything."

She nudged him with her elbow and watched his look of surprise. "But you were thinking about it. Go on, admit it."

Ignoring Lexie, Gunner inspected his knife and fork and gave them a wipe down.

"He is fastidious." Luna licked her paw. "Perhaps he does have some redeeming qualities."

"Is he growing on you?" Lexie laughed. "No, don't answer. I think you're merely identifying with everything you find familiar."

Luna blinked. "Are you, by any chance, suggesting I am like him?"

Jonathan chortled. "I love it when you two bicker. It means you're not bickering with me."

Lexie took the last bite of her burger and eyed the coffee machine.

"Coming right up," Jonathan said.

"His mood has changed," Luna remarked. "I wonder what that's about?"

"Jonathan is probably grateful for the entertainment we're providing."

"I think you might be right. " Luna craned her neck and said, "Have you noticed how Gunner eats? He cuts a portion of everything, and then he arranges it on his fork. You tend to start at one end, and work your way to the other, regardless of the food you have on your plate."

"Let me guess, I remind you of a pig sticking its snout in the trough." Lexie fixed her attention on Gunner who appeared to be having a conversation with himself. At first, she thought she'd imagined it, but then she saw him nodding, as if agreeing with himself.

"He must be conversing with the O'Rourke detectives," Luna said. "It shows how conscientious he is, treating this as a working lunch."

Jonathan set a cup of coffee down in front of her.

"I think Luna is about to tell me off for not knuckling down and solving my case." She shrugged. "I'm stuck." And mystified. Why had the elements nudged her into action?

"Perhaps because you recently connected with them and, without realizing it, opened the channels for dialogue. You should call Octavia," Luna suggested. "She's a fount of knowledge and is bound to have a ready explanation."

Lexie patted Luna on the head. "Who needs a thinking cap when I have you."

Within seconds of Lexie mentally calling Octavia, she appeared at the door leading to the back room. She peered around her and, straightening her jacket, she strode casually toward them.

Jonathan smiled at Lexie.

"Yes, yes. That's how to make a discreet entrance."

"I came as soon as I heard you calling me," Octavia said. She took the barstool beside Lexie and mouthed, "Who's he?"

Lexie rolled her eyes. "Gunner." To her surprise, Octavia curled her lip. Her personal assistant had a pristine record for performing admirably in her job and always maintaining her professionalism.

"What's wrong with him?" Octavia whispered. "He's like Dodge... yet, he is nothing like him."

Octavia's recent encounter with another O'Rourke detective, Dodge, had been intriguing to watch. They'd both hit if off and while Lexie hadn't pushed Octavia for information, her personal assistant appeared to be happier than ever before.

"He has no sense of humor." Lexie shrugged and wondered if she should ask Octavia about Dodge...

"Oh, I see. How odd."

"I believe he's about to give us an update. Meanwhile," Lexie filled Octavia in on everything that had happened. "Do you have any idea why a gust of wind would intervene and lead me right to a murder scene?"

"You recently engaged with the elements," Octavia said, "Now they're at your disposal."

"That's what Luna said. Am I likely to hear from the elements every time there's a crime in the city?"

Octavia sat back and tapped her chin. "That's unlikely since you'd be facing a hurricane every day. This must have happened in response to your search for the cat."

That made sense. "Hang on. So why didn't the gust lead me straight to Frederick?"

"His disappearance and his owner's death must be connected." Octavia gave a small nod. "Find the killer and you'll find the cat."

Lexie tried to play around with the idea of one person being responsible for both crimes, but she failed to come up with a reasonable explanation. She drummed her fingers on the counter. "That's your cue to suggest something, Gunner."

He looked at her and straightened. "I've just received a report about the Hargreaves' finances. There are no unusual activities and no sudden loses. Oscar was an astute investor."

"Okay. I guess we need to look at who gets to benefit from his death. Maybe someone killed him for his money. Or, if we're going to tie in the murder with the missing cat, maybe someone wanted to use Frederick as leverage to force Oscar's hand... Help me out, people. I'm fresh out of ideas."

"There are no children," Gunner said.

"So his wife stands to inherit everything."

Gunner shrugged. "It would be a safe assumption but we won't know for sure until the will is read."

"We'll have to speak to the office staff. They might have some useful insight about the Hargreaves."

Gunner shook his head. "It's already been done. They were a happily married couple. Every Monday the personal assistant took care to organize a dozen red roses for Mimi Hargreaves. Oscar Hargreaves personally handwrote a card for his wife, which was then delivered to the florist to be included with the roses. If he worked late, he always called ahead to let her know. Every other night, they dined out and every other day, they met for lunch. Weekends were spent at home, and once a month they trekked out to their beach house."

"And all that is supposed to convince me Mimi is innocent?" Lexie asked.

Gunner checked his watch. Noticing the way he rested his hand on it, Lexie suspected he wanted to make sure it was still there.

"The only way you'll find Mimi Hargreaves guilty of anything is if you frame her," Luna murmured.

"I'd like to know how the husband felt about Frederick." To the outside world, Oscar and Mimi might have come across as being blissfully happy, but Frederick had gone missing on the day Oscar Hargreaves had been killed. "Hypothetically, if Oscar disliked Frederic, do you think Mimi would be capable to killing him?"

Luna tilted her head from side to side. "I believe she could be capable of committing a crime of passion."

"I'm waiting for you to ask me about the murder weapon," Gunner said, his voice flat.

Lexie looked at Luna. "In his place, how would you phrase that?"

"My eyes would twinkle with amusement. I'd clear my throat." Luna gave a feline shrug. "Set the scene and make some sort of snooty remark about you missing the obvious clue."

Lexie said, "In other words, you'd use the opportunity to banter with me."

"Of course. Otherwise, it's no fun."

She turned to Gunner. "See?"

"Actually, I don't. Are you suggesting there's something wrong with the way I express myself?"

"You could try relaxing a little. Also, you might want to stop looking down your nose at us."

"My eyes are above my nose."

Lexie chortled. "And what's with the three piece suit?"

He gave his jacket a tug.

"And that tugging. When Octavia tugs her clothes it's because she means business. When you do it..." She gestured with her hands. "Help me out, Luna."

"He is a man with great discerning taste. I suspect he is thinking of the quality of his clothes and bemoaning the loss of good taste."

"You just took a stab at my preference for denim."

Luna's whiskers twitched. "Sorry, I couldn't help myself."

Lexie turned to Gunner. "And that's how it's done. I know how Luna feels about my poor taste in clothes, but I never feel inferior. With you, however... I get the feeling you're on a mightier than thou trip."

"Yes," Luna said, "He's a proverbial detractor. If he had to rate you, I'd bet anything he'd struggle to give you a half star."

"Nonsense." He checked his watch.

"Relax. I'm not going to tamper with your clothes again." Lexie rose to her feet. "We should hit the pavement and start pounding on some doors."

"Aren't you forgetting something?" Luna asked.

"Oh, the weapon."

Gunner said, "A cast iron doorstopper in the shape of a cat."

"Do you really think he'd only give me half a star?" Lexie asked.

Luna brushed her little head under Lexie's chin. "I'd give you ten stars and my opinion is the only that counts."

Mimi Hargreaves had sunk into a catatonic state and refused to receive visitors. Lexie didn't blame her.

"If she's catatonic, then how is she communicating her desire to be alone?" Luna asked.

"I have no idea. I only know we need to find Frederick." Lexie strode out of the 5th Avenue building and swirled around. Where would she start looking? "Security cameras in the area."

"Already checked," Gunner said.

"Check again, please." Lexie smiled at his raised eyebrow look. "Well? You wanted to work with me."

"You seem to forget I had no choice in the matter."

"Anyway, as I was saying," Lexie continued, "I think we should start widening the net. What if someone from their past came back to haunt them? Everyone has a past."

"Did you know you're still wearing you Santa hat?" Luna asked. "It's lovely to see you getting into the spirit of it all. As this is our first Christmas together, I am slightly apprehensive. Everyone has different customs and traditions. For instance, my previous companion enjoyed opening gifts on Christmas Eve. I believe that is a tradition the English royal family adhere to."

"Was your previous companion an anglophile?" Octavia asked.

Luna nodded. "She loved tweed and it was always gin and tonic time for her." Luna looked up at Lexie. "Are we getting a tree?"

Lexie hadn't given it any thought. Her Christmases had always been spent at the theater helping out with one of her mom's productions. Also, every year, her mom organized a Christmas Eve dinner for the cast and crew. That was as far as their celebrations went. Since moving to the city, Lexie had spent her Christmases working at O'Connor's Bar.

"I guess the answer is no?" Luna asked.

Both Gunner and Octavia raised their eyebrows at her.

"What?" she asked, her tone defensive.

"We should have a Christmas tree," Luna purred. "A little one would suffice. My previous companion loved the holiday season so much she was non-denominational and even celebrated Hanukah. That's eight days of gift giving. Oh, and to avoid the post seasonal slump, she also celebrated Epiphany. That falls on January 6th. That's when the three Wise Men brought me more gifts."

"I've just detected a pattern," Lexie said under her breath. "Just how many presents are you used to getting?"

Luna blinked and purred deeply. "My previous companion was very thoughtful and generous."

Lexie sighed. "I'll see what I can do."

Octavia nodded and scribbled on a small notebook. "I've made a note of it and will start browsing for suitable feline companion gifts."

Gunner gave her a small nod of approval.

Really? "Can we please focus on one cat who might not be celebrating this Christmas?" She looked up at the building. She didn't think Frederick would jump from the tenth floor. If he had, surely Smithers would have noticed.

"I think we've already established that his disappearance and Oscar Hargreaves' death are linked," Luna said.

"Let's not cross anything off the list." Lexie looked up and down the street trying to spot anyone acting suspiciously. There were a few people walking dogs, but no cats. She turned to Gunner. "What about Oscar's building? Surely there must be security cameras there."

He nodded. "Everyone, including you, has been cleared."

"Did you check the previous couple of days? Someone could have gone into the building and found somewhere to hide, waiting for the right moment to strike." Lexie raked her fingers through her hair and nearly dropped Luna.

"You're clearly frustrated," Luna said. "Relax."

"Easier said. What if the killer has been hovering around the office, working undercover? He overheard Oscar saying he needed to stay behind and chose the moment to strike. We need to follow up on anyone new working in his office."

Luna looked at Octavia and Gunner. "Well? What are you waiting for? Hop to it."

CHAPTER FOUR

Octavia strode into the living room saying, "I've crossed off—"
Luna hushed her. "Can't you see Lexie is meditating?"

"Sorry," Octavia mouthed and looked at Gunner.

He sat by the window shaking his head. "She's been at it for an hour and her cat keeps glaring at me."

Luna hissed.

"You really shouldn't refer to Luna as a cat," Octavia warned.

Lexie winced. She'd been sitting in her quiet place, going through everything she'd seen and heard over the last couple of days. Calling on the elements to help her, she'd sensed a light breeze sweeping around her mind, clearing the debris away and leaving behind an imprint of everyone she'd seen when she'd emerged from the 5th Avenue apartment. She insisted the killer might have been lurking somewhere in that crowd of people strolling by. Drawing in a deep breath, she emerged from her meditation and opened her eyes. Lexie yelped. Gunner and Octavia stooped down almost nose-to-nose with her.

"Well?" Gunner asked.

"Purple." The color had popped up several times. "I'm hungry."

Gunner straightened. "We could go over the security footage. Maybe it'll show up. Do you remember where you saw it?"

"A Coat." Lexie held her hand up. "Don't ask me why I saw a coat. Everyone's wearing them." She checked her cupboards for food. "There's nothing here. Let's go out."

Gunner and his fellow detectives hadn't come up with anything substantial either. The Hargreaves were universally liked. Oscar's employees had been with him since he'd gone into business. The most recent recruit had been working for him for over a dozen years and she'd had nothing but praise for her boss. Besides, they'd all been accounted for as they'd all been having lunch.

At the Kitty Café, Lexie ordered her favorite comfort food, a pizza with the lot. As she watched Luna mingling with the other cats, she tried to think of suitable Christmas/Hanukah/Epiphany presents to give her. "Gifts." She hated shopping. "Octavia."

"I know what you're going to say. I'd love to—"

"Thank you. That's a load off my mind."

"Wait. You didn't let me finish. I'd love to, but I think Luna would like the gifts to come from you."

"She doesn't care where they come from, so long as she gets numerous boxes containing things she'll probably play with for a minute and then discard."

Octavia patted her hand. "I guess Christmas is not a big deal in your family."

Not really. Her mom was always so busy with her theater group, Lexie had grown up thinking of it as another day she had to put in making an appearance and pretending to be happy hanging around the theater, all the while knowing her mom would love nothing better than for her to take up acting. If she had spent more time grooming Lexie for her role as a High Chair and less time making her memorize lines, Lexie wouldn't be playing catch-up. She unclenched her jaw and steered away from casting blame. After all, she'd been the one to ask for a sabbatical from her "witch" duties and her mom had been nice enough to grant it.

"Octavia, please remind me to get a tree."

"And ornaments," Gunner surprised her by saying. "Glass ones can be eye-catching. And you must have tinsel. Have you thought about a color scheme?"

Lexie tried to speak but no words came out. She wore denim jeans and T-shirts, killing several birds with one stone as every morning she only needed to reach inside her closet and pull out some clothes without thinking. She'd never been any good at making selections.

Octavia smiled. "I think that's too much for Lexie to process."

"How are you going to wrap your gifts?" Gunner asked. "Personally, I prefer satin ribbons."

Octavia nodded in agreement. "I'm great at tying bows so I can help you with that."

"We could start after you finish your meal," Gunner suggested. "We'll have a tree up for you in no time."

Either Gunner was trying to make himself more likable or he was showing his true colors...

"I think you're forgetting something," Lexie said.

"I have my people working on it," Gunner assured her.

Lexie crossed her arms. "I want access to that security footage. They're missing something. Someone walked into that building and killed Oscar. Either that... or someone is lying."

Gunner chortled. "Lying to an O'Rourke detective? That's unheard of."

"Did you use your compelling voice on everyone you interviewed?"

He nodded. "The O'Rourke detectives know when to employ their voices for major effect."

"Are you suggesting I shouldn't tell you how to do your job?"

"We're the ones with the detective badges." He shrugged. "Legitimate badges."

"And yet, I'm the one with a lead."

"A purple coat."

"That's a start. It's more than you have." Lexie's tone betrayed her frustration.

"So we should scour the city and employ our compelling voice on anyone wearing a purple coat."

Lexie wanted to say it might work if she cast a spell on his voice to single out the culprit. While she'd been surprised by her increasing confidence, she still doubted its reliability. She knew that attitude worked against her, but maybe if everyone had been less sketchy with information and more helpful with providing a how-to instruction manual...

Sighing, she made a mental note to practice meditating and spell casting.

Lexie looked over her shoulder. "I hope Luna's networking pays off." Luna appeared to be in deep conversation with a group of cats. "Maybe the kitty grapevine will provide us with a solid lead."

Gunner harrumphed.

"If you have issues, I suggest you take them up with Luna."

"And risk having my eyes scratched out?" he mumbled under his breath.

Luna strode toward their table, her nose lifted in the air as she eyed Gunner.

Lexie pushed back a chair for her to sit on. "Well? Did you find out anything useful?"

"Everyone has their Christmas trees up and the gifts are beginning to pile up."

Lexie knew Luna had tried to sound indifferent, but her voice had been loaded with yearning. Scooping Luna up, she said, "Okay, people. There's nothing more we can do today. I..." Lexie swallowed, "I need to shop for a Christmas tree."

Octavia and Gunner looked at each other and both said, "We'll come too."

Half an hour later, Lexie stood in the middle of Elf Kingdom, a local store selling nothing but Christmas decorations. Gunner and Octavia both displayed their superior shopping experience by grabbing shopping carts.

"What do you think?" Gunner asked. He held two sets of ornaments and, apparently, he expected Lexie to select one or the other. "The Shatterproof Peacock Feather Balls or the Drop Ornaments."

"Is there a reason why we can't have both?" Lexie asked, her voice faint.

"We could get the set." Gunner looked over her shoulder. "But we should select the tree first. Traditional or quirky?"

"Maybe we should let Luna decide. Yes, in fact, run everything by her first."

"Good call," Octavia whispered. "Oh, I saw those baubles but at 4.99 each, I didn't think you'd go for them. We are going to have so much fun decorating the tree. I can't wait."

Counting the ornaments Gunner had piled up in his cart, Lexie swallowed.

Gunner went off, murmuring under his breath, "Christmas tree. Tinsel. Lights. More ornaments. You can never have enough ornaments or tinsel. Silver? Gold? Where's that cat?"

"He's getting into the spirit of it," Octavia remarked. "I would never have guessed."

"Yes, I can see you're both possessed. Before you dash off into a shopping frenzy, could I borrow your notebook, please?"

Shoppers streamed in and out of the store, their eyes bright with excitement. The upbeat sounds of a Christmas tune mingled with the shoppers' chatter and the hoot of a toy train winding its way around the store.

Lexie stood in the middle of the hubbub, scribbling a few ideas. "Inside job." She thought she'd heard Octavia say she'd crossed someone off the list. "Must be the maid, Marcie." Lexie decided they should look at people associated with Marcie. Someone might have put pressure on her to gain entry into the Hargreaves' home. Then there was the matter of linking the stolen cat to Oscar's death...

She looked around her. Seeing Gunner emerging from between two large trees, she strode up to him. "Time of death."

"Between nine and midday. Spruce, fir or pine?"

"Huh?"

"I can't find Luna. Someone has to decide." He swept his hand across one side of the store. Tree after tree were lined up, with and without ornaments.

Shrugging, Lexie pointed at one. "That's pretty."

"Really? What about the one next to it?"

"Yeah, I like that one too." They all looked the same to her.

Gunner picked up on her thought. "They're not. There's the Noble Fir. The needles turn upward, exposing the lower branches. The stiff branches make it a good tree for heavy ornaments. Then there's the Virginia Pine. The branches are stout and woody and respond very well to trimming. The Douglas Fir is one of the top major Christmas tree. It's my personal favorite. It comes in dark green or blue green."

Frowning, Lexie asked, "You just happened to know that?" She could see him struggling to answer so she added, "Don't worry." She mentally hollered Luna's name.

She came sprinting across the store, a huge kitty grin lighting up her face. "I've never seen so many pretty lights. Which set are we getting?"

"Can you help Gunner pick a tree?"

Luna glanced at the display. "So many to choose from."

She left them to it and found a corner to sit down. Hypothetically, someone could have snatched Frederick, raced down 5th Avenue and killed Oscar. But why?

"I talked him into getting the Noble Fir," Luna said as she leaped up onto her lap, "But I don't think he's happy about it. He was displaying childlike stubbornness, so I had to put my paw down and remind him this was all about me. Can we put the tree up tonight?"

"I'm sure Gunner and Octavia will love that."

"But what about you? I wouldn't want you to feel left out."

Gunner rushed toward her, his shopping cart full to the brim. "I've just received word, Mimi's cat has turned up. Gold or silver tinsel?"

"Balance is everything. See, you have two blue ornaments together," Luna explained and pointed to the ornaments. "Is it that you don't understand, or you don't want to understand? You can't have the same colors next to each other."

Lexie looked up from her notebook. "Play nice, Luna."

Octavia chuckled under her breath. "Poor Gunner, he's actually doing a terrific job decorating the tree, but Luna's a hard taskmaster."

"Wait until he has to put the tinsel on." It had taken him an hour to set up the lights to Luna's specifications. That had involved Luna prancing around the tree and making sure she'd be able to see lights from every vantage point.

Before that, he had decorated her apartment with Nutcracker

soldiers, red candles, wreaths, and a couple of reindeers, but that had happened after he'd set up the tree next to the fireplace with ample space for the presents.

"Do you think Luna would enjoy a spa day?" Octavia asked.

"I thought you'd finished your on-line shopping. Do we really want to spoil her?"

"It's just once a year. Which reminds me... Are you doing lunch or dinner? I'm good with either one."

Really? "I haven't thought about it, but what about your family?" Lexie had assumed Octavia would want to spend the holidays with her nearest and dearest.

"As you know, I'm working very hard to reinstate our coven. They're not helping, in any way. And they've all opted to spend Christmas in Hawaii."

"If you had a falling out with them, this is the time to kiss and make up," Lexie suggested.

Octavia lifted an eyebrow. "Are you spending the holidays with your mom?"

"She's bound to drop by." Lexie scrunched up the page she'd been scribbling on. It didn't make sense. "Gunner, did your people give you any more details about Frederick? A cat that size should have been reported wandering around the streets. He can't have just turned up. Someone must have dropped him off."

He shook his head.

Lexie turned to Octavia. "Earlier, you started to say you'd crossed someone off. Who was it?"

"Oh, the office staff. Gunner put me in touch with his people and we coordinated our efforts. You wanted everyone cross-referenced and double-checked, so I got onto it. I even pushed to have their relatives and friends scrutinized. They're all in the clear."

"And yet, someone managed to get inside the building and kill Oscar." As for Frederick disappearing...

Lexie flipped through the pages she'd been filling up with every idea that came to her. "Gunner, what did Oscar have scheduled for the day he was murdered?"

"Only a business call, and then he planned on joining the others for lunch."

"Who was the business call with?"

Gunner shook his head. "Oscar was killed before he took the scheduled call."

"Yes? But... Do we know the name of the person he was dealing with?"

Gunner put down the tinsel he'd been holding. "His personal assistant will know. I'll... I'll get someone onto it straightaway."

"We have to talk to Mimi Hargreaves."

"Now?" they all asked.

Lexie and Luna emerged from the alley where they'd landed and strode around to the front entrance of the 5th Avenue apartment block. "I told Octavia and Gunner to meet us out front." Unlike her, they had no trouble whisking from place to place. "Do you see them?"

"No, but I see the old woman in the purple coat and hat. She's pushing that stroller again."

"Let's follow her."

"What about the others?" Luna asked.

"I'm sure Gunner will have no trouble finding us."

Luna cleared her throat. "I think you're forgetting something."

"Let me guess, you want me to carry you." Lexie caught Luna as she leaped up.

"I don't mean to be pushy, but a pair of kitty boots would really help."

"I dread to think what you'll be like when it snows."

Luna curled up in her arms. "I wouldn't know. I used to gaze out the window and think what fun it would be to try to catch a snowflake but my previous companion never took me outdoors in winter."

A gust of wind swirled around them. Lexie had no idea if it was a regular gust or one carrying a message. It didn't seem to be impeding her progress or encouraging it. That might mean she was on the right track.

"I can sense your mind juggling a few thoughts," Luna said.

"I've been trying to join the dots. Do you remember seeing the display of snow globes in Oscar's office?"

"I might have caught sight of them, but I can't be sure. At the time, I was consumed by Gunner's disturbing presence. FYI, he appears to have grown on me. Perhaps we were too hasty in judging him."

"He's still odd, but in a surprisingly amusing way. The festive season must bring out the best in him." Lexie craned her neck and tried to keep the woman in sight. "She's setting a cracking pace."

"Why did you ask me about the snow globes?"

"Oh, I nearly forgot. We saw them at Mimi's apartment and that woman had one in her stroller."

"I thought you might have been trying to determine if I'd like one for Christmas."

"Yeah, that too."

"Purple seems to be the color of choice," Luna remarked as several people strode by wearing purple coats.

Two blocks along and the woman showed no signs of slowing down. "Where is she going? Hang on, where is she?"

"There," Luna pointed. "She stopped outside that store. I suggest you slow down because she's looking over her shoulder. She might be onto you."

Lexie ducked behind a group of late night shoppers. When she emerged, she saw no sign of the woman in purple. "Now what?"

Luna bobbed up and down.

"What's wrong with you?"

"I'm running on the spot and trying to keep warm. Can't you hear my teeth chattering?"

"Okay, we'll head back now and hopefully meet up with the others." As she turned, she caught sight of the purple hat. "She's in that store." Trying to keep out of sight, she edged toward it. "It's a florist."

"Huzzah. Now can we go?"

"What is she doing in there? This can't be a coincidence."

"You're about to tie it all in to Frederick's disappearance and Oscar's murder. Great. Now can we go?"

Lexie peered inside the store in time to see the old woman striding toward the back room. With each step she took, she seemed to straighten. By the time she reached the doorway, she was standing tall and...

"Her gray hair."

"What about it?" Luna asked.

"It's lusciously thick and brown now."

"Call for back-up," Luna said. "Call. For. Back-up."

"When did you become a scaredy-cat?"

"I'm being practical, cautious and sensible. You haven't come into all your powers. That woman just transformed herself from a street person to... possibly the owner of this establishment and mastermind of crimes. That is, assuming she is linked to Frederick's disappearance and Oscar's death. What do you propose doing? Please call for back-up."

Lexie stepped inside the store. Her nose crinkled. When she felt a sneeze coming on she tried to hold it back.

"I don't care for this pungent smell of flowers. It's... it's overpowering." Luna shook her little head and sneezed. Not once, but twice.

As Lexie took a retreating step, she heard the woman call out, "I'll be with you in a moment."

"I hope you have a game plan," Luna said and buried her face in the crook of Lexie's arm.

"You." The woman appeared and pointed a finger at Lexie.

"And," Luna added, "If you have a game plan, you should put it into motion right about now."

Lexie straightened and sneezed. "Hi."

"That's it?" Luna curled up into a tight ball. "Don't take this the wrong way, but self-preservation compels me to make myself invisible."

"You followed me," the woman accused.

Lexie lifted her chin. "And just as well I did. You have some explaining to do."

The woman appeared to become even taller. When she raised her hands, Lexie knew she had to act quickly. She only had two choices. She could either beat a hasty retreat, or... she could call on her powers.

Emptying her mind, she focused first on shielding them from whatever the woman was about to do to them, but then Luna cut in on her thoughts.

"Bind her. Bind her."

In that split second, Lexie's mind filled with images of shiny crimson red satin ribbon, but only because she'd caught sight of a roll of it on the counter.

As the ribbon swirled around her mind, the ribbon on the counter began to unwind.

"Oh, that is so cool."

When she saw the woman's fingers lighting up with sparks, Lexie mentally scrambled to hurry up the process. Instinctively, she used her finger to draw a circle. The ribbon flew around the woman. Lexie made a pulling motion with her hand and the ribbon tightened, securing the woman's arms in place.

"Tighter. Tighter, and faster. Yes. Faster." Luna yelped.

Lexie kept winding the ribbon around until the woman resembled a bright red cocoon.

Luna bounced up and down in her arms. "Now, just in case she frees herself, run for your life."

As Lexie took a tentative step forward, the store door open. Gunner stormed in followed by Octavia.

"Ah, the cavalry has arrived," Luna's head emerged from hiding. "You'll be pleased to note we have secured the killer. Now handcuff her and watch out for her hands."

"What's going on?" Gunner demanded.

"I'm not sure." Lexie shrugged. "Where did you two get to?"

Gunner and Octavia exchanged a sheepish look. Octavia shifted and said, "We stopped at Elf Kingdom to pick up some more ornaments."

Lexie rolled her eyes.

"So who is she?" Gunner asked.

"We've seen her hanging around Mimi's apartment building and followed her here. That's when we saw her transform herself from an old woman. Feel free to use your special voice on her. She's definitely guilty of something."

"Unbind me," the woman hollered.

Ignoring her, Lexie strode up to the counter and picked up a business card, which read: Gloria Winchester, Florist.

Turning, she noticed a snow globe. As she had a closer look at it, she said, "She had one in her stroller."

Gloria Winchester screeched. "Put that down."

"Hey, there are little figures in this one." She turned to Gunner. "Did you hear me?"

Gunner pressed his finger to his ear.

Luna leaped up onto the counter. "I think he's communicating with his group."

Moments later, Gunner turned to her. "The back-up will arrive shortly."

Sighing, Luna purred, "See, normal people call for back-up. Please try to remember that."

Rounding the counter, Lexie inspected the shelves. "Look, more snow globes." Each one had a unique scene. A comfortable fireplace with a sparkly chandelier. A beach house with a yacht moored off the jetty... "A jet. Who'd want a snow globe with a jet plane in it?"

"Plenty of people," Gloria blurted out. "And they're all willing to pay a pretty penny for it."

"Huh?"

"Put it down. It's mine."

"Threaten to drop one," Luna said, "She'll confess in no time."

"Gloria Winchester is a what?" Lexie asked.

"A peddler of desires." Gunner picked up a snow globe. "The young version of her runs the flower shop and the old one does the peddling. People buy desires from her, as in, stuff they want. She created them in these little snow globes." He shook it. "Dream home? Coming right up. A new yacht? Here you go."

"And people paid her for it?"

He nodded.

"But this is all stuff people can buy."

"She paved the way for an easy way of getting it all."

"I still don't get it. You went through all the security footage. How did she get inside the building to kill Oscar?"

"She's the florist and regularly goes there to freshen up the flower displays. No one suspected her. When she went into Mimi's apartment, she disguised herself as the old woman, which practically made her invisible. No one notices people like her."

She did... "So why did she kill Oscar?"

Gunner sighed. "She thought the Hargreaves had reneged on their deal so she took Frederick. Then she confronted Oscar who threatened to report her to the Coven Disciplinary Board because he insisted he'd made the payment in full. He called her an old hag. That's when she lost it and hit him with the doorstopper."

Lexie frowned. "So Oscar knew her as the old... woman and the young one?"

"Yes. He's been dealing with her for years."

"Hang on. How did he know about the disciplinary board?"

"We gained access to his safe and found a document dating back to the 1770s when his family first settled nearby. They purchased favors from a local witch and the family prospered. It's been going on for generations."

"You mean, every snow globe Mimi has represents a new acquisition?"

He nodded.

Luna's eyes widened. "Everyone seems to be doing well out of the witchcraft business except us."

Lexie slumped back against the counter. "Well, I guess that's that." The front door eased open and a gust of wind swept in, swirled around Lexie, and swept out again. "Yeah, I still can't get my head around that one." One with the elements? "Thank you," she called out as the door closed.

CHAPTER FIVE

"The Christmas tree looks lovely, thank you." Luna snuggled against Lexie. "Are you awake?"

Lexie brushed Luna's tail off her face. "How long have you been asking me that?"

Luna purred deeply. "A while. I can almost see the first slivers of daylight."

"Who needs to set the alarm when I have you to wake me up." Lexie groaned. "I dread to think what you'll be like on Christmas day."

"Before I forget, I should tell you it's the thought that counts."

"I'm still half asleep so I'm not even going to try to decipher that." While Octavia had gone ahead and spent a small fortune on presents, she'd insisted Lexie had to do her own shopping. That had taken some doing, but Gunner had been surprisingly helpful, offering to keep Luna busy by finishing decorating the apartment. As a result, her apartment looked like Santa's alternative pied-à-terre.

"Perhaps Santa will be especially generous with you this year," Luna said. "After all, you caught a killer."

Lexie brushed her hand across her forehead. "I seem to recall you spotting the woman with the purple hat and coat first."

"Yes but you were the one to follow your intuition and chase after her. Also, you insisted it had to be an inside job." Luna jumped off the bed. "If you're not going to get up, you should go back to sleep. I'm going to go admire the tree."

Lexie plumped up her pillow and pulled the blanket over her head.

A peddler of desires.

What would she have wished for... in exchange for an exorbitant amount of money?

Lexie's eyes danced around her bedroom. She loved her small apartment but Luna had been badgering her to find something to accommodate her frenzied sprints. She had a closet full of her favorite jeans and T-shirts. Her inheritance provided her with more than enough to live on, although Luna thought of that as chump change.

Shrugging, Lexie decided she liked everything as it was. Although, she wouldn't mind having a few days of peace and quiet...

With all the shopping done and nothing else to do, she drifted off back to sleep only to be stirred awake by the chatter coming from the living room.

"You're missing all the fun," Lune said as she scurried into her bedroom. "The day is already half gone."

"Have you been talking to me in my sleep again? I swear I heard you."

"I might have asked a question or two," Luna said, "I don't know. The morning's been hectic."

"Give me a minute to pull myself together."

Half an hour later, she strode into the living room and found Octavia roasting chestnuts by the fireplace. She wore a bright red Santa hat matched with a red sweater and black tights.

"Are you moonlighting as Santa's helper?" Lexie asked. "And where's Dodge?" Belatedly, Lexie clamped her hand over her mouth.

"It's okay. You can ask about him. He's helping out with a case so he's going to be tied up for Christmas." Octavia's cheeks colored slightly. "I hope you don't mind me dropping by."

"The more the merrier." Lexie had no idea what she meant by that, since she hadn't actually planned anything.

Gunner emerged from the kitchen, two mugs in hand. "Oh, there you are. I've just made some mulled wine."

Gunner? Here? Lexie stared at his reindeer sweater and raked her fingers through her hair. "I haven't had breakfast yet." She looked for Luna. "Did someone remember to feed Luna?"

Octavia put her hand up.

"Thank you." Turning to Gunner, Lexie asked, "Is the case closed?"

He nodded. "Gloria Winchester is in custody and awaiting the Coven's wrath."

"That's an interesting way of putting it." Lexie hoped she never had to face the Coven's wrath. "Which version is actually guilty?"

"They found the young version you bound innocent of all charges. The older version, however, insisted she'd been within her rights to kill Oscar because no one got to call her an old hag. I believe she is going to plead temporary insanity. Too many years of shifting from her old version to her young version have played havoc with her mind."

"You actually buy that?"

"It's not up to me to decide. The powers that be will determine her future. She's definitely out of the florist business and she won't be permitted to peddle desires any more."

"Did she say why she returned Frederick?"

Gunner nodded. "She wanted to get rid of the evidence and released him outside the apartment building."

Lexie sniffed. "What's that smell?"

"We're having turkey for lunch," Octavia piped in.

She looked over at her small table. There were four place settings. "Um, are we expecting someone else?"

Right on cue, the front door opened and her mom, the current High Chair of the Mackenzie Coven, swept in, her arms laden with gifts. She wore a bright red coat with fur trimming and her dark brown hair cascading around her shoulders.

Luna leaped into action inspecting all the presents as Morgana set them down under the tree.

Morgana smiled at her, "I thought I'd surprise you."

"How wonderful, mom."

"I hear you've been busy. I can't wait to hear all about it." Her mom turned to Gunner. "Who is this charming man?"

Lexie made the introductions. To her surprise, her mom and Gunner hit it off straightaway.

"I love what you've done with the place, Lexie. Although it still feels a little cramped." Even as she spoke the walls shifted and her apartment gained a couple of feet of space.

"Mom?"

Morgana waved her hand. "Oh, don't worry. No one will notice." She bent down and picked up one of the presents. "You can open this one now. It might help you get into the festive mood."

A red sweater... with a snowflake on it. "Um, how did you manage to get away from the theater?" Lexie asked.

Morgana gave another breezy wave of her hand. "Nothing's more important than spending a special day together with you."

"Really?"

Luna raced up to her. "You mustn't make her feel uncomfortable. She might be your mom, but she's still the High Chair and she brought presents." Luna's ears twitched. "I hear someone else coming. Oh, more presents."

Jonathan strode in carrying a couple of shopping bags. "Hello, I hope I'm not late."

Lexie hid her surprise. Normally, Jonathan spent the day working behind the counter at the pub.

"Morgana, I didn't expect to see you here today," Jonathan said in a forced tone.

Whatever history her guardian and sometime employer had with her mom remained a mystery to Lexie. While she hoped they'd put aside their differences, she couldn't help saying under her breath, "This can't end well."

Octavia edged toward her. "Don't worry. I got them all presents on your behalf. You should stop looking so apprehensive."

"I can't help it. My mom just made my apartment bigger."

"I'm sure she'll put it back before she leaves."

Jonathan set his bags down and discreetly murmured, "No one told me she'd be here. If Morgana turns me into a monkey, it'll be on your head."

"Oh, look. Snow." Luna rushed to the window and pressed her little nose against it.

Morgana smiled. "I thought it might set the mood. Oh, here come the other guests."

"Other guests?"

"More presents." Luna hurried to the door. "They all come bearing gifts. How attentive."

Lexie recognized the actors from her mom's theater group.

"I hope you don't mind, darling. They're like family and since you couldn't come to us, I thought we'd all come to you."

"Sure, the more the merrier."

"You actually meant that," Jonathan murmured.

Lexie smiled. "I guess all those years being an understudy have served me well." In reality, she did mean it. Most of the cast members in her mom's theater group were people who would otherwise not have anywhere to go during the holidays. The fact they all looked a little dazed meant her mom had woven her magic in getting them here.

Luna leaped up into her arms and brushed her little face against her cheek. "Thank you for making our first Christmas together magical. Now can I open a present?"

Lexie wove her way toward the tree; the distance twice as long as it had been before her mom had decided to weave her magic... "Sure."

"What did you get me? Wait. Don't tell me. I'd like it to be a surprise. Although I think I know what it is. Did you get me an Amish quilt? You did. You don't have to answer. My heart's pounding with excitement. I'm sure I'll like whatever you got me... and if I don't, I'll just pretend I do..."

ABOUT THE AUTHOR

Sonia wrote her first mystery at sixteen and was encouraged to pursue a career in writing. Instead, she listened to her art teacher and earned a B.A. in Fine Arts. She has no idea how as she spent most of her time reading and writing fiction. Further studies followed in information technology and marketing management but she spent most of her time writing stories. After dabbling in the romantic comedy genre, she found her way back home and now writes lighthearted contemporary and paranormal cozy mysteries with quirky characters and fun dialogue.

Follow Sonia Parin online:
    Website
    Twitter
    Facebook

DEAL OR SNOW DEAL

The Mystic Snow Globe Mystery Series: A Prequel

M.Z. ANDREWS

SUMMARY

Whitley and Esmerelda Snow have but one wish this Christmas: to find beautiful gowns to wear for the Winter Solstice Snow Globe Ball in their hometown of Everland Cove. But when their down-on-his-luck father, Felix, strikes up a deal with an unlikely stranger, things take an interesting turn.

Deal or Snow Deal, the prequel to The Mystic Snow Globe Mystery Series, can be found EXCLUSIVELY in the Spells and Jingle-bells anthology.

CHAPTER ONE

"Come on, Joey. Your order is down thirty percent this month. Last month it was down twenty. I'm sensing a trend here."

Joseph DeMarco wiped his greasy hands on the front of his white cotton apron before scratching the blue-black stubble on his chin. "I'm sorry, Felix. I don't know what to tell ya."

Felix Snow stood stuffed between the bread proofer and the commercial grill. Pots and pans clanged together around him as waitresses hollered orders over a stainless-steel warmer. The rapid fire of a knife mincing veggies thudded on a cutting board. He inhaled a shallow breath of moist air seasoned with freshly baked bread and simmering marinara sauce. His stomach rumbled inside his potbelly. It had been a very long day, and he hadn't had a bite to eat since the cinnamon raisin bagel he'd snatched from his first customer of the day.

"Tell me this is just a passing thing, and the numbers are gonna come up again next month?" begged Felix.

"Excuse me," interrupted a young man in a white jacket and hat who carried a large cardboard box. "Mr. DeMarco, what do you want me to do with this?"

Joey glanced at his new assistant chef and cocked a thumb over one shoulder. "Just put that down over there, Sam." He turned to look at

Felix again. "I wish I could tell you what you want to hear, Felix, but things ain't carved in stone in the restaurant business, ya know?"

Felix rubbed a hand through his dark, wavy hair. "It doesn't *look* like things have slowed down around here."

Joey threw two thick, sausage-fingered hands out on either side of him. "Listen, Felix. Business is good. I ain't gonna lie to ya. Unfortunately, ya ain't cuttin' me the deals that other guys is cuttin' me."

Felix's jaw fell open. "You're cheating on me, Joey?"

Joey sighed. "Don't look at it like that, Felix. We've known each other for, what, twenty-five years? You're a pal, and I owe ya a lot, but I gotta watch out for my bottom line here."

Felix couldn't help but nod. He understood bottom lines more than anyone else. "Of course, Joey. I can't blame you. How about you give me a chance to make the numbers right for you?"

"But, Felix. Those otha guys. They're bigga! You're like a mom 'n' pop compared to them. You just can't match the prices."

"Be straight with me, Joey. Are you leaving me altogether? Is this a breakup?" Felix asked as a wave of unease turned his stomach. What would he do if he lost his biggest client? Things would go from bad to worse. It wouldn't take long. He'd been in the business long enough to know how these things went.

Joey's head wobbled on his shoulders. "Not right now. You still got the best prices on veal. I don't know how ya do it, but ya do. You still got the best prices on lotsa stuff. So until ya don't, I can work with ya."

Felix grimaced as he wondered how much longer it would be until he couldn't beat the big guys' prices anymore. The words he wanted to say to the man in front of him snagged in his throat. What Felix *wanted to say* was that his company had been the first one to give Joey DeMarco credit when he'd first opened and hadn't had two nickels to rub together. Not only did Joey *owe* the success of *this restaurant* to Felix's fortitude in talking the big bosses into extending him credit, but Joey *also* owed the success of his other restaurants to it as well. But as a salesman, Felix knew he had no choice but to swallow back the betrayal he now felt. He offered his old friend a tight grin. The kind where his cheeks lifted into apples beneath his eyes, but his lips didn't part. Felix tipped his head to the side and tucked his clipboard beneath the perspiration-stained armpits of his blue-collared shirt.

"Yeah, alright," said Felix. He tapped the clipboard. "I'll get this order placed. You should have it by the end of the week."

"Thanks, Felix," said Joey, clapping the shorter man on the back. "I'm sorry I couldn't do more for ya. It's just that I got mouths to feed. Ya know?"

Felix lifted his old company coat up off the stainless-steel table and tucked it under his other arm. "I know what ya mean. I have a couple of those mouths to feed myself."

"Okay, well, listen, Felix. God bless ya. Have a merry Christmas."

"Thanks, Joey. You too. Give Valentina and the girls my regards." Felix looked longingly at the sauce in the pot on the top of a warmer as he tugged on his coat.

"Hey, Felix, you, uh, want me to have my guys make you a plate before you go?" asked Joey.

Felix shoved a hand into his pocket and felt the thin, folded lump of cash. He flicked through it, rubbing the bills silently. He knew there wasn't enough in the budget for a plate of food *and* what he really needed. Not after this new round of bad news.

Felix shook his head, his gaze skimming over Joey's head and then hitting the floor. "Nah, I ate at my last stop. I'm solid."

Joey lifted his chin towards a basket of bagged bread on a shelf. "Well, at least grab a loaf of Val's bread on the way out. For the road, ya know? It's on the house."

Felix pulled his red QFS work coat higher around his neck as he walked down the bustling city street. It was dark, and the snow fell around him wet clumps, chilling him to the bone and making the sidewalks and streets thick with grey sludge. As he crossed an alley intersection, Felix's loafer disappeared into a hole in the road, soaking his foot from his toes to just above his ankle. He threw his head back. *Just great! Par for the course.*

Without setting the other foot down, Felix hopped towards the slushy sidewalk to lean a hand against a tan brick building beneath a red-and-white-striped awning. He growled as he leaned over to pull off his wet shoe and dump out the half-snow, half-water mixture. Looking down at his sock, he debated taking it off but decided against it. Instead, he wedged the wet sock back into the wet shoe and wished he were anywhere but here.

As he straightened himself and enjoyed the brief reprieve from the elements that the awning provided, he read the vinyl in the window. *Arabella's Mystic Treasures.*

Felix took a step back to peer into her storefront to see just what kind of *mystic treasures* Miss Arabella was peddling. Two beautiful ball gowns sparkled in the window. His eyebrows lifted. "Well, I'll be," he whispered as a soft smile slowly lifted the corners of his eyes.

Almost by force of nature, Felix walked towards the door and pulled it open. Sensing his presence, a melodic chime sprang to life, filling the dark entryway with song. He stuck his head inside and peered around. The storefront was dark and overloaded with display racks covered in odds and ends. *Ah, it's an antique store!* Immediately, he questioned his decision to go inside. It probably wasn't open anyway, and he had only a few hours to spend hunting down ball gowns for his daughters; this looked like a waste of time. Just as he pulled his head out of the doorway, he heard a woman's lilting voice call out to him. "Come in! Come in! We're open!"

Felix let out a heavy sigh. His daughters, at least one of them, anyway, would likely *kill him* if she knew her dress came from a second-hand store, no matter how beautiful the gown was. "Oh, thank you. I was just dress shopping, but I didn't realize this was an antique store," he called back to the mysterious voice.

"Oh! Well, you came to the right place. I have dresses! Did you see the lovely gowns in the window?"

Felix eased further into the shop, trying to find the person behind the voice. "I did. That's actually why I came in. I thought that perhaps this was a dress shop."

"I sell many lovely items. Some are new. Some are used. The dresses in the window are new. They've never been worn. Would you like to look at them?"

Lights flickered further inside the shop, casting strange shadows across a rack of dark garments, and as he took another step further inside, he realized the lights were candles flickering on a glass counter. "Your lights are off. Are you sure I'm not catching you at a bad time?" he asked, craning his neck in search of the woman.

"Oh, not at all, Felix. This is a mystical shop. Everything here has been hand-selected and has a story to tell. I feel that the candles preserve the aura of the items."

Felix cocked an eyebrow up. "Felix? You know my name. It seems you've got one up on me. Have we met?"

Her giggle swirled around him in the darkened room. He heard the floor creak, and a woman appeared seemingly out of nowhere. She was tall and thin with dark skin. Her head was bound with layers of colorful cloth, and she wore bangle bracelets up both arms. Despite her exotic beauty, Felix frowned. "I'm afraid I don't recognize you."

"Forgive me, Felix. You're correct. We've never met. I'm Arabella. I'm a mystic." She tipped her head to the side. "I'm clairvoyant. I know a bit about every person that enters my shop. In fact, I've been expecting you, even before you needed a pair of dry socks." She walked assuredly behind a glass counter filled with medallions and rings that seemed to glow from within and pulled out a pair of black dress socks. She held them out to him.

Felix shook his head, waving a hand at her gently. "Oh, I couldn't."

"They've been here, just waiting for you to arrive." She waved them at him, insisting he take them. "You'll catch cold in those wet socks."

With an appreciative smile, Felix took the socks and sat on a small bench. "Very kind of you. Do you mind if I browse barefoot so my shoes might have time to dry?"

"Not at all! In fact, let me grab those dresses you saw in the window. Esmerelda and Whitley are size fours, yes?"

Felix smiled uneasily. Arabella's clairvoyance was a bit unnerving. "They gave me specific instructions. Esmerelda wants a size two or smaller, and Whitley wants a size four."

Arabella stopped moving and turned to look at Felix with one lifted brow. "They're identical twins, aren't they? They don't wear the same size?"

Felix laughed. "You know a lot, but obviously you don't know their personalities. Esmerelda likes her dresses tight. Whitley prefers to be able to breathe in her clothing."

Arabella winked at him. "I had an idea, but I wasn't sure. You know your girls well."

He couldn't help but chuckle. If there was one thing he knew, it was his daughters. "Oh, I know everything about them. Ask me anything!"

"Which one was born first?"

"Esmerelda! And she *never* lets Whitley forget it!"

"Which one got her powers first?"

"They got them on the same day. The day their mother passed."

He had to swallow back the lump in his throat. Even though that was years and years ago now, it was still painful to speak of.

"I'm so sorry, Felix. Yes, of course, they inherited their mother's *gifts*. How insensitive of me."

He nodded but found he couldn't bring himself to speak for fear of breaking down. It had been a long, emotional day, and he needed to focus.

Arabella's lips formed a tight line. It was obvious she'd touched a nerve. She tried to change the subject by bringing up a bouncier topic. "Whitley's your seamstress and amateur sleuth, right?"

Felix cleared his throat and forced a smile. "Yes. She's my little people pleaser. She loves nothing more than helping people."

"Tell me about Esmerelda. What are her interests?"

"Oh, my Esmerelda," he sighed. "She doesn't really have a lot of hobbies. Unless of course you call *dating* or playing with makeup a hobby. She's a very talented singer, passed down to her by her mother, but she doesn't use her talent. And then, of course, she got her power of enchantment from her mother."

"Oh, Felix, your girls sound lovely. Now, just wait until they see these unbelievable gowns I have for them! They are just going to adore them!"

Felix could hear the woman pulling down mannequins in the window. "Do you need any help?" he hollered.

"I've got it!"

It wasn't long before the two exquisitely dressed mannequins stood in front of him in the flickering candlelight. "They're absolutely stunning," he breathed. "Are they their sizes?"

Arabella winked. "But of course."

They were perfect. His girls would be ecstatic if he came home with the gowns. He stuck his hand back in his pocket and felt the small wad of bills again. He was scared to ask. "How much?"

"Four hundred a piece," said Arabella unapologetically as she fluffed the skirt of the emerald-green dress. "You won't find a more amazing deal in all of the city."

Felix swallowed hard. He had three hundred dollars in his pocket, and to his name. "They're lovely, but I'm just not sure my girls would approve. Girls can be very picky, you know?"

Arabella stopped fluffing and turned to look at Felix. "Too tight for your budget?"

He let out the heavy breath he had dammed in his lungs. His shoulders slumped. "Yes."

She nodded primly. "Indeed." She held up her index finger and nodded her head knowingly. "I have other dresses."

Felix felt the weight of a two-ton elephant on his heart. He didn't have the time or the energy to look at other dresses that he knew he couldn't afford. He tried to smile at her. "No, thank you. I should go. I've taken up enough of your time."

As he turned, Arabella magically appeared in front of him. "I'm known as a woman who likes to wheel and deal. I enjoy a good trade."

"A trade?" Felix looked down at his beat-up work coat, the mud on the cuffs of his khaki trousers, and his new black socks. "I have nothing to trade, I'm afraid. And I'll be honest. I have very little money."

"What if we didn't trade for money? What if I requested your help with an obligation I have?"

Felix looked at her blankly. What could a Quality Food Supply salesman possibly offer a mystic help with?

"I can see I have your attention," she said before he could speak. "I recently received a load of dresses. Like I said when you entered—

every item in this shop has a story behind it. Some things have mysteries attached. Mysteries that the universe wants solved."

The weight of the day fell heavily around Felix's shoulders. His droopy eyes looked up at Arabella. "I'm not following you."

"You have a daughter that enjoys solving mysteries, yes?"

He nodded. "Yes. *Small* mysteries."

"And you have a daughter who...how should I put this...can be *very persuasive?*"

Felix's face tingled with heat. He shifted uncomfortably and then nodded.

"Give me just a moment!" Arabella turned on her heels and practically floated towards the glass counter, where she disappeared behind a nearly invisible black curtain.

Felix looked around the room helplessly. What would he tell his daughters when he came home empty-handed? They'd given him *one job*: to find them ball gowns for the big gala to be held on the winter solstice in their small town. He ran a hand through his thick hair. He'd just have to give Whitley his last three hundred dollars and let her buy material to sew their own dresses. He only hoped there would be enough time for her to start from scratch. He shuddered at the thought of Esmerelda's reaction. His highly stubborn and opinionated firstborn had already put her foot down on more than one occasion. She wanted a store-bought dress, not some simple creation her sister had sewn for her.

"Felix, do you mind giving me a hand?" called out Arabella's voice behind the curtain.

He rushed around the counter and peeled back the curtain to see Arabella holding two handfuls of dresses on hangers high above her head. Felix lifted the hangers from her thumbs.

"Just drape them over the counter, Felix."

With a smile on her face, Arabella took a step back and threw her hands on her hips. Her bangles made a little clinking sound as they slid together on her wrists. "What do you think?"

Felix looked down at the myriad of dresses. "Think about what?"

"Do you like them?"

He lifted his brows and stared down at the pile of garments. "There are at least a dozen dresses here."

She nodded. "More than a dozen, in fact. You can have them all. Then the girls can have their pick."

"I can have them all?!" he replied, nearly choking on his words.

Arabella nodded emphatically. "Yes. They are previously owned, but I think you'll be pleased to see that they are all still in pristine condition. And like I said, I'm willing to trade."

Felix's mouth hung open. "A trade for what? I have nothing to offer you!"

She pointed at the dresses. "All I want is the mystery behind each of these dresses solved."

"You want my daughters to solve their mysteries? But how?" he asked, befuddled.

Arabella lifted her brows and tipped her head to the side. "When the time comes, they will figure it out."

"But what if they don't want to solve the mysteries?"

"Then either return the dresses untouched, or you'll have to repay me in some way."

His jaw dropped open. "I don't have the money to pay for all of these dresses!"

"Then you can repay me with something truly valuable to you."

"*Anything* valuable to me?" he asked. His mind raced. He had his spare truck to offer. Of course, Whitley and Esmerelda used it for driving into town when he was gone. *I'm sure Essy would be happy to part with the old jalopy*, he thought. *She never did like it anyway.*

Arabella waved a hand at him dismissively. "I don't think we need to fret about minor details, Felix. I know it'll work itself out."

He looked down at the pile of dresses. He was sure there was *bound* to be something useful in there. Whitley could surely dress them up with her flair for fashion and her sewing abilities.

His eyes slowly moved up to meet Arabella's. He couldn't believe he found himself considering accepting this peculiar woman's offer. It felt a bit surreal, like he was being propelled along in a dream. He held a tentative hand out to Arabella. "Deal."

A smile poured across her face like slow-spreading honey. "Very good," she said, holding her bejeweled hand out to shake his. "Let me get these dresses packaged up for you, and then you can be on your way!"

A weight seemed to lift off of Felix's heart, which moments ago had been heavy and full of anxiety. Now it suddenly felt buoyed in his chest. His girls were going to be so excited! He could barely wait to get home and show him their good fortune.

CHAPTER TWO

Pulling aside the sheer curtains in her bedroom, Whitley Snow's breath caught in her throat as she rubbed her fist against the frosted windowpane. Delicate snowflakes fell from dark grey clouds, covering the ground below her second-story window like an undisturbed white blanket. Whit's emerald-green eyes, fringed with eyelashes like chocolate-colored awnings, sparkled excitedly. "Oh, Essy!" she breathed. "It's snowing! I didn't think it would! Do you know what this means?"

Lounging across Whitley's neatly made lavender bedspread, her sister Esmerelda rolled onto her back and flipped her long brown hair out of her eyes before groaning. "That it's going to be muddy next week?"

Whitley let go of the gauzy material, threw her arms out wide, and pirouetted across the room. "No, silly. It means we'll have real snow for this year's Winter Solstice Snow Globe Ball!"

Esmerelda lifted an arm into the air and twirled her finger. "Woo-hoo," she replied in a monotone voice.

Whitley grabbed a small carved wooden wand off her desk. An orb-shaped bloodstone was held in place by a spiral of copper wire atop the smooth cherry-stained wand. She gave the stick a slight swirl in the air, and a cream-colored cashmere scarf magically plucked itself from an oversized wooden wardrobe on the other side of the bedroom and floated towards her. When it landed lightly in her hands, Whitley wrapped it around her neck and peered into the mirror. "Essy," she admonished. "You need to cheer up. Saturday is going to be the best day of the entire year! Maybe even the best day of our lives!"

Esmerelda sat up straight on the bed. Her perfectly manicured brows dropped and she curled the corner of her ruby-red lip in disgust. "Tell me how it's going to be the best day of our lives, Whit. It's a *ball*, not a wedding. And besides, we have nothing to wear! You know we'll be stuck wearing something we've worn before! What kind of statement does that make? I'll tell you! It tells the world that we're *paupers! That's what kind of statement it makes!* Do you know how embarrassing that is?"

Whitley cocked her head to the side as she glanced at her sister. "Why are you so worried about our dresses? Dad promised he'd bring us the most beautiful dresses he can find!"

"I'm sorry if I don't put a lot of faith in *Dad's shopping skills*. What does *he* know about fashion? Or about buying dresses for a ball?"

Whitley turned to face her sister, putting her fisted hands on either hip. "I offered to make us dresses. You should have just let me do it."

Esmerelda groaned. "Are you crazy? I don't want a homemade dress! I don't understand why you couldn't just zap us up some fabulous gowns like Cinderella's fairy godmother did!"

Whitley giggled. "Just because I have a wand doesn't make me a fairy godmother, Es. My powers don't work like that."

Esmerelda's green eyes darkened. "Ugh, I wish they did."

"Listen, give Dad the chance to show you that he can do this. I know he'll come through for us."

"I just wish Everland Cove had a decent shopping mall. Then we could have bought our own dresses, instead of sending Dad!"

Whitley put a hand on either side of her sister's shoulders. "Relax, Es. Dad's got this covered. Have faith. And if he doesn't bring back something you like, I'll figure something out. I always do!"

Esmerelda crossed her arms defiantly across her chest. "You mean you'll make us dresses?"

Whitley nodded.

"I don't want a homemade dress. I think that just might be worse than re-wearing last year's dress!"

Whitley felt a pang of unappreciation squeeze at her heart as her eyes swept across her sewing machine and the large pile of fabric next to her desk. She'd sewn their own clothing for years. Why, at twenty-two years of age, Essy was suddenly opposed to wearing one of her custom creations, Whitley wasn't sure. "Okay," she whispered.

Tired of talking about their father and her lack of a dress, Esmerelda sighed before changing the subject. "Do you have a date yet?"

The side of Whitley's mouth crooked up into a half-smile as she stood up straight. "No, but I assumed Ash and I would go together. He doesn't have a date either." Whitley plucked absentmindedly at the puff sleeves on the hand-made blouse she wore.

"Oh, Gawwd," drawled Esmerelda. "Why in the world would you go to the ball with Sebastian Everett? He's soooo boring! The *only* good thing about him is that his father is positively *loaded*."

Whitley's green eyes widened as she gasped. "Ash isn't boring!" She lifted the matching cashmere sweater off the back of her desk chair and tugged it on over her blouse. "He's amazing! We have so much fun when we're together!"

Essy rolled her eyes. "If you have so much fun with him, then why don't you marry the man already?"

Whitley felt heat rush to her cheeks. She most certainly had no interest in discussing her love life, or lack thereof, with her nosy sister. "You know it's not like that with Ash and me. We're just friends."

"See? Boooring," sang Esmerelda. "You won't catch me going to the ball with some *platonic friend*." She spat the words *platonic friend* from her mouth as if they tasted like Brussels sprouts. But, of course, Whitley expected that from her sister. Aside from handsomeness, there were three qualities Esmerelda Snow looked for in a man: she liked them fast, reckless, and rich.

The Snow twins were well-known in Everland Cove. Not just because they were enchanted witches, but because of their remarkable beauty. With their petite features, their long, dark hair, fair skin, and brilliant green eyes, they were a magnet for men. Esmerelda attracted the majority of the suitors, however. Not because she was any more beautiful than her sister—they were identical, after all—but because Esmerelda Snow was, quite simply, a party girl. She changed men almost as often as she changed her underwear. Picking one out in the morning, she often had selected a different one by the evening.

Whitley didn't mind that her sister wasn't as virginal as she was. Sleeping around wasn't her cup of tea, but if having loads of boyfriends made Esmerelda happy, then it made Whitley's life that much better. She, on the other hand, was quite content being single. She had her sister and father, her best friend Ash, and her fashion design to keep her company.

"I'd rather go to the ball with a friend than with some random," said Whitley with a shrug.

"Hello?! That's called dating, dear sister!" bellowed Esmerelda. "It's fun. You should try it. How do you ever expect to find a husband if you're not doing it?"

Whit shrugged. "Who said I'm looking for a *husband*? I'm only twenty-two. I want to go to fashion school someday and live in a big city. What I don't understand is why *you* would you want to find a husband this early. Then you have to give up your wild and lazy lifestyle and be someone's *wife*."

Esmerelda was quiet for a moment. "I just want my life to begin. I'm tired of waiting for it to happen."

Whitley gave her sister a soft smile. "Essy. I'm afraid you can't see the forest for the trees!"

Her twin lifted the corner of her lip. "Huh?"

"This *is* your life. Quit waiting for it to start. It already has!"

Esmerelda rolled her eyes. Whitley knew she probably didn't get it. She never would. Her sister was too self-absorbed to see the big picture. Esmerelda lifted her chin towards Whitley, who had begun to pull on her winter coat. "Where are you going?"

"I have to run into town. Do you want to come?"

Esmerelda cast a glance out the window. "But it's almost dark," she whined.

"And?"

"And it's snowing."

"So?"

"I just curled my hair."

Whitley groaned. "Come on, Es. It'll do you some good to get out of the house."

Esmerelda looked at the white cashmere hat Whitley was just about to pull over her own freshly curled hair. "Let me wear your new hat and scarf, and I'll go with you."

Whitley peered at her reflection in the mirror. She loved the matching set her father had found for her in the city during his previous work trip. He'd been so proud of the good deal he'd negotiated with the street vendor that he couldn't wait until Christmas to give her the gift. "Dad got you a set too. Wear yours," suggested Whitley.

"Mine's *pink*."

"So? I happen to like pink."

Esmerelda smiled sweetly. "Then trade me!" She shrugged as if that were that.

Whitley frowned. She liked pink, but she liked her cream set better. Then she looked into her sister's hopeful green eyes and sighed. "Oh, fine. I'll let you *wear* mine today, but I'm not trading. Dad gave me this set. I don't want to give away the gift he gave me."

Esmerelda pulled Whitley's scarf from her neck and wrapped it around her own. "Oh, thanks, Whit, you're the best," she gushed before throwing her arms around her sister.

Whitley sighed. If only her sister truly thought she was the best, she'd have treasured the hug because it came from her heart. But Whitley knew the truth. "Alright, let's go, then."

CHAPTER THREE

T he rusted-out Ford pickup truck thumped into every pothole on the way into town, causing Whitley and Esmerelda's heads to jerk sideways in unison. The wipers squeaked as they chased each other back and forth across the windshield, struggling to keep up with the heavy snow blanketing the outskirts of Everland Cove.

"I hate this truck!" whined Esmerelda. "Why can't Dad buy us a new car? All the girls our age have new cars."

"All the girls our age also have jobs, Essy. I'm sure Dad would love it if you went out and got a job. Then you could buy *yourself* a new car."

Esmerelda crossed her arms across her chest and peered defiantly out the window. "Oh, who wants a dumb old job? Not *all* girls our age work. *You* don't have a job."

Whitley turned the steering wheel towards town and looked at her sister out of the corner of her eye. "I do too have a job, Es. I'm a seamstress and a budding fashion designer."

"You hem old women's pants and replace broken zippers. I'd hardly call that a job."

Whitley pursed her lips. "You know I've done more than that. I've sewn all of our clothes for years. *And* I'll have you know Mrs. Huntley hired me to make all new curtains for her *entire* house, and if that goes well, she said she'd recommend me to the women in her garden club."

"Big whoop," said Esmerelda. "I still don't consider that a real job."

"It's enough for me," said Whitley. "I'm putting away every cent so I can go to fashion school in the city in a few years."

"School," she spat, rolling her eyes. "Even worse than getting a job. At least you get *paid* when you have a job. No one pays you to go to school!"

The old truck bounced through the streets of the small village, passing by the familiar downtown shops, whose lights were just beginning to shut off one by one. It was nearly dusk, and the streets were lit by cheerful Christmas lanterns and colorful old-fashioned bulbs. Whitley pointed to a brightly lit tree in the center of town. "Look, Es, Everland Cove put up their Christmas tree!"

Esmerelda put a hand to her chest in mock surprise. "Alert the media!"

"Oh, Es. Why must you *always* be such a downer?" asked Whitley, wrinkling her nose.

"Why must you always be such an upper? No one can *possibly* be this perky all the time." Her eyes widened dramatically.

"*I can*," chirped Whitley as she pulled the truck in front of Fiona's Fabrics at the end of the row of shops. She hopped out of the truck before her sister could say another cross word to her.

"Good evening, Fiona," sang Whitley as she pushed open the heavy door. The warm scent of Fiona's apple cinnamon candle blasted her in the face. "Thanks for staying late. I see all the other shops are starting to close up for the night. I'm sure glad I called ahead."

"Oh, not a problem, Whitley," said Fiona with a hint of a tremble in her voice as she kept one eye trained on Esmerelda. While Whitley and Fiona had formed a friendly relationship over the years, Whitley could tell Fiona, like many of the women in Everland Cove, was intimidated by her sister. Whit couldn't blame any of them. Es charmed her way through the men in Everland Cove, but to the women, she was rude and demanding.

"Mrs. Huntley said you'd have the fabric she picked out all ready for me?" Whitley smiled warmly at Fiona.

Fiona nodded and moved to the other side of the counter. "I sure do."

"Have you gotten in that new fabric you'd mentioned ordering?" Whitley asked as she examined a simple grey flannel adorned with white snowflakes.

"The mystery fabric?" asked Fiona. "I did! And what a fabulous idea that was! Thank you! I think it's going to be a hit. I ordered the Sherlock Holmes pattern and the Murder on the Orient Express pattern. Can't you just picture a pair of Agatha Christie slip-covered throw pillows for the chair in the den? How precious!"

Whitley heard Esmerelda's condescending puff of air from across the room but ignored it. She was debating buying a few yards of the flannel to make her father pajamas for Christmas. Then she saw a navy-and-grey-plaid variety and immediately knew it was perfect for her father. She picked up the bolt of fabric and carried it to the counter. "Six yards of this please, Fiona."

Esmerelda reeled around to look at her sister's purchase. She lifted one brow skeptically as she eyed the plaid material. "Ew. Why would you buy flannel? Gross."

"It's for Dad. For a Christmas gift."

"Just don't make me something out of that. Can we go now?" demanded Esmerelda. "I'm cold. I thought we were coming into town to go somewhere *fun*."

Just then the front door chimed, and two familiar people walked into Fiona's Fabrics.

Whitley smiled warmly at the pair. "Ash! Mrs. Everett!" she said excitedly.

"Whit!" he said as a smile spread across his handsome face. "I saw your dad's truck out front. I figured you'd be in here. What are you doing in town?"

"Just getting some fabric for a few projects. I think we're supposed to get some serious snow tonight. I didn't want to be snowed in at the house tomorrow with nothing to do!"

Sebastian Everett shook his dirty-blond hair out of his eyes. "Didn't I tell you, Mom? Whit's always got to be doing something to keep busy."

The Amazonian woman with the stacked brown hair pulled her handbag closer to her stomach as she slipped past a rack of brightly colored fleeces. "Yes, you sure do sing Whitley's praises to me all the time," sighed Mrs. Everett. "I commend you, Whitley. Idle hands are the devil's workshop. I'm glad to hear you've found your calling. And how about you, Esmerelda?"

Esmerelda looked up to stare at Ash's mother with a dry look that read, *I'm sorry, were you talking to me?*

"Do you keep busy as well?" she asked.

Esmerelda puffed out her breath. "I most certainly do keep my calendar full."

"She meant with work, Es. Not dates," scoffed Whitley.

Fiona's eyes widened as she measured out Whitley's flannel, but bit her lip.

Esmerelda glowered at the three of them. "I *know* what she meant, Whitley."

Mrs. Everett cleared her throat as she poked her head around a corner to look at Whitley. "Oh, Whitley," she began. "I know you're busy with your sewing projects and such, but Sebastian is always boasting about what a terrific sleuth you are."

Whitley smiled and lifted a brow towards Sebastian. "Oh, is he?"

His face flushed. "I've only mentioned a few of your many cases. Like the Marshall case."

"I don't know that I would consider a case of a missing high school football jersey worthy of mention," said Whitley, more than slightly embarrassed.

"Neither would I!" snapped Esmerelda with a pout twisting her otherwise lovely face.

"Well, what about that little girl that went missing last summer while she was camping with her parents?" chimed in Fiona from across the room.

"Oh Gawd, do we really have to talk about *that* again? That's all I *heard* about last summer," snapped Esmerelda.

Mrs. Everett tilted her head. "Yes, I do remember Sebastian telling me about that last summer. You returned a little girl to her parents. That was a pretty big deal if you ask me."

"I suppose." Whitley felt heat creeping into her face. Discussing her victories made her self-conscious. She'd been reading mystery novels her entire life, but it seemed that it was her witch's intuition that seemed to make solving mysteries come so naturally to her. Her father always agreed that sleuthing was just one of her many *gifts*.

"Anyway, I have a case that I'd like to hire you to solve."

Both Whitley's and Esmerelda's eyes widened. "*Hire me* to solve?" Whitley repeated. She'd never been *hired* to solve a case before.

"Yes. Sebastian's father bought me a Norwegian forest kitten. It was an early Christmas gift. She's a *beautiful* creature. Just gorgeous. With long grey hair, she's just the *perfect* little ball of fur. I absolutely adore her."

Whitley nodded, anxious to hear the mystery surrounding this kitten.

Mrs. Everett pulled a snapshot from her purse and handed it to Whitley. "Oh, she *is* adorable!" cooed Whitley, showing Esmerelda the photograph.

Esmerelda rolled her eyes but didn't say a word.

"I've only had Sophie for a few weeks, and last Friday she went missing. Well, stolen is actually more precise. Now with this big storm that's coming, I'm just worried sick about her. I'd like her returned."

Whitley blanched. The thought of finding a little kitten in all of Everland Cove sounded daunting. After all, footprints in the snow weren't exactly the kind of clues she was used to searching for. "Perhaps he just got out of the house, Mrs. Everett. It might be hard to find him if he's found a place to get out of the snow," Whitley suggested. "But, I mean, I can certainly come over and take a peek around your house for you."

Mrs. Everett shook her head. "He didn't just get out of the house. He was *stolen*. I'd put him in his little cage to keep him safe during the night, and when I went to retrieve him at breakfast time, his entire cage was gone."

Fiona sucked in her breath. "Someone broke into your house?!"

Mrs. Everett nodded sadly. "Mr. Everett admitted he forgot to lock the back door the night that poor little Sophie went missing."

"I can't believe someone would break into your house to steal your cat!" said Whitley. The thought of such a thief running around Everland Cove made Whitley sick to her stomach.

Mrs. Everett frowned. "Mr. Everett said he spent a thousand dollars on Sophie. She's a very valuable cat. Someone in town knew *exactly* what they were doing."

Whitley's eyes scanned Sebastian's face for signs of approval.

He shot her back an encouraging smile. "I'll help you, Whit. We'll find Sophie together. What do you say?"

Whitley's tiny nose wrinkled excitedly. "I say, Mrs. Everett, you've hired yourself a pair of sleuths!"

CHAPTER FOUR

"Essy, look! Dad's home from his trip!" said Whitley as the old beater truck pulled into the driveway in front of the Snow family's modest country home.

Esmerelda's eyes widened and a genuine smile blazed across her face. "Eeee!" she squealed, clapping her hands excitedly. "Our dresses are here!"

"Is that seriously all you care about? Dad's been gone for a week."

Esmerelda waved a hand, pooh-poohing her sister. "Oh, you know what I mean. Of course I'm happy to see Dad too. I just didn't know if he'd get here in time." She threw open her door and burst out of the truck. Without bothering to shut it, she hollered back at her sister. "Come on, Whit! First one inside gets first pick!"

Whitley sighed as she shut off the ignition. Was her sister serious? Since they had been old enough to speak, Esmerelda had *always* gotten first pick. Walking away from the truck, she pulled her wand from her pocket and waved it at the truck. Without turning around, she heard the door slam shut.

Inside, Whitley unbundled herself, dropping all of her wet clothing onto the floor. Then, wand in hand, she flicked her wrist and her garments all lifted off the ground and hung themselves up on their proper hooks to dry, and her boots marched themselves underneath the bench. Then she headed upstairs in search of Esmerelda and their father. "Dad?" she shouted through the halls.

"Whit! We're in here!"

Whitley's heart lifted at the familiar sound of her father's voice. She raced into her bedroom, where she found her sister sitting on her bed next to an enormous cardboard box. "It's about time!" cried Esmerelda. Then her eyes swung up to meet her father's. "Oh, Daddy, Whit's here. Can we open it now?"

He laughed. "First things first, Es." He turned to face his youngest daughter. Wrapping his arms around Whitley's shoulders, he gave her a little peck on the cheek. "Hello, sweetheart, it's good to see you!"

Whitley melted into her father's embrace. It felt good to have him home. *Finally* it felt like the holidays! "Oh, Dad, I'm so glad you're back. I was worried the storm would keep you away."

His head bobbed. "I was worried too. I left a day early just to beat the weather."

Esmerelda pounded the pads of her feet against the carpet. "Okay, enough chitchat. Can we *puh-lease* see our dresses now?"

Whitley looked down at the enormous box on the bed. "Our dresses are in there?" She pointed to the box.

He nodded excitedly. "I can't wait for you to see what I found for you!"

"Then let's open it already!" pleaded Esmerelda.

Their father smiled gleefully, a web of wrinkles crinkling the corners of his eyes. His head gave a little nod. "Open it!"

Whitley didn't even have to touch the box; her sister plowed into it with the enthusiasm of an eight-year-old on Christmas morning. When she'd peeled back the cardboard and the layers of tissue paper, Esmerelda reeled back in horror. "What is this?!" she demanded.

Curious, Whitley peered into the box. A pile of dresses lay carefully folded together, ensconced in tissue paper. With a flick and swirl of her wand, Whitley lifted out a large portion of dresses. "What is this, Dad?"

"Dad! They look *old*," spat Esmerelda as the dresses magically emerged from the box one by one and hung in the air. "And *used!*" She turned to face her father with a hand on her hip. "*Tell me* you didn't buy us used dresses, Dad!"

Their father's face went ashen. "Well, the woman—uh-hum." He cleared his throat. "At the shop, she said you'd love them."

The dresses kept coming, spreading out shoulder to shoulder around the room. Whitley's stomach swayed. "This is a lot of dresses. How in the world did you afford this many dresses?"

"Because they're *used*, Whit. Dad went to the *junk store* and bought us rags to wear to the Snow Globe Ball!" she cried, running two hands through her long brown hair and pulling at her roots.

"It wasn't a junk store, Esmerelda," began their father. "It was a mystical shop, and listen—I *almost* bought the two of you these brand-new ball gowns..."

Esmerelda stopped pacing the floor and threw her arms down by her side. "Well, why in the world *didn't you?!* Do you hate us *that much?!*" she demanded.

"Essy, that's terrible to say! Dad doesn't hate us!" admonished Whitley.

He shook his head. "Let me explain, Es. I certainly don't hate you. Those dresses were four hundred dollars apiece. I didn't have that kind of cash. When I didn't, she offered up these dresses for free! Well, almost for free."

"For *free?!*" Esmerelda gasped. "Dad! You're a salesman! You've always told us that you get what you pay for! *What were you thinking?!*" She returned to pacing the length of Whitley's bedroom floor.

Whitley let out a heavy sigh and took in her father's downtrodden face. Her heart hurt for him. He was only trying to do something nice, and her sister was making it horrible for him. "Oh, Daddy. I think the dresses are just lovely! And what a deal! Free? That's amazing!" She flicked her wand, and the dresses all marched single file into the over-sized wooden wardrobe next to her bed.

He winced. "To be honest, they didn't cost me any *money*. But they will cost you girls a little time."

"What do you mean?" asked Whitley, ignoring her sister, who had taken to muttering profanities under her breath.

"I got the dresses from a mystic's shop in the city," he explained.

"She said each of the items in her shop had a story behind them. These dresses, in particular, all have mysteries of one type or another to solve. She asked for your help in solving them."

Whitley's eyes widened as she put a hand to her chest. "*My help?!*"

"Well, you and your sister's help."

Esmerelda sucked in her breath. "I am *not* lifting a finger to help that woman! I don't even *want* those dresses!"

He rubbed the heel of his hand against his forehead. "Yes, I see that now."

Whitley looked at the dresses crammed into her wardrobe. There were some lovely items in the lot. Oddly, there were a few wedding dresses and some interesting costumes, but there were also some very fine ball gowns. With her seamstress abilities, she knew she could make her and her sister look phenomenal for their big event. Of course it would take a bit of work getting Esmerelda on board, but she knew she could do it. But to solve the mysteries of some old dresses? "Dad, I wouldn't even know how to start solving the mystery of an old dress."

He threw his arms up in a dramatic shrug. "That's what I told the woman. She insisted that it would all become obvious over time and that everything would present itself to you. It really didn't sound like a very big deal to me."

Esmerelda shook her head wildly when she could see Whitley relenting. "No, Whit! Do *not* tell Dad we'll take the dresses. Tell him to take them back and find us new dresses!"

"Es, it's *Thursday!* The ball is in *two days!* There just isn't time! This storm is going to hit and then the highways will all be closed. We won't have time to get new dresses. And there really isn't time for me to start two new dresses from scratch." Whitley began rifling through the dresses in her wardrobe. "Essy, there are some really fabulous gowns in here."

To demonstrate, she pulled out a gorgeous ruby-red A-line chiffon dress with a ruffled split front. "Picture this with your silver heels, Es. I'll adjust the top, so it's off the shoulder. With your dark hair and eyes, you'll absolutely pop in this dress."

Esmerelda stared at the dress hatefully but didn't speak. Whitley knew that was a sign that Esmerelda could see her vision, but was too stubborn to admit it.

She pulled out a floor-length silver charmeuse gown with a plunging neckline next. "Oh, Essy! How gorgeous is this one? It's a little too big, but I can take it in. You'd look amazing in this one too. Give them a chance? Dad tried really hard for us."

Esmerelda wrinkled her nose, balled her hands into fists, and pounded them into her thighs before dashing out of the room in a huff.

Whitley's heart broke for her father. She threw her arms around his shoulders. "Don't worry, Dad. These are perfect. We'll solve the mysteries and keep the dresses. Thank you!"

He tried to smile, but the corners of his eyes didn't crinkle up as they had before. Whitley could tell that her sister had crushed his spirit.

Whitley peered up into his eyes. "You know Es. She'll come around. Don't worry. I'll talk with her, alright?"

He nodded before kissing Whitley's cheek. "I'm going to see about supper. I'm in the mood for soup and grilled cheese. You?"

"Soup sounds great, Dad. I'll be down in a minute to help."

Her father was only gone for a few seconds before Esmerelda appeared in the doorway again. Whitley didn't have to look up from the dresses in her wardrobe to know that Essy wore a scowl on her face.

"You know what Mom always said," Whitley chastised. "Smiles make friends. Scowls make wrinkles."

"This is all your fault, you know?" clucked Essy as she fell onto her stomach next to the cardboard box.

"*My* fault? How is this *my* fault?" Whitley's eyes narrowed into pinpricks as she reeled around to stare at her sister.

"If you didn't like mysteries and sewing so much, Dad would have *never* taken those dresses. Instead he would have bought us new ball gowns."

Whitley groaned and turned her back to her sister. Esmerelda's constant negativity exhausted her. "Go away, Es," she sighed.

"You're kicking me out?" demanded Esmerelda, sitting up on the bed and knocking the box full of tissue paper to the floor. The sound of a heavy object clunking as it hit the floor made both girls stare down at the box.

"What was that?" asked Whitley.

Esmerelda clambered off the bed and lifted the box.

Whitley reached inside and pulled out a heavy object wrapped in scads of tissue paper. She peeled back the nearly transparent layers. "It's a snow globe!" she said with surprise.

Esmerelda smiled for a half-second as she looked down at the ball. "Dad got us a snow..." Her eyes darkened as she realized it was empty. "There's nothing in it!"

Pulling the remainder of the tissue paper back, Whitley's nose crinkled. The base of the heavy globe was a burnt copper color with an ornately carved swirling pattern dotted with stars. She gave it a shake and watched as a snowstorm ravaged the watery world. Aside from the snow, Esmerelda was correct. The globe was empty. She'd never seen an empty snow globe before. She tipped her head to the side. What a funny thing for their father to bring them home from his trip.

Esmerelda's face reddened as Whitley set the globe on her nightstand. "Ugh!" she hollered into the air. "He couldn't even buy us a snow globe with *something in it*! I've had it with this family!"

CHAPTER FIVE

That night, nearly a foot of snow blanketed Everland Cove and the surrounding countryside. Whitley holed up in her bedroom and worked tirelessly through the night and into the next day to make something out of the assortment of dresses their father had brought them.

It was nearly dark again when Whitley's door burst open, and Esmerelda flounced into her room in a panic. "Whit! Carter Langdon just called and *canceled* our date for tomorrow night! Now what am I supposed to do? I can't go to the Snow Globe Ball *alone!*"

Whitley's heart nearly leaped from her chest as she bolted upright in front of her sewing machine. "Es! You scared the living daylights out of me!" she cried, quickly throwing a blanket over the dress in front of her. Then she leaned backward and scratched the back of her neck nonchalantly as her pulse throbbed wildly in her veins. "That's kind of last-minute. I'm shocked you didn't use your magical powers of persuasion to change his mind."

Esmerelda groaned. "I tried," she pouted. "My powers don't work through the phone."

Whitley tipped her head to the side. "Why did he cancel?"

"I don't know," whined Esmerelda, throwing herself down onto the

612

bed. "He's on vacation with his family. Something about bad roads and not wanting to risk his life. Lame, right?"

Bleary-eyed from staring at her sewing machine for the last eighteen hours straight, Whitley slumped back in her chair. "Yeah, totally lame," she quipped, shooting her sister a sardonic grin.

"So what am I supposed to do?!" demanded Esmerelda. "I can't go to the ball in a horrible dress with no date! I'll be the laughingstock of the entire town!"

Whitley rolled her eyes and puffed air out her nose. "I really think you should have become an actress, Es."

Esmerelda stopped pouting and furrowed her brows. "Because I'm so beautiful?"

"Because you're so dramatic! Just ask a different man to take you. Have you forgotten you're a witch with the powers of enchantment? It shouldn't be that difficult. Now if you'll excuse me, I have a lot of work to do if our dresses are ever going to be done in time for the gala."

"You're so selfish, Whit," snapped Esmerelda, leaping off the bed and heading for the doorway. "I come to you with a problem, and you mock me. Why Dad always says *you're* the good one, I'll never understand."

Whitley groaned as her sister disappeared out the door. She threw the blanket back onto the floor and attempted to refocus her attention on the dress she had been working on before Esmerelda had come in. She'd only managed to put in a few more stitches before her father poked his head around the door.

"How are the dresses coming?" he asked with a smile.

Whitley relaxed backwards in her chair and rubbed her eyes with the balls of her hands. "I'm so close to being done with this one," she sighed.

"Are you hungry? I'm just about to go start supper."

"Famished!" said Whitley. "But I don't want to take a break until I get Essy's dress done."

He pulled up a seat next to her little sewing desk. "Oh, you're working on your sister's dress first?"

Whitley flashed him a brilliant smile before lifting the pressure foot and raising the needle so she could slide the dress out.

She held the red gown up to her chest. "Isn't it gorgeous, Dad?"

He nodded and pointed to the off-the-shoulder sleeves she'd added to the dress. "Absolutely stunning! I love the little beads on the sleeves!"

"I know, right! I removed them from one of the other dresses. I feel like it makes the dress a little bit more regal. Not that she would actually *say it to me,* but I think Es is going to *flip!*"

Suddenly, Esmerelda's head was in Whitley's doorway again. "Did you say my name?" she demanded, her eyes scanning her father's and sister's faces.

Whitley immediately dropped the dress to the floor and her heart pulsed in her ears. She was pretty sure her father's body had covered the dress, but she couldn't be sure. "Oh, I was just telling Dad about Carter canceling on you," she lied.

"Oh," she said, her face crumpling. "I was just starting to forget about that jerk. Why'd you have to bring up his name again?"

"You asked!" snapped Whitley. She swept her fingers in Esmerelda's direction. "Can you please shut my door?"

Esmerelda rolled her eyes, let out an overly dramatic sigh, and pulled the door closed, leaving it open a crack.

When she appeared to be safely out of earshot, Felix bent over and lifted the dress off the floor. "I really think you made a good choice, Whit. This was the best of all the dresses in the pile."

Whitley's face brightened as she took the dress from her father and held it to her own slim figure. "I thought so too. And it's going to fit like a glove," she added, swaying her hips and the dress from side to side.

"Oh, absolutely. Once again, you've outdone yourself, sweetheart!" He beamed at her. And then just as suddenly, his face sobered slightly. "Now, Whit. Don't forget, you and Es have to solve the mystery of these dresses. It was part of the bargain, and now you've altered them, so I can't take them back to the shop."

Whitley winked at her father. "I know, Dad. I'll do whatever I need to do."

He let out a breath of relief. "Good. And I know I tell you this all the time, but you really are the most thoughtful and caring girl I know."

Whitley's face brightened. "Aww, thanks, Dad. But you have to say that, you're my dad."

He shook his head. "No, no. I mean it. You're the most selfless person I know. Your sister would do well to take lessons from you."

Whitley waved a hand dismissively at her father. "Oh, Dad. You put me up on a pedestal. I'm really not *that* great. Es is a very good person. Deep down. Way, way deep down. She's got a warm heart."

He chuckled. "I know she does, sweetheart." He kissed her forehead and headed for the door. "I know you don't want to quit until the dresses are done, but you have to eat. Why don't you finish up and come downstairs and take a little break?"

Whitley gave him a soft smile. "I will. Just a few more minutes and I'll have this all done."

He opened the door to leave, and the duo heard a rustling sound just outside her door. Felix peered into the hallway.

"Is Esmerelda out there?" asked Whitley.

He shrugged and shook his head. "Nope, must have been the wind."

CHAPTER SIX

With one arm laced inside the crook of Sebastian's elbow and the other arm propped up on her hip, Whitley scanned the snow-covered neighborhood in front of the Everett family home. Her brows were furrowed and her mouth set in a straight line.

Sebastian took one look at her and let out a deep belly laugh.

Whitley looked up at him from beneath her chocolate-brown bangs, smashed down onto her forehead by a pink beanie. "Why are you laughing?"

He pressed his free hand against her shoulder playfully. "You!" he chuckled. "You should see yourself!" He tried to mimic her serious expression, but only managed to make himself laugh harder. "You look so serious!"

Her slow smile caused her green eyes to soften. "When I'm on a case, I take things very seriously," she explained. "I'm trying to use my powers to sense where Sophie is."

He followed her gaze and attempted a somber expression. "I see that!"

Ignoring his amusement, Whitley pulled her magic wand from the pouch of her sweater and waved it at the houses across the street.

Obediently, every shrub kindly lifted its foliage like a woman lifting her skirt and revealing the knobby knees below.

"See anything?" she asked, tilting her head towards Sebastian.

"Nope. No kittens."

Lowering the foliage with another flick of her wrist, she then pointed one mittened hand towards the houses across the street. "Now, is there anyone in the neighborhood who your parents don't get along with?"

He shrugged and followed her gaze. "My mom has issues with lots of women. She's a bit overbearing. Some people find that to be a turnoff."

Whitley smiled to herself. It sounded like someone else she knew. "Anyone in particular?"

He tipped his head backwards to the house behind them. "Mrs. Vorman next door wasn't too thrilled when Mom returned a baggie of her dog's droppings and told her that her dog couldn't relieve himself in our yard anymore."

Whitley nodded excitedly. "So you think she might have stolen Sophie to get even?"

Sebastian's warm brown eyes widened. "You really do get into this sleuthing thing, don't you?"

She nudged his side with her shoulder. "Of course I do! Especially when it's *your mother*! And there's an adorable kitten missing!" She held up the photograph of Sophie that Mrs. Everett had given her. "We need to get serious, Ash. We don't have much time before I need to go home to start getting ready for the ball."

He raised a hand to his forehead and saluted her. "Yes, ma'am!"

Seconds later the two of them stood in front of the Vormans' red front door, waiting for someone to answer.

The door opened and an older woman in a pink floral muumuu carrying a miniature two-tone grey schnauzer in her arms answered. "May I help you?" she asked, looking directly at Whitley.

Whitley flashed the woman her sweetest smile. "Yes, we're looking for a missing kitten. We were wondering if perhaps you've seen her?" Whitley held the photograph out to show the woman.

Mrs. Vorman took a look at it and then looked back at Whitley and up at Sebastian. "You're Donna's boy?"

Sebastian nodded. "Yes, ma'am."

She lifted her chin, pursed her lips, and hugged her dog closer to her chest before looking pointedly at Whitley. "Haven't seen her."

"But you knew she was Mrs. Everett's cat!" said Whitley.

Mrs. Vorman lifted a shoulder and smoothed her dog's grey fur as he relaxed contentedly in her arms. "Of course I did. Donna came running over here the day Justin bought her that cat, bragging about how much Sophie cost him." Mrs. Vorman leaned forward. "A thousand dollars is far too much to spend on a silly little kitten if you ask me," she hissed conspiratorially.

Whitley looked at the schnauzer. "What did your dog think of Sophie?"

"Norman?" she asked. "Oh, my Norman cannot stand cats! He didn't like her for a second. He positively would not stop barking when Donna brought Sophie over."

Whitley sighed. "I see. Well, as you can imagine, Mrs. Everett is heartbroken because Sophie is missing, as I'm sure you would be if Norman ever went missing. Would you please let her know if you see her?"

The mention of Norman being in a similar situation softened Mrs. Vorman. Her shoulders dropped slightly, and her expression relaxed. "Yes, of course I will."

"Thank you," said Whitley with a smile.

"Thanks, Mrs. V.," said Sebastian as the door slammed behind them.

Together they walked down the sidewalk towards the street. "Well? What do you think?" pressed Sebastian.

Whitley shook her head. "It wasn't her."

"You're sure? She could have been lying."

"She could have been, but I don't think she was. I can verify with your mother how Norman reacted when she brought Sophie over, and she knows that. If there were a kitten in that house, Norman wouldn't have been so content."

Sebastian beamed down at Whitley. "You're brilliant, you know that, Whit?"

Whitley rolled her eyes. "I'm not brilliant, Ash. That was just common sense. Now come on. We're going to show this picture around to the entire neighborhood and see what we come up with. We better get moving. I only have another hour before I have to head home."

"Then what are we waiting for? Let's get knocking!"

When they'd finished knocking on every door on both sides of the street, they headed back towards the Everetts' house. Whitley's shoulders slumped in defeat.

Sebastian put his arm around her and pulled her in for a side hug while they walked. "Don't worry, Whit. We can search for Sophie tomorrow, after the ball."

Whitley sighed. "I know we can look tomorrow, but my senses were going crazy when I woke up this morning. I just had this *feeling* that we were going to find her today!"

"Maybe your powers were telling you something else?" he suggested with a light shrug.

"Maybe," she agreed.

They were quiet for a few long moments when Sebastian finally chimed in. "Did you finish your dresses for the ball?"

Whitley brightened. "Yeah, I finished hers late last night and mine early this morning. I can't wait to get home and show Es her dress. She was sleeping when I left to come into town, but she's literally going to flip when she sees it."

"What about your dress?" he asked gently, looking down at his feet as they walked.

Whitley stopped walking and turned to face Sebastian. "Oh my gosh, Ash! It's *gorgeous!* It's this silver iridescent material, and the neckline goes down to here." She traced the outline of the plunging neckline with her finger, stopping just between her breasts.

Ash swallowed hard. "That's kind of low-cut, huh?"

She nodded with wide eyes. "It's *super sexy*," she admitted. "Not my usual style. In fact, I almost picked a different dress, but I know red is Essy's favorite color, and the rest of the dresses needed so many modifications that I just didn't have time. That one was almost perfect the way it was. I just had to take it in a little and shorten it."

"It sounds really beautiful," he whispered. Then he reached out and took her by her mittened hands. "Of course, you're beautiful in everything you wear."

Whitley felt tingles of heat color her cheeks. "Aww, Ash. That was sweet!"

He swallowed hard again and gave her fingers a gentle squeeze. "So...I wanted to ask you a question..."

"You can ask me anything, silly. Shoot!" she chirped.

He cleared his throat. "Well. Whitley Snow. I was wondering if I could take you to the Snow Globe Ball tonight."

She lifted one eyebrow. "Of course you can. Wasn't that the plan all along?" she asked, tilting her head to the side.

"Oh, yes, of course," he stammered.

Whitley could see his face reddening slightly. He looked so cute with those pink cheeks and pink ears. "Unless you wanted me to drive into town? I mean, I'm sure Dad would let me drive the truck in. Would that be easier for you?"

He swung their arms together. "Oh, gosh no, Whit. That's not what I meant," he stammered. "I want to drive out there to get you. What I meant was, umm, can we go *together*? Like *together* together."

Her body froze as her mind tried to play catch up. Had Ash just asked her out? "Like a couple?"

A slow smile crept across his face, and the pink that had colored his cheeks was now a full-on frostbite red. "Yeah, like a couple," he said quietly.

Dazed, Whitley stood in front of him with her mouth agape. She struggled to make her brain think of something to say that wasn't completely idiotic. "Oh, well, yeah. I mean, sure, that would—uh." It was her turn to swallow hard. "That would be great, Ash."

"Really?" he breathed.

Her head bobbled excitedly as it hit her what had just happened.

Sebastian Everett had just asked her out on a date! "Yeah, really. I think it'll be fun to go as a couple."

He let out the breath he'd been holding. "Oh, good. I wasn't sure what you'd think of that. We've been friends for so long, and I just haven't...well, I didn't want to..." He waved a hand at her dismissively. "What time should I pick you up?"

"How about seven?"

He let out a big sigh of relief. "Seven it is."

CHAPTER SEVEN

Practically floating on air, Whitley bounced up the stairs. She could hardly wait to tell Esmerelda that Sebastian had asked her to go to the ball with him as a *date* and not just as a friend. She was still in shock over what had just happened! She and Ash had been friends since high school, and while there were times she'd found herself crushing on him, she'd never let herself get that carried away as to dream about the two of them being together.

With her hand hovering over the door handle, Whitley paused just outside her bedroom. She felt a sudden strange sensation that she couldn't quite place. But at that moment, it occurred to her that her sister didn't have a date anymore, and telling her about Sebastian's request would only make Esmerelda jealous.

No, I can't tell her. I'll give her her dress instead. That should make her feel good! Whitley squealed to herself and then threw her bedroom door open.

Inside, Esmerelda stood hunched over, breathing heavily in the center of Whitley's room, surrounded by long shredded strands of ruby-red fabric. Her long brown hair frizzed out wildly around her face, and her eyes glowed like foxfire in the dark.

Whitley slowly walked into the room with her mouth agape. She stepped across tiny beads that she knew to be the ones she'd sewn on Esmerelda's gown and stared at the piles of red fabric that lay in sad heaps across the floor. "Essy!" she breathed with her hand to her heart. "What have you done?!"

Esmerelda straightened her spine and dropped the last of the beautiful red dress Whitley had toiled on for hours. "I've *had it* with you and Dad!" she raged. "Everything is about *you! You're the good one! You* get the best clothes! *You* have the most talent! *You* got the best powers from Mom! What did I get?!" she demanded. "I got *nothing!*"

"Oh, Essy! How could you?" Whitley's heart throbbed against the inside of her chest. Her heart hurt for her sister, and for herself. All of her hard work was for nothing! "You destroyed the dress I made for you! Why? I don't understand!"

"The dress you made for me?! No! I destroyed the dress that you made for *yourself!*"

Whitley's head shook violently. "No, Es. That dress was for you! I made it for you! Red's *your* favorite color! It was going to be a surprise!"

Esmerelda's hand shot out as she pointed her finger at Whitley. "Don't lie! *I heard* you and Dad talking about how the dress would fit you like a glove, and it was the best of all of the dresses! *You always get the best!* It's not fair!"

"Esmerelda Snow! You were listening in on my conversation with Dad?!"

"You bet I was! Some sister you are! Saving the best dress for yourself! Why Dad thinks you're the good one, I'll *never* understand!"

Whitley shook her head. "You didn't hear the whole conversation, then! I told Dad that that dress would fit *you* like a glove! Not me!"

"Liar!" she raged.

"I'm not lying!" Whitley pointed to the silver dress hanging on one of the posts of her canopy bed. "*That's* my dress. I altered the red dress for you because red's your favorite color!"

"I don't believe you!" she screamed with her hands in her hair.

"It's the *truth*, Es! I wouldn't lie to you!"

Esmerelda stepped over the shredded remains of the dress Whitley had spent hours on and strutted past the bed and towards the door. "Why? Because you're so *perfect?*" she demanded. Then she mockingly added, "Because sweet little perfect Whitley would never tell a lie?"

"Es, I'm not perfect! I never said I was." She threw her hands out on either side of her and then dropped them to her sides again. "If you don't believe me, go ask Dad. He'll tell you the truth. I told him the dress was for you."

"No! I never want to speak to Dad again! Or *you*, for that matter! I'm over it! I want out of this family!"

"Oh, Essy! You don't mean it!" gasped Whitley.

Esmerelda trained her wild eyes on her sister. "Oh no. I do mean it! You're Dad's favorite. You always have been and always will be. You were Mom's favorite too! That's why she gave you all the *good* powers. She gave me the ability to charm men. *What good is that?!* I can charm men, and yet *I'm the one without a date!*"

"You'll meet someone at the ball. It'll be more fun without a date," pleaded Whitley. "You'll get to dance with all the single men and have your pick!"

Esmerelda's head bounced. "Right. Because that doesn't look desperate, does it?!"

Whitley didn't know what else she could say to make her sister understand. "It won't look desperate. I swear!"

Esmerelda lowered her chin and glared directly at her sister. "I don't want to hear another word out of your lying, scheming mouth!" She turned to open the bedroom door and then stopped, swiveled on her heels and padded over to Whitley's bed, where she lifted the silver dress off the bedpost. "I'll just take *my* dress."

"Esmerelda! That's *my* dress!"

Esmerelda tilted her head to the side mockingly. "Oh, Whit. Don't make me laugh. Do you know how I know that you're lying?"

Whitley's brows scrunched together, but she didn't say anything. She knew her sister would never believe her.

"Because Whitley Snow would *never* wear a dress with this low of a neckline. Never! She's just too *basic.*" She looked at the dress with a sardonic smile one last time before throwing it over her shoulder and strutting towards the door. "This dress is for a woman with style. Not some meek little mouse like *you*. Goodbye."

Whitley tried to run after her, but the door slammed in her face, leaving her alone in her bedroom with the remnants of a once-beautiful gown and no dress to wear to the ball.

CHAPTER EIGHT

Thoroughly disheartened by the whole chain of events, Whitley threw herself onto her bed and sobbed like a five-year-old. Not only was her sister mad at her, but now she had nothing to wear on her first real date with Sebastian. *And* the perfect dress that Whitley had made for her sister was destroyed! She suddenly wished she didn't live in the bedroom next door to her miserably unhappy sister. She wished she lived in New York City and went to some fabulous design school. She wished she were anywhere but in Everland Cove.

When the sobs that racked her body finally eased, she opened her eyes. Nothing had changed. She was still in the same old bedroom she'd woken up in for the last twenty-two years. Slowly she sat up and reached for a tissue from her nightstand. She blotted her tears, wiped her nose, and assessed the damage in her room. Little pieces of red material were everywhere. It hurt her heart to realize that the very thing she'd thought would bring her sister happiness was the same thing that had enraged her so much.

Whitley threw her crumpled tissue back onto her nightstand and was just about to stand up and begin to tidy up her room when she caught sight of the snow globe that had been in the box of dresses her father had brought home. She picked it up and sat back down on her bed. Pulling her legs into pretzel style, she set the globe down in her lap to examine it more closely.

What a peculiar snow globe, she thought as she gave it a good shake. She watched the tiny particles of fake snow glisten as they floated through the water, hanging precariously before slowly drifting downwards. Where were the little ice-skating people set in an idyllic Christmas village? Where was the simplistic snowman or the Christmas tree with presents? She would have even been happy with a wintery cityscape of tall buildings or a simple cardinal on a tree branch. But *empty*? Why would anyone even *make* such a thing? She set it on the bed in front of her and stared at it. *What a boring snow globe. No wonder it wound up in a secondhand shop. Who would want a snow globe with nothing but snow inside?* she wondered.

But something about the snow globe mesmerized her. She leaned forward, picked it up again, and shook it. Then she shook it again and again, entranced as the snow whipped and swirled about. Then the floor of the watery world began to sparkle. Lights glittered upward and began forming letters and then words! Whitley's eyes narrowed into slits and her nose wrinkled as she brought it closer to her face. She thought she could make out the words.

"*There's no star too far away*," she whispered before the swirling snow covered the floor in the globe again, obstructing the words. She shook it one more time to reveal more of the words.

"*And no wish too grand*," she added before having to shake the globe yet again.

"*Shake the snow globe and make a wish. The magic's in your hands.*"

Whitley put the globe down, stunned to find the mystical words hidden beneath the snow. Not quite sure what to make of it, she stared at it—almost scared to touch it. She swallowed hard and thought about her biggest wish. Was it to fall in love? Was it to go to fashion school? Could she really do that? Could she leave Esmerelda, Dad, and Ash behind for good for the big city?

She glanced over at her alarm clock and suddenly realized how late it had gotten. She barely had enough time to shower and do her hair, let alone enough time to try and remake an old dress so she had something to wear on her date.

Whitley looked down at the globe. *You don't find happiness by wishing for it,* she thought, *you find it by working for it.* With that thought firmly in place, she hopped off the bed and set to work. She had a dress to make!

Esmerelda smoothed the waves of her long brown hair and adjusted her breasts to show as much cleavage in her silver gown as possible. She tilted her head from side to side and looked down her nose at her reflection in the long foyer mirror. With kohl-rimmed eyes, flawlessly contoured cheekbones, and carefully sculpted brows, she looked impeccable. She patted her nose with pressed powder and then tossed her compact into the little silver clutch she'd found buried in her closet.

Esmerelda lifted the truck keys from the small foyer table. She hated the idea of having to drive herself to the biggest winter solstice event in Everland Cove, but she had no choice. Her Prince Charming wasn't about to just ride in and sweep her off of her feet.

But then, as if it were a miracle, there was a knock at the door. She opened it to find Sebastian Everett in a tuxedo staring back at her.

"Sebastian!" she said with surprise. She'd almost forgotten her sister even had a date.

"Whit!" he said, casually tossing back his dirty-blond hair.

She opened her mouth to speak, to clarify that *she* was most certainly *not* her boring younger sister. But before she could, Sebastian took her by the hands. "Oh, Whit. I've never seen you look so lovely!" he said. His eyes practically sparkled as he spoke. If Esmerelda didn't know better, she'd say that Sebastian Everett almost looked moony-eyed.

"I do?" she asked, stunned.

"Absolutely. You're glowing! And that dress!"

Esmerelda noticed a little blush rise up into his cheeks. "What about my dress?"

"It's stunning. And," he whispered, "every bit as sexy as you told me it would be. I'm going to have to fight off all the other men at the gala tonight!" He chuckled.

"Riiiight," she drawled, as it suddenly dawned on her that the best way to exact her revenge was to steal her sister's date and let Whitley find her own way to the dance. She dropped the keys on the foyer table. "So should we go?" she snapped. She wanted to get out of there before Whitley showed up and stole Sebastian from her.

"You don't want to say goodbye to your dad?" he asked, looking around. "Or Es?"

Esmerelda shook her head. "Oh no. *Es* left already and Dad's, umm, napping," she lied.

Sebastian's eyes widened. "Oh, really? I thought for sure you'd want him to take some pictures. I mean, technically this *is* our first real date."

"Real date?" asked Esmerelda. This was new information, considering Whitley had told her they were just going as friends. "You mean as just friends, right?"

Sebastian lowered his brows and looked slightly hurt. "Oh. Did you change your mind?"

Esmerelda cleared her throat. She was so confused. "Change my mind?" She waved a hand at him playfully. "Oh, you. I was just joking, of course."

He looked at her curiously then. "Are you feeling alright, Whit? You don't sound like yourself."

"What? No, I'm fine. I'm just a little tired." She threw both arms into the air and faked a yawn and a stretch. "You know, long day."

"Oh, I know!" he agreed. "It's too bad we didn't find Sophie before the dance. That would have made today perfect."

"Sophie?" snapped Esmerelda, forgetting the character she was supposed to be playing. "Who the hell is Sophie?"

Sebastian grimaced and dropped her hands. "Sophie. You know, Mom's kitten. We went looking for her today? You really aren't yourself. Did something happen that you're not telling me?" He looked at her suspiciously.

Esmerelda panicked. There was no way she'd be able to impersonate her sticky-sweet sister all night long without a little magic. She sighed. It was time to bring out the big guns.

She began to hum a simple little melody. Then she reached her hand out to Sebastian. "Oh, Ash, take my hand," she begged sweetly.

Awkwardly, he accepted her hand. "Maybe we should just wake your dad up. He should know you're leaving."

But Esmerelda didn't want him to talk. She held a finger up to his lips to shush him. "*Under the light of the moon,*" she sang.

He tipped his head to the side and looked at her curiously.

She continued to sing to him. "*You're my destiny. Run away with me. Into the light of the moon. You hung the stars for me. It's my solemn plea. Run away with me.*"

Slowly Sebastian pulled Esmerelda closer. "Oh, Whit," he whispered. "Let's run away together!" he said, as if he didn't realize that she'd just put the idea into his head.

Esmerelda nodded excitedly. "Yes, yes, let's run away together. But first, take me to the Winter Solstice Snow Globe Ball, Ash? Please?"

"Yes. I want to take you to the Winter Solstice Snow Globe ball," he repeated with a smile plastered on his face.

Esmerelda squealed and shoved him towards the door. "We should go."

"Yes. We should go," he agreed.

Suddenly footsteps sounded behind them.

Esmerelda's heart thumped wildly in her chest as she slowly spun around.

"Whitley?" asked her father from behind her.

Esmerelda's face froze. Her father would be able to see right through her little charade if she wasn't careful. She turned to Sebastian. "Wait for me in the car, Ash?" she asked sweetly.

He turned woodenly and opened the front door without a word to Felix. "I'll wait for you in the car."

Felix rushed towards them, holding a hand up. "Wait, wait! I'd like to get a picture before you go!"

But Sebastian was already gone.

Esmerelda turned to face her father. "Sorry, Daddy, we're in a bit of a hurry, got to go."

"Esmerelda?" he asked, his mouth agape.

Dammit. She threw both hands on her hips and tilted her head to the side. "Yes?" she asked impatiently.

"But—I thought Whitley was wearing the silver dress? She told me she altered the red dress for you."

Esmerelda paused for a moment. *Of course Whitley told him to lie! They always stick together. She's his favorite after all!* She puffed air out her nose. "Oh, please, Dad. Don't lie. You and Whitley can have each other!"

"What are you talking about, Esmerelda?"

Her left eyebrow peaked as she put a hand on the doorknob. "You know perfectly well what I'm talking about. You and your perfect little angel can just *have each other!* I'm leaving!"

CHAPTER NINE

W hitley had barely finished dressing in a navy-blue floor-length dress when her father came peeling into her room.

"Dad! What's going on?"

Felix took one look around the room and sucked in his breath. "Whit? Is this Esmerelda's dress?" He kneeled down and picked up a handful of long pieces of red material. "What happened? It's destroyed!"

Whitley had to swallow hard to fight back the tears that threatened to ruin her makeup. "I know, Dad. Es did it. I got home from hanging out with Ash earlier, and she was in my bedroom destroying the dress."

"Why would she do that?!"

"She said she overheard you and me talking last night. She thought the red dress was for me and that I'd picked the best dress for myself. She thought I was being selfish and that you didn't see it."

He shook his head with his mouth hanging open and his eyes wide. "But that's not what happened!"

Whitley gave him a half-smile. "I know, Dad. We know that, but Essy doesn't. I just need to give her time to cool down."

"How can you be so calm and collected? Look what she did to your room!" he said in shock.

"It's alright, Dad. I've had time to relax. I'll clean it all up tomorrow."

He shook his head firmly and grabbed the empty cardboard box that all of the dresses from Arabella's Mystical Treasures had come in. "No, this is all my fault. I'll clean this mess up." He scooped up a pile of red fabric and shoved it in the box.

"Oh, Dad, you don't have to do that!" said Whitley.

"How can you be so forgiving? She was wearing *your dress*. You let her get away with everything, Whit. It's time you stood up for yourself!"

Whitley held her arms out and spun around. "It's okay. It was just a dress. I found this one from a couple of years ago. It almost fit me," she said with a chuckle. "I just had to let out the seams a little, but it'll work. It's not as beautiful as the silver dress I loved so much, but I'm sure Ash will like it just the same."

"Ash?" Felix's brow wrinkled.

Whitley picked up a small purse from her bed and pulled the thin strap over her shoulder. "Yeah. He's my date," she admitted with a bit of a blush. "He's supposed to be picking me up any minute now. He's actually a few minutes late. I haven't heard the doorbell."

"Sweetheart, Ash was here already."

Whitley's eyes brightened. "Oh, he's here? Great!" she hurried towards the door, but her father put up a hand to stop her.

"He left. With Esmerelda."

Whitley stared at her father in shock. "What?!"

"They're gone."

Whitley's head shook in horror. Ash took Esmerelda to the dance instead of her? This had to be a mistake! "No, he wouldn't have!"

"I'm sorry, sweetheart. I saw them leave. Esmerelda was pretty upset."

Whitley's stomach did flip-flops as she strutted past her dad and into the hallway. "Oh, Dad, I have to go."

He nodded. "Take the truck. The keys are in the foyer. I'll have your room clean by the time you get back!"

"Thanks, Dad, I love you!"

All the fanciest cars in town lined the streets in front of the Winter Solstice Snow Globe Ball, but Whitley didn't care that she pulled up to the curb in her father's old beat-up pickup. She threw open the door, lifted the hem of her long navy tulle skirt, and hopped out of the truck.

"I'll be right back," she hollered over her shoulder at the valet, who watched her run in her heels up the red carpet.

Inside, white Christmas lights sparkled all over the posh interior, giving the room a magical glow. She pushed her way through the crowd, trying desperately to find Sebastian.

Finally, she caught sight of him and Esmerelda, climbing the wide circular staircase to the second floor. Whitley dodged and ducked the party guests, and as she got to the bottom of the stairs, she looked up to see Sebastian pull on Esmerelda's arm to stop her from going any further up the stairs. Esmerelda turned and looked down at him. He took one step up so that he and Esmerelda were eye to eye. Whitley felt her heart stop beating in her chest as he gently leaned forward and kissed her! *NO!* That kiss was supposed to be hers!

From several steps down, Whitley felt paralyzed. Why was Sebastian kissing Esmerelda? Had things changed *that much* since earlier in the day?! What was going on?

"Ash, NO!" she finally managed to holler up the stairs.

At the sound of her voice, he suddenly pulled his head back and looked down the stairs at her. "Whit?" he whispered. His eyes blinked several times as if he were coming out of a trance.

Whitley nodded her head as tears sprang forth from her eyes. "How could you, Ash? With my sister?!"

Sebastian turned to look at Esmerelda, who now grinned from ear to ear.

She wiggled her fingers in a little wave at him.

"She—she *tricked me!*" he said, stunned.

"How could she trick you, Ash? How could you not know it wasn't me? You've always been able to tell us apart."

"I—I did know, but then I didn't know..." He looked back and forth between the two identical women. "She messed with my head, Whit!"

"Esmerelda Snow!" breathed Whitley. "Did you enchant Sebastian?"

Esmerelda lifted one shoulder. "If I did, it's only payback for *what you did*."

"I didn't do anything to you! I've had it with you, Es. You ruined the dress I made for you. You stole the dress I made for myself. And now you're trying to steal Ash from me! I'll never forgive you!" cried Whitley as she ran back down the stairs. Sobbing, she pushed her way back through the crowd and out the front door, where her father's truck waited for her.

"Whit, wait!" Sebastian yelled before chasing after her.

"Sebastian Everett! Do not chase after her!" Esmerelda shouted and then found herself chasing him.

CHAPTER TEN

Ten minutes later, Whitley blasted back inside her house in a fit of tears. The walls shook as she slammed the door behind her and hollered into the silent house. "Dad!"

Not waiting for a response, Whitley's feet pounded up the stairs. She'd had it with her sister! Always taking things that weren't hers and ruining her relationships. Why couldn't she have had a *normal sister*?!

Inside her room, Whitley discovered that in the short time that she'd been gone, her father had cleaned up all the tiny beads and the pieces of fabric from the floor. She stared down at the pile of material inside the cardboard box, and her eyes filled with tears once again.

She plucked two tissues from the box on her nightstand and rubbed furiously at the streaks of mascara on her cheeks. She felt like her life was over. She wanted *out!*

Suddenly, her eyes caught sight of the pink hat she'd worn to meet Ash earlier in the day. That wasn't *her* beanie. Esmerelda had *her* beanie. The one their father had given *her*, and she suddenly realized she wasn't going to give Esmerelda *everything* that she wanted!

Whitley rushed down the hall to her sister's bedroom. Clothes were scattered everywhere, tossed over chairs and strewn about the floor. What a mess! Whitley pulled her wand from her purse and waved it around the room. Her sister's dirty shirts and rumpled jeans all lifted into the air. She shook her wand, and the clothes shook, but no beanie seemed to appear.

Whitley's eyes scanned Esmerelda's dressing table, which was covered with half-eaten cookies, piles of makeup, and pieces of lingerie. She even dug through her hamper, which had fewer clothes in it than the floor, but to no avail. Her hat and scarf set was nowhere to be found.

Setting her brows in a straight line, she opened her sister's closet and flipped on the light. Immediately, she heard a tiny noise coming from beneath a rack of clothes. Whitley stopped moving and listened carefully. *Meow.* There it was again! She was sure she heard it this time. It was a cat's meow!

Whitley used her wand to shove aside the hanging clothes, which revealed a small pet carrier nestled underneath. She lifted the carrier out of the closet and set it on Esmerelda's bed. Reaching inside, she pulled out a small grey, long-haired kitten and curled it to her chest. Her eyes widened. *It can't be!* "Sophie?!" she asked.

The cat only meowed back at her. But Whitley knew it was Sophie. It was the exact kitten that had been in the picture! Her pulse beat wildly in her ears. Her sister had stolen Mrs. Everett's cat? It didn't make any sense! What would Esmerelda want with Mrs. Everett's cat?

She carried the cat back down the hall into her bedroom. The poor thing shook, even as Whitley held it tightly to her chest, cooing soft words to it and smoothing its soft fur. "It's going to be alright," she whispered. "I'm going to take you home to your momma."

"Like hell you are!" Esmerelda screamed from the doorway. "I found her, and *I'm* taking her back!"

Whitley grimaced. "You *stole* Mrs. Everett's kitten? How could you, Es?" asked Whitley, her eyes damp with tears. "After everything you've done to me and stolen from me. Now you're stealing kittens too?"

"I didn't *steal* the dumb cat. I *found her*," snapped Esmerelda.

Whitley's head tilted to the side. "Really? You just found her? How, Es? She was in a cage! She didn't just *wander off* in her cage!"

Esmerelda's eyes narrowed. "One of the girls we went to high school with posted the cat on her Instagram story. I recognized the dumb thing from the picture Sebastian's mom showed us. So I went and got it. I was *trying* to do something nice."

Whitley shook her head. "No, you weren't! You were *trying* to solve the mystery yourself because you're jealous of the fact that I've gotten attention for solving mysteries and you haven't!" Whitley countered. She looked around. "Where's Sebastian? I'm giving him Sophie to take home to his mother."

Esmerelda sneered at her sister. "I wouldn't let him come in. I sent him home."

Whitley sighed. She was almost thankful that Sebastian hadn't come in. There was just too much going on in her mind at the moment to deal with what had happened between Ash and her sister. *Ugh, Ash and Esmerelda*. The thought nauseated her. "How could you, Es? You're my sister! How could you steal Ash from me?"

Esmerelda rolled her eyes and swept her hands together in front of her. "You stole my dress; I stole your date. All's fair in love and fashion."

Whitley's tears came fast and hard then. "For years, I've taken care of you, Es. I've done everything you haven't wanted to do. I've mothered you. I've been there for you. And you don't appreciate *any* of it. *You* are the selfish one. *You* are the hateful one. Well, I tell you what, Es. I'm over it. I'm not doing anything for you anymore! I'm not making your food. I'm not sewing your clothes. I'm not driving you anywhere. I'm not even going to be your friend anymore. I'm done!"

Esmerelda didn't look the slightest bit concerned, and if she was, she was too stubborn to show it. "Fine by me! I don't care!"

Whitley caught sight of her wardrobe overflowing with the mysterious dresses. "And now that you solved the mystery behind Sophie's disappearance, you can just solve all of these mysteries on your own too! I did my part. I made you a dress, and *you ruined it!* There's no way I'll be helping you with any of this mess either."

Esmerelda furrowed her brows. "Solve the mysteries of the dresses? I'm not solving any mysteries! I didn't want those dumb old dresses! I told you to tell Dad to take them back! So you think I care that you're not going to do it? Fine. Don't solve them. But neither am I!"

Whitley heard her father's words replaying in her head. *You let her get away with everything, Whit. It's time you stood up for yourself!* Whitley wiped away her tears with the back of her hand. "Well, I'm certainly not going to do it for you! I didn't even wear a single one of those dresses to the ball because of you!"

Esmerelda shrugged. "Fine, then the mysteries don't get solved!"

No sooner had the words come out of her mouth than suddenly the snow globe on the nightstand began to tremble, its feet rattling on top of the dresser. The girls looked over at it in astonishment. Neither of them knew what was going on. And then, out of nowhere, it began to snow in the bedroom.

"What's going on?" asked Esmerelda.

The snow, which had begun as a light flurry, was now a full-on snow storm, just like the storms inside the globe. Whitley's eyes scanned the ceiling. She had no idea what was going on either.

Esmerelda reached out and took Sophie from Whitley's hands. "That's it. This is creepy. I'm outta here."

"Wait! I'll take Sophie back..." began Whitley. Her words were halted by an earsplitting sound and a sudden flash of light radiating out of the snow globe. Whitley stood staring at it in shock, but Esmerelda and Sophie ran for the bedroom door.

And then, suddenly, everything inside of Whitley's bedroom magically appeared inside the snow globe. A replica of what was in her room was now inside the globe.

Whitley rushed to look inside of it. Lifting the globe to her face, she stared down at the miniature furniture. Her sewing desk. Her bed. Her wardrobe stuffed with gowns. Everything was in there.

"It's my room!" she said in shock.

Esmerelda stood in the doorway with Sophie still in her arms as another light burst forth and wrapped itself around Whitley's body.

"Es!" screamed Whitley as she saw the fingers of light around her waist. She reached her hand out to her sister for help, but before Esmerelda could assist her, Whitley was sucked into the snow globe!

"Whitley!" Esmerelda called out, lurching to catch her hand. But it was too late. She was gone. And the snow globe that Whitley had just held seconds ago fell into the folds of material inside the cardboard box next to the bed.

Suddenly, Esmerelda heard another cracking sound. Worrying that perhaps the sound would pull her into the snow globe next, she rushed to the door. No sooner had she stepped over the threshold of the bedroom than she found her own body covered in the same bright light.

Her eyes blazed wild. "Help!" she screamed, scared for her life, holding the kitten up to her face to shield herself.

The fingers of light grasping Esmerelda pulled her into the little grey puff of fur she held in her hands. As the kitten landed on the ground with a gentle thump, the snow in the room magically disappeared. The only light in the room was from the dim glow of the moon outside, and the whole house went silent—as if it had never happened.

CHAPTER ELEVEN

Later that night, Felix returned to the house with a bag of takeout. He saw his old truck parked outside and assumed that Whitley had returned. He hoped everything had gone alright at the ball.

"Whit, I'm home!" he called out, running up the stairs two at a time. Poking his head in her bedroom, he found it empty. He poked his head in Esmerelda's room next. It was also empty.

"Huh," he said. "Maybe they worked things out and brought the truck back."

Satisfied with that explanation, he went back into Whitley's room. He'd forgotten to take the cardboard box he'd loaded up earlier out to the trash. *Whitley won't want to look at this dress anytime soon*, he thought, folding the flaps together. *Garbage comes tomorrow. I better get it taken out to the mailbox before it gets too dark. Maybe then we can all just forget any of this ever happened.*

Slinging the box up onto his shoulder, Felix didn't notice the tiny grey kitten hiding beneath the bed. Nor did he notice the tiny grey kitten following him down the stairs and out the front door. And he certainly didn't notice the grey kitten following him all the way down the driveway, where it hid behind a shrub until he'd gone.

The minute he was gone, the kitten scratched and clawed its way into the box. Undoing the box flaps, it dug through the material until it found the snow globe buried inside.

The kitten blinked her bright emerald eyes down into the watery world, where a miniature Whitley Snow stood staring back at her, pounding on the glass, pleading with silent screams to be set free.

If you enjoyed the prequel, short-story *Deal or Snow Deal*...check out *Snow Cold Case*, the first full-length novel in the new *Mystic Snow Globe Mystery Series* by M.Z. Andrews

ABOUT THE AUTHOR

M.Z. Andrews lives in the Midwest, United States with her husband. Together they have six children, three have flown the coop, and the other three are up and coming. Aside from writing, M.Z. enjoys gardening, canning salsa, KC Chiefs football games, and DIY projects.

M.Z. writes cozy mysteries, both regular and the magical kind. If you enjoyed this story, please check out one of her many other works.

The Mystic Snow Globe Mystery Series
The Witch Squad Cozy Mystery Series
The Coffee Coven's Cozy Capers Series
The Witch Island Series

Follow M.Z. Andrews online:
Website
Facebook
BookBub
Amazon

AUTHORS' NOTE

TWO MAGICAL BONUSES FROM US TO YOU!

We hope our stories bring extra enchantment to your holiday season! We had such a great time writing these for you that we decided to add two fun bonuses.

A Magical Scavenger Hunt

We've chosen a single holiday object and woven it into each of our stories so that it appears in every story at least once. Figure it out for a chance to win an Amazon gift card and free books!

14 Days of Christmas

From December 10 through Christmas Eve, five random entrants per day will win a full-length book from one of our authors.

Go to this page to enter both contests or visit our Facebook page to enter and spend the holiday season with us!

Made in the USA
Coppell, TX
21 December 2021